Family Ties

Rowena Summers

Family Ties

First published in Great Britain in 1988 by Severn House Publishers Ltd by arrangement with Sphere Books Ltd

This edition published in the United Kingdom in 2020 by

Canelo Digital Publishing Limited
Third Floor, 20 Mortimer Street
London W1T 3JW
United Kingdom

A CIP catalogue record for this book is available from the British Library.

Print ISBN 978 1 78863 847 0
Ebook ISBN 978 1 78863 469 4

Printed and bound in Great Britain by Clays Ltd, Elcograf S.p.A.

This book contains views and language on nationality, sexual politics, ethnicity, and society which are a product of the time in which the book is set. The publisher does not endorse or support these views. They have been retained in order to preserve the integrity of the text.

For my family and all the loving ties that bind us.

Chapter One

Morwen Killigrew gazed out of the long drawing-room windows as the children's chatter died away. The governess took little Charlotte to the nursery, and the others were taken off to school in the carriage after bidding their mother a noisy goodbye. Through the open windows, Morwen breathed in the fragrance of rose petals as a soft breeze tossed a scattering of them on to the dew-drenched lawns, as if to herald the end of summer.

Another season gone, another one beginning. And into Morwen's mind came the thought that soon they would start loading the clay blocks from the works on the moors on to the sturdy trucks of what everyone called Ben Killigrew's railway.

Just for a second, no more, Morwen felt an enticing tug of nostalgia. To be up there on the moors, dancing in the wild wind, glorying in the scents of heather and yarrow. To be part of it all, amid the twice-yearly rituals of moving the clay from pit to port that she had once known so well. To cheer the loads away with the Pit Captains and the clayworkers, the kiddley-boys and the fresh-faced bal maidens, as she herself had once been…

There were some clayfolk who still maintained stoutly that, despite the good that the railway had done to St Austell town, there was nothing to compare with the sight of the old clay waggons, piled perilously high with blocks, careering through the steep, narrow streets of the town, a danger and an excitement to all in their path as the iron wheels struck sparks off the cobblestones… it was easy to speak of it fondly in retrospect, when all such danger was past.

Ben's rail tracks were well-established now, their route safely redirected since the disaster ten years ago that had caused one death, and the subsidence from old rogue tin workings on the moors had questioned the very future of Killigrew Clay. But undoubtedly the railway had made the clayworks and its ever-growing white mounds of waste more acceptable to those who once bitterly resented the constant flurries of clay dust that used to hang like a pall over town and people alike, drying the mouth and dulling the hair and clothes.

'Folk should be grateful for it,' Morwen's father, Hal Tremayne, used to chuckle. 'They're getting a free supply o' medicine by swallowing the clay dust. 'Twill stop their belly-aches and freshen their breaths, if not their tongues!'

Morwen smiled now, remembering the flashing blue eyes of her father, inherited by all his family. But Hal's eyes were not quite so lustrous now, she thought, with a stab of anxiety. Nor was Hal's voice as hearty as when he'd roared for the clayworkers to rally to the side of the new young owner, Ben Killigrew, when times were bad.

Hal had been justifiably proud of his status as Pit Captain, and then Works Manager for Killigrew Clay, Morwen thought lovingly. But, lately, much of her father's old fire seemed diminished…

The door of the drawing-room opened behind her, and she turned quickly to smile at her tall, handsome husband. As if suddenly in need of reassurance from a shadow she couldn't quite dispel, she moved quickly to his side, hands outstretched. And Ben took her instantly in his arms, still as captivated by her as when he'd first seen her defying his haughty aunt in the streets of St Austell in what seemed a lifetime ago.

He hadn't realized then, of course, that the fascination he'd felt in those moments would turn to love. He'd little thought that Morwen Tremayne, bal maiden at his father's clayworks, would become so all-important in his life.

She had known it though, Ben thought, a little smile teasing his mouth.

Morwen, with her fey Cornish ways, still vowed that it was meant to be, that when his gentleman's pin had scratched her cheek as she lurched against him in the street, he had branded her with his mark.

It was no more than a charming tale… and one that a hard-headed businessman should not dwell upon, perhaps. But when Morwen was in his arms, he was never the clay boss that his workers knew and respected, as they had respected his father before him, but ever her lover and husband, champion and friend…

'Well, dar?' he said softly, using her own parents' private endearment that they had claimed as their own. 'Why such a look of sadness? Do you hate the damp mornings so much? You were very pensive at the window—'

'It's nothing. A goose walking over my grave, perhaps—'

Ben tipped up her chin and looked steadily into her face. Fine lines fanned out from the lovely, expressive eyes, but her mouth was as full and mobile as ever. No glint of silver yet highlighted the glossy blue-black of her upswept hair, but there was a maturity in the face of a once-lovely girl who was now a beautiful and sensual woman, and the mother of his children.

And he knew her too well…

'What's worrying you, Morwen? I insist that you tell me.'

She heard the old imperiousness in his voice, and was reminded of a time when she was a child, and the snot-nosed owner's son had come to Clay One pit years ago with his father, old Charles Killigrew, inspecting the Works and the clayfolk there as if they were specimens on a glass plate. And she and her brothers, and her Daddy and Mammie too, had all guffawed at the young man in the stiff college clothes who didn't know what it was to dirty his hands by an honest day's work. Now they all knew differently, and Morwen's eyes softened, knowing that Ben's irritation with her was because he cared. She gave a small unconscious sigh.

'I just wish I knew what ailed Daddy, Ben,' the words were almost dragged from her. 'He's been acting so strangely of late. He's slowing up, dar, and I see it more and more every day. I don't know how my mother would live without him—'

It was out in the open now, no longer a silent fear in her own head, but a shared thought. And although there was no one in the world she would rather share it with, once voiced it became a real threat to the serenity of her world.

'I'm sure you're imagining things, Morwen.' But he spoke briskly, and by that small fact alone she knew he was disguising his real opinion. She felt a lump clog her throat as he went on talking with false cheerfulness.

'If it makes you feel easier, I'll try to persuade him to have a word with Doctor Pender. Better still, try to persuade your mother. Bess could always get round him. It's something we men have to put up with from our Tremayne women.'

His teasing brought the ghost of a smile to Morwen's mouth, and Ben capitalized on it.

'And in case you're thinking it's a pity your witch-woman of the moors can't give you some of her evil potions to spirit away whatever's wrong with Hal, then good riddance to her is all I can answer to that!'

She bristled against him, as he had expected. He didn't mind a good argument with his wife. It invigorated him, and they usually finished up in each other's arms, with neither the victor, which was a very satisfactory arrangement.

'You didn't always scoff at old Zillah.' Her voice was a sweet breath against his cheek. 'She said I'd marry a tall, dark-haired man, and that came true, didn't it, my 'andsome!'

She lapsed into the sing-song patois of the Cornish, as glad as he was to lighten the atmosphere. Ben laughed, holding her tight in his arms, and kissing the tip of her nose before his mouth eventually found hers.

No matter that the Master and Mistress of the house still found delight in such informality in the sedate drawing-room, for there was none to see, and Ben Killigrew would have cared little if there had been observers. Even so, such sweet moments had become rarer over the years, and were therefore more precious to Morwen.

'I sometimes think there's something of the witch about you, my dar,' Ben said. 'But only in the sense that you can twist me around your finger without my even noticing it.'

'Can I?' she wheedled unconsciously. 'Then you'll agree with what I was saying last night—'

He let her go abruptly, and it was as though a chill little wind blew into her heart as she saw him frown.

'Morwen, why are you so unreasonable about this? Any woman should be overjoyed at the chance to go to London. I can show you all the places you've ever heard about—'

'I never heard of any on 'em,' she said smartly, annoyed that her old speech patterns betrayed her anxiety. What would she do in London? Out of her depth; out of place; even as Ben Killigrew's wife, while he revisited places he'd known as a college boy, invited now to return and be made an Honorary Governor.

She caught her breath. It sounded so grand: Ben Killigrew a Governor of Ormsby College. It was a great honour for one of barely thirty-five years to be offered such a position, and it was all due to the success Ben had made of Killigrew Clay. But what of his wife, Morwen wondered? One-time bal maiden, who had married the young boss, and was now expected to be his hostess in the smartest of London sets for the brief time they were there…

Her heart went cold at the thought. Here in her own domain, it was possible. But in London, far away in upcountry England, which might as well have been an alien land to her, she would be all fingers and thumbs. Besides, the children would miss her, and her father wasn't well, and her mother relied on her company more and more now all the boys had left home… oh, there were endless reasons why she shouldn't accompany Ben to London…

'You're being ridiculous, Morwen,' Ben was as distant as a church steeple now. 'You're coming to London with me, and that's final. It would be the height of discourtesy to refuse.'

'I couldn't go if I was ill, could I?'

'But you're not ill, and you're not going to be, are you?' His dark eyes dared her to fabricate sickness to prevent the journey. She shook her head quickly, and the sleek dark coils of hair threatened to break loose from their pins into the flyaway wildness of the moorland girl.

'No, Sir.'

Her sarcasm was lost on him. There were more important matters to attend to. A clay boss was always beset with worries, even though there was a boom in the demand for china clay right now. Ben was experienced enough to know that when prices could rise so dramatically in a fluctuating market, they could fall just as quickly, and it was well to keep plenty in the coffers for such an eventuality.

As an afterthought, before he left the house for his weekly discussions with the Killigrew accountant, Ben gave his wife the news he had been saving.

'I thought we might go to France for a short holiday next year. I can't spare more than a couple of weeks at most, but once the spring despatches have gone, I daresay Killigrew Clay won't fall apart without me—'

He couldn't say more, because Morwen was back in his arms again, her eyes as brilliant as sapphires. Ben's throat tightened with love for her. She was sometimes so beautiful he could hardly believe she was real, and his, all his…

'Oh Ben, you know how I've longed to go abroad! Can we really go in the spring? What of the children? They'll miss us so much – or can we take them all with us—?'

He stopped her hurtling words with a laughing kiss.

'All five of them? I think not, dar! Your mother will have a wonderful time looking after them. We'll ask her and Hal to live here while we're away, then everything will run as smoothly as if we were still here. It won't be too hard on your family. Think about it, my love, and perhaps it will soften the blow of going to London!'

He threw her a last kiss and was gone, while Morwen was still going over his words in her mind. It was bribery, of course, she thought wryly. He knew how she longed to see France and the beautiful fairy-tale chateaux she had read about. That was the bargain: play the lady in London, and the reward would be a holiday in France.

Morwen bit her lip. She *was* a lady, she reminded herself. She was Killigrew's lady... and after fourteen years of being Ben's wife, she should know how to behave like one! She had learned the art of taking tiny bites of food, of playing the pianoforte moderately well, of making polite conversation with the most boring of people. She had tidied up her speech, as she preferred to call it, and remembered to say Mother instead of the familiar Mammie when she spoke to Bess – at least, in public.

She idled the morning away. It wasn't so hard to be a lady, she thought, with a glimmer of a smile, even though some of them were so starchy they didn't seem to be living at all, but more like waxwork figures. She had made Ben laugh many times by mimicking some of the townsladies who came to her afternoon teas. *Soirées*, she reminded herself, the smile turning into a wide grin. What she gave at Killigrew House were *soirées*...

She wondered how many other young matrons did the same thing most afternoons at four o'clock. Her brother Jack's wife in Truro often did so. Annie was a Boskelly, daughter of the Boskelly boat-builders, in which Jack was now a partner. Annie had been brought up to do things right, and invitations to her little tea parties were much sought after.

Morwen's mother never put on such airs, Morwen thought affectionately. Bess Tremayne took a back seat in everything now, letting the world pass by, and revelling in the fact that her family was thriving. Once an industrious seamstress, glad of bits of sewing work for the gentry, Bess contented herself now with making small items for the grandchildren, having no need for the scrapings of finer folk.

Only two things jarred in Bess Tremayne's life: the death of her eldest son, Sam, in the terrible rail disaster ten years ago; and the loss of her best-loved son Matt, to the gold-fields of California.

Not that Matt was dead, Morwen thought quickly, although he had seemed so during the years when they never heard from him. But then he had made contact again, and for all the Tremaynes it was as if the sun had begun to shine once more, although there had been no more than a spasmodic correspondence between them ever since.

Did Matt's wife, Louisa, give little tea parties in their Californian mansion, Morwen wondered? Did their son, Cresswell, act the polite little man, with the same dreams in his eyes that his father used to have? Cresswell would be ten years old now, the same age as her own Justin. Morwen often wondered about him, all those thousands of miles across the sea, and whether family bonds made the two boys anything alike.

–

'Mrs Killigrew, there's a person here to see 'ee.'

She started as the housekeeper made the announcement. Mrs Horn didn't like visitors so early in the day, and Morwen hid a smile, thinking that at times the elderly woman acted more as if she owned the house than Morwen did herself. She took the card from the salver, frowning at the strange name.

Wainwright… Randell E Wainwright… she was sure she knew no one of that name… and yet somewhere in her memory it sounded vaguely familiar…

The gentleman who was ushered in was unknown to her. He was as tall as Ben, but leaner. His clothes were obviously expensive, and he had the air of someone well used to good living. He was a fine-looking man, in his early thirties, Morwen guessed in those first inquiring seconds, and probably a little older than herself. His eyes were deep brown, with a velvety look about them. Morwen caught her thoughts up short with a little shock, for never, since the heady days of falling in love with Ben, had she really noticed or cared about another man's appearance. The self-knowledge made her cooler than usual with a visitor.

'Good morning, Mr Wainwright. I'm afraid my husband is not at home at present, and he won't be back until late this afternoon—'

'As a matter of fact, Ma'am, it's not your husband I've come to see. It's you.'

His voice was deep, interrupting her sudden flurry of words. But it wasn't just the voice that made her pause… it was the accent. It wasn't the slow and melodious Cornish, nor the rounded vowel sounds of someone city-educated like Ben. Nor was it the clipped flat Yorkshire voice of Tom Askhew, one-time reporter on *The Informer* newspaper. Morwen couldn't place it at all, and then she realized what the man had said.

'To see me?'

Randell Wainwright smiled. Oh yes, he was very good-looking, Morwen thought faintly.

'I was told that you were beautiful, but I hadn't been prepared for quite such a pleasurable surprise, Mrs Killigrew. Nothing I was told about you did you justice.'

Swift, hot colour rushed to Morwen's face. The shock of such a blatant compliment from a stranger made her overlook his earlier words for a second or two. This was not the way people behaved in polite company! Morwen had learnt that much since becoming one of the St Austell society ladies… but there was undeniably something in this man's demeanour that intrigued and attracted her, despite herself.

Perhaps it was his very candour that was akin to the naïvety of the moorland folk; the clayworkers who had no need of arch comments and decorous remarks that meant nothing, and believed in good plain speaking and judged a man by his ability to be fair and honest.

Undoubtedly, Mr Randell Wainwright knew what he liked and wasn't above saying so. And he was making it plain by his smile and the admiration in his eyes that he liked what he saw very much indeed. Morwen dismissed the thought immediately. She was Ben Killigrew's wife, the mother of his children, and as such she had no right to be standing here like a gauche bal maiden, practically glowing with pleasure at sensing what almost amounted to desire in a young man.

'Someone has spoken of me to you?' Morwen was unsure whether this was something she cared to hear. Ben would certainly not approve.

'Why yes. Your brother Matt.'

She sat down quickly, motioning the man to do likewise. Until then she had hardly registered what he had said.

'You know my brother Matt?' She stared at him in astonishment. 'Then you are from America, perhaps?'

'I am indeed, Ma'am.' Again, that quaint little word that was so like the way Morwen had always addressed her own mother: Mammie... the word she was trying very hard to avoid now, since Ben had said quietly that it was a mite countrified.

'How is Matt? Is he well? And Louisa, and little Cresswell? You know them all?'

Suddenly it was as though Matt had stretched out his hands across oceans and continents, linking them all through this man. She had felt that way once before, when Killigrew Clay's fortunes were in danger of collapsing, and Matt's gift had arrived to set them all on the road to prosperity again. Morwen could still hardly believe that her dreaming brother had become a rich man in the California gold-fields.

'I should say I do! I haven't seen them for a while, since I moved to New York. Matt doesn't know I'm here, but I couldn't resist taking the liberty of calling. I hope you don't think me too presumptuous, Ma'am.'

The stranger looked awkward for the first time, but suddenly the half-remembered name fell into place.

'Of course! Wainwright! I should have remembered. Matt's wife was called Louisa Wainwright. And she had a small brother.' She looked at the elegant young man sitting opposite her. 'But you cannot be the small brother,' she stated.

He laughed out loud. 'A fair deduction, Ma'am. No, the small brother is away at college and, as you surmise, I am rather older than my cousin Philip.'

'Then you are Louisa's cousin?'

'And Matt's, and therefore a kind of cousin of yours also, if you'll pardon me for saying so.'

Morwen smiled delightedly. The impropriety of chattering with a stranger without a proper introduction had not escaped her. Ben would not have been pleased… Ben was surprisingly stuffy about such things… but if Randell E Wainwright was a kind of cousin, then that made everything all right. At least, she hoped that it did.

There were cousins and cousins, of course. Ben's own cousin, Jude Pascoe, would be shown the door of Killigrew House if he ever dared to set foot near it. Thankfully, Jude was out of their lives for ever, Morwen thought, superstitiously crossing her fingers behind her back for a moment.

Years ago, Jude Pascoe and her brother Matt had fled the country in dubious circumstances after a wrecking along the treacherous Cornish coastline when a man had been killed. Neither Morwen nor her mother could think of that awful time without pain, even now. To them, America was no more than a great expanse of land on a map, although Morwen had taken a great deal of interest in it since communicating with Matt. Of Jude's whereabouts, she didn't know, and didn't care.

And this stranger came from over the Atlantic Ocean, he had lived there, he knew the land and her American family. He knew Matt. He was a link with her past.

'You're very welcome here, Mr Wainwright.' Her soft Cornish voice was warm and generous.

'Thank you. But please – my family and friends call me Ran. It would give me much pleasure if you would do so too.'

'I don't know if I should.'

'Why not? We're cousins, aren't we? And – forgive me again if I'm too bold, but I already think of you as Morwen. Your name has charmed me for many years, ever since I first heard it. I never thought I would see the lady in person, but now I know that your name fits you perfectly. Mysterious and beautiful, and as fey as the Cornish are reputed to be, I suspect.'

'Mr Wainwright, please!' Morwen had never heard such artless flattery. Even from Ben, whose education allowed the words to charm a lady flow easily, there had been nothing like this. She wasn't sure if she should be listening to it, or whether such devastating frankness was frightening or even a little suspect. She didn't always trust such smooth tongues.

Once long ago, an old acquaintance of Ben's had come to stay at the house. A man with a plausible patter and a slickness of manner, and that man had been so nearly caused her young brother Freddie to lose his reason with his foul words.

'I'm so sorry – have I offended you?'

She heard Randell Wainwright's concerned voice, and realized that her shudder had been obvious.

'No – of course not. I'm just – not used to colonial ways.' She blushed as his eyebrow raised slightly. 'Now I must apologize. It's the way my husband refers to Americans, I'm afraid. I've never been sure if it's complimentary or otherwise.'

He laughed, a deep throaty sound. 'I'll forgive you on one condition. That we forget this ridiculous protocol and agree to call each other by our Christian names. We're family, aren't we? What do you say, Morwen?'

She liked the sound of her name on his lips. He was the most refreshing person she had met in a very long time. She had become steeped in domestic affairs for too long, in the little tea parties she was obliged to give as Mrs Ben Killigrew, and smothering her own identity in the process of being businessman's wife, and mother. Randell Wainwright brought a breath of fresh air into the house. It was almost – almost like a moorland breeze blowing through it, and she followed her instincts about him, feeling her soft mouth curve into an answering smile.

'I think that would be very nice – Ran,' she said, a little awkwardly. She stood up quickly. 'I'm forgetting my manners. You'll have some tea, won't you? And of course you'll stay to lunch? I want to hear everything about Matt.'

She pulled the bell-rope for Mrs Horn. Randell stood up too, holding out his hand to shake hers in a formal greeting.

'Thank you. And I hope we can be friends as well as cousins,' he said gravely.

Her hand felt small and delicate in his. She had long ago lost the roughness of a bal maiden's hands. They were a lady's hands now and she was absurdly pleased to register that fact. She felt the strong male fingers curl around her own in a protective gesture. She felt warmed by them, then a feeling that was akin to an odd little panic made her almost snatch her hand away from his as the housekeeper entered the room.

Chapter Two

Jack Tremayne was in a black humour. He had been at loggerheads with his boat-building partner, who was also his father-in-law, over the purchase of paints and materials; he had bickered with his wife Annie all last night, because she wanted to invite his sister Morwen and her family for tea on Sunday, and it meant Jack riding all the way to St Austell with the invitation, and he was just too busy; his five-year-old twin daughters had upset their nurse by tipping their breakfast all over her, and had since been sent to their room in disgrace. And the doctor had asked Jack to call at his office that day and told him bluntly and in no uncertain terms that Annie was not to have another child.

Sometimes it felt as though the whole world was against him, Jack thought darkly. He strode angrily through the streets of Truro that bleak September afternoon, after seeing the doctor, then sorting out the building materials problem less satisfactorily than he would have wished, though they had come to some arrangement, at least.

The bickering with Annie was no more than was normal among married people after eight years or so, and he supposed he'd eventually give in and ride over to Killigrew House with the invitation to Sunday tea. And his little daughters were only being naughtier than usual because they had a new nurse. But this other thing… this straight-talking by that fool of a doctor… that he must be celibate from now on, or risk his wife's health… what did he take him for? Jack was a healthy, vigorous man of twenty-seven, not a monk! He had no intention of tying his breeding tackle in a knot for the rest of his life because of Doctor Vestey's say-so!

The man wasn't human. It wasn't natural to lie in wedlock with a woman and not want to love her. It gave more dignity to the beasts in the fields that they could follow their instincts while he was supposed to lie mute every night, think of other things, and let his baser male urges die. Those were the fancy words the doctor had used, but they didn't change the bald and unnatural facts.

Jack scowled unseeingly at the young Truro matrons who nodded at him as he passed. Such a splendid man he'd turned out, some sighed. And how lucky Annie Boskelly was to have captured him. The bolder of them avoided each other's eyes so as not to see the flush on each delicate female cheek, as each wondered secretly how it would feel to be pinned beneath that strong young body and be locked in wanton embraces with him…

'Heyo, Jack, what's got into you today? You nearly knocked me over!'

He heard the laughing voice, and cleared his vision rapidly. He had been too incensed at his own bad luck, too upset by the misery of his future to notice anything or anyone. His brother Freddie was grinning at him, as tall as Jack now, and should surely be looking for a wife himself soon. Freddie was gone twenty-two, so it was high time he got himself wed.

If it wasn't such a damnable embarrassment, he'd warn Freddie to look for a wife with good child-bearing hips who didn't drop a child before it was halfway to being born every couple of years. He was immediately ashamed of his thoughts. He loved Annie to distraction. That was the hell of it. That was definitely the god-damned bloody hell of it…

'Sorry, our Freddie. I was hard in thought.' He used the old familiar term without thinking. Hard in thought and hard in body… Jack groaned. From now on, everything was going to be a torment to him.

There was really no one he could confide in, he thought bitterly. Freddie was not the one. A younger brother never was. Matt was God knew where in California… and Sam… Jack swallowed painfully. The memory of Sam, his best-beloved brother and god, could still twist his gut whenever he thought of him lying among the rubble of the railway cave-in on the moors. Even after ten years, the memory of it could still catch him unawares, making him sick at heart and he missed Sam more as the years went by. He could have confided in Sam, and he swore beneath his breath in bitter frustration that his oldest brother wasn't around to listen and sympathize.

Freddie walked easily beside him. Where there had been one handsome Tremayne man, now there were two, and Jack didn't miss the way the Truro misses eyed up this perky young echo of himself.

'It must have been something important to make 'ee so all-fired miserable-looking.' Freddie tried to coax Jack out of his mood by responding in the old way.

'No, it wasn't,' Jack said shortly. 'Nothing I can't put right, anyway.' If there were ways, he didn't know of them. Only one way… and the thought of turning his lust upon a painted moonlighter for his own relief revolted him.

'Good. Then I've got some news for you.'

Freddie never wasted words. If somebody didn't want to invite his confidence, it was a waste of energy trying to persuade them. He hadn't learned that at St Austell school, but in the private tuition which the teachers had insisted he deserved. Freddie had always been a bright boy, and he had grown into a man with a good business brain.

He'd begun as an apprentice with Boskelly Boats, following in Jack's footsteps, but he now had his own flourishing chandlery shop near to the Lemon river where the tall ships anchored, and both they and the busy little sea and river craft kept him busy with their endless requests for supplies of every kind. Freddie had found his own niche without anyone's help.

'What sort of news?' Jack snapped. His own was so bad, he didn't see how anybody else could smile on such a day as this. His sister Morwen had once said caustically that he was the most selfish of her brothers, wallowing in his own misery almost as if he enjoyed it… if that was being selfish, then so he was, he thought with a darker scowl.

Freddie stopped walking as his brother strode on almost at a run, and Jack was obliged to turn round and wait for him.

'That's better. I thought we were in some kind of race or summat. Now listen. Morwen's had a visitor from America—'

Jack's mouth dropped open at that, his thoughts temporarily diverted from his own troubles. 'Not our Matt! I don't believe it—'

'Shut up a minute, Jack. No, 'tis not our Matt. I called at Killigrew House yesterday when I was visiting Mammie – who wouldn't mind a visit from you and Annie sometime, by the way – and there's this tall fellow staying with 'em. I thought for a minute it might have been one of Ben's college friends, but he calls himself Ran Wainwright, and he's Matt's wife's cousin.'

He kept his voice quite steady as he mentioned Ben's college friends. It was a small test he set himself every now and then, and he'd passed it again. The very phrase 'college friends' held horror for Freddie. If he lived to be a hundred he would never forget seeing Captain Neville Peterson in an embrace with Morwen's piano tutor… the immediate shock of it, added to the abuse hurled at him afterwards by Peterson, had been overwhelming.

It lingered now, whenever he thought of any kind of intimate relationship. Freddie longed for a normal happy life like his brothers and sister, but a deep underlying fear of failure made him wary.

'What's he doing here?' Jack said in astonishment, pulled out of his own misery for the moment.

'Who? Oh – Randell Wainwright – uh, he's going to study European business methods for a year, and then he'll decide whether to settle here or go back to California. He dabbled a bit in the gold mining, I understand, same as our Matt, but didn't stick with it.'

'What sort of business methods?' Jack was already losing interest in this stranger who could mean nothing in their lives.

'Anything legal, I suspect.' Freddie grinned. 'I think Ben's quite keen to fix him up with Daniel Gorran. The old boy can't go on much longer, and it would be useful to have a sort of relative in the family firm who understands the rudiments of mining, even if 'tis not quite the same.'

'Gorran's is not a family firm—'

'He's been the Killigrew accountant ever since anybody can remember—' Freddie said. 'That makes him sort of attached to Killigrews, wouldn't you say?'

'And you think it's a good idea to have a stranger knowing all about the Killigrew fortunes, do you?' Jack was still determined to be objectionable about everything. 'Ben ought to have more sense, and I'm surprised that Morwen wants anybody else staying at the house wi' that brood of children of theirs.'

'Morwen's very taken with him,' Freddie commented. 'And I'd say he's more than taken with Morwen too.'

Jack laughed out loud. 'Now you're being mist-touched, our Freddie. Morwen's got eyes for nobody but Ben Killigrew, and it would take more than one fancy American to turn her head!'

They had reached Freddie's shop, where the black lettering proudly proclaimed the name of F. Tremayne, Proprietor, over the door.

'See for yourself on Sunday. We're all invited to tea, the lot of us, in honour of our American cousin. I was coming to tell you, but now I've seen you, it's saved me the bother.'

Jack groaned. 'Next Sunday?'

'That's right. I've given you the message, so you and Annie and the girls had better be there, or Morwen will never forgive you. And nor will Mammie,' he added meaningly.

He swung into his shop, the doorbell jingling behind him, and Jack swore softly beneath his breath. This was none of his fault. How was he to know some American would be arriving to thwart Annie's own tea party? Or that Morwen would be acting the fine lady and having a grand to-do with all the Tremaynes and the Killigrews under one roof, when it wasn't even Christmas? He sighed heavily, making his way home to break the news, knowing it wouldn't be welcome.

-

Morwen was indeed charmed by this new arrival into her life. Not for worlds would she ever have admitted openly that life at Killigrew House could sometimes be deadly dull. She was appalled that such a thought even drifted into her mind at times when she was less guarded than usual, because marriage to Ben Killigrew was everything she had ever wanted… and she rarely allowed the thoughts to form that life to a clay boss, however beloved, wasn't always the easiest form of existence.

Ben was her life… and so were the five children: Walter and Albert and Primmy… and now Justin and Charlotte. Neither parent showed any preference for either group. The older three were legally adopted by them after Sam's terrible accident and Dora's subsequent death, which Morwen privately attributed to a broken heart rather than the fatal attack of measles.

It had seemed a miracle at the time, in the midst of such misery, for Morwen to discover so soon afterwards that she was pregnant at last, when she had almost given up hoping. Justin was born while the wild celebrations at the end of the Crimean War were still going on up on the moors, and Morwen had been obliged to miss the bonfires and the dancing and cavorting.

Four years later, Charlotte had arrived to make their happiness complete. She was just a slow starter, Morwen had told Ben happily. If he still wanted more children, there was plenty of time, and to produce a child every four years wasn't so bad! And it gave them all the delicious time in between to themselves…

Only now Justin was ten, and Charlotte six, and there was no sign of another child, nor any reference to either Ben or

Morwen wanting one. Had they slipped so far apart, she sometimes wondered sadly? Was it really possible that two people who loved as they had done, could find it so hard to talk to one another, except for superficial things, or the doings of Killigrew Clay, that all-important factor in their lives?

And now Randell E Wainwright had come into their lives, and his presence was a delight and a respite. While he was in the house, Ben lost the dour expression that so often spoiled his handsome good looks, turning him into an old man before his time. Ran could cajole and tease, and make everybody laugh, and the children adored him.

'I can't think why Matt hasn't brought Louisa and Cresswell for a visit in all these years,' he said one evening soon after his arrival. 'Louisa's own parents died some years ago, and I know she's always been interested in her husband's Cornish background.'

'Oh, I wish you could persuade him, Ran!'

Morwen clasped her hands together, the thought of a visit from Matt making her eyes moisten, the thought that this delightful man could be the catalyst to bring her adored Matt home again, making him her champion.

Randell watched her across the dinner table, her glorious eyes like blue fire in the candlelight, her mouth open and inviting in that wonderful smile of hers, the deep neckline of her russet gown accentuating the soft curves of her breasts and her tiny waist. Dear God, he thought, did she know what effect she could have on a man? Did her husband not know, or appreciate such a woman? He glanced at Ben, teasing the enchanting six-year-old Charlotte into eating her meat pie, and felt a sharp envy of this man who had so much, so much…

'Ben, did you hear what Ran said? He'll write to Matt and suggest a visit to us. Wouldn't it be marvellous?'

'Have we got many American cousins, Mother?' Walter asked eagerly.

At fourteen, he was so like his own father, Sam Tremayne, that it sometimes took Morwen's breath away. Already Walter was tall and broad, and destined to break a few girlish hearts, she guessed. And mad keen to work at the clayworks, alongside his grandfather Hal.

So far Ben had refused to allow it, even though the clay was in his blood, as it was in all of them. Walter was the son of the clay boss, and therefore couldn't be given the menial job of kiddley-boy, making the tea and running around at everyone's beck and call, no matter that that was the way all Morwen's brothers had begun. If Walter did want to work with the clay, it must wait until he was older. Besides, he had his schooling to finish, and there might be a college place for him yet.

Undoubtedly, the old stories about the clayworks intrigued all the children. None of them was aware that the real parents of the older three were dead. They were brought up as Killigrews, and it had been decided long ago that they would take the Killigrew name. It was simpler for everyone.

'Only one, I'm afraid,' Morwen gave Walter his answer. 'He's the same age as Justin—'

'Only ten! He won't want to play with cissy things, will he?' Albert added scornfully, which brought an immediate retort from Justin.

'*I* don't play with cissy things!'

'When will he be coming, Mother?' Primmy clamoured, her pretty flushed face already showing signs of the lovely young woman she would be, even at eleven years old.

'Will he talk funny, like Uncle Ran?' Charlotte piped, at which they all laughed, and once again Randell envied them their closeness, their private circle in which he sometimes felt very much the outsider.

As if suddenly aware of this, Morwen smiled into his eyes.

'I don't think Uncle Ran talks funny, Charlotte. Just differently, that's all. If everyone talked exactly the same, we'd never be able to tell people apart, would we?'

Ben spoke coolly from the end of the table. 'My wife has a special kind of philosophy all her own, Ran. You'll grow to understand it in time.'

He understood it now. It was warm and funny and wonderful, and it was one of the things that had charmed him from the first moment he saw her. And showing how much her every word and gesture delighted him was one of the things he had to keep under control whenever she was near him. She didn't belong to him, and never could. But it didn't stop him wanting her.

'But when will Cresswell come to Cornwall?' Justin said impatiently, his handsome young face betraying the impatience of both his parents. Morwen sighed. He was her darling, yet he could try her patience more than any of the others. Justin wanted the moon, and he wanted it now…

'Nobody said he was coming,' Ben said. 'Why don't you listen? All Randell said was that he'd write and suggest it. Are you incapable of understanding plain English?'

'Ben, please—' Morwen hated the way he belittled their son. It was almost as though he forced himself into doing it, in his determination to show no favouritism towards his own. It was ridiculous and unnecessary, and, as so often happened, it caused a wave of embarrassment to go around the dinner table. It was even worse because Randell Wainwright must be able to sense the sudden atmosphere.

'I shall write tonight,' Ran said quickly to Justin. 'And if you wish, you may write a little note to your cousin Cresswell, and I'll send it with my letter.'

Justin's face beamed with pleasure. 'Will you really? Thank you, Uncle Ran!'

Ben scraped his chair back from the table.

'Well, if we've all finished, it's time the children went to bed. You must wait until tomorrow to write your note, Justin. It's too late now, and it will keep the others awake while you pore over your spelling. Tomorrow will be soon enough.'

Sometimes, Morwen thought silently, you can be a prize pig, Ben Killigrew. She caught Ran's eye and turned away quickly. Disloyalty in one's own head was one thing. Knowing that another person was aware of it and sympathized, was something else.

–

'Jack!' Morwen said in pleased surprise next morning. 'We don't often get a visit from you! Is Annie well? And the twins?'

'Everybody's well,' Jack hid his impatience, knowing Morwen's small show of sarcasm was deserved. He wasn't one for visiting. 'Freddie seemed to think it was time I called on Mammie, so I thought I'd kill two birds with one stone and tell you we'll be glad to come for the tea party on Sunday.'

'Good. Then you'll be able to meet our American cousin.'

'Isn't he here now then?' Jack was disappointed.

'Ben's taken him to see Daniel Gorran this morning. Ran's quite keen to work with him for a while, and Ben says Mr Gorran's been saying he'll have to give up soon and hand over to a younger man. It's possible that Ran will take over Gorran's Accounting Chambers.'

'Can he add up in pounds and pence then? I thought he'd only know about those new-fangled dollars—'

Morwen burst out laughing. 'Oh Jack, you are funny. Dollars aren't new, only to us, that's all. Ran was explaining it all to the children last night—'

'Your Ran seems to have charmed everybody from the looks of it.' He watched her closely, and noted how her colour rose.

'He's not *my* Ran, Jack, so don't be so silly.' But just as it was hard for her to hide anything from him, she saw the anxiety in his face, and smothered her defensive tone. 'Shall we have some tea? The children are at school and Charlotte's having a nap, so we can be cosy the way we used to be.'

'In this barn of a place?' At her reproachful look, Jack's prickliness vanished. 'All right then, our Morwen, let's be cosy.'

'And you can tell me what's wrong,' she said calmly.

'Nothing's wrong.'

'Then tell me what's right, and I'll try to work out why a man with nothing wrong should be frowning at his sister whom he's ridden miles to see.'

She rang for Mrs Horn to bring the tea, and when they were settled with it, and a plate of fruit scones baked that day, she tried once more.

'Are you going to tell me, or are we going to sit here making petty talk the way the fine townsladies do?'

Jack grinned. 'Do 'ee remember how you used to call Jane Askhew "Miss Finelady", Morwen? When you thought she and Ben were going to be wed, and you were all hoity-toity because of it—'

'I was not!'

'No? What about the night we first set foot in this house, when old Charles Killigrew asked us to supper, and you nearly died with shame because your Miss Finelady Jane asked you what a bal maiden did?'

Morwen hadn't thought of that night in years. Her life had changed so dramatically since then. She had never imagined then that one day she would be Ben Killigrew's lady. She had been so certain that his heart was already lost to that young Truro girl who was born a real lady, whose white hands caressed the pianoforte keys as though she touched a lover's skin.

'I didn't know you boys even noticed such a thing,' Morwen murmured.

Jack laughed wickedly. 'Oh, we did. Well, Matt was too taken up with Jude Pascoe, I daresay, and Freddie was too young to care for anything but the food. But Sam and me—'

She saw the sudden look of pain on Jack's face.

'You still miss him, don't you?'

''Course I do. That's a daft question to ask, our Morwen. Didn't you miss your friend Celia for years after she drowned herself in the claypit? Time makes no difference to missing people, do it? Ask Mammie about that, and see how her eyes soften when she thinks of our Matt—'

'All right, I understand!'

Jack didn't often go on so. There must be something troubling him, something he couldn't talk about, not yet. As if the small silence forced him to speak, he muttered almost beneath his breath.

'And if our Sam were here, he'd know what I should do. I could tell him things—' he stopped abruptly.

'Tell me,' Morwen said simply.

She saw her brother's face redden. He saw his sister, serene and beautiful, fulfilled as she was always meant to be, a lovely young wife and mother, and everything seemed to curl up inside him. He got to his feet, clattering his cup in his saucer.

'I can't. You're not a man,' he said brutally.

'Then tell Ben,' she said swiftly, and got no reply.

-

Long after Jack had gone back to Truro, Morwen brooded on his words. She had thought there might be some small domestic trouble. Jack was the kind to let problems fester instead of bringing them out into the open, the way Morwen always did. Though she had to admit she had been reluctant to share her anxiety over her father with Ben.

But now she believed Jack's worries went far deeper than some slight disturbance at home. She ached for him, but if he wouldn't tell her, she couldn't force him.

Perhaps on Sunday there might be some opportunity for Ben to take him aside and get him to confide in him. She prayed so. Ben hadn't always had much time for Jack. She shrugged, hoping things would sort themselves out, and in the meantime she was going to see her mother that afternoon. Bess may have got some sense out of Jack.

Once a week, Morwen and her mother met at Fielding's Tea Rooms in St Austell. It was an arrangement they had continued for years, a little outing in the middle of the week that they each looked forward to enormously. Bess was there first that day, which was unusual. Morwen always tried to get there before her, to order the tea and fruit buns, and to settle the bill in advance before her mother had a chance to do so.

'Hello, Mother,' Morwen said warmly, kissing her soft cheek in greeting. Bess was comfortably rounded, a little stiff in the joints, as she put it, but still going on fair to middling, thank you.

'Did you see Jack yesterday?' Morwen went on, nodding to Miss Fielding to bring the refreshments. Bess gave a small snort.

'That I did, and why he bothered to come, I can't think. All he did was mope about the house as if he'd lost sixpence and found tuppence. Your Daddy wanted to see 'un, but Jack couldn't wait for the end of his shift, said he had to be back in Truro before afternoon.'

'He does have a business to run, Mammie—'

'Oh aye, the boat-building,' Bess said vaguely. 'Well, never mind all that. I daresay we'll be seeing him and Annie and the little 'uns on Sunday. Has Ben said anything to 'ee, Morwen?'

Morwen looked at her in exasperation. 'Well, we do talk to each other! What about?' Her sarcasm was lost on her mother.

'Your Daddy says there's been uproar at Bult and Vine's because of some scaggies working nights and pinching clay loads for their own gain.'

'What? They wouldn't be so stupid—'

'They would. I don't need to tell 'ee that some of the young clayworkers are reckless enough to do anything for an extra shilling or two. Bult and Vine's took on some roughnecks from over Redruth way a while ago, and they'm inciting the rest of the young 'uns to do a bit of scaggying. Ben's afeared it's spreading to Killigrew Clay, but he can't prove nothing yet.'

Morwen shuddered, remembering the last time such a thing had happened at Killigrew Clay. All those years ago… she remembered the hysterical tales of the badly-loaded clay waggons hurtling through the town and the resulting disaster, with lives lost, and the destruction of the very bakery that was now Fielding's Tea Rooms in which they were sitting.

'But there's plenty of work now. The clay is fetching a fine price—'

'That's as may be, but there will allus be they who are greedy, my lamb. A few of the scaggies were sacked when they was discovered at it, but some of the regulars refused to work wi' the rest, and left of their own accord. Bult and Vine's needed men for the spring despatches, and stupidly took the bad 'uns on again and hoped for the best. The whole business is causing a lot of unrest among our men. So Ben hadn't told you?'

'No,' Morwen said shortly. 'How long have you known of it?'

Bess thought back. 'About a week. I daresay you've all been too taken up with your visitor for Ben to think of it.'

Morwen looked at her sceptically. Too taken up with visitors to mention something that could be significant in their lives? Too self-contained to share such a turn of events with his wife, with whom he had always shared the good times and the bad, especially those concerning Killigrew Clay?

Morwen felt as though an icy band was settling somewhere around her heart, wondering just how far apart they had really grown, so imperceptibly that she had never even noticed it was happening.

Chapter Three

'Why didn't you tell me about the scaggies!'

Ben looked at the flushed and angry face of his wife when he arrived home that evening. He had spent a wearisome afternoon trying to determine if any of Killigrew's clay was being filched from under his nose, and the last thing he wanted was to be met by accusations and female tantrums.

'It's men's business,' he said coldly. 'Will you please pull off my boots for me?'

She ignored the dusty, booted foot thrust up on to the foot-stool, and folded her arms tightly across her chest, glowering down at her husband.

'Is that all you think I'm good for? To tug at your boots and grace your table and tuck your children in bed at night? I'm not a skivvy, Ben—'

'Then act like the wife of a gentleman, and pull off my boots before the circulation is cut off completely.'

The edge in his voice now took away any suggestion of teasing in the words.

She reached down, tugging at one boot and then the other, and flinging them across the elegant drawing-room.

'That's a very childish action,' Ben snapped. 'And more worthy of young Charlotte than my wife—'

'Your wife – your *wife*!' She was incensed now. 'I'm *Morwen*, Ben! I'm flesh and blood, not a possession to be brought out and then tidied away when it suits 'ee. I'm the one you share your troubles with – or so I always thought.'

She couldn't hide her hurt, especially over this. Didn't he know – was he so blind that he couldn't see – that her heart and soul was still entrenched in the fortunes of the clayworks?

And not because of how grand the Killigrews could become when the demand for clay went well, or if he said jocularly that they must draw in their horns a little if demand fell. The clay was part of her life, and had been long before she met Mr High-and-Mighty Ben Killigrew…

Her own thoughts appalled her. But Ben – even Ben – had come into the works long after Morwen. His father had been the mighty clay boss while Ben prettied his time away in a fancy London college. While Morwen and all her family – every one of them – had been gouging out the soft white substance from the earth to make the Killigrews rich. Oh yes, she was very much a part of it all, and how dare he forget it for one minute.

'I think you forget your place,' Ben said icily.

'I do not! I forget nothing!' She flashed at him, deliberately misunderstanding. 'I remember all the years my Mammie and Daddy gave to Killigrew Clay. I remember how my brother Sam died for it. I remember how Jack and Freddie and me wore our fingers to ribbons in cold and rain and mist to keep your family prosperous. And all for the pittances you saw fit to pay to the likes o' we!'

She bit her lip, furious that her lady's manner was slipping badly. Her heart beat sickeningly at recognizing in Ben's eyes the disgust at her outburst. Disgust… when once he would have laughed and thought her Cornish ways quaintly charming, folded her in his arms and kissed away the quarrel…

'What is it you want to know?' He spoke with insulting politeness. 'Perhaps we had best get it said, and then we may present ourselves for dinner in a reasonable state of harmony. The children will be sent down from the nursery soon, and your visitor will be returning from Gorran's Chambers.'

Oh God, when did he become so pompous? Morwen clamped her lips together rather than make an angry retort that Ran Wainwright wasn't merely her visitor. She knew well enough that it was Matt Tremayne's sister the American had come to see. Not only her, she thought quickly, but she admitted there was a small truth in Ben's tart remark.

And it was Matt's parents he now knew and who found him pleasantly agreeable, and nothing like the wild colonials that Ben had teasingly told them lived beyond the ocean. It was Matt's family he was so taken with, and Ben Killigrew was a mere accessory to the Tremaynes. It was a novel situation, and if he felt it a blow to his pride for one moment on that account, she guessed that he would dismiss it as being ridiculous.

'I want to know if it's a serious matter at Bult and Vine's,' she said, trying not to let her mouth tremble. Any suggestion of scaggying or strikes or wild-running among the clayworkers was always serious. Morwen had always seen it as an omen for herself too. When things went wrong with the clay, somehow they invariably went wrong for her. She knew better than to try to explain that to Ben. He would call her as moonstruck as the old hag on the moors, whose cottage had gone up in smoke with her in it a year or so ago. For which most folk had thankfully and guiltily said good riddance.

'Discontent among workers is always serious,' he said shortly. He caught her eye, as mutinous as only Morwen could look when she knew she wasn't getting a straight answer. Damn her need for honesty, Ben thought sourly. Hadn't she learned yet that in business, as in life, there were some things that were best glossed over?

'All right. There's been some scaggying—'

'I know that. My mother told me. Daddy told her a week ago.' She let this sink in with a little pause. 'So how will it affect us?'

'I won't hold with scaggying or striking, and that's one thing on which I'm certain,' Ben was suddenly more like his old self, the pomposity stifled as his eyes gleamed. 'Killigrew clayworkers get fair dues for their labour, and I shall read them the riot act to make them realize it. They're better off now than they ever were, and I'll not stand for it!'

'Bravo,' Morwen said tremulously. 'Your father wouldn't have stood for it either. Whatever their grievances, stop them swiftly and sharply, he always told Daddy. Tell them to work or get out. There's no place here for wastrels.'

He was suddenly still, listening to her. It was like listening to the ghost of old Charles Killigrew, giving his lion's roar to his Pit Captains, to Hal Tremayne and Gil Dark, and the others from Pits Three and Four. His wife was no social butterfly, flitting about the society set of the town with her head full of fripperies and nonsense. And he knew instantly how badly he had hurt the woman who was inextricably a part of him, of the clay, and of his life.

He moved across the room to her in long strides. He took her in his arms, and held her against his chest. The beat of her heart was his heart, her sudden glimmering tears echoed inside him. He felt her trembling body and hated himself.

'Forgive me, dar,' he murmured roughly. 'It's sometimes too easy to forget the important things.'

'It doesn't matter, Ben,' she whispered against the warmth of his body. 'We are what we are.'

Someone else had once said as much. Someone she wished hadn't come into her thoughts just then: Captain Neville Peterson. And one of the reasons she didn't want to go to London with Ben was because of the risk of seeing Neville Peterson again.

And what was more likely? Peterson was one of Ormsby College's Crimean heroes. He had not an ounce of sensitivity about the way Ben had sent him packing after his disgraceful behaviour with the piano tutor, and he would undoubtedly be present at the new Honorary Governor's inauguration. Seeing him again would be more than an ordeal for Morwen, but she had never revealed her dread of it to Ben.

She was as guilty as he for keeping secrets… thankfully, the London visit was still some weeks away, and Ben was too fully occupied with the crisis at the clayworks to dwell on it. He admitted to himself, if not to Morwen, that there was a crisis.

–

He called a meeting at the works for Monday morning. Hal Tremayne, Works Manager, grizzled and a little stooped, still had enough voice to bellow at the boisterous clayworkers gathered at Clay One pit to keep some order while the boss had his say-so.

The pit was surrounded by the white spoil hills, the depth of the pit wider and deeper now than when Ben had first taken over from his father. The pool, filled with the slurry from the clay, was a pale milky-green in the September day. The autumn loads had been sent to Charlestown port on Ben's railway, and the turnaround in the preparing and drying and blocking of the clay should be starting now for next spring's despatches.

Ben's handsome face darkened. This should be a good time in the clay calendar. One load safely gone, the next swinging into production in line with the seasons. Instead, he faced an unsettled mob.

Clayworkers, young and old, squelching from foot to foot to keep from sinking into the mud in their thigh-length leather boots; the wild young kiddley-boys racing hither and thither, bootless and often shoeless, their feet hardened to the moors; the white-bonneted bal maidens, clustered together like fluttering moths, the long black hair of the younger ones streaming out; the older matrons seeming to have no hair at all beneath the all-embracing bonnets. And over faces and clothes, the clinging white clay dust that made phantoms of them all.

Except for the shouting and cat-calls, Clay One was eerily silent. There was no rumbling of the little trucks taking the waste to the sky-tips. The pumping-house was quiet, the beam engine still. The fire-hole no longer roared with the furnace heat and the blasphemies of the men stripped to the waist and glistening with sweat.

For an instant, Ben remembered the day he had taken his turn in the fire-hole at his father's insistence. The acrid smell of men's bodies, the unbearable heat, the searing of flesh, drying of eye sockets and throats, the bulging of muscles, were all as vivid to him now as it had tormented him then.

'Let's have silence, you buggers!' Hal shouted above the din. His son Sam had always added his voice to Hal's when needed. It was Ben's voice now that roared alongside him.

'Let's have a spokesman to air your grievances. We'll get nowhere while you're all hollering at once.'

He might as well have tried to stop the tide from filling Charlestown port twice a day.

'We want some assurance that our jobs be safe.'

''Tis our bellies that'll be empty if the clay demand falls off because of these bastards sellin' it off cheap—'

'Have I given any of you your marching orders?' Ben said angrily, having little patience with rumours and the way they made sheep of sensible men.

'Bult and Vine's have—'

'We're not Bult and Vine's,' Ben shouted back. 'Tell me your grievances, and I'll set your minds at rest—'

'I mind your daddy said that once,' one of the older clay-workers spoke up loudly. 'Next thing we knew we was on strike and our babies was starving.'

Ben looked at him coldly. 'We want no strikes here, and there's no need for them. You're paid a fair wage for a fair day's work. But I promise you, here and now, that the first one I catch scaggying will be out on his ear, and if he's living in one of my cottages he'll be turned out without a roof over his head.'

There were mutterings among the men, and cries of disapproval from the women.

'You'd turn out innocent babbies, would 'ee, Ben Killigrew?' One old harridan shrieked. 'Shame on 'ee for saying such an evil thing. 'Tis not what Morwen would want from 'ee. She'll not have forgotten her days in one of Killigrew's cots wi' her mammie and daddy. You go back to your fine house and tell Morwen what you've told we and see if 'ee don't get tongue pie for supper!'

The woman's words drew howls of laughter from the rest. Ben felt the anger tightening up in him. This was what he hated. There was no respect among these people. Couldn't they see that Morwen had moved on, even if they had not?

Morwen was his wife. She was no longer the prettiest bal maiden who ever worked at Killigrew Clay, turning every young clayworker's head. She was Mrs Killigrew, and these fools should remember it. He was about to tell them so, when he felt Hal's hand on his arm.

'Leave it, Ben. 'Twill do no good to let personal pride get in the way of what you've come here to say.'

Ben knew the sense of it well enough. He gave a small nod, waving his arms about for quiet.

'We all want the same thing,' he shouted, appealing to their common sense. 'We want Killigrew Clay to continue and prosper, and if some scaggies have begun disrupting Bult and Vine's, that's no concern of ours. His pits may be in a state of upheaval, but ours are not. And as long as you do your work, I'll do mine—'

'So long as those soft hands o' yourn don't get dirtied, I daresay—' a lone voice jeered, to be shushed by the majority.

Ben spoke loudly now that he had got their attention. 'It's time the clay bosses got together and stamped out this threat to all our livelihoods. What affects one pit affects all the rest. It's time we made certain rules and obligations between us all, and I'm going to ride over to Bultimore and Vine's right now to see if a proper meeting can be set up among the bosses. I shall propose that Hal Tremayne and the four Pit Captains attend, so that they can report back all that's said to you. Is it agreed? You can trust your Captains, and you know you can trust Hal Tremayne.'

The mutterings now were generally approving, unaware of the sarcastic note in his voice. They would trust Hal Tremayne in preference to trusting the man who put the bread in their children's mouths.

'Get back to work then, or there'll be no dues to put food in your children's bellies at the end of the week.' His voice held the smallest threat. They recognized it, and dispersed rapidly.

'That was a bit o' quick thinking, Ben. Though now you'll have to see it through,' Hal grunted as they made their way to his Works Manager's hut.

Ben smiled grimly. 'It wasn't said on the spur of the moment, Hal, even if it sounded that way. It's time for a reckoning with the rest of the bosses, and time we all stood firm. You'll know what a union means?'

Hal gaped at him. 'You're not proposing to unite the two clayworks, Ben? Your father 'ould turn in his grave. He built Killigrew Clay from nothing—'

'No, I'm not,' Ben said impatiently. 'But there should be rules for every pit, and we should all abide by them, to rid ourselves of the dangers of scaggying and striking.'

'You'll never do that. Not while men breathe and have minds o' their own. You can't be the voice for every clayworker, Ben. You know well enough that a Cornishman is fiercely proud and independent, and don't take kindly to rules.'

'They'll have to take to mine,' Ben retorted. 'There can be only one boss in any business.'

Hal looked at him thoughtfully. 'Yet you'm about to see Bult and Vine to make these daft suggestions?'

Ben flushed angrily. 'Daft suggestions? You forget yourself, Hal. You may be my father-in-law—'

'But that don't give me the right to say my piece, is that it? I think you'm forgetting summat too, Ben. A legal bit o' paper that says I've as much right to discuss these things as you, and if I think my partner's acting daft, I shall say so!'

They glared at one another across the hut, and then Ben grinned, holding out his hand for Hal to take.

'Damn it, man, it's me who's the bloody fool. You insist on keeping our partnership so well-hidden I'd all but forgotten it myself. You do well to remind me.'

'Well, now forget it,' Hal muttered. 'I don't bring it up to make trouble, and the dividends paid into the bank every year are frightening enough—'

Ben laughed good-naturedly now, slapping Hal on the back.

'By God, Hal, you're the only one I know who's frightened of accumulating wealth. Do you and Bess ever spend a fraction of what you make?'

Hal shrugged. 'I doubt it, since our needs are simple enough, and I can't make head nor tail of the accounting figures, and don't want to neither!'

Ben shook his head in disbelief. If he wanted to, he could swindle this simple man out of his fortune, and Hal would never be the wiser. He would never do it, of course; Hal was Morwen's father, and his good friend. But he knew that the naïvety of this man was echoed in all the moorland folk who worked the clay. They were honest and hard-working… except for the few…

'Did you never think of taking Bess to America to visit Matt?' Ben said abruptly. 'It would mean the world to her, and you have ample funds. And it was Matt's gift that made our partnership possible, so it would seem right—'

Hal's face was shadowed. 'Our Matt left us. He's made amends by writing and putting his mammie's mind at rest, but it's his place to come to us, not the other way around. Besides, if Bess and me suddenly sported fares to America, the rest on 'em 'ould wonder where we got the money, and know of our partnership arrangement, and we swore to keep it private, didn't we?'

There was no way such a dogged man could be changed, and the Tremayne pride was leaps and bounds ahead of the Killigrews', Ben thought, as he rode off towards the other large clayworks in the district. That damnable pride that could keep families and lovers apart, and made a mockery of the honesty they all admired so much.

-

It was evening by the time he got back to Killigrew House. He had called at Hal's house to tell him that the other clay bosses had been all too eager to go along with Ben's suggestion for certain rules and agreements. No scaggies were going to skip from one claypit to the next and keep their own bit of shiftless work going. The general meeting with Works Managers and Pit Captains was fixed for two days' time, at Bult and Vine's.

He felt more than satisfied. It was for the good of everybody, and Morwen could get that worried look off her face now. He loved her, but he wished she wouldn't concern herself quite so much with what went on at the works. Ben was nothing if not a man's man, and his need to take care of the business without any female interference was absolute.

There was already one woman who had inherited her husband's clayworks, and was said to be running it single-handed. A load of poppy-cock, Ben thought sourly. Did she stoke the fire-hole? Did she stack the clay blocks all by herself, when a team of bal maidens worked for the whole year to prepare the twice-yearly loads in every pit he knew? Did she wheel the little trucks and tip the waste?

No, much as he loved Morwen's nimble mind and undoubted intelligence, and the wisdom that was sometimes uncanny, her place was here in his house, caring for his children and being his woman… just as she herself had asked him so scathingly, he thought, with a small grin at her impertinence.

She ran to greet him as he entered the house. Her eyes were shining, and as he held her close, he thought how beautiful she was tonight, and how easily his hands spanned her waist, and how delightfully her softly curving body nestled against him.

Desire flared within in him as it hadn't done for some little while, and he smiled down into her glowing face.

'You'll never guess what's happened, dar!'

'Then you'll just have to tell me,' he teased. 'Quickly, before the little hordes rush in and spoil this moment.'

Already they could hear the sounds of high-pitched voices, laughing and squabbling, from somewhere in another room.

'Oh, it's all right,' Morwen laughed. 'They're too busy playing charades with Ran. He came home ages ago with such exciting news! They'll be bursting to tell you too, and will no doubt get it all wrong!'

So, all this exuberance was because of Ran Wainwright. Ben held Morwen slightly away from him, watching the rapid rise and fall of her breasts in the rose-coloured gown she wore. When had she last looked this excited for him? The unexpected thought disturbed him.

'What news?' he said, a little distantly.

'Ran's bought out Prosper Barrows!'

Ben stared at her disbelievingly.

'He's going into clay-stone quarrying? But he knows nothing about it! What kind of foolhardy scheme is this?'

Morwen's smile slipped a little.

'Ben, I thought you'd be pleased! It means Ran has decided to settle in Cornwall, and not only that, his business and ours will have connections. It will be almost like having Matt home again.'

She was so charmed at the thought that she didn't notice her husband's darkening features.

'He decided to settle here pretty damn quickly, didn't he? What happened to the accounting post I arranged for him at Gorran's?' Resentment oozed out of him, and Morwen spoke impatiently.

'He intends to carry on with that for the time being. He wants to leam all he can about business methods here. He's putting money into Prosper Barrows, but he will leave the actual production to his stoneworkers. My guess is that Ran means to be there as often as he can, all the same. He says that a boss without his finger in the working pie is no boss at all.'

'He says that, does he? You seem to know a great deal about it. And I suppose the children know it all as well? Everyone knew but me.' He growled the words, knowing they sounded petulant and irritated, but that was suddenly the way he felt.

Prosper Barrows had been a going concern until the owner gambled his assets away. Since china-stone had as steady a market as clay, if not more so, the quarry-workings only needed a good injection of money behind it to make it highly competitive in the alternative industry.

Entrepreneurs from up-country England had taken over more than one such quarry, left it to the Pit Captains to work the china-stone with new and more efficient equipment, and sat back in their city mansions, reaping in the profits.

Ben had never considered that the American would speculate in the same way, and for some reason he found the news less than agreeable. He saw Morwen's astonished face.

'Lack of communication seems usual between us lately, Ben.' Her voice was soft and steady. 'I don't recall you telling me so fast about the scaggies. And since I only heard of Ran's business venture this afternoon, you hardly expected me to ride up to Killigrew Clay to tell you, did you?'

Before he could answer, the children came rushing into the room, clamouring with Ran's news. Ben saw the way little Charlotte was held tightly in the man's arms, and how eleven-year-old Primmy gazed up adoringly into the handsome American's face. To the three boys, Ran was clearly a hero, and jealousy ran through him, as keen as a knife.

'I hear I've to congratulate you, Ran.' He spoke with false heartiness. The American gave an apologetic laugh.

'I would have liked time to consult with you on it, Ben, but the chance came this afternoon when the owner walked into Gorran's Chambers. There were two others in the running, so

I had to make a quick decision, and fortunately I was able to top their offers. I hope it's the right decision.'

'I hope so too.'

Morwen's eyes flashed at her husband.

'Oh Ben, can't you be more positive? It's simply wonderful, and there will be even more reason for Matt to come home now. Louisa and Cresswell will have relatives on both sides of the family to visit!'

'Yes, it's wonderful,' Ben said steadily, hoping that the sparkle in Morwen's eyes was on account of this fascination with seeing her brother again, and not for the enjoyment of having Randell Wainwright around permanently. But not here at Killigrew House, surely! This new thought occurred. As if Morwen was reading his mind in her uncanny way, he heard her speak sweetly.

'Ran will be looking for a house of his own in the district, Ben, and I've said it will be my pleasure to help him choose and to arrange the decor for him. It will be such fun, and the girls are going to help too, aren't you, my darlings?'

'So are we!' Walter and Albert and Justin shouted in unison, as the little girls squealed with delight. 'We're all going to help Uncle Ran in his new house, and we can visit him there as often as we like. He told us so!'

They laughed and joked and made plans, all through dinner and for the rest of the evening until it was time for the children to go to bed. And still Morwen hadn't asked what had happened at Killigrew Clay that day. It seemed that she was too taken up with these new happenings to take any further interest. So much for her avid concern, Ben thought savagely.

In the end, he interrupted the gleeful plans his wife and the American cousin were making as to colour schemes and carpets and furniture, discussing them just as though they were a newly-married couple. Ben told them shortly all that had happened at the clayworks meeting that day, and of his preliminary meeting with Bultimore and Vine's before the all-important one in two days' time. Morwen gave him all her attention u... something still nagged vaguely at Ben's gut.

It was a feeling he didn't like one bit. It was as if he needed to break through some invisible barrier erected against him. And it was Ben Killigrew now who, for once in his life, felt very much the outsider looking in.

Chapter Four

Mrs Horn had lit a fire in their bedroom that evening. The late September nights had turned cold, and the welcome flames leapt in the fireplace. Morwen held her nightgown in front of it to warm it for a few minutes, undressing in front of the comforting glow. Her long black hair was free from its pins, and fell in cascading waves over her bare shoulders. Through its tresses Ben could see the firelight, and it was though the flames danced in the silken strands. It made of her a wood-nymph, a creature of nature, which to Ben she had always been.

She was unconsciously voluptuous. She had never had need of stays or bodices. She was firm and rounded and supple. To Ben she had hardly changed since the first heady days of their marriage, despite having had the children. He knew every soft contour of her. He knew the scent and the feel of her, and the answering caress of her fingers on his body. And the sudden need to make her his, to possess her and be possessed by her, was overwhelming.

As though aware of his growing desire, she turned her head slowly. Her profile was etched against the orange glow of the fire, her arms poised to pull the nightgown over her head.

'Leave it, love,' Ben said softly. 'Come to me.'

He held out his arms, glorying in the nakedness of her. And Morwen, with that extra perception that made her uniquely Cornish, knew of his need that went beyond the urges of the flesh. She ran her hand expressively over the deep pile of the carpet on which she half-lay.

'You come to me, dar,' she murmured.

Ben moved swiftly to her side, lying beside her on the Axminster that was warmed by the fire, making a lovers' bed of it. Morwen lay back, her glorious hair fanning out around her head, the dark triangle between her thighs inviting him in. He ran his questing hands slowly over her breasts, feeling their quick response, hearing her breathing grow heavy as her desire rose to meet his in an instant.

It was always so. It had always been so. No thoughts of anything beyond these four walls, and the love that soared within it, entered either of their minds from that moment on. Ben leaned over her, his flesh hard and familiar on hers, his arms holding her, wanting, every pore in him aching for fulfilment with her. His mouth sought and found hers, and when he spoke his breath was no more than a fraction away from her.

'It seems a long while since I told you I loved you, my Morwen.' His voice was husky with passion. 'How can something so important be so overlooked?'

She touched her fingers to his lips to hush him.

'What need is there for words when you tell me of your love every day of our lives, just by being with me, dar?' she whispered back. Right then, it was never so true. What need for words, when feelings, emotions, desire, said everything that was needed to be said?

She felt the sweet pattern of their loving begin; the seeking hands; the teasing kisses on every part of her that changed so quickly to passion; Ben's touch that was lust and love combined, rousing her to something approaching ecstasy.

'Oh Ben, I want – I want—' she said faintly.

If it was unladylike to let a man know how much a woman could want him, such thoughts didn't form part of Morwen Killigrew's make-up. If he ever considered that such behaviour was unladylike in a wife, it was never now, never when his Morwen moved so erotically beneath him, bringing him near to his own state of rapture.

The time for such delightful play was over. He parted the soft black tangle of body hair, knowing that she would be ready for him as always. It was almost fulfilment enough to slide inside that warm inviting place, to know that he was so wanted and welcomed there. In all the world there could never be such a feeling as this, this oneness, this perfection, this love…

And afterwards, the sweet lethargy of lying motionless, still locked in love, with the fire's warmth gently suffusing them, almost lulling them to sleep where they lay.

Ben wished that life could always be this beautiful, and at last he realized the fire had died, and only a few embers still glowed in the grate. He kissed Morwen's soft lips and dream-closed eyes, lifted her bodily and lay her between the bedcovers without attempting to pull the cumbersome nightgown over her head. She would be warmed enough in his arms.

–

A week later an urchin kiddley-boy ran all the way down to St Austell town, to summon Ben with all speed to Killigrew Clay. The boy's eyes were saucer-round, awed at the sight of the big house, and ready to spill news of its grandeur to all those who had never seen it.

'You must know what's wrong, boy,' Ben snapped in annoyance, when the child seemed almost dumb-struck and could barely stammer the necessary words. 'Is it scaggying or what?'

'I dunno, Mr Killigrew, Sir. I was just told to run and tell 'ee to come at once.'

Morwen had heard the rumpus downstairs, and came into the dining-room, where Mrs Horn was tut-tutting over the boy's unshod feet and the mud oozing on to her clean floor. Morwen took in the scene at once, and went to the boy's side.

'It's Billy Dare, isn't it?' she said. 'Get your breath back a minute, lamb, and try to tell us what's to do. Take a deep breath, and Mrs Horn will get you some lemon to drink and a fruit scone to fill your belly.'

Mrs Horn looked scandalized, but Morwen ignored her. She knew how it felt to be poor and hungry, and to be so overcome by the trappings of rich folk that the mouth dried and the legs turned to jelly. She knew how young Billy Dare would be feeling at coming here, when his family lived in one of the meagre cottages on the moors. A cottage where you could see the stars through the slates on the roof, and where the wind blew down the chimney and put out the peat fire, filling the rooms with a choking stench in minutes. Morwen remembered such a cottage where she had been born, remembered it with a fierce loyalty and love for those families who had nothing but the weekly wages packets from the clay bosses to feed their ever-growing broods.

'Morwen, leave this to me—'

'You frighten him, Ben,' she retorted. 'Tell us what's happened, Billy. Is it fighting, perhaps?'

She took a wild guess, and to her surprise the boy nodded vigorously. He sucked noisily at the lemon drink Mrs Horn thrust at him, and nearly gagged on the hot fruit scone.

'There's fighting summat awful, Missus!' he said at last, spluttering crumbs and currants in his eagerness to say it and be gone. 'Two bal maidens started it, and then more on 'em joined in, and my daddy says they'm like a lot o' she-cats scratching and screeching and gettin' no work done—'

'Bal maidens fighting!' Ben's voice was furious. 'Do you mean you've been sent all this way to tell me about women's squabbles, instead of doing your work?'

Billy Dare looked at him, scared and white-faced now.

''Tweren't my fault, Boss! Mr Tremayne told me to come.'

Morwen was angered by the derision in Ben's face, as if women's quarrels were unworthy of his attention. She was angered too by the way he had turned on the unfortunate child, no more than eight years old. She was unable to resist thinking how different life might have been for her own Charlotte, if she too had been born in a clayworker's cottage instead of in the loving comfort of Killigrew House.

'If Daddy thought it was necessary to send the boy, it must be so, Ben,' she said in a clipped voice. 'It must be more serious than just women squabbling!'

She didn't need telling how quick the bal maidens could be to fight when provoked. It was all part and parcel of the lusty freedom of the moorland life, women and children working alongside the men, and no doubt each side would have a proper supportive group cheering them on by now…

'I shall ride up there immediately.' Ben was clearly put out, and didn't need his wife to point out what was obvious enough to him.

He looked at the wide-eyed child. 'You'll find your own way back, and I'll expect you to go straight there, or you'll be docked a penny from your wages for dawdling.'

He slammed out of the room without another word, paused to collect something he needed from the study, and left Morwen speechless at his arrogance. He had a great deal of worry on his mind, but this was too much… too much…

''S'all right, Missus,' she heard the boy say with an unconcerned sniff. 'I ain't afeared of getting my feet wet. Me dad says they'm ducks' feet by now, anyways.'

Morwen felt her throat constrict. Years ago, her parents had used the same words about her brothers when they too were doing the cheap and cheerful jobs at Clay One.

'Wait a minute longer, Billy,' she said. 'You'll just sit down and finish that scone properly. And nobody's going to take a penny from your wages.'

She knew Mrs Horn was hovering outside the open door, no doubt wondering if the scallywag would pocket anything he shouldn't. Morwen sent for Fanny, and when the maid came and bobbed enquiringly, her nose wrinkled at the sight of the clayboy perched on one of the best dining chairs, bare feet swinging.

'Fanny, go to the closet in Master Justin's room and find an outgrown pair of boots that look as though they might fit Billy

Dare. Hurry now!' She added the words as the maid's mouth gaped open, the same as Billy Dare's.

'I never had no boots, Missus,' he said nervously.

Morwen smiled generously, but tears threatened at the backs of her eyes.

'Well, you're going to get some now. They may not be the best fit, but they'll keep you warm and dry. You may tell your mother that it's not charity, but that Mrs Killigrew had no more use for them, and can't abide waste.'

She hoped that the last remark would soften the indignity of passing on used boots. For all their need, clayworkers could be almighty proud when they chose. Ten minutes later, Billy Dare went clumping awkwardly out of Killigrew House, and Morwen prayed that he wouldn't have blisters by the time he reached the clayworks. She doubted it. The poor little feet already resembled tanned leather. She dismissed him from her thoughts with an effort, knowing she had done all she could for him, bursting with anxiety to know what was happening up on the moors.

–

Ben wondered if he had come upon a fairground wrestling match. The two bal maidens who had originally started the fight had long ago exhausted themselves. It had been taken up by half a dozen others on each side, and the women slithered and scratched, punched and pummelled... but they were hardly recognizable as women any longer. They were caked in the slop of the clay slurry and the sinking mud of the pit. Light-coloured skirts and bonnets were caked with it, the fabric clinging to their bodies and revealing young shapes or pendulous breasts, all to the jeers and cheers of the clayworkers gathered round. Pennies that could ill be afforded were being tossed in the air as wagers to see which side would win.

'What in God's name is going on here?' Ben roared into the hullaballoo.

Nobody heard him at first, and then those on the outskirts of the group shuffled their feet and fell silent, as he forced his way through. He remained mounted to give himself authority, his horse whinnying at the clamour all around, and frightened at the oozing mud beneath his hooves.

'Hal Tremayne!' Ben bellowed next, too intent on keeping his balance to think first and speak later. 'Where's that damn-fool Works Manager? I don't pay him to let my workers act like ruffians instead of getting on with their work.'

He caught sight of Hal's furious white face a minute later, and realized what he had said. But it was too late. The words were said. And if Hal didn't like it, then he was a bigger bloody fool than he needed to be, Ben thought wrathfully. There was no need to play the game he did. Why not come out in the open and say he was part-owner, take life easy and spend his days in easier pursuits than pacifying these scruffs?

He suddenly remembered he had done nothing about persuading Hal to see Doctor Pender. But if the man couldn't look after his own health, he shouldn't expect somebody else to do it for him. Ben's small twist of guilt vanished.

Hal pushed his way through the crowds closing around him and Ben in a way that was almost menacing. Ben shrugged off the feeling. This was his clayworks. He was the boss here, and if they wanted to collect their pay dues, they owed it to him to do their work.

'There's big trouble, Mr Killigrew,' Hal snapped.

Mr Killigrew? What was this? Ben looked at him sharply, seeing the angry pulsing in Hal's throat. There was obviously trouble here. There was also going to be a reckoning between the two of them later, he guessed.

'I'm not blind, man! Who started it?'

The women began screaming abuse at each other at once. The clayworkers hollered, backing either side. The kiddley-boys screamed with laughter, dancing a jig in the mud and enjoying a respite in the daily boredom.

Without warning, a cracking shot rang out, blue smoke rising into the air from the pistol in Ben's upthrust hand. The screams were of terror now, and then the entire crowd was hushed except for the sounds of muted sobbing from those nearest to him. The horse jerked beneath him, but Ben dug his heels in tightly to the animal's flanks, and gripped the reins with his free hand.

'If any of you buggers want to argue with me further, you'll find the next bullet aimed at somebody's head,' he roared. 'Now, you'll let Hal Tremayne be spokesman, or you'll know what to expect.'

He looked down into the disbelieving eyes of Morwen's father. Never, in all the years old Charles Killigrew had been boss of Killigrew Clay, had he fired a shot at the men. The pistol had remained in its case in the study, being cleaned and oiled at intervals to ensure its efficiency. It had never been needed, and Charles Killigrew's proud boast had been that it never would. But Ben had spoiled all that. Ben had different ideas.

'Two bal maidens had a disagreement,' Hal said savagely. 'One accused the other of walking out with one of the scaggies from Bult and Vine's. T'other 'un said didn't she know there were scaggies at Killigrew Clay already, so what did it matter, and the first was only jealous of her having a young buck. There was name-calling and mud-slinging, and next thing we knew they was wallowing in the mud, and t'others was joining in. It started out as a bit of a lark and caught fire.' He had said his piece and his lips clamped shut. He had never felt ashamed of Ben before. Hal had been proud and honoured to call him son-in-law, but he was shamed by Ben's action today. To fire on a bunch of clayworkers, even over their heads, was demeaning.

But Ben wasn't listening any longer. His attention was caught by that one phrase: Didn't she know there was scaggies at Killigrew Clay already…

'Do any of you buggers know anything about scaggies in my employ?' He bawled at the clayworkers.

There were shuffling feet, mutterings and growlings, but nobody answered. The bal maidens were sullen, shapeless masses of filth, and Ben was suddenly sickened by the whole lot of them.

'Then if I can't trust you to work without supervision, I shall make it my business to be here every day in future. I'll see to it that no clay leaves this pit but what's accounted for to me. If you want to act like children, then you'll be treated like children. Hal, I'll see you in my office in St Austell after your shift.'

He twisted the horse's neck in his eagerness to get away from here, regardless of the animal's protesting cry. He ignored Hal's outraged look at being summoned to St Austell instead of thrashing things out here in his hut. He was so sick of the whole clay business he wanted to ride as hard and long as he could, away from the dankness of the clay and on to the free open moors where he could get some good clean air in his lungs.

He didn't need telling that he had done wrong in firing the pistol. Other bosses may have done the same, but that didn't make it better. It was a bully's way, and Ben didn't want to dwell on that. He had never been accused of bullying... into his head came Morwen's softly accusing voice, 'Why must you teach the boys that awful fighting art, Ben? It's so cruel, and I'm sure they'll hurt themselves. You're a bully to insist on it!'

He rode hard, unheeding of the way the horse foamed, until the heaving flanks beneath him made him slow down to a trot. He patted the sweating neck, speaking shortly to the beast as he slid from his back and let them both recover.

Was it cruel to insist on teaching his boys to defend themselves from whatever they came across in life? Was he a bully to want no evil to come to them? He swore violently as he stubbed his foot on a hidden stump, and recognized the soaring granite mass of the Larnie Stone nearby.

He had no idea he had ridden as far as the mystical Cornish standing stone, through whose hole could be seen the distant sea at St Austell. The stone where Morwen and her friend Celia had danced at midnight after swallowing a witch's potion, hoping to see the faces of their true loves. Celia had seen the wicked laughing face of his cousin Jude, and Morwen had seen Ben Killiigrew, and the pattern of their lives had been set.

Did she sometimes wish that day had never happened, Ben thought suddenly? Was Hal Tremayne wishing right now, as he dealt with the furore Ben had left behind, that Ben Killigrew had never entered their lives at all, but had stayed a dandified college boy who wouldn't soil his hands with the clay?

Ben wished his thoughts away. There was no place for sentiment in business, and Hal must realize that. His married life was totally separate from his business life, and the Tremaynes must accept that too. He simply refused to get caught up with these petty personality crises on top of everything else.

A small breeze blew through the coarse bracken, like a sorrowing sigh. The mist would soon be rising, swirling about the moors and creating ghostly images. The late afternoon sky was already darkening, and Ben had no wish to be up on the moors in an October mist. A man could lose his way and his footing, and some said his reason too, when he was mist-touched.

He turned the horse more gently and rode at a fair pace the way he had come, knowing he still had to face Hal's pride and Morwen's questions. And half wishing he too had never heard of a family called Tremayne.

'So you've chosen to use violence, have 'ee, Ben?' Hal faced him across the stout oak desk at Ben's office in the town. Ben had had to wait a long time for Hal to arrive, and it hadn't put him the best of tempers. Nor did he like being put on the defensive.

'Violence? I didn't fire directly at anyone, and you know it. Nor would I have done—'

'Not this time. But pistols are a coward's way, Ben, and I never thought to see 'ee resort to such a thing.'

Ben scowled. His own father was dead, and he didn't need Morwen's father taking on the role of guide and mentor.

'And what would you have done?' he asked sarcastically.

'Tried reasoning. Diverted 'em. Anything other than what you did,' Hal retorted.

'When I want your advice, I'll ask for it.'

'I thought you just did.'

They glared at one another, the first time he and Hal had acted more like enemies than friends. There had always been respect on both sides. Now Ben knew to his regret, that there was little respect in his father-in-law's eyes today. He resented the fact keenly. Hal was still a clayworker at heart. He might understand those like him, but he was no scholar, nor a young boss, and as such didn't understand the fine line he sometimes trod to keep that status.

'For God's sake, man, sit down,' Ben said irritably, as Hal began stifling a cough and going puce in the face at the effort. 'We'll gain nothing if you collapse in the middle of an argument. Have you seen a doctor about that cough?' It was out now, bluntly and without preamble, and he heard Hal swear beneath his breath.

'I don't hold wi' doctors,' he growled.

'Perhaps Bess won't hold with having a dead husband. I'll ask Doctor Pender to call at the house and see you tomorrow morning. Take the day off. I'll be at Clay One, so there'll be no need for you to be there for once.'

Hal's blue eyes flashed. 'And have the men say I've backed down because of all the fuss?'

'Don't be bloody stupid. You'll see the doctor and there's an end to it. I'm not having you hacking and barking all winter and getting my head snapped off by my wife for not making you see sense. Tremayne women usually get their own way, in case you haven't noticed.'

Hal gave the glint of a smile.

'I've noticed. So what's to do about the trouble then?'

Ben leaned back. He knew he'd gained a small victory. Hal would see the doctor, though Ben knew very well he'd be at the works the minute the man had gone. The two of them had calmed down a little; but there was one more thing that needed saying.

'Let's get one thing straight first of all. I apologize for the way I referred to you, Hal. It was unforgivable. If you'd just end this farce and tell everyone that you're my partner—'

'*No*. I'll continue working until I drop, so we'll hear no more o' that.' He was doggedly adamant. 'And we'd best forget one chance remark. 'Tis less important than what's to be done.'

He had clearly had time to think too, and Ben breathed a little more easily. The last thing he wanted was to have Hal as an enemy. He gave a shrug.

'For the present, it will be as I said. I'll be at the works every day. We'll work together, which is as it should be.'

'And what of this journey to London that our Morwen's been on about? Don't that come up soon?'

Ben swore beneath his breath. He'd completely forgotten the forthcoming trip to London and the honour to be bestowed on him at his old college. He couldn't refuse to go. He didn't choose to refuse, anyway. But the plans would need to be altered. It was no longer feasible to spend several weeks away from Cornwall. God knew what might happen if he did.

There might very well be no clayworks to come back to if he left it in the hands of fools. He didn't look directly at Hal. He never meant to think of his father-in-law in those terms, but when all was said and done, there were men born to lead and others born to follow, and Hal Tremayne was most definitely one of the latter.

'My plans will have to be changed,' Ben said abruptly. 'I doubt that Morwen will be too disappointed if I don't take her with me, since she was never over-keen on the idea. I shall be away for the minimum of time, Hal. A day to reach London, a day for the presentation, and a day to get back. Three days in all. I daresay the works won't fall to ruin in that time.'

'I daresay they won't,' Hal said evenly.

Ben shot out his hand and Hal took it grudgingly. Without realizing that he did so, he echoed his daughter's thoughts; Ben Killigrew had changed. He was no longer the young and dashing clay boss, but a man borne down by worries and frustrations. He had grown hard, and if that was what responsibility did to a man, Hal wanted none of it.

'Do as I told you, Hal,' Ben warned him as they parted company. 'I'll want to hear what Doctor Pender had to say when I see you next.'

'Mebbe,' Hal grunted, and left the younger man to glower at the implacable stiff walk of his wife's father.

Morwen was waiting for him when he got home.

'Well?' She said at once. 'How serious is it?'

'Serious enough that I've decided I can't spare so much time in London. I need to be on hand to keep my eye on them. They act like spoilt children half the time.' He spilled out his rage, fully aware of the flare of hope on Morwen's face at his words. He related what had happened, leaving out the ignominious firing of the pistol, and the angry exchange with Hal.

'By the way, I told your father I'd get Doctor Pender to call on him tomorrow morning,' he added casually, taking her mind off the troubles immediately.

'And he agreed?' she asked in astonishment.

Ben spoke grimly. 'He had to. I shall be at Clay One tomorrow morning and every morning, and I told your father I want a full report of what the doctor has to say.'

'But if you're to be there every morning, what about our time in London?' Morwen said carefully. It was coming close now.

He gave a short laugh. 'Your eyes give you away, my sweet. Have no fear, you'll not be expected to accompany me. I can barely take the time to go myself, but I'm damned if I'll let clay-workers' squabbles dictate to me, and ruin a splendid occasion. I shall go alone, and be back in three days.'

When she said nothing, trying desperately to disguise the enormous relief she felt, Ben walked to where she sat on the sofa, leaning down and tipping up her chin with his finger. It was less a gesture of love than of mockery.

'Will you exist without me for three days, my love? I'm sure that you will, especially with the dashing Ran to keep you company. I daresay you'll hardly miss me at all!'

He strode off to put the gun back in the study, wishing he'd never seen the damnable thing. And Morwen sat very still, her eyes suddenly pricking. Once, Ben would never have spoken to her in such a way.

There was spite and hurt and frustration in his voice. And whatever he had intended by his words, Morwen realized blindingly that there was truth in what he said, so much so that she hardly dared to face up to it.

Chapter Five

The doctor gave Hal some linctus for his chest, saying that it was no worse than for any middling man, and would see him well into old age, providing he took reasonable care. Morwen breathed a little more freely when her mother told her, though she added tartly that for a Works Manager to go tramping about in the damp clay-clogged earth at all hours probably went completely against the doctor's warning.

But there was another bit of cheerful news. There was to be an October Fair in Truro at the end of the month. Details were announced in *The Informer* newspaper, and the Killigrew children were agog with excitement when they discovered it.

'Oh, please can we go, Mama?' Primmy pleaded. 'Please say we can! Uncle Ran will take us, even if Papa says he's too busy like he usually does! Uncle Ran will let us have fun!'

Morwen laughingly shushed her, egged on by her other eager little daughter. Charlotte's blue eyes shone like jewels as she climbed on to her mother's knee, mindless of Morwen's freshly-donned dress, all ready for afternoon tea with several town dignitaries who had been invited to meet Randell.

Thankfully, both he and Ben were still upstairs, for Ben would be none too pleased at hearing his daughter's careless dismissal of her father's presence, however innocently said.

'I'm sure we can go to the Fair, and I'm just as sure that your Papa will want to take us,' she said.

Justin pulled a face. 'If he's in his usual bad humour, I'd rather it was Uncle Ran,' he muttered.

'Justin, that's enough,' Morwen said sharply.

'Well, I don't care who takes us as long as we go!' Primmy put in airily. She paused in front of the mirror, on her way to the pianoforte, which she was learning with considerable dexterity, and Morwen noted with sudden alarm how vain the girl was becoming. She was eleven years old, but sometimes she behaved with an elegance that was far beyond her years.

'If we do go to the Fair, you'll stay with the adults at all times,' Morwen assured her. 'There are rogues and pickpockets at these places, and there will be no slipping away to watch puppet shows or hurdy-gurdy men on your own. Is that understood?'

'It sounds as if you've been to plenty of Fairs, Mother,' Walter added his piece grumblingly. 'You've never let us go before, and we're not babies—'

'Well, I've said you can go to this one as long as you all behave, and there's an end to it.'

She knew she was being tetchy, and she wondered that Albert wasn't clamouring about the Fair too. But he was more taken up in watching the progress of a beetle across the mist-spangled lawn outside. Albert would happily go wherever anyone else directed. He was the least complicated of the children, the nature lover.

As for the rest of them… there were plenty of arguments between them. Walter, the eldest, couldn't seem to get along with Justin at all, though Morwen admitted that it was usually Justin who picked the fight. And the girls… Primmy was growing up too fast, and little Charlotte at six years old was beginning to want her own place in the family. She was no longer a baby, Morwen thought, with a small stab of regret. They were all moving on, and there was nothing anyone could do to stop it.

But all this talk of Truro Fair was making her think backwards, not forwards. She had avoided its lure for years. Yet she only had to see the words on posters or in the newspaper, and she was instantly a girl again, with the smells and the colour and the excitement of Fair-day filling her senses.

She was one of the rich pageant of bal maidens who flocked to the Fair, walking miles across the moors and thinking nothing of it, decked out in bright colours and frilled bonnets, all hoping to catch the eye of a good-looking young man for a stolen kiss in a hay-loft or behind a cart, thrills and excitement spiced with daring and danger.

Her friend Celia had once found such kisses at Truro Fair. The memory could still twist Morwen's heart, remembering how pretty Celia had taken too much of the heady potent sweet-drink and been cajoled into more than stolen kisses with Jude Pascoe, Ben's cousin. While Morwen herself had stumbled into Ben's arms, pushed by the crowd. She had looked into his dark eyes and known in an instant that their destiny was somehow going to be linked.

'Mama, why have your eyes gone all funny?' She heard Charlotte's curious voice, and felt the child tugging at her skirt. She looked down quickly, feeling the heat in her cheeks, her mind and her soul still filled with those wondrous, turbulent, terrible days…

'They're not funny, little chick,' Randell Wainwright's strong voice said, swinging the child up into his arms and making her squeal. 'Your Mama's eyes are beautiful, just like yours!'

Morwen blinked swiftly as Primmy crashed the notes on the pianoforte, sitting bolt upright, and the boys started jumping up and down saying that carriages were approaching.

It broke into a moment that could have been charged with emotion, and Morwen was glad of the intrusion, even though she promised to speak to Primmy severely in the near future. The girl was definitely getting above herself.

Later, the dignitaries and their wives were seated as if in some elaborate tableau in the drawing-room, replete with tea and little cakes, and Primmy was performing for them beautifully, her slender fingers tripping over the keys.

And as Primmy turned to accept their applause and praise, her face glowing as if with rapture, it was only then that Morwen recognized the need in her.

'We should have seen it long ago,' Morwen said to Ben, when at last they were alone in their room that night. 'Sam's children will always be fighters. It's born in them. Justin and Charlotte won't have inherited this drive, this need to prove themselves, because they have their heritage—'

'You're talking absolute rubbish as usual,' Ben interrupted irritably. 'The older ones don't even remember their real parents, so how can they feel any differently? We treat them all the same. And aren't you forgetting Albert? There's a dreamer if I ever saw one. He reminds me more of your brother Matt than Sam! Nothing will disturb Albert, my dear. I sometimes wonder if there's anything inside that head of his, apart from bees and insects.'

She came to his defence passionately. 'You're being unfair. And if you do liken him to Matt, well, Matt hasn't done so badly, has he?'

'All right. But I really don't want to have a lengthy discussion about the children at this hour, Morwen. The afternoon was tedious enough, without all this nonsense about Truro Fair.'

Morwen rounded on him. 'Ben, you will take them, won't you? I promised them we'd go—'

'Then you shouldn't have promised before asking me. How dare you promise on my account?'

His anger rose so swiftly she could hardly believe what was happening. She knew the scaggies were still troublesome, and that the men resented the boss being at the works every single day and treating them like naughty children, but he didn't have to vent his spite on his family…

'I dare because I thought it was what you'd want,' she said tremblingly. 'Families go to the Fair, Ben, and I thought we were a family—'

He chose to ignore her distress. Either that, or they had grown so far apart that he simply wasn't aware of it.

'Well, this family will have to go without me,' he said shortly. 'You've clearly overlooked the fact that it coincides with the time I shall be in London. I'm sure it will be no hardship for our American cousin to take you and the children to Truro Fair, my dear, and that it will be infinitely preferable to you than going to London with me!'

He turned out the gas-light abruptly and slid into bed beside Morwen. She lay there, unmoving, slow tears streaking her face.

'You haven't asked me about London since you decided to take so few days off, Ben—'

'Would it have made any difference? You've made it perfectly clear that you've no wish to do your wifely duty—'

She turned sharply towards the darkened profile beside her. Handsome and unrelenting, and grown so hard that she grieved for the old Ben, the Ben she had loved so wildly, not this stuffy, pompous man who took himself and everything else too seriously.

'*Duty!* Since when did you and I talk about *duty* to one another! That's not the way I think of our marriage.'

'Then perhaps you should. You allow your social graces to slip at times, Morwen. I noticed it this afternoon when our guests were here. It does little credit to our name, and sets a bad example to the children.'

This was too much. Morwen ripped off the bedcovers and slipped out of the bed, standing beside it in her nightgown, hands clenched, eyes blazing, consumed with an anger greater than she had ever known.

'*I* set a bad example to the children, do I? When you have so little patience for your own son that you constantly beat him down with words if not with blows. If that's what you think, then 'tis a good thing you're not coming to the Fair wi' us, for I might forget myself and go funning along with the bal maidens. 'Tis all I'm good for, wouldn't you say – *Sir*?'

Her breasts heaved with the effort not to cry as she looked down at him. Knowing and hoping that there was still a chance, even now, for all this to end in a tumble between the sheets, for Ben to leap out of bed and catch her in his arms. For the laughter to begin, and the loving to melt all the hurt…

'Try to control yourself, Morwen, for pity's sake. Do you want to waken the entire household with your ravings?' Ben snapped.

At his words, something inside her died. She reached for her dressing-robe with shaking hands. Her voice was brittle, her throat aching with unshed tears.

'That would never do, would it? 'Tis not how a lady should behave. I apologise for being myself, Ben. I won't keep you or anyone else awake a moment longer.'

She turned swiftly and sped out of the room, along the corridor and into another bedroom. It hadn't been used for a while, it was cold and faintly musty, the sheets unaired. Morwen didn't care. She cared about nothing but the enormity of realizing that she and Ben seemed to have reached a crisis point in their marriage, and he wouldn't or couldn't recognize it.

Morwen crawled between the cold sheets, still wrapped in her dressing-robe, shivering violently. She couldn't think sensibly. The long night stretched ahead, dark and dreary. Somewhere out at sea she heard the eerie moan of a ship's fog siren, echoing the emptiness inside her.

She had the children she had longed for, to make her life complete... but somehow in the process she had lost her husband. She couldn't think of anything else. She had lost Ben, and he didn't seem to care.

She turned her face into the unfamiliar pillow, stretching out her arms towards the empty place beside her as if in supplication, and wept as though her heart would break.

–

St Austell market-place had always been a thriving source of servants' gossip. Many a young serving-girl came rushing home with a tasty tid-bit of news for her mistress about some other lady in the town, some scandal or other to brighten servants' eyes and enliven a dull day for their gentlefolk.

'I'm telling 'ee 'tis true,' Fanny from Killigrew House said indignantly to the young parlour-maid from Oakville Manor. 'Mrs Killigrew's bin sleeping in that spare room for six nights now, and goes about looking like summat's wrong wi' her face, where she's bin crying so much.'

'And what about 'im, then? Do he allow such goings-on from his missus?'

'Ain't got no choice, 'as he? Mrs Killigrew's got a mind of her own, though why anybody 'ould want to leave the Master's bed to sleep on her own, I can't think.'

The other girl sniggered. 'Ain't 'ee offered to warm it for 'un yet then, Fanny? You'm slipping!'

'I'm thinking on it,' Fanny said airily. 'Mr Killigrew's going away to Lunnon for three days next week, and she ain't going with 'un, neither.' Her eyes gleamed as she thought of another item of news. 'I'll tell 'ee summat else too. I don't think the American gennulman's too upset by all the goings-on.'

'Oh-ho. Fancies your mistress, does he?'

Fanny nodded vigorously. ''Tis as plain as the nose on your face, Edie, and that's plain enough for anybody—'

She ducked laughingly as Edie's hand came up to give her a playful swipe. The stallholder swore loudly at the two prancing maids as they knocked a trayful of cabbages flying, and none of them noticed the person turning to stare thoughtfully after them as they disappeared into the Monday crowds. None of them would have recognized him anyway.

-

Jude Pascoe had come home to Cornwall, after what some might call a long exile in America. He didn't see it that way, even though he hadn't come home a rich man. He hadn't prospered in the way his companion Matt Tremayne had done, apparently, from the whispers that had come Jude's way. Even in New York, it wasn't so difficult to get news of what was happening on the far side of the continent in California.

He knew Matt had struck gold, and for a while he had toyed with the idea of going west to seek him out. Matt owed him something. If it hadn't been for Jude, Matt would probably be dead by now, hanged as a murderer for his part in drowning the foreign sailor in the midst of the wrecking.

Jude easily dismissed the fact that if it wasn't for him, Matt would never have got caught up with the infamous wreckers in the first place, and that it had been Jude's hand, not Matt's, that delivered the final death blow to the sailor. Jude was adept at forgetting things too uncomfortable to remember.

He assessed the situation cannily. Matt wouldn't welcome him in his new-found wealth, and Jude doubted if he'd get a penny out of him, for all his blusterings. Jude knew very well that he didn't cut too fine a figure any more. His youthful, rugged good looks had succumbed to heavy drinking and a lusty appetite, and he knew he was gross and unattractive. Matt's wife would probably show him the door, and that would be that. Far better to try his luck elsewhere.

And why not his old home, where his mother was still besotted by her errant son, and his uncle wouldn't risk the good name of Killigrew by turning him out on the streets? Charles Killigrew would give him money and shelter, however grudgingly, until he decided what to do next.

It hadn't taken Jude more than a day in St Austell to discover that both his mother and uncle were dead, that his cousin Ben was now in control of Killigrew Clay, and married to that damnable black-haired imperious bal maiden, Morwen Tremayne. And there was a whole brood of children at Killigrew House.

Ben hadn't wasted much time, Jude thought. He himself had always been the lecherous one of the two, but he didn't blame Ben for getting on with things. From what he remembered of the passionate Morwen Tremayne, and her luscious friend, Celia Penry…

Jude's thinking had paused for a moment in the cheap, smoke-filled kiddleywink where he was lodging. Celia Penry…

he hadn't thought about her in years. His mind flashed over the events as if he was seeing them through a kaleidoscope.

Pretty doe-eyed Celia with her come-hither glances that could curdle a man's guts with pleasure… plying Celia with sweet-drink at Truro Fair while Miss Haughty-face Morwen looked down her nose… fondling Celia and seeing the promise in her eyes, and getting the secret out of her that she and Morwen were visiting the Larnie Stone with the old witch's potion to make them see their true loves through the stone…

And the rest of it, persuading Ben to go with him, to go funning with the maids at midnight on the moors. Celia screaming with laughter as he went chasing her, and when he found her, the sweet piercing of her maidenhead and soaring inside her and spilling out his seed… and Celia screaming, and screaming…

'Be 'ee looking for a night o' pleasure, my 'andsome?'

Jude's hand jerked on the ale-pot as an inviting female voice spoke alongside him. The whore slid along the wooden seat to press close against him, the cheap, sickly scent enveloping him for a moment. The woman's hand squeezed his leg, moving towards his thigh, and he felt himself rise. He pushed the memory of Celia Penry's terrified eyes out of his mind, and smiled into the painted face.

'If you think you're up to the best night you've ever 'ad, lead on, babe,' he said coarsely. He gave a soft chuckle as he saw her eyes widen with delight.

'Be 'ee from over the sea then, my dear?'

'That's right. All the way from America, just to see you, with more'n a sixpence to pay for a good time.'

Nobody took any notice of the whore hugging his arm as they moved towards the stairs. If she thought he was American, so much the better, Jude thought with satisfaction. Local girls seemed to have the notion that the Americans were bigger and better than anyone else, especially in the breeding tackle department, and he wasn't about to disprove it.

And as well as this night of enjoyment, he had this other news to ponder about. Cousin Ben and his wife weren't getting along, and there was somebody else in the running – he was an American too, if the maid's words were correct. And Ben was leaving his wife, whom Jude still thought of as the clayworker's daughter, alone for three whole days… Jude wasn't too sure yet what he was going to do with the information, and it needed some thinking about. But one thing was certain. Jude Pascoe was back all right.

–

One by one, the children hugged their father and kissed him goodbye. They lined up like a row of little soldiers, Morwen thought with love. And Ben was so perfunctory with them all, as if he couldn't wait to be away from them. But it wasn't them, of course. It was her. It was Morwen he couldn't wait to be away from.

Ever since she had moved out of their bedroom, Ben had only spoken to her when it was absolutely necessary.

Then he was cold and polite, and it was so obvious Morwen was quite sure the servants must know, and it only added to her humiliation.

She wasn't sure just how much Randell Wainwright knew, or guessed. He still remained in the house as their guest, but he had seen a possible house just outside Truro that he might consider purchasing, and Morwen had promised to look over it during their visit to Truro Fair.

The children were all invited to an early tea with Jack and Annie and their children, and Morwen and Ran would join them later when she had given him her opinion of the new house. It was something to look forward to. It helped to shut out the fact that nothing was resolved between her and Ben, and it seemed as though it would remain that way.

And she just couldn't bear to see him leaving like this, so cold and unforgiving, when she had done nothing wrong…

She caught at his hand when he would have turned to leave, unable to believe that he would snub her in this way, and not bid her a tender good-bye in front of the family and servants. Her eyes pleaded with him, and then he bent to give her the coolest peck on the mouth.

'I hope you have a wonderful day at your college, Ben,' she said tremulously. 'We shall all be thinking of you, and I shall be so proud of you.'

He looked at her stonily.

'Thank you, my dear. At least you won't be lonely. You have family and friends around you, and the delights of Truro Fair tomorrow. I know you'll enjoy it. Now, if you'll excuse me, I must leave.'

He might have been speaking to a stranger. Morwen's eyes were blinded with tears as she caught sight of Fanny nudging Mrs Horn's arm as they each bobbed in turn as Ben strode past them. They all know, Morwen thought. They all pity me, or laugh at me, and it's all so unfair…

'Don't look so sad, cousin,' Ran said gently. 'Three days isn't so long, and he'll be back before you know it.'

How could Ran not see the change in Ben… but why should he? He hadn't known the old Ben. Ran had only ever seen the cold clay boss that Ben had become. Even towards her own father… Hal had been so bitterly hurt at Ben's treatment of him. He hadn't held it back from Bess, and Bess had told Morwen, filled with indignation and anger…

At such times, Morwen's family loyalty was as fierce as ever. She was still Morwen Tremayne, despite all the fine trappings Ben Killigrew had showered upon her. And knowing how he had insulted her father, she had been shamed by him.

Now she smiled brilliantly into Ran Wainwright's eyes, so brilliantly that he caught his breath for a moment.

'You're right, Ran. I refuse to be sad. None of us must be sad. Let's all have tea together and then play charades. What do you say? Do Americans know how to play charades, or do my clever little daughters have to teach you?' she added, as Primmy and Charlotte clapped and jumped up and down, the gloom of their father's departure diminishing in seconds.

Ran laughed. His teeth were so tidy when he opened his mouth, Morwen thought unexpectedly. White and tidy, and not with ugly gaps in them like half of the men she knew.

'Oh, we Americans know plenty of parlour games, coz. We're not as uncivilized as you seem to think!'

Primmy caught one of Ran's hands and one of Morwen's, the young-old composure slipping for once. Charlotte did the same, jumping up and down in her excitement and linking the four of them in a small, intimate circle.

Morwen was very aware of it. She was aware too, of the undisguised admiration in Ran Wainwright's eyes, and her laugh was slightly breathless.

'Run and tell Mrs Horn that we'll have tea served up immediately, then, Primmy, and you boys can be thinking up some words to mime.'

She turned away from Ran's gaze in some embarrassment. Ben had gone away and left her in his care, and it was good to have a relative as a chaperone and bodyguard in the house, but she could never really think of Ran as a relative. He was too different, too unlike anyone she had ever known before. Too masculine and attractive for her peace of mind.

And she would be a fool not to know that he was attracted to her as well. She did know it, and sometimes it was like a balm, and at other times it disturbed her more than she admitted.

Morwen threw herself into the game of charades, as much to keep up the children's flagging spirits at their father's departure, as to keep herself busy. While she was occupied, however simple the task, she could temporarily forget that something between her and Ben was dying… and that something else was imperceptibly coming to life between her and Randell E. Wainwright.

She smothered such thoughts as best she could while the children shrieked and clapped at the sight of Ran on hands and knees silently growling like a tiger, and easily guessed the animal he was miming. Then it was Morwen's turn. She had prepared her mime, and moved in a stately fashion around the room, her head held high, graciously touching one child's shoulder and then another with an imaginary sword.

'Queen Victoria!' shrieked Primmy. 'I knew you'd do that mime, Mama. You always do it!'

Morwen laughed into her beautiful, sparkling eyes.

'That's because I'm so good at it,' she said airily. 'I was always meant for noble things, didn't you know that?'

They all laughed and teased, and Ran joined in, and it was the most joyous day Morwen could remember for a long time. And after their tea, they all sat cosily in front of the fire while Primmy played for them, and as the music flowed all around them Ran looked down into the flushed face of his Cornish cousin, and thought he had never seen anything so lovely.

'Being noble in the ways of the world wouldn't become you, Morwen, and I mean no disrespect,' he said softly, out of earshot of the children. 'There's no merit in being what you're not, and you don't need the trappings of society women. Your charm was born in you. Don't ever lose that.'

She was startled at his frankness. She knew by now that American gentlemen were eloquent, and uninhibited by prissy protocol. The knowledge touched a spark in her that was in danger of becoming a flame, and Morwen suddenly felt afraid.

'I was forgetting that you will know all about my background from Matt,' her tone was light, deliberately misunderstanding him, 'and we country folk should never aspire to be kings, is that it?'

'It is not, and well you know it,' Ran said gravely. 'In my country we set little store by a person's birth. It's what he does with his life that's important.'

Morwen stood up abruptly.

'Goodness me, how serious we've all become,' she said quickly. 'Play something lively, Primmy, and we'll all sing.'

She moved across to the pianoforte, and the children clustered around her. Ran remained where he was, lighting a cigar and leaning back on the sofa, wreathed in an aromatic scent, watching and listening to the little family group, to which he'd become more attached than he had ever expected or intended.

One thing was abundantly clear to him. Ben Killigrew might be the head of this house, but Morwen was its heart, and to Randell Wainwright, she would always be a queen.

Chapter Six

Jack Tremayne's humour was definitely improved. He had discovered that there were other ways of preventing a wife becoming pregnant than by enforced celibacy for the rest of one's life. In desperation, he had begged Doctor Vestey to put him out of his misery and suggest something other than visiting street women, which would shame him and Annie too.

Jack's pleas were eloquent. He was in dire need. He would die without the comfort of his wife, which he had been assured of in the marriage vows. He would probably end up cutting his wrists or throwing himself in the Lemon River or beneath the wheels of a waggon if he didn't get help...

Finally, the doctor had obliged, after much hawking in his throat, with details of appliances that made Jack wince at the very idea of them. There were further instructions about times of the month that made him scarlet with embarrassment, having always thought that these were women's doings, and nothing that should concern a man, except for the inconvenience if he wanted her to perform her marital duty.

Jack had gone home to Annie, apprehensive of her reaction to all that he had to tell her. The doctor had supplied items that would seem to deflate any man's ardour, and a chart on which Annie was to record her monthly happenings, to be doubly sure...

He stumbled and stammered in trying to explain to his wife, while Annie turned the unfamiliar appliance over and over as though it was red-hot. Her mouth began to twitch, and to

Jack's astonishment she began laughing and gasping, and he was laughing just as hysterically.

'Then you don't think too badly of me for finding a way, my lamb?' he said roughly, when the mixture of tears and laughter subsided.

'I would never think badly of you, Jack.' She smiled through tears. 'I'm touched more than I can say that you swallowed your pride and asked Doctor Vestey to put things right for us. It proves how much you love me.'

All the aggressive male feelings he'd had to suppress for weeks began to stir in him. She was his girl, his woman, and he wanted her now.

'If 'tis proof that you need, then we'd best try out this new-fangled affair, afore I go off the boil,' Jack teased.

'And hell will freeze over before that day ever comes,' Annie replied, and opened her arms to him.

-

And now it was Fair-day, and all the younger Tremaynes and the Killigrews were going to be together. The morning was crisp and bright, the excitement rising as coats and bonnets were fastened and boots were laced with shaking fingers. Morwen forgot everything but the excitement of Fair-day: the noise, the colour, the smells, the magic. They would be meeting Annie and Jack and their two little girls, and, hopefully, Freddie would leave his shop in the care of his assistant and join them all. The Tremaynes and the Killigrews were going out on the town.

Ran was going to drive the carriage himself. He had been used to driving heavier vehicles than this in California, he assured Morwen. It would be no problem to control the reins of the two horses, and since the carriage would be left at Jack's yard, it would be perfectly safe without a groom.

'Besides, when I take you to show you my house, I don't want anyone else around,' Ran added with a smile. 'I want to be the only one to see your expression when you see what I'm going to buy.'

'It sounds as if you've already decided on it,' Morwen said, ignoring the dangerous little glow his words gave her. 'I thought this was to be an inspection to give you my feminine views on the house.'

Ran laughed. 'So it is. But I don't have any doubts on that score. I'm perfectly sure that our opinions will be in perfect harmony.'

A little thrill ran through Morwen at the confident words. She couldn't deny that in most things they were in perfect accord. Their tastes coincided in so many things. They liked the same kind of music, not too heavy, but something with a swing to it. They liked walking on the moors with the wind in their faces, or along a stretch of virginal sand and making their footprints the only ones to mar its surface. In short, they liked everything Morwen had always liked sharing with Ben, the things that Ben had no time for any more.

But this was no day for such unhappy thoughts. The children could barely contain their excitement as the carriage took them away from St Austell and along the high road towards Truro. They merged into a seemingly endless procession of fine carriages and humbler carts, and frequently scattered those who were doggedly walking the twelve miles to Truro in aim of a day's pleasure.

'See there, Mama!' Primmy pointed ahead of them. 'Are those women the bal maidens from the clayworks? How common they look in their loud clothes.'

Morwen's anger was as sharp as a knife at the girl's thoughtless remark. She rounded on her at once.

'There's nothing common in doing an honest day's work, Primmy, nor in dressing up in finery when once they get away from the claypits. 'Tis no pleasure to be working in damp and muck for half the year, and covered in clay dust for the rest of it.'

'Well, I still think they're common,' Primmy said mutinously. She tossed her dark hair, glaring at the three boys giggling at her. Charlotte put her small hand in her mother's.

'I'm going to be a bal maiden when I grow up,' she said confidently. 'There's more room for people on the moors.'

The boys hooted at this, while Primmy mocked her small sister, annoyed that she seemed to be getting the worst out of all this.

'Don't be a ninny, Charlotte. Daughters of Killigrew Clay owner's can't be bal maidens. That's for people who don't have any money and live in miserable cottages.'

Morwen felt panic. How could she and Ben have been so foolish not to let the children know of their origins before this? Primmy had been a baby when their parents had died, Walter and Albert still very young, and for them the memory of their old life had faded very quickly.

'Sometimes I wonder if we ever lived in a cottage,' Walter said suddenly. His eyes were troubled, and Morwen felt a swift sorrow for him as Primmy burst out laughing now, ridiculing him.

'What nonsense! Of course we never lived in a cottage! Papa's father built Killigrew House, and Charlotte was named after him. How stupid you are today!'

Morwen saw Ran's hand leave the reins and cover hers for a moment. It didn't help. This was something she had to do alone, and she had to do it now. It didn't matter where they were. In fact, it was probably better that they were in a fine carriage on their way to Truro Fair, because there was nowhere the children could run and sulk or weep or rage…

But when she started to say the words, they wouldn't come, and she could only tell part of it after all. The enormity of the knowledge that the older three were her brother Sam's children, and had been born in the humble cottage on the moors, was too much for them to take in on a sunny October morning without Ben's support.

'You're turning into a snob, Primmy, and it's something I don't want to see. As for living in a cottage, there's nothing so terrible about that. I was born in a cottage, and I lived there with my parents and brothers for many years until I married your father. You can be just as proud of being half Tremaynes as you are Killigrews, all of you.'

At least that wasn't a lie, even though the Tremayne half didn't come from her, Morwen thought swiftly. After the first stunned silence, came the choking words from her elder daughter.

'I don't believe it! Papa would never have—'

Morwen turned to stare at her reddened face, her eyes steady and unblinking.

'Papa would never have what?' Morwen's voice was hard as steel. 'Married someone so far beneath him? Someone as common as those bal maidens walking all the way to Truro Fair? Is that what you were about to say, Primmy?'

'Mother, she's just being silly,' Walter said uneasily. 'But you should have told us. It's not right for families to have secrets—'

'I think it's a bit special, for Father to have picked Mother out of a poor cottage,' Albert said stoically.

'It's not special, it's awful, you milk-sop!' Primmy was near to tears now. Justin said nothing, and Charlotte merely looked frightened at this upset in what began as a perfect day.

'You children need your backsides spanked,' Ran suddenly put in calmly. 'Your mother is the most gracious lady I've ever met, and what does it matter if she once lived in a hovel or a castle? It all happened before you were born.'

'Just as long as she wasn't one of those women!' Primmy was still vindictive, still determined to have the last word, but in that, she was out of luck. Morwen's lips tightened. Her chin lifted, and if Ben Killigrew had been there, he would have recognized someone who had once charmed him into wanting her with all the passion he possessed.

'I'm sorry to disappoint you, Primmy, but that is exactly what I was when I first knew your father,' Morwen said. 'My family all worked for Killigrew Clay. Your Grandma Bess and I were bal maidens, Granddad Hal was Pit Captain of Clay One, your Uncle Freddie was a kiddley-boy, and your – other uncles – were all clayworkers. Now, if you've anything more to say about it, let's have it now, before the whole day is spoiled.'

Her chest ached. She had so nearly said 'your father had been a clayworker until the proud day he took over from Hal and became Pit Captain of Clay One'. If that knowledge had come out now, on top of everything else, she was sure it would have destroyed Walter and Albert and Primmy. As it was…

'Mother, we should have been told this before,' Walter said angrily. 'We're not babies any more. You had no right to keep us in the dark all these years.'

'No, my love. You're not babies any more.' Morwen knew the truth of it as she looked into the fiercely blue eyes of Sam's eldest. The pain inside her deepened. Someday they would need to be told all of it. That they weren't even of her flesh, nor Ben's.

It was something they had avoided mentioning all these years, wanting to compensate for the fact that the three little ones had been left orphaned. And Morwen had wanted them so much, and had looked on them as her own for so long…

She realized that Ran had turned the horses and was driving the carriage away from the main stream of traffic, on to a waste patch of land. He pulled the horses to a stop, and turned round in his seat to study the belligerent young faces.

'You've all had your say, and now I'm going to have mine,' he said. 'Just because I talk with a funny accent and come from a different country doesn't mean I'm not concerned with what happens to you. I haven't known you long, but I love you all as my family. Do you agree with that?'

'Of course we do,' Primmy said. 'It's not you who's deceived us, Uncle Ran—'

He smiled gently at her proud young face, so like Morwen's at that moment that a family relationship was unmistakable.

'Get those pompous words out of your head, honey, and think hard about what I just said. I come from a different background and I talk differently, but it doesn't change the person I am, and I hope, the person you love and respect. It doesn't change what your mother is to you either.'

Morwen was silent, seeing the way Ran's mind was working, and praying the children would understand. All this had blown up in a moment, and she was still reeling with the shock of it all. But she needed someone else to cope with it now. She needed Ran's common sense. She saw Primmy glance at her uneasily, and knew the battle was half-won, temporarily at least.

'I still think we should have been told,' Primmy muttered stubbornly.

'Sometimes grown-ups do things that they think are for the best. Your parents did it to protect you. Have they ever been cruel to you, or hurt you? Haven't they always been loving parents?' Ran went on relentlessly.

'Oh, can't we forget it, Primmy? Why do you always have to question things?' Albert was getting impatient. 'What does it really matter if Mother was once a bal maiden? She doesn't dress in that funny way now, does she? She doesn't talk as funny as Grandma Bess!'

'That's true,' Walter managed a grin, echoed by Justin.

Morwen felt her mouth twitch. Oh, if they only knew, how hard it had been to train her voice to that of the cultured lady deserving to be Ben Killigrew's wife! It had been easy enough for the young Walter and Albert to lose the rough accents they didn't even remember now, but it hadn't been so easy for Morwen.

'Mama's never cruel,' Charlotte said indignantly. 'She's lovely and soft and pretty.' She climbed on to Morwen's lap, winding her chubby arms around her mother's neck. She hugged Morwen so tightly that the stinging tears threatened to fall.

'Well, if everybody's agreed on that, what do you say we all go to Truro Fair and enjoy ourselves?' Ran spoke briskly. 'If we don't hurry, the day will be half over before we get there, and this lovely, soft, pretty lady deserves a day off from being at your beck and call all the time.'

Justin leaned forward. 'We do love you, Mother,' he whispered in her ear, and sat back hastily before the others would think him too feeble for words.

But Morwen treasured the moment, and resisted the uneasy knowledge that it was her own son, and her own sweet Charlotte, who had been the most generous. Sam's children were still Sam's children after all.

–

A couple of hours later, the Killigrew carriage had been safely stabled at Boskelly's boatyard in the care of Jack's stable-lad. Jack and Annie had welcomed the St Austell relatives, and their little girls, Sarah and Tessa, had immediately turned painfully shy until coaxed out of it by Charlotte's artless chatter.

And Morwen began to breathe a little easier at last. There had been bad moments earlier in the day, and she had missed Ben more than she could say. It had been his place to soothe and calm, and she was enormously grateful to Ran for his tactful handling of the situation, and for not interfering until the time was right.

But now they were all walking the short distance to where the streets of Truro sang with noise and glowed with colour. Truro Fair was a hotchpotch of vendors and stalls selling everything from boot black to exotic silks; there were stilt men, performers of tragic plays, pierrots, hot potato sellers, cheapjacks, magicians, clowns. There was something for everyone, and it was a heady mixture of sights and smells and impressions.

'There's Uncle Freddie!' Justin shouted. He ran nimbly away from the family group, twisting and flying among the crush of people as he glimpsed Freddie Tremayne's tall handsome figure some distance away. In seconds he was swallowed up in the crowd.

'Damn the child!' Jack exclaimed. 'Why didn't you keep more control of him, Morwen?'

'I thought he was right beside me,' she said indignantly.

'He won't be far,' Ran soothed her. 'I'm sure Freddie caught sight of us, and the two of them will be heading towards each other.'

'I hope so,' Morwen said, suddenly apprehensive.

Ben had always been against the children coming here. If anything went amiss now… Her eyes searched frantically for the dark head of her son, bobbing amongst a sea of other heads.

For some crazy reason, she thought of the young, vulnerable boy Freddie had been. How easy it would be for a young boy to fall prey to rogues and abductors in the midst of a raucous crowd. She could almost hear Ben's words saying as much on the many times the children had tried to persuade him to change his mind. This time, he had given in almost too easily. As if he had too many other things on his mind to be bothered with the responsibility of his own children…

She shook herself angrily, knowing she was letting her imagination run away with her. She did Ben an injustice. And surely there was nothing here to fear on this bright day, and old ghosts were best left undisturbed.

'Stay right here with everyone else, Morwen,' Ran ordered. 'I can see Justin near the hurdy-gurdy man. I'll fetch the boy back, and give him a good talking-to on the way.'

He thrust his way through the people pressing from all sides, and Morwen saw Jack and Annie glance at one another. She could interpret the look very clearly. The American cousin took a very proprietary interest in the Killigrew children…

Morwen ignored it. As long as Justin was brought back safely, it didn't matter who reprimanded him, and if Ran was acting like a substitute father, then it was Ben's own fault for not being here with his children…

Morwen drew in her breath. Dear God, today was Ben's important day. Today her husband was being honoured by his old school and would become Honorary Governor of Ormsby College. And this was the first moment she had even thought of it. Guilt and horror overcame her. Her eyes sought to find the missing members of her family, as if to blot out the realization. How *could* she have forgotten.

A new shock held her gaze as if riveted for a second. A face she had hoped never to see again seemed to drift in front of her vision in the crowd. A fleshy face with dark piercing eyes, whose owner quickly turned and appeared to melt away. Morwen stood as if stunned. It couldn't be Jude Pascoe. Not unless he had come back to haunt her...

'Mama, Uncle Ran's found Justin and Uncle Freddie too,' she heard Primmy shout with relief. 'Can we go and watch the puppets now, Mama? Can we, please?'

Primmy reverted to being Primmy the child again, and Morwen hugged her at once, and said of course they could, provided they all walked in crocodile-fashion, each keeping hold of another.

'I want to go with Uncle Freddie.' Justin yelled, quite unrepentant at being hauled back to his family.

'And I want to stay with Uncle Ran,' Charlotte howled.

'We'll all stay together,' Ran said. 'And no nonsense from any of you, do you hear?'

'Remember what we're saying, and just don't go rushing off out of sight,' Morwen said weakly, unable to think clearly any more.

'Are you going to take some sweet-drink later on, Morwen?' Freddie grinned. 'Or is it too potent for you now that you're such a fine lady?'

She glanced down at Primmy, who would read the significance in the words now, where once she would just have taken them for more of Freddie's nonsense. The girl hesitated for a second, and then to Morwen's surprise, she felt Primmy's hand curl around hers.

'My mother's always been a lady,' she said, making Morwen's eyes prickle. And then the haughtiness fell away from her as a painted youth came prancing around them, announcing that the puppet show was about to begin.

'You go and watch the puppets, while Annie and I take our little ones to see the monkey on a stick and we'll buy you all toffee apples and come and find you,' Jack said.

He was well away from his brother and sister and the American, with the five children trailing along with them, when he spoke thoughtfully to Annie.

'Well, well. It looks more and more as though Ben will have to take better care of his wife, wouldn't you say? The American seems pretty well inclined towards our Morwen, and I get the feeling that his attentions aren't too unwelcome.'

Annie looked troubled. 'I'm sure you're wrong, Jack. Morwen never had eyes for anyone but Ben. You used to tell me how besotted they were with one another.'

'They *were*,' Jack stressed. 'But I don't see Ben here now, do you? And afore you start telling me he had to go away to that fancy college of his, tell me the last time you saw him and Morwen being lovey-dovey together.'

'I can't remember. But you don't think Morwen would—'

He gave her slender waist a squeeze, knowing a great satisfaction that his wife was still healthily disposed towards him, and that his anguish at not being able to express his love for her until recently, was her anguish too.

'I think our Morwen's as passionate as the rest on us,' he whispered in her ear under cover of the general babble all around them. 'And if Ben Killigrew don't act the proper husband towards her, then why shouldn't she look elsewhere?'

'Jack, that's scandalous talk!' Annie hissed at him, praying that people wouldn't hear. And wondering if this didn't echo some dark fear inside himself. Had he perhaps wondered if his own wife might not look around for some other partner if her husband stuck too closely to the doctor's blunt warnings?

It was ridiculous to think so, and it was for Annie's own sake that Jack had been forced to lie rigidly beside her and think of something other than his own lusty urges… as she remembered those tormented nights, Annie felt a great wave of love for this tall, aggressively masculine husband of hers. She held his arm tightly to her side.

'Forget about Morwen, dearest,' she pleaded. 'The girls can't wait to see the monkey on the stick, and that's all we need think about right now, isn't it?'

He laughed down at her, and scooped up a squealing, giggling child in each powerful arm, as they sought out the man with the monkey dressed in a glittering little green waistcoat and red trousers, and the tiny fez ludicrously stuck on top of his head. This was the important thing, he agreed, seeing his children happy, and his wife's pretty face filled with pleasure.

By the middle of the afternoon they were all exhausted. They had eaten toffee apples, and home-made cakes from the countrywomen's stalls, drank lemon cordial and tasted various mixtures of sweets and biscuits, and Charlotte was looking decidedly pale.

'I think it's time we took them back to Jack's house,' Morwen said anxiously to Ran. 'They left an hour ago, with the girls asleep in Jack's arms. And before you boys protest, remember that there'll be a fine tea waiting for you, if you've got room to stuff anything more inside you.'

'Of course we have,' Walter and Albert and Justin said at once. Morwen raised her eyebrows at Ran and Freddie, commenting that she hoped they wouldn't have five sickly children to take home to St Austell that night.

'Why take them back?' Freddie said at once. 'There's room at my house and at Jack's to accommodate you, if you'd prefer to stay until tomorrow morning. Jack said as much earlier in the day, and 'tis far better than travelling after dark. Some of the clayworkers can take a message to Killigrew House so that Mrs Horn won't be expecting you back tonight.'

It was too tempting to refuse, and the children were charmed by the idea, already squabbling over who would stay with which brother. Freddie settled it.

'I could take the three boys if they don't mind bunking in together in my bed, and I'll sleep on the sofa,' Freddie said. 'Jack and Annie have room for you and Ran and the two girls.'

'What do you say, Morwen?' Ran said. 'I think we should. Let the children start afresh tomorrow morning.'

She nodded in agreement. It would be strange to sleep away from home, especially without Ben. Even though she hadn't moved back into their bedroom since their terrible quarrel, he had always been there, except for these three nights when he was in London. Neither had thought that she would be away from home for one of those nights as well. But why not? It would be as much an adventure for her as for the children.

Freddie sought out several of the Killigrew clayworkers he knew of old, who promised to deliver the note to Killigrew House, touching their caps to Morwen in respectful recognition.

Now they could set off for Jack and Annie's house with the children, the girls already arguing excitedly now over which bed they would sleep in and what they would wear for nightgowns. Once they were settled in the house, Ran and Morwen left them there, driving off in the Killigrew carriage to view the splendid new house Ran intended to buy.

And once again, a silent watcher hovered near, curiosity really taking hold of him now, as Jude Pascoe saw his cousin's wife being apparently whisked off in the diminishing daylight to some unknown destination away from Truro town, without a chaperone in sight.

Chapter Seven

Morwen looked in open-mouthed pleasure at the elegant house that Ran pointed out. Bathed in the last rays of the evening sunlight, it seemed to welcome her. It was quite grand, sitting on top of the low moors, with lawns sweeping away towards the sea, yet without the more austere appearance of Killigrew House. She exclaimed with delight as Ran trotted the horses forward through the wrought-iron gates with symbolic stone lions as guardians atop massive pillars at either side.

'Ran, I never dreamed it would be so magnificent!' Morwen exclaimed. 'It's the house of a man who means to settle. Are you very sure about this?'

She hardly realized how much, how very much, she hoped that it was so, or how his smile reassured her.

'A man with a good business at his fingertips would be foolish indeed if he didn't remain near his acquisition,' he said lightly, careful not to reveal how he revelled in Morwen's glowing pleasure. He was careful too, not to betray how dear she was becoming to him. Dangerously dear, Ran admitted, and the sooner he moved out of Killigrew House and into an establishment of his own, the better.

Even to finding a wife of his own… but each time he contemplated such a move, the only face that floated in and out of his dreams was the lovely face of Morwen Killigrew.

'I hope it all comes up to your expectations and meets with your approval, Madame.' He went on, teasingly, because it was obvious to him now that asking Morwen to help furnish his home might not be such a good idea after all. It was what he wanted, of course, but he would always be thinking of her being here with him, his possessions her possessions, her life entwined with his, and it was an impossible dream that was best strangled at birth…

He felt her soft hand on his arm as the horses stopped in front of the house, and he was unaware that he sat motionless for a few seconds as the dream enveloped him.

'Ran? Are we going inside, or are you too awe-struck by your own cleverness in finding such a beautiful house?' Morwen laughed into his face.

He jumped out of the carriage, holding out his arms to lift her down. She was more than feather-light in his arms. She was warm feminine flesh and substance, and as his hands spanned her waist, he felt a fierce protective desire for her. And a brief anger at the short-sightedness of Ben Killigrew, who was more concerned with ambition than the priorities of family life.

He brushed such thoughts aside as he let her go and watched as she picked up her skirts to walk lightly up the steep stone steps at the front of the house. He was probably all wrong, anyway. He was a stranger, seeing things too acutely with a stranger's eye, the way he was wont to do. Such keen vision had served him well in the past, but it had never been so coloured before, and Ran freely admitted that his feelings for another man's wife were beginning to trouble him greatly.

'The house has been unoccupied for some while,' he said prosaically, to keep his mind off the memory of holding her in his arms. 'Several of the rooms need attention, and there is some exterior repair work to be done—'

Morwen stopped abruptly. 'So I see!'

The tiled balcony along the front of the house was broken in several places, most notably right in front of the door, where a large tiled area was cracked and sunken. She might have caught her toe in one of the cracks and fallen, if Ran had not caught at her arm at the same moment.

'I'm sorry, I should have warned you—'

'It's all right, Ran,' she began to laugh. 'I'm not made of cotton. I can step over the cracks.'

'Wait a minute.'

He stepped over the broken tiled area and opened the heavy door with an ornate key, then turned back to her.

'Will you allow me to emulate Sir Walter Raleigh, my lady?' He made an elaborate bow, and the formal words in the American accent sounded funny to her ears. 'As one of your colonial cousins, I'd like to prove that we've inherited a few manners from the mother country!'

'Oh Ran, you are a ninny,' Morwen giggled, but before she could protest, he had swept her up in his arms and was striding through the door into the entrance hall. She bumped against his body as he carried her right inside, involuntarily clinging on to him at the unexpectedness of it all. Ran still held her, and she was very aware of his rapid heartbeat against her breast.

'Are you going to put me down?' she protested, still laughing. 'I feel suspended up here!'

He looked down at her, and even in the dimness of the house she could see the sudden change of expression in his eyes. It matched something deep inside her that she couldn't immediately identify. Longing, fear, need...

'Put me down, cousin,' she said quietly, using the term deliberately, because of all the new and turbulent emotions churning in her veins.

'Not until you pay me the fee for entering my house,' he was unrelenting, unheeding of her words.

'What fee? Ran, please—'

'It's an old American custom,' his voice was soft now, his breath on her cheek. 'A lady is expected to give a gentleman a kiss when she enters his house for the first time.'

'I don't believe it. You're making it up—'

'Would you insult your cousin by not accepting a well-known custom of his country?' he mocked her.

And before she could protest any further, his dark head was bent towards hers, and his hands held her fast to him. Still in his arms, Morwen felt as though she were literally floating in space as his mouth touched hers. Gently at first, and then with a restrained passion that she could no longer mistake.

And her arms that were clinging to his neck seemed to have a life of their own as they held him tight, wanting more of him, wanting all of him. The sudden small whinnying of a horse brought her back to reality, and she dropped her arms, pushing her hands against him as she wriggled out of his embrace.

'I think that is sufficient fee for any cousin to extract,' she spoke breathlessly, not wanting him to guess how much she had wanted the kiss to continue, and for love to grow and flourish between them. Such thoughts were wrong, but they were suddenly, gloriously, the only thoughts in her head at that moment…

Morwen turned away in a small burst of embarrassment. Had he guessed? He mustn't, not ever. Not while she was Ben's wife, and it was to Ben that her duty lay. Shocked, Morwen registered that her first thought had been of duty towards Ben, not love. It was a thought that filled her with pain, because she always believed that love lasted forever, even beyond the grave. But perhaps there was no such thing as forever…

'Are we going to look at the house while there's still a bit of daylight, Ran? That was our purpose for coming here, wasn't it?'

'Of course. There are some oil-lamps, Morwen. I'll light one and we'll explore. We should have got here earlier, perhaps this morning, and brought the children as well.'

She watched as he found the oil-lamp and lit the wick, throwing the house into a warm rosy glow. Her thoughts were as jerky as his words. Brought the children this morning? And if they had, she suspected that the so-called old American custom would never have been mentioned, and she wouldn't have been held in his arms and kissed so rapturously.

She mustn't think of it that way, either. She was a sensibly married woman with a loving husband and a houseful of children. She was content. She had everything that a woman could want, and the dreams that came in the night, when a woman was a girl again, and all of life and love were hers for the taking, were nothing more than dreams… and everyone knew that dreams seldom came true.

She followed Ran through the house, trying to imagine it filled with the sounds of laughter, instead of the cold echoing rooms through which they moved. But it had potential. It could be a lovely family home. It was a house that ached to be filled with children, a house of dreams…

'I'm sure it will suit you very well, Ran,' she spoke abruptly, when they had finished the tour of it all. 'You've had an architect's report on it, I believe?'

'Oh yes. Everything's sound enough, or will be when the repairs are done. And you'll help me to decide on colour schemes and furniture as we agreed?'

Morwen bit her lip. Was it wise, or would she merely be indulging herself, fitting out a house for some other woman to live in, in a way she herself had never done? But if it was Ran's wish…

'I'd be glad to, providing we come here next time in daylight, so that I can give you some sensible opinions,' she said evenly.

'Daylight will be best,' he agreed. 'We should bring the children, and Ben, and your entire family, perhaps.'

Morwen turned away. 'I think you make fun of me, Ran. Perhaps I'm not quite as ready for your colonial ways as you seem to think.'

'Morwen, isn't it time we forgot those ridiculous labels we put on each other? We're just people, you and I, just a man and a woman. And given other circumstances, a man and a woman who could mean a great deal to one another, and I make no apologies for my background for saying such things to you.'

'Then I think you should. 'Tis not the way a gentleman should speak to a lady – or perhaps despite your fine words, you're still labelling me as a clayworker's daughter!'

She goaded him, hardly knowing why. Would he have said such things to Miss Finelady Jane? The insidious thought crept into her mind, and she tilted her chin higher. She heard Ran give a contemptuous laugh, and before she knew what was happening, she was pulled into his arms again. His hands moved swiftly upwards from her waist to cup her face. She felt the soft sweet caress of his fingers, and it seemed as if all her flesh moved beneath her skin at his touch.

'You idiotic woman,' his voice was rough now. 'Do you think I care a damn what you were? It's not the way we think in my country. We're not hide-bound by such pomposity, and all I care about is what you are. All I ever want is what I know I can't have.'

She couldn't avoid his kiss without the risk of having her neck snapped in two. And she didn't want to risk that… nor could she deny the surging thrill of his words, the wanton passion flooding through her at the pressure of his mouth on hers, and the evidence of his desire in every part of his body that touched hers.

At last he let her go, and it was Ran who stood silently for a moment, while Morwen trembled at the force of her own sexuality.

'I've never stolen another man's wife, Morwen, nor do I intend to start now. But I'd be a hypocrite if I denied that I would give the world to make you mine. I'm sorry I burdened you with my secret. I had hoped to keep it mine alone.'

'Let's speak no more of it, Ran,' she said unsteadily. 'It was a moment's madness, and we both know what our relationship must continue to be—'

For a second he spoke bitterly. 'Yes. The American cousin daring to buy Cornish land and Cornish business, allowed into the Killigrew household because of distant family connections. I'll try hard to remember it, but don't insult my feelings by calling them no more than a moment's madness.'

'I have to,' Morwen whispered. 'Don't you see? Otherwise, I can no longer come here with you, nor would I feel comfortable in my own home whenever you called. I would feel guilty every time I looked at you.'

'I do see,' he said at last. 'So I must continue to think of you as my dear cousin and nothing more. And you?'

'It's what you are to me,' she said simply, knowing it was the greatest lie she had ever spoken. Because in those illuminating moments, she knew that Randell E Wainwright had become so much more. The knowledge was new and frightening. She wanted to run away from it, but there was nowhere to hide from the thoughts inside her head. He blew out the oil-lamp, and the pungent aroma enveloped them for a moment, the wispy smoke enclosing them in a small private world.

'I had better get you back to Truro, Morwen.' He was once more the considerate gentleman, and she gave a sigh of relief. 'The road will be busy with people going home from the fair, and will be relatively safe, but if we're out too long after dark, I'm sure your brothers will start to worry.'

'And you'll see the agent about the house soon?' She was thankful to be outside of it, stepping carefully around the broken tiles without waiting for assistance, and talking of less emotive subjects.

'Tomorrow,' Ran said. 'When I want something, I see no point in wasting time. If I did, I would have missed the chance of buying Prosper Barrows, and that promises to be a good investment.'

Morwen nodded as he helped her into the carriage. The words were innocuous enough, but she felt an unaccountable shiver run through her. He had made it very clear that he wanted her, but she believed him to be an honourable man, and that he would never try to take her from Ben. But no amount of honour ever stopped a man wanting, or a woman loving.

–

All the way back to Truro, they felt as though they were salmon trying to swim upstream as they were caught in the crush of carriages and groups of walking revellers going in the opposite direction. As they left the grounds of the new house, Morwen had the strange feeling that someone was watching them, and she couldn't forget the moment when she had thought she had seen Jude Pascoe. She had been thinking of dreams, but the thought of that man was a nightmare…

They reached Jack's house safely, and discovered that Freddie had already taken the three boys to his own house to spend the night. Annie had put the girls to bed with the twins, and she and Jack were eager to hear details of the fine new house Ran was buying. Morwen plunged into descriptions of it, praising the design of the architecture and the superb sea and moorland views, and Ran's luck in finding it.

'I'd say luck shines quite often on 'ee, Ran. What do you say?' Jack said lazily, sprawling by his own fireside with all the complacency of a man well-pleased with life.

'What an odd thing to say, Jack,' Annie exclaimed.

'Why should it be odd? Here's a man come from across the sea, and in a very short time he finds himself a ready-made family, a business, and now a fine new house. Wouldn't you call that luck? There's many a man who spends a lifetime looking for those things, and never finds 'em.'

'Jack, you're not being very tactful!' Morwen said.

Her brother looked honestly surprised. 'What's tactless about that? I'm all for a man who bends his luck to suit himself, that's all, and if a body's got more'n his fair share of it, good luck to him—'

He and Ran began laughing at the same time as the words tripped over themselves.

'You ladies don't need to take offence on my account,' he said easily. 'I know just what Jack means, and he's right. A man still needs to make use of his luck, though, or it's wasted.'

'Do you mean to stay in Cornwall forever then, Ran?' Annie enquired, the interested hostess.

'I'm not sure I believe in forever,' he said with a smile. 'Today is more important than some shadowy future that can be taken away in a minute if the fates are against you.'

Morwen listened with something like panic. He echoed so much of her own thinking it was uncanny. If she let her control weaken, she might admit that the hard-headed American businessman and the fey Cornish girl were kindred spirits after all.

She kept quiet, drinking in the night sounds of the little household. Jack and Annie were so suited, still so much in love, talking and listening politely to their guests. And she and Ran... they were part of the family, but they could almost be just another married couple on a visit, while all the children slept upstairs... her thoughts veered away at once.

After an hour or so, lulled by the warmth of the fire and the pleasant conversation, she gave a stifled yawn. She was suddenly very tired, not only from the Fair, but from the emotional time afterwards.

'Morwen, do you want to go to bed? I think we should all have an early night,' Annie said, to which Jack agreed at once. Morwen didn't blame them, and nor did she miss the glances between them. They were sweetly familiar to her, the kind of glances she and Ben used to exchange. The salt tears pricked at her eyes, because such moments were increasingly rare between them, and she was infinitely sad that something so beautiful could disappear without anyone realizing it or being able to hold it back.

She went upstairs to the bedroom she was to share with her two sleeping daughters, and it was the first time she had been obliged to listen to someone else's breathing besides her own or Ben's in the darkness. Since she and Ben had been using separate rooms, Morwen hadn't realized how another person's snuffling little noises could disturb her. It was difficult to sleep, and evidently the girls found it difficult too, from their constant tossings and turnings, probably due to over-excitement and the strangeness of a different atmosphere.

And in the settling sounds of the night, Morwen found herself drifting into dreams. Not the somnolent kind that had their excuse in unconsciousness, but waking dreams that were far more disturbing, because her brain was alert, her mind active, and the dreams were all of Ran Wainwright. She tried desperately to subdue them.

It was the house Ran had taken her to see, she told herself in a kind of panic. No more than the house, and the intriguing thought of helping Ran plan and furnish what went into it. It was like a new beginning, and she had always been excited at the thought of something new, a legacy from the far-off days when her life had been no more than a dull pattern of days spent scraping and stacking the clay with no prospect of anything ever changing it.

But her life had changed beyond measure. Marriage to the man she loved so fiercely had been the culmination of an impossible dream, and to have all the children around her was the final fulfilment. And yet… and yet…

'Oh Ben,' she found herself whispering the words, her hand stretching out to the empty pillow beside her, aware that there was dampness on her cheeks. 'Why have we drifted so far apart, and why can I never reach you in spirit any more?'

She tried to conjure up his face, but it remained tantalizingly out of range, like a water-colour painting that was indistinct. As if it didn't want to be recognized, the face was shapeless and distorted, and with a little sob, Morwen closed her eyes tightly against the vision, as if it was some kind of omen.

–

Daylight came as a relief. Morwen felt as though she had hardly closed her eyes all night, but the girls were awake and chattering as soon as the people of Truro went about their business, and begged their mother to let them go along the waterfront to see the tall ships at anchor.

'Perhaps Uncle Matt will come home on one of them one day,' Primmy said eagerly. 'Uncle Ran says he might. What will he look like, Mama?'

Morwen felt her eyes soften.

'He'll be tall and dark and as handsome as your Uncle Jack and Uncle Freddie.' She smiled, glad to talk of something so familiar and ignoring a small pang that she couldn't include her brother Sam in the description.

Sam, who was Primmy's real father, and about whom the children should be told someday. A feeling of unease filled Morwen whenever she thought about the telling, wondering what the reaction would be. She was reasonably sure that the middle boy, Albert, would take it all calmly enough. The eldest, Walter, might be belligerent at not knowing the truth earlier. While Primmy… Morwen eyed her wilful adopted daughter. Sam's daughter, yet more like the fiery young Morwen Tremayne than anyone might have expected. Primmy's reaction was unpredictable, and the time for telling must be carefully judged.

'Your eyes have gone all faraway, Mama,' she heard Primmy say curiously. 'Do you still miss Uncle Matt?'

Morwen gave her a quick hug. 'When you lose somebody dear to you, darling, time makes no difference to how much you miss them.'

Morwen knew that she was referring not only to Matt, but to Sam, and to Celia, her dearest friend…

'Did Uncle Matt look like our other uncles, Mama?' Charlotte jumped up and down, clearly enchanted by the thought of someone across the sea resembling any of them.

Morwen laughed, her voice a mite husky as she urged the girls to refresh themselves at the wash-basin and get dressed quickly for breakfast.

'He was even more handsome, but don't you dare tell the others I said so,' she said lightly. 'He had blue eyes like all the Tremaynes, and I pray that one day you'll all get the chance to see him. It will be the happiest day in Grandma Bess's life.'

'Will she be happier than seeing us?' Charlotte pouted.

Morwen teased her.

'Well, my lamb, she can see you any day, can't she? So it will be a bit more special when your Uncle Matt comes home.'

'I don't think I shall like him,' Primmy announced imperiously.

Morwen lost the patience that seemed to be always teetering dangerously of late. 'Don't be ridiculous, Primmy. And don't put ideas into Charlotte's head. Everyone loved Matt—'

'Did you love him better than Daddy?' Charlotte said in her curiously perceptive childish way. Morwen's heart lurched.

'We love people in different ways, Charlotte. Matt is my brother, so I feel specially close to him, but it's different to my love for your Daddy—'

'Why don't you sleep in the same room any more then?' Primmy suddenly asked. 'You always used to share things but you don't seem to do that any more. Daddy's always cross, and you don't even talk to each other very much.'

Morwen turned slowly from her attentions to Charlotte's neck with the wash-cloth. She met Primmy's too-knowing eyes, and the glib words died on her lips. Primmy was growing up too fast to be fobbed off. The boys might never notice such things, but a daughter was different. She left Charlotte's side and went swiftly to the older girl, standing tense and taut as Morwen put her arms around her.

'Darling, people don't always have to be saying sweet things to know that they care for each other,' she chose her words carefully. 'Sleeping in separate rooms is something that lots of married people do after a while—'

She *was* fobbing her off, Morwen thought helplessly, not knowing what else to say. Primmy wriggled out of her embrace and looked at her accusingly.

'Grandpa Hal and Grandma Bess don't!'

'Oh Primmy, just don't question things you don't understand,' Morwen said softly, kissing the top of her shining black hair. Primmy glared at her.

'Daddy says you never find out anything unless you ask,' she said rudely. 'But when I ask, I never get any proper answers. You're all the same.'

'Don't shout at Mama,' Charlotte said, suddenly frightened. Morwen turned to her quickly.

'It's all right, love. Nobody's shouting, and if we don't go down to breakfast soon, we shan't have time to see the tall ships before Uncle Ran takes us back home.'

'When we get home, Daddy will be there, won't he?' Charlotte cheered up at once. How little it took when you were only six years old, Morwen thought enviously.

'He'll be back later tonight,' she promised.

It seemed a long time off. It seemed an eternity since she had seen Ben, and it scared her to know how little she had thought of him since he had been away. Once, his absence would have devastated her. Once, it would have seemed that her whole life came to an end until he returned. She forced herself to think of Ben, where once she would have been totally unable to keep him out of her mind.

Tonight, Ben would be home again, and she knew guiltily that he must be missing her by his side in London. She owed it to him, and to all of them, to put any other madness out of her mind, and to restore happiness to Killigrew House. For the sake of the children, and for their marriage, Morwen knew that she must move back into their old bedroom that night before it was too late.

Chapter Eight

The ceremony at Ormsby College was over, and Ben Killigrew had been installed as Honorary Governor, to the applause of pupils past and present, and the comment by one of his old acquaintances that the college never did things by half. Ben laughed agreeably, feeling expansive and mellow at the surprisingly formal proceedings. Celebrations had gone on far longer than he had expected too, and it was already dark before anyone began to leave the splendid main hall of the college.

'You're right, Desmond. I thought it would be some private and dreary meeting in the Dean's study and it would all be over in minutes.'

'Instead of which, you're the hero of the hour, old boy,' Desmond Hartley-Hogg grinned. His rotund, bewhiskered face beamed at his old friend. 'Tell me, what d'you do now in that heathen corner of England?'

'You mean Cornwall,' Ben corrected. 'Never refer to a true Cornishman's land as England, Piggy! They bristle at once.'

'All right, then, Cornwall,' Hogg said lazily. 'So what's to do there apart from fishing and staving off these murderous wreckers one occasionally reads about in the newspapers?'

Ben laughed. 'You townies are all the same,' he commented. 'Once out of London you think we're all barbarians and have no social graces.'

'I must say, I can't say that for you, Killigrew,' Hogg conceded. 'Besides, I travel up and down from town, and have my share of country life as well.'

'Oh yes – a gentleman farmer, aren't you?' Ben grinned. 'Living off the fat of the land while your labourers do the work, I suppose.'

'What's the point of being rich if you don't make use of it?' Hogg said airily. 'Whatever game you're in, you do the same, I'll wager.'

'True enough. I produce china-clay, and some of it probably reaches your table in fine chinaware.'

'Is that so?' Hartley-Hogg was already losing interest as an idea struck him. 'I say, why not make a night of it, Killigrew? You can stay at my town-house tonight, and I know a very interesting little establishment. You were a deft hand with cards and dice in the old days.'

'I haven't gambled in years,' Ben said shortly.

Hartley-Hogg guffawed and dug him in the ribs. 'I don't believe it. Once a gambler always a gambler. Or did the little woman rumble you and put the blocks on it? Is that it? Got your bollocks nipped, have you?'

Ben felt his skin bristle at the unconsciously patronizing tone. He had never been over-keen on the boisterous Desmond Hartley-Hogg, though he was definitely preferable to Neville Peterson.

To his relief, Peterson had kept noticeably absent in the personal congratulations to the new Governor, though his Captain's uniform was prominent among his old cronies. Ben thought sourly that a man who corrupted boys, as Peterson had done when he threatened Freddie, was a disgrace to any uniform.

Ben pushed away these thoughts, and rose instead to Hartley-Hogg's challenge.

'All right. Why not? The club where I've booked rooms is as dreary as hell. Why not make a night of it?' Hogg clapped him on the back. 'Now you sound more like the old Killigrew. Let's get out of here.'

It was only as Ben finally reached the door that he turned and saw the calculating eyes of Neville Peterson watching him, surrounded by his old cronies. He muttered beneath his breath as he followed Hartley-Hogg out to his waiting carriage and climbed in beside him in the cold night air.

'What's that, Killigrew?' Hogg said in amusement. 'You never used to curse so readily!'

'Perhaps not, but I know a bastard when I see one,' Ben said tersely.

'You mean Peterson, I suppose? He always boasted he had a score to settle with you someday.' He guffawed again, coarse as ever, and Ben wished he'd never mentioned the man.

He was thankful when the carriage eventually stopped at a London pavement, where a flight of steps led down to a discreet doorway. Hartley-Hogg gave a coded knock on the door, which opened and admitted them at once. The door closed behind them swiftly, and the seductive fighting in one part of the place told its own story, while the bright fights above the gambling tables told another.

'Whatever your pleasure, you can find it here, Killigrew,' Hogg's voice was lecherous. 'If you'd rather keep pure for that little gel of yours back in darkest Cornwall, that's your affair, but I mean to start off with one of the delectable French mamselles they've imported from gay Paree!'

Ben's immediate reaction was to snap at Hogg that he'd be happy enough with an hour's gambling, and would probably return to his club after all. His second reaction came suddenly, as the high-class prostitutes began circulating round the room at the appearance of new clients, wafting expensive French perfume in their wake.

He might have known that Hartley-Hogg wouldn't bring him to some low-class whore-house, but to a place where the clientele moved in high places in the city from the looks of them…

And why not indulge himself for once, for God's sake? The thought came to him savagely. His wife didn't want him. She had made that plain enough lately. She cared nothing for the way a man needed his woman, for the unbearable ache in his loins and the resentment he felt that she could demean him so in his own house, where all the servants must be aware that they no longer slept together. If he enjoyed a prostitute tonight, then it was Morwen's own fault. If she had been here with him, he would never have been tempted...

'Can I do anything for you, Sir?'

He heard a soft voice beside him, and looked down into the smoky-black eyes of a velvet-skinned Malaysian girl. Her mouth was painted into exaggerated curves, and her teeth were very white against her lips. She wore a white floating gown with feathers at the neck and hem, and the effect of the white fabric against the dark skin was sensually arousing. At her inviting smile, Ben felt himself rise in a way that was acutely pleasurable, a feeling he hadn't known in many weeks, and saw the girl run her tongue slowly over her glossy top lip in expectation of his reply.

'I do believe you can,' Ben said thickly, and allowed her to lead him away to the seclusion of a rose-coloured room where nothing mattered but the touch of his flesh on a woman's, soft lips exploring his skin, gentle fingers searching and finding, and the blotting out of everything but sensation and sensuality.

And then the urgency of a primitive need to forge his body into the one beneath him, thrusting with reckless abandonment, until the final exquisite moments when his seed spewed out from him, and he lay spent against the girl's glistening body.

'I think you were badly in need of that, Sir, and I believe I recognize your accent. It is from Cornwall, I think. A Cornishman visited me once who spoke the way you do. If you are ever this way again, may I remind you to ask for Darianna.'

The girl's oddly cultured voice, and her first attempt at conversation, seemed to reach him through a cloud. He hardly knew where he was any more. He had fornicated with a prostitute, and, Ben thought guiltily, it hadn't been distasteful at all. It had been glorious, defying description, and if he died in her arms, he would die happy. Indeed, it might be better if he did die now, a tiny sane part of his brain told him, because very soon he was going to be riddled with remorse…

'You will pay Madame,' Darianna went on coolly. 'Just give her my name and my fee, and she will then direct you to the gambling tables. My gentlemen usually finish off their evenings there, and may I wish you good luck.'

Ben leaned up on his elbows, looking down at her. She still lay imprisoned beneath him, her breasts small, smooth copper-coloured globes. Her belly was taut, the black mass of pubic hair tangled and damp. The musky sexuality of her body was without question, but it was the remoteness of her eyes that arrested Ben now. When he looked into her face, it was mask-like. All the required passion, real or simulated, was gone, and just as quickly he was sickened and revolted.

He eased himself off the silken sheets, unwilling to look at her any longer. He felt unclean, knowing that whatever the excuse, he had betrayed Morwen and their marriage. If he sometimes felt guilt at neglecting her, his guilt would be ten-fold now.

'I'll see that you're well-paid,' he growled, pulling on his clothes with all speed.

'And you'll visit me again, Cornishman?' she suddenly smiled, all the beauty back in her face.

'No. I can safely say that I shall never visit you again,' he said, and left her staring at him in surprise.

He paid the Madame, and looked around for his companion. Hartley-Hogg was nowhere to be seen, and Ben decided to while away his time at the gambling tables, partly because he could hardly leave without saying goodbye to the man, and partly because the lure of the card-games was beginning to make his fingers itch. And it would take his mind off his infidelity.

It was a long while since he had gambled, but tonight seemed to be a night for renewing old enemies, and he knew that the fever could soon take hold of him again. He could control it, of course. He'd always been able to do so, and he would never be like some of these raddled old men, pathetic in their last gasp attempts to win back their losses… Ben had always been lucky.

–

'Jesus, old boy, you've made a packet!'

He couldn't have said how long he'd been sitting there, numb and tense, but with adrenalin flowing in his veins, when he heard Hartley-Hogg's voice. His neck and shoulders ached as he flexed them, but the pile of bank-notes in front of him was mountainous.

'Are you joining me?' Ben realized that his throat was dry from holding his breath. Every turn of the card was an excitement, every win a boost to his ego. Hogg shook his head.

'I think not. My stomach's empty and I shan't be able to concentrate. I suggest we go back to my house and rouse my manservant to cook us some breakfast.'

'Breakfast?' Ben said in surprise.

'It's nearly four in the morning, old boy. If you're planning on going home to Cornwall today, you'd better get an hour's shut-eye, at least.'

'All right, Piggy. And thanks. It's been a good night,' Ben said expansively, the memory of Darianna's attentions already fading. If he tried hard enough, he could forget it ever happened, at least when he was so weary he could hardly see straight. He stuffed the bank-notes into his pocket and the two of them stumbled out into the freezing morning air.

It was still dark, but a thick, choking, yellow fog hung about the streets. For a moment Ben was disorientated. He was totally lost in any case, not knowing how many streets Hogg's carriage had taken them. He heard Hogg say he'd call for his man to come and get them, when suddenly it felt as if all the demons in hell had descended on them.

Though not on Hartley-Hogg, except when he got in their way and tried to help Ben… even as he heard himself screaming at the vicious punches to his guts and his tender parts, and felt the searing slice of a knife on his cheek, Ben realized it wasn't Hartley-Hogg for whom they had come. It was for Ben that the six of them had been patiently hiding in the darkness…

'I've waited a long while for this, you Cornish prig,' he heard Neville Peterson scream in his ear. 'I knew there'd be a time for me to get even. You won't find your breeding tackle so comfortable, nor will your stuck-up wife find you so pretty when we've done with you.'

Two of his companions held Ben's flailing arms while Peterson aimed his boot into Ben's crotch. Others aimed at his face and chest. There was nothing he could do. All the expertise in the world couldn't stop them, and he felt his teeth rattle in his head as blow after blow found its. His groin was one mass of pain, and when he realized Hartley-Hogg had fled, he wondered bitterly if he had been a party to it.

Minutes later, he knew thankfully that it was not the case, when the man returned with several constables, the sounds of their whistles piercing the night. Before there was any danger of them being caught, Peterson and his cronies ran off, swallowed up in the London fog, and Ben lay groaning in agony in the filth of the gutter.

'Are you all right, Sir?' one of the constables asked.

'No, I'm not bloody all right,' Ben lashed through badly cut and swollen lips, his voice a blur of sound.

'You'd best get him to hospital, Sir,' another constable said to Hartley-Hogg. 'He looks fair injured to me, and there'll be statements to be made, and charges made—'

'No!' Ben said as sharply as he could, despite the fact that his chest hurt every time he breathed, and he felt as though every bone in his body was broken. 'There will be no charges—'

'Ben, you must!' Hartley-Hogg exclaimed. 'They've got to pay for this!'

'You'll do as I say! But I'd be very obliged if you'd get the carriage and get me some medical attention, for I fear I'm about to black out at any minute.'

The entire universe seemed to be dancing about in a haze of yellow fog. The constables' helmets floated in circles of blue above him, their faces pale moons of light. God, he wished he could black out. He wished he never had to feel the pain… just as long as he had impressed the need for no charges to be made. Nothing that would mean court appearances, and newspaper reports, revelations of where he had spent the last hours, the mention of Captain Peterson's name, and the shame and the horror of it reaching Morwen, and Freddie…

'I'll take care of him, Constable,' he heard Hogg's strong voice say. 'The culprits will be far away by now, and there's no point in trying to pursue them.'

'Very well, Sir,' the man said in frustration. 'Just get your friend attended to, for he looks in a real bad way.'

They helped Piggy lift Ben into the carriage, an ordeal more excruciating than he let them see. His face felt split wide open, and the cold night air made it sting as if from a hundred needle-points. And then he remembered nothing more until he awoke in a hospital bed with two doctors inspecting his body. There was an agonizing tightness on his cheek, and when he touched it, one of the doctors spoke sharply.

'No, Mr Killigrew, your face is stitched. It will be less painful in a few days when the stitches are removed.'

'How long have I been here?' And why in God's name did he feel so sluggish and drugged, as if everything around him was happening in slow motion?

'Three days,' the doctor said. 'Your friend has given us details of your accident, and has been to visit you daily—'

'Three days! Dear God, I should get home!'

He made to sit up, and the room swam as pain rushed into every part of him. The second doctor pushed him back on the pillow, and spoke impatiently.

'My dear Sir, you will not be going anywhere until your wounds have healed. You were very badly beaten up, and whatever it is you've been rambling about will have to wait.'

Ben answered furiously. He was enveloped in pain, he realized, and it even hurt to breathe. His head felt as though it was stuffed with sheep's wool. He was irritated by the doctor's reference to his rambling. It wasn't a word he liked to associate with himself, but the devil of it was, he couldn't remember what it was that was so all-fired important for him to attend to.

He wasn't an idiot, and nor had he lost his memory. He knew his name and his business… he forced his brain to respond…

'The scaggies!' he groaned. The medical staff glanced at one another, clearly thinking their patient might be demented to be uttering such strange words. Ben made himself sound more authoritative.

'Patch me up and arrange for a carriage to take me to the railway station,' he ordered. 'It's imperative that I get back to Cornwall immediately. My wife will be sick with worry—'

Morwen had been a secondary thought. It had been the clayworks that were all-important, but a wife should realize that a man's work was the mainstay of all of them. He brushed aside his guilt, and was obliged to listen instead to what these fools of doctors had to say. He felt impotent and vulnerable while they towered over him.

'Mr Killigrew, please listen. Your friend has sent a messenger to inform your wife of what's happened, and to say that you will be confined in this hospital for a week or so while we make sure you are fit to travel, and make certain tests.'

'Nobody's keeping me here for weeks!' Ben felt as though he roared, but the stitches in his cheek tugged and smarted so keenly that he had to speak through tight-clenched lips. 'And what tests, may I ask? A few cuts and bruises won't kill me—'

'No, but a faulty heart valve might.'

Ben stared at the man, his gimlet eyes daring a patient to argue with his suspicions. Faulty heart valve? What nonsense was this? He was as strong as any man…

All his arguments made no difference. They let him rave for a while and then simply turned and left him alone in the small white room, having been assured by Hartley-Hogg that there were ample funds to pay for private attention. Ben stared at the ceiling, refusing to believe what he had heard. He was a young man in his prime, with a beautiful wife and five healthy children. Heart defects were for old men, and he had every intention of living until he was ninety.

For the first time in his life, stirrings of fear seeped into him as he lay quite alone, and realized that, whatever his intentions, he was too weak and in too much pain to simply get dressed and walk out. He was as helpless as a child, and the thought of submitting to medical tests was making him less arrogant by the minute.

-

Two days after Truro Fair, back at Killigrew House after the excitement of staying away from home for a night, Morwen was informed that there was a visitor from London. She looked up from her sewing in surprise. It was someone to see Ben, presumably, and he should have been back yesterday.

Her father had already been to Killigrew House in some annoyance, with news that the Pit Captains were incensed that Ben was still away gallivanting when a boss should be at hand whenever there was a crisis brewing. It was the first time Hal had referred to the state of Killigrew Clay in crisis terms, and Morwen knew it must be serious for him to do so.

She had tried to play down the fact that Ben was still away, her own annoyance coupled with the feeling of guilt over her feelings for Ran Wainwright making her pompous and sharp with her father.

'Really, Daddy, you shouldn't let the men rule you. If Ben wants to stay away a bit longer he has every right to do so. He's the boss, after all—'

'Oh ah, and he'll be a boss without a clayworks if he don't keep his eye on what's afoot,' Hal said grimly. 'And don't come the high-and-mighty boss's wife wi' me, Miss. You'm still my daughter, and I don't need 'ee telling me how to behave.'

She bristled for a moment and then her blue eyes laughed back at him.

'I'm sorry, Daddy, but I'm sure Ben has a perfectly good reason for staying away. He has strong ties with his college and now he's so important, they probably expected him to stay and be sociable.'

She tried not to notice her small shiver. The ties with Ormsby College included Ben's hatred of Neville Peterson.

And if her father was angry, then Morwen was angry too. It piqued her to know that just when she had decided that harmony must be restored to their marriage, and had every intention of moving back into the marital bedroom, Ben stayed absent.

And now there was a visitor from London. She waited curiously until Mrs Horn showed the man into the drawing-room. He seemed not quite at his ease, though looking mildly surprised to find a luxurious house in good taste so far away from London. Morwen hid a smile. Cornish folk were not all rogues and vagabonds, despite what those from upcountry England thought.

'Forgive me for disturbing you, Madam, but I bring news of your husband.'

Morwen was alarmed at once. 'Of Ben? What's happened? I was expecting him home yesterday—'

'May we sit down, Mrs Killigrew? I think it would be best.'

After a startled second, she sat down abruptly, motioning him to do the same. Her heart pounded. There was clearly something wrong, and she prayed that Ben's quick temper hadn't landed him in any trouble with the law.

'My name is Hartley-Hogg, and my brother is an old friend of your husband. They were re-acquainted at the governor's ceremony at Ormsby College, for which my congratulations on your husband's behalf, dear lady.'

Now that he was here, he was acutely embarrassed, knowing it was best that he kept some of the details from this beautiful young woman. Though why Ben Killigrew should want to visit a high-class brothel and gaming establishment when he had such a wife at home was beyond Royston Hartley-Hogg. He wished he had not volunteered to come here, and let his brother Desmond send the telegraph instead. But it had seemed so cold and brutal to inform her that way, and Royston had been vastly curious to see this strange, wild corner of England and had decided to spend a few days exploring it.

'Will you please tell me why you have come, Mr Hartley-Hogg?' Morwen said quietly, fighting down the sudden desire to laugh at the ludicrous name.

'I'm afraid your husband has been slightly injured in a street brawl, Mrs Killigrew, when some ruffians set upon him. He's not badly hurt, but he needed some stitches and is badly bruised, and will have to stay in hospital for a short while—'

'Dear Heaven!' Whatever she had expected to hear, it wasn't this. 'He's in hospital? Then it must be serious—'

'No, no!' Her distress made him agitated. He prayed that she wouldn't faint. He was a respectable bachelor by choice, and women's infirmities were out of his range of experience. 'My brother has sent you a letter explaining everything. Please read it, Mrs Killigrew.'

He thrust it under her nose, thinking that even her sudden pallor became her. She read the letter quickly. According to his friend, Ben had been grossly unfortunate. It was a risky business being out and about in London in a thick pea-souper, whatever that was, and the villains had set upon them before they could shout for help. Hartley-Hogg assured Morwen that he would visit Ben and send daily telegraphs on his progress until Ben himself was able to send word that he was coming home.

'Have you seen my husband?' she asked her visitor.

He was unused to such directness in a lady's gaze, and found it both disarming and alluring. And it did not allow for any prevarication.

'I am not acquainted with the gentleman, Madam,' he said. 'But I assure you my brother will carry out any task you wish. You have only to send a telegraph back to him.'

'You're very kind.' Now that the initial shock was lessening, Morwen remembered her manners. Ben was obviously in good hands, and the letter had reassured her a little.

'Forgive me for neglecting to offer you some tea, Mr Hartley-Hogg. You must be in need of refreshment after your journey.'

'Thank you, no. I will be on my way.'

He rose at once, to Morwen's great relief, for if she had to repeat the name once more, she was sure she would succumb to hysterical laughter, and that would be appalling. She thanked him again and rang for Mrs Horn to show him out. The hysterical laughter was still dangerously close to the surface as she folded the letter carefully and bit her lip, feeling it tremble.

Ben… her dearest Ben… was in some strange hospital, lying hurt and bruised, and probably in the very moments that the attack had been happening, she had been on the brink of a delicious flirtation with an American cousin…

'Morwen, what's happened? Darling, you look stunned. Has something happened to one of the children?'

She heard Ran Wainwright's voice as if from a distance. The cool American accent was something she found undeniably attractive, and her new awareness of the caring look in his dark eyes now, all added to the feeling of guilt that overcame everything else. He touched her arm, and she wrenched it from him as if stung by a hornet.

'It's nothing to do with the children. It's Ben. He's been hurt and he's in hospital in London, and I must go to him!' She hadn't considered it until that moment, but now she saw that she must. She saw something else too. 'And I'd ask you please not to call me darling! I'm not your darling, and I'll thank 'ee to remember it!'

The words tumbled out, and when they were finished, she crumbled. Without another word Ran took her in his, and held her sobbing body close to his heart. And each of them was acutely aware that nothing could ever change this magnetism between them, not guilt nor anguish nor duty…

Chapter Nine

'I shall take you to London,' Ran said calmly, when Morwen had shown him the letter.

'It's not necessary—'

'Don't be ridiculous, Morwen. You can't travel alone. I would be a poor cousin if I couldn't chaperone you.'

She gave the glimmer of a smile. And who was going to chaperone the chaperone? But there were more important things to consider, and she was thankful, after all, for Ran to take over and to help reassure the children and her parents.

If Ben was to be away longer than expected, it was up to Hal now to pacify the men and keep Killigrew Clay running as smoothly as possible. He and Bess hugged their daughter as she and Ran prepared to leave for London the following morning, after a whirlwind of packing for the few days Morwen assumed they would have to stay.

'Don't worry about anything here, my lamb,' Bess said. 'I'll see that the children don't run wild, so just you go and satisfy yourself that Ben's all right. Thank God you've got a responsible relative to look after you.'

Bess wholeheartedly approved of Randell Wainwright. What would her gentle mother think, Morwen wondered uneasily, if she knew of her daughter's unbidden dreams about the handsome American? However unprovoked, Morwen knew they were adulterous dreams, and now she was being brought sharply back to reality in this rush to be at her husband's bedside, as though it was a punishment. She hugged Bess tightly.

'I shan't stay any longer than I need to, Mammie,' she whispered. 'Once I see for myself that Ben's going to be all right, I shall come home.'

Now that the time was here, she was shaking with nerves. London was so far away, the city where vice and wickedness went hand in hand. She had never been on a train before, except on Ben's little railway, nor had she stayed in an hotel before, which was what she and Ran would be obliged to do. It hadn't been so difficult after all to insist that she couldn't leave the children and accompany Ben, yet now she was being thrust into it without any choice.

'I'm sure Ben's injuries aren't too serious, Morwen. We would have heard otherwise.' Ran's voice kept telling her the same thing throughout the journey. He was keeping his distance, she realized miserably. Ever since she had raged at him last night, he had been strictly impersonal towards her. It was what she wanted, what had to be…

'The thought of London has always unnerved me,' she told him, once the journey had begun. 'And now I'm going there voluntarily. Ben wanted to take me for several weeks, and I hated the idea of it. I counted the trouble at the clayworks as a mixed blessing, because it meant Ben didn't insist on taking me. It sounds so terrible now.'

'Nothing you do could be terrible to me.'

'And yet I would dearly love to see foreign countries,' she rushed on as if he hadn't spoken. 'I wouldn't be so afraid there, because they would all speak in languages I couldn't be expected to understand. Whereas in London, as soon as anyone hears me speak, they'll know me for the country ninny that I am.'

She stopped, realizing how she had been babbling, and that she had revealed her fright at last. Not even to Ben had she been quite so self-doubting. Her pride seemed to be in tatters, and she was furious at herself for appearing so vulnerable in front of Ran Wainwright. Him of all people… yet only with him, of all people, could she feel so unfettered by convention.

'Calm yourself, Morwen,' Ran said. 'I refuse to go on telling you how beautiful you are, for you must see it in my eyes every time I look at you. Every man in London will envy the man who escorts you, and your voice is charming. You need have no fears, my dear.'

'I suppose I must be comforted by that, coming from a man of the world,' she tried to respond lightly, while her heart quaked as they travelled nearer to the city, and she felt as though every bone in her body was being fractured. They travelled first-class, but even so, there was little comfort. But by the time they reached Paddington Station late in the evening, the relief of alighting from the carriage, and walking past the monstrous engine belching smoke and sparks and steam, overcame much of Morwen's apprehension.

And after all, the people milling about looked much like themselves, weary travellers. Glancing around the platform, she saw poor flower-sellers huddled in corners with their meagre winter displays, and a few ragged children darting about begging for coppers, reminding her of the kiddley-boys at home.

Ran had called for a porter to carry the baggage, and instructed him to call for a taxi-cab. The horse-drawn vehicles were patiently waiting to collect any passengers with means to pay, and again Morwen was awed, but with more interest than fear. She must remember everything to tell the children, because apart from her reason for coming, it was all a bit of an adventure… and she should have been sharing it with Ben, she thought guiltily.

Ran gave the hospital address to the driver, and they sped off into the dark November night. The driver agreed to wait for them, calculating that the gentleman was well prepared to pay for his services, and afterwards to take them to a respectable hotel nearby.

They reached the hospital after a short journey made longer by constant stops to let other vehicles pass. Morwen had never seen so much traffic, not even on Truro Fair days. She reversed her idea of an adventure, remembering Ben had been accosted in these very streets. The sooner they were safely indoors, the better.

Her heart began to thud as they went inside the hospital with its pungent mixture of smells, pleasant or objectionable, that made her wrinkle her nose. She gave her name to the starched nurse sitting at a desk, and she and Ran were taken by a much younger nurse to a small room at the end of a corridor.

'Private patient, ain't he, ducks?' the girl said. 'All right for some, ain't it?'

Morwen murmured that it was. She had expected someone in a nurse's uniform to be very solemn and correct, yet she spoke in a perky rounded accent that Morwen could hardly follow. And then she forgot all about such peculiarities as the nurse opened the door and showed them inside. And the figure in the bed, battered and bruised, and with the ugly gash that had split his face in two now hideously stitched together, was Ben…

'Oh– Ben—' Morwen felt a wave of faintness wash over her. She gritted her teeth and clenched her hands. What a fool she would be to faint now… she was aware that Ran was propelling her gently towards the bedside, and that the nurse was pushing a chair beneath her… she was even more aware that Ben was glaring at her in disbelief.

'What the hell are you doing here?' he growled. 'There was no need for you to come. I'll be all right in a day or two when these bloody doctors have finished prodding me about.'

Morwen felt her face go scarlet. She couldn't believe Ben could be so uncouth and so ungrateful. And not only that – so displeased to see her! Her eyes filled with tears. After that appalling journey, to find him like this…

'I was so worried about you, Ben,' she said in a choking voice. 'Of course I had to come. What would you have thought of me if I hadn't?'

'I'd have thought you used your common sense,' he snapped, though every muscle in his cheek hurt as he did so. 'What were you thinking about to bring her, Wainwright?'

'I was thinking you'd want to see your wife and assure her of your swift recovery,' Ran said, the glint in his eyes daring Ben to demean her any more. Ran couldn't imagine what had got into the man. It was obvious he was in pain, but to treat Morwen so shabbily was unforgiveable.

'So my wife overcame her dislike of travelling,' Ben ignored him and spoke obliquely to her. 'I must remember to get beaten up more often, then perhaps she'll rush to my bedside again, which is also something of a novelty.'

'Ben, please!' Morwen said, humiliated. 'Won't you tell us what happened, and if we can do anything for you?'

At her words, Ben's head was filled with another soft voice, cultured in the precise manner of foreigners who had learned another language, 'Can I do anything for you, Sir?' And the tumbling between the sheets, with Darianna's warm and pliant body beneath him, welcoming him, albeit that he paid for the privilege. His guilt at the memory, when his beautiful wife's distress was obvious, made him even sharper.

'You can leave me alone. I'll be fit to travel in a week, they tell me, and I'll hire a comfortable carriage instead of taking the abominable train, so there's no need for you to wait around. Get back to the children, Morwen, and whatever else fills your days.'

He insulted her with every word. And she had come to London for this! She rose stiffly, leaning forward to kiss him, but his voice stopped her.

'Don't touch my face, please. It stings hellishly, and I'm best left alone.'

Ran pulled her away, feeling her tremble. His instinct was to hit out, verbally and physically, at the man in the hospital bed, but that was a feeling best kept to himself.

'We'll come back tomorrow, Ben, when, hopefully you'll be in a better humour. We're putting up at a hotel nearby.'

Ben didn't answer, but stared stubbornly at the ceiling. There was nothing else for the visitors to say or do. The nurse hovered outside. From her sympathetic look, Morwen knew she had heard everything.

'Don't be too upset, ducks. They often get that way when they've had bad news. It'll wear off soon.'

'Bad news?' Ran said sharply. 'What do you mean? The cut on his face will heal, won't it?'

'Oh yeah, the cut will heal.' The girl looked frightened, as if she had said too much. 'I don't know nothing, sir. The doctors are the big-wigs round 'ere—'

'Can we see a doctor then?' Ran said immediately. Morwen let him talk, blown by the wind, hardly knowing what was happening. The nurse took them along more corridors and left them outside a larger room.

'Doctor Mosley's office,' the nurse said. 'But I dunno if he'll see you—'

'He'll see us.' Ran knocked at the door and went inside without waiting for an answer. Morwen followed.

The doctor looked up in irritation from his discussion with a colleague. Ran told him who Morwen was, and saw the men glance at one another. A feeling of unease swept through Morwen. There was something wrong, and she knew it with certainty. They were invited to sit down, and Doctor Mosley shuffled some papers about on his desk.

'Well, Mrs Killigrew, I'm glad to tell you that your husband's injuries as the result of the unfortunate brawl are beginning to heal nicely. His face will be scarred, of course, and that's something he will have to get used to.' He paused.

'*But?* I would be glad if you will please tell me the rest, Doctor Mosley,' Morwen said quietly.

He looked at her through narrowed eyes. During Ben's ramblings he had deduced that the fellow had been to a brothel. He didn't condemn him for that. Prostitutes' clients came from the highest in the land as well as the lowest. But he was mildly surprised at seeing this dark-haired vision in front of him now, with those startlingly beautiful blue eyes looking unblinking into his, and wondered why Ben Killigrew had felt the need to stray, unless it was for sheer lecherous indulgence.

'The rest, dear lady?' he prevaricated.

Morwen gave him her direct gaze. 'Doctor Mosley, I am Cornish, like my husband. We Cornish have an uncanny instinct at knowing when something is wrong. If Ben's health is at risk, I insist on being told.'

'Mrs Killigrew has a right to know,' Ran put in. 'And we shall not leave here until you give us the information.'

'And you are, Sir?'

Ran became impatient. 'My identity is immaterial, but I am the lady's cousin, and concerned that she is told the truth.'

The doctor hesitated. His usual practice was to tell the wife nothing, but there was a clarity in this one's eyes that made him feel she could see right through him. That whatever he said, she would have the truth, in the same way her husband had dragged the truth out of him that very morning.

'Your husband has a heart defect, Mrs Killigrew,' he said deliberately. 'The heart is an organ in the body the same as any other, and some people can live for years with a problem—'

'Dear God! And how long for Ben, Doctor?'

This time he was uncertain. The entire truth or a half-truth? He finally muttered the usual platitude that such a strong man would have a long life ahead of him yet. He simply couldn't face a scene if he said brutally that Ben Killigrew had a serious heart condition that could kill him at any time. It could happen tomorrow, but it might not happen for years. It was like a death sentence… it was *exactly* that, the doctor thought grimly. But he saw the narrowed look come into Morwen's eyes, and gave a small sigh, sensing that she hadn't done with him yet.

'How long, Doctor?' She persisted doggedly.

He was angry at having to impart dire news and saw her face whiten as he did so. 'No-one can give a true estimate of life, but your husband has youth on his side,' he added.

'Does my cousin know all this?' Ran said, shocked to know Ben's days were numbered.

'The doctor sighed again, remembering the angry exchanges that morning. 'Oh yes. With such a strong character as Mr Killigrew, we could hardly keep him confined under false pretences. He is not the easiest of patients.'

'Then he has a right to his ill-humour,' Ran went on as Morwen continued to stare blankly at the floor.

'Most certainly.' Doctor Mosley was grateful now to the stranger with the nasal voice for turning the attention from Ben's medical condition to a social one.

'May we visit my cousin tomorrow?'

'Of course.'

There was nothing else to say. They left the hospital and went back to the waiting carriage outside. Once the vehicle began to move, Morwen sagged against Ran, mumbling incoherently.

'I can't believe this is happening. Ben will hate to know he has an illness. He always wants to be so strong – and what am I to say to the children? And God forgive me, but seeing him there, as hateful as usual, even with that hideous injury on his face, it all seemed such an anti-climax. I know it's wicked to feel that way, but I can't help it!'

He longed to put his arms around her and comfort her, but he sensed that it was the last thing she would want.

'Strong men always hate illness, love,' he dared to use the gentler endearment. 'You must know that. He can't help his reaction any more than you could help rushing to his side.'

'I do know it,' she nodded. 'I remember it in his father. Charles Killigrew was a great lion of a man, but when he was struck down with his stroke, he was as pathetic as a child.' She shivered. 'I couldn't bear to see Ben like that.'

Ran tried to reassure her. 'Doctors can always be wrong, Morwen. It may be the shock of the beating that has temporarily affected his heart. I remember such a thing happening to a boxer in New York. It was reported in all the newspapers, but the man recovered completely.'

'Really? You're not inventing the story?' She turned to look at him in the darkness, and he was glad she couldn't see his eyes. The boxer had recovered, but that had been temporary too…

'I'm not inventing it,' he said. 'Now let's register at the hotel and get some food. You must be starving.'

'I am,' she said in surprise. It was hours since they had eaten, but Morwen hadn't been able to think of food until now. The driver of the taxi-cab took the baggage in for them, anticipating a generous tip from the American, and was not disappointed.

'Is it a double room?' the hotel clerk enquired of Ran.

'No. A room for myself and another for the lady,' he replied. 'And we'd like some food, please. Anything will do, and some hot coffee.'

The clerk looked irritated. It was no business of his, but from the look of these two, he'd hoped for a spicy bit of gossip to pass on to his lady-friend. It was said that the Americans were known for their prowess in the bedroom. Pity… it had been a boring night so far…

'The dining-room's closed, sir,' he said, shortly.

'Then send up sandwiches and coffee for us both to my room, and also a bottle of brandy and two glasses.'

Ran gave an order rather than a request, and the clerk handed over two keys ceremoniously, winked broadly, and said it would be attended to at once.

'What a detestable little man,' Morwen breathed, when they had climbed the two flights of stairs to the adjoining rooms, Ran carrying their few pieces of baggage himself.

'Forget him,' Ran said roughly, knowing that in different circumstances he would wish for nothing more than to be in a hotel bedroom with Morwen Killigrew.

After the doctor's news, Ran's thoughts were in a turmoil. The news had been a tremendous shock, particularly the fact that there was no way of knowing if Ben was going to die in a week, or in fifty years from now. And was he unnatural to be wondering which it was to be? Would he be a fool to consider remaining unmarried indefinitely in the tantalizing thought that one day Morwen Killigrew might be free, and would agree to be his wife? Or was he tempting fate in a horribly ghoulish way to even think of it? Honourable or not, such thoughts buzzed in his brain and refused to go away.

It was obvious that Morwen was still very shocked. Only a cad would take advantage at such a time. They would eat the sandwiches, he must insist that she take some brandy to calm her nerves, and he must then see her safely to her own room. His intention was of the highest order.

An hour later, somewhat more relaxed, Morwen said that she would try to get some sleep. It had been a long journey, and Ben didn't want her in London after all, she thought miserably. Nor did she want to stay, except for seeing her husband. London still frightened her. It made more sense for her and Ran to return to Cornwall once they had made the hospital visit tomorrow. What was the point in doing otherwise, when Ben had made his feelings clear?

And Morwen knew that her feelings had changed too. She still loved Ben, and always would, but no longer with the all-consuming love of a woman for her man. It was rather the settled love between old friends, and she knew it with an unbearable sadness.

She stifled a sob in her throat as she rose from her chair in Ran's room, and the brandy made her head spin. He steadied her, his hands gentle on her shoulders, and slowly she looked up into his face, seeing all the emotions there that he found impossible to hide.

'Ran, please—' she said faintly.

The warmth of her in his arms made all his good intentions vanish, and it was as if the words were torn from him.

'Don't go, my dearest one. Stay with me. Be with me tonight.'

'I can't. You *know* that,' she said in panic. 'Ben—'

He was brutally honest. 'Ben doesn't want you, Morwen. I do. I can give you all the love you'll ever need, and no one will ever know. Just this one night, my Morwen.'

'It's wrong. We both know it's wrong—'

But something stronger than her own will was telling her to take this brief happiness while it was being offered. Here was a man who loved and cherished her, and it was so long since she had felt that kind of commitment from Ben. So long since she had felt wanted and desired…

'I always believed that loving someone is never wrong, and I'm not asking for forever, Morwen. We both know the futility of that word. But the memory of these few hours with you will remain with me forever. Will you deny them to me, darling?'

His mouth was touching hers, his body tense with the desire he had controlled with such difficulty, and she could deny him nothing. She swayed against him, her body heavy and sensuous against his, and he carried her in his arms towards his bed.

It reminded her of when he had carried her over the threshold into his house… but this was a very different kind of threshold they were crossing, and there was no turning back.

She didn't remember the moment when Ran turned down the gas-light until there was just a soft popping sound from the lamps. Nor quite how she came to be without her clothes until she became aware of the sudden release of the restricting garments and felt the erotic sensation of cool air on her flesh.

And then the coolness was replaced by warmth. Ran Wainwright's warmth, bringing her back to life again, releasing all the tension and hurt, and reminding her that she was a woman with a woman's needs…

She could see his dark shape over her, and wanted him with a fierceness that obliterated all else. There was a time for gentle love-making, and a time for every animal instinct to be aroused. And they had waited too long for this…

With a small cry, Morwen welcomed him into her body, exalting in pleasure from that very first touch. He moved slowly against her, and she felt every pore ripple in response as the hunger within her matched his.

Her fingers dug deep into his shoulders, revelling in the powerfully hard-muscled flesh. And as if sensing her needs perfectly, they moved rhythmically together, pleasure mounting higher and higher until Morwen felt they must almost reach the stars. And finally all conscious sensation merged into a state of exquisite unreality as they soared towards the peak as one.

Ran still lay against her, and Morwen buried her head into his neck, feeling the dampness of his exertions. It was impossible to describe how she felt, yet she wanted to imprint it on her memory, so that during the darkest days she could remember exactly how it felt to be so loved…

As if thinking her silence might be due to remorse now, Ran turned his head towards hers, and his voice was soft against her cheek.

'You still belong to Ben, Morwen. But now a little part of you will always belong to me, even if it's all I can ever have. This night will be my talisman.'

She felt her throat thicken. It was her husband who was the Cornishman, and Ben with whom she shared the affinity of her race, yet this stranger from across the sea reached into her soul like no other man ever had or ever could. She touched her lips to his, knowing it was goodbye, and her voice was husky-soft.

'And mine too, my love. Our talisman, and our sweet memory of all we can ever have.'

She couldn't say it any plainer. She needed to get away from him now, to be alone and to come to terms with what she had done. She was an adulteress… yet the word had no meaning. She was a woman who was loved and cherished, and that love must remain a secret for all time.

'Ran, I'm going to my own room now,' she said in a low voice, praying that he wouldn't expect her to stay. To spend the night in his arms was a dream she wouldn't allow, and he moved away from her at once. He put her long cloak around her shoulders for modesty's sake. The sweet incongruity of his thoughtfulness after all they had been to one another, made her eyes prickle.

He opened the door between their rooms and lit the gas-light. It threw soft shadows around the room, and silhouetted Ran's nakedness, and Morwen felt a wave of tenderness rush over her that this strong and powerful man should be hers. Whatever happened in the future, for those wild sweet moments, he had been hers and she his, and that was irre-versible.

'Until tomorrow, my dearest.' He ran his finger gently down her cheek, then turned quickly back to his own room. Morwen stared blindly at the closed door for a second before the sudden sting of tears overwhelmed her.

Chapter Ten

Daniel Gorran looked at the sheets of figures in front of him with growing alarm. As accountant for Killigrew Clay, he had become used to the fluctuations of the clay industry, the periodic dip in prices, the falling off of demand, and then the sudden bursts of prosperity. The last few years had been good ones, regardless of all the grievances of the clayworkers. Gorran brushed them aside. Clayworkers were notoriously temperamental, and arguments were only to be expected from such men.

Once the turmoil over the railway tracks had been put to rights, and the route redirected after the court case that had so nearly been disastrous for Ben Killigrew, it should all have been plain sailing for Killigrew Clay. But it definitely wasn't, and the sooner the man looked to his business affairs, the better.

Gorran frowned, comparing the Ben Killigrew of old with the one he had met briefly in the town that morning. A different man now, he acknowledged, not only in demeanour and appearance but, Gorran suspected, in habits as well. He gave a small sigh, remembering the eager young man who had come home from his London college and decided that his birthright was worth fighting for after all. And Gorran realized that it was since this latest return from London that Ben seemed to have changed so much.

'What can you expect?' Doctor Pender had commented recently, when they met socially. 'The boy suffered a painful attack, and he won't thank the villains for the loss of his good looks. He'll have that ugly scar down his face for the rest of his life.'

However long that life was to be, he added silently. The grim letter from the hospital consultant was a private matter that he was bound to honour, but the knowledge of Ben Killigrew's heart condition weighed heavily on his mind. He turned the conversation quickly.

'I thought we were having a friendly game of backgammon,' he reminded Daniel Gorran. 'Though I confess your parlour's so warm I'm nearer to sleeping than playing. I think I shall have to retire to my bed soon, Daniel.'

'One more glass of porter then,' Gorran suggested. 'We both seem to have lost our appetite for the game tonight.'

Backgammon was harmless enough. As he poured the drinks, Gorran's thoughts kept returning to Ben Killigrew, and wondering if his pursuits were as harmless. There were rumours in the town. When Ben first came home from London he had kept very much to himself, and since the activities of the so-called scaggies had been silent, he hadn't bothered to go to the clayworkers more than once or twice.

But Christmas had come and gone and another year had begun, and with it, Ben Killigrew had asserted his presence in the town in a different way, acting quite the dandy. That was fine enough, as long as he didn't ignore his business. It would never have done in old Charles Killigrew's day. A man needed to know the state of his finances if nothing else, and when Ben Killigrew was acquainted with his, he would need to think seriously. Gorran hoped too, that Ben's home-life would improve. He didn't know the truth of it, of course, but there had been stories about that too…

–

Morwen went through a mixture of emotions after her brief stay in London. She had lain with a man other than her husband, and it had been the most wonderful experience of her life…

the thoughts rushed at her, shaming her one minute, filling her with joy the next. She was too honest to deny the pleasure of Ran's love-making, too honest not to admit that she wanted it to happen again… but that was where the dream ended. She was Ben's wife, and her loyalties were to him.

But that was all. She dreaded the thought of moving back into the bedroom with him now, where she had once been so determined. She would be living a lie to pretend a passion for a man who had changed so dramatically.

His attackers had done more than they realized, she thought bitterly. They had put fear into Ben. She sensed it every time one of the children knocked him playfully, and his arms went up to guard himself. He was afraid of the wounds re-opening, especially the jagged cut on his face, and he was afraid of his heart condition. She'd told him briefly that she and Ran knew the truth, and from then on none of them mentioned it again.

Because of the fear, he made no mention of his wife resuming marital relations with him. By day they got along tolerably well, but at night they remained apart.

-

Some weeks after Ben returned home, he had been urgently summoned to Gorran's chambers on a business matter, and Mrs Horn had brought a note to Morwen, holding it away from her as though her fingers were fire-tongs and she held something abominable.

'This was pushed under the kitchen door, Mrs Killigrew,' she said with a sniff. 'It's addressed to you, but I suspect 'tis some rubbish, and if 'ee don't want to read it, I'd burn it straight away—'

'Thank you, Mrs Horn,' Morwen said, with a smile. The woman had a fierce concern for her mistress's well-being, and Morwen had had to listen to much shielded advice on powders to help her sleep and potions for reviving her spirits, that had nothing to do with Doctor Pender's medical practice.

She took the crumpled note curiously. Her heart leapt when she saw the name on the envelope. Morwen Tremayne. No one had called her by that name for years.

Yet in an instant, the sight of it could make her revert to being Morwen Tremayne, bal maiden at Killigrew Clay, who dared to think a boss's son could marry her. Her hands trembled as she pulled the piece of paper out of the envelope, glad that the children were away from the house and that she was quite alone. As though the walls had eyes and were watching to see her reaction…

The words were written in large capitals with no beginning and no end to the message, nor any signature. Morwen's eyes blurred as she read it swiftly:

> IF YOU DON'T WANT YOUR HUSBAND TO KNOW WHAT WENT ON AT YOUR FANCY-MAN'S NEW HOUSE AFTER TRURO FAIR, BRING FIVE HUNDRED POUNDS TO THE BEACH THIS AFTERNOON. LEAVE IT IN A BAG UNDER A ROCK AT THE FOOT OF THE STEPS AND DON'T WAIT.

Morwen gasped in horror and fury. She crushed the note in her hand, and then opened it out to read it again, as if the words weren't already imprinted in her brain. Her mouth was dry as dust, her heart pounded so hard it made her feel faint. Truro Fair was a few months past, and since then the children had always accompanied her when they went to Ran's house, now nearing completion and ready for the furniture to be installed.

And nothing had happened there after Truro Fair, nothing that could warrant this piece of filth! The brief kiss had been innocent… but what had happened in a small hotel in London was not so innocent, and the guilt of it all made her shake all over. She stared at the note again, remembering the strange feeling at Ran's house that day, that someone was waiting and watching… someone wanted money, and had discovered a way of getting it… but she had no money!

Morwen's head began to throb. She was Killigrew's lady, but she never concerned herself with money. There was no need. When she wanted something she went to Ben and he gave it to her. How could she possibly get hold of five hundred pounds!

The sounds of the children returning from their morning lessons startled her. How long she had stood there, completely disorientated, she didn't know. She sped along to Ben's study, the one place in the house they never entered unless invited, and closed the door behind her. She leaned against it, closing her eyes, more frightened than she had ever been in her life.

Blackmail was a criminal offence and should be reported, but how could she report this without Ben learning of it? In his present mood, he was capable of believing anything, and she was afraid of what a scene might provoke. If it brought on a heart attack and killed him, her guilt would be even more paramount.

She felt trapped. Already in her mind was the insidious thought that somehow the blackmailer must be paid. She had no choice. To save herself and to save Ben. She tried to think logically, but the demand outweighed all other considerations, and it must be met. But how?

She stared around the study as if hunted, her eyes taking in the sight of the long boxes on one of the wall-shelves. Ben kept money in those boxes. How much or how little, Morwen didn't know. But she could find out… her fingers were all thumbs as she took the boxes down.

'My God!' she whispered, minutes later. She was stunned. The boxes were stuffed with money, more than Morwen had ever seen. There must be several thousand pounds here in old bank-notes. Her heart thudded wildly. If she took some from each box, Ben would never miss them, she thought desperately. Before she could think of the consequences, Morwen had begun counting, taking exactly the five hundred pounds demanded and not a note more.

She was shaking even more violently when she left the study. She was a thief, but if Ben's money was also hers, then she believed her action was justified. It was to save Ben pain, she told herself over and over.

Luncheon with the children seemed endless. They squabbled and she was short-tempered, and very conscious of the money now hidden in her room in a small leather bag.

'When will we see Uncle Ran, Mama?' Charlotte pouted. 'You always send us to bed before he comes home. He spends so much time at his other house or at his new office in Truro or his works, and Papa's always so grumpy with us—'

'You'd be grumpy if you looked like an ape!' Justin sniggered.

'Justin, that's a wicked thing to say,' Morwen snapped at him, silently agreeing with the children that Ran spent a great deal more time away from Killigrew House now than before he had taken her to London. 'Your father was badly hurt, and his face will heal in time, and he does *not* look like an ape!'

'He's not so nice-looking though,' Primmy sighed, very much at a romantic stage of adolescence. 'The girls at my school always thought he was so handsome, and now they look away whenever I mention him.'

'It's what a person is inside that's important, not what he looks like,' Albert stated. Morwen threw him a grateful glance. Albert was becoming very dear to her. Sam's second son was so like Matt in his gentle ways… the resemblance struck her again.

'And what do you say, Walter, since everyone else has joined in this debate?' Morwen challenged the eldest boy.

Walter shrugged. 'I dare say Albert's right for a change,' he said, to a cat-call of cheers. 'Justin's an idiot as usual, and I'm going back to school.'

Walter the diplomat, Morwen thought, as he ducked away from his youngest brother's swipe. He would do well at Killigrew Clay, given the opportunity…

For once the thought of it didn't fill her with nostalgia. Not with the memory of the anonymous letter so vivid in her mind, and the sickeningly uneasy certainty about the writer. Whose image had haunted her ever since she thought she saw his face floating like a spectre at Truro Fair? Who would address her after all these years as Morwen Tremayne? Who else but the one person she loathed more than anyone else in the world? She prayed that she was wrong, but knew instinctively that she was not. And yet, in one way, she hoped it would be him. Because through all the turmoil in her mind, Morwen had one trump card to play that would send him out of her life for ever.

January was sticky and mild, with none of the cold snow that plagued up-country England, and the house was stuffy and airless. She informed Mrs Horn that if any callers arrived, she was out riding. The housekeeper would assume that Morwen intended visiting her mother or taking a gallop on the moors. Instead of which, when the mare was saddled, Morwen turned her towards the shore, the bag of money safely fastened inside her cloak.

The sands were virginal at that time of year, the expanse of ocean like a rippling sheet of cold steel. But the soft breeze at sea-level was bracing, and for ten minutes Morwen raced the mare along the sands, feeling the exhilaration of it, and almost able to forget why she had come. If the hidden watcher was frustrated by her apparent inattention to his demands so much the better. She was perfectly sure he was there somewhere among the rocks or caves.

'Whoa there, Sheba,' she breathed at last to the mare, reining her to a halt near the sandy steps carved into the cliffs. 'It's time for the pretence to end.'

She slid from the mare's back and took the bag from her cloak, making it obvious. No one was visible. Her hands shook as she placed it in a crevice in the rocks, looked around as if fearfully for a moment and then remounted, racing the mare back the way she had come, up and over the cliffs until the sound of hoof-beats would be lost to anyone below. Then she tethered Sheba to a stump and crept carefully down one of the many well-worn footpaths to the beach below.

A heavily-set man was already bending over the fissure at the foot of the steps, retrieving the leather bag. Morwen moved swiftly from her vantage point behind an outcrop of rock, giving him no chance to get away.

'Jude Pascoe.' She spoke his name, and her voice throbbed with all the hatred she had ever felt for Ben's cousin. He turned with a start, his eyes narrowing as he saw her, his already-florid face flushing a duller red.

'So you twigged who it was, did you, Morwen Tremayne?' He leered, recovering himself at once, and stuffing the leather bag inside his jacket.

'My name is Morwen Killigrew, and has been for the past fifteen years,' she snapped.

'Oh, ah. Well, you're still no more than a miserable bal maiden to me, though you were always a comely wench, I remember.'

'You remember that, do 'ee?' The grammatical slip incensed her even more, and so did the fact that Jude Pascoe was grinningly aware of it. 'Perhaps you remember another bal maiden at Truro Fair and afterwards—'

Jude laughed coarsely now.

'Am I supposed to recall one wench among so many? But she does come to mind,' he nodded carelessly. 'Connie or Celia, or some such name, was it? A pretty wench with bedding eyes and a fine way o' teasing a man—'

'She's dead,' Morwen said baldly, unable to bear the sudden reminiscence in this lout's eyes. He said nothing for a minute, and then he spoke more sharply, a hint of suspicion in his voice.

'So she's dead. What's that to do wi' me? I went to America years ago with your brother Matt, though God knows what he's been up to since we parted company.'

Morwen's knees were shaking, and she suddenly realized the danger of being here alone with this man, but she had to go on now.

'My brother's well rid of you. It's not him I'm here to talk about. It's Celia Penry.'

'What about her? Did you bring me the money or have you put a packet of newsprint in the bag?'

He scrabbled in his jacket to check, and immediately Morwen saw what a fool she had been. She hadn't stopped to think, but Jude's own words told her all she had needed to do. She could have tricked him with wads of newsprint. Instead of which, she had taken Ben's money to pay him off… but if she succeeded, then it would be worth it.

'The money's there, and it'll be the first and last that you'll get.'

He gave a taunting smile. 'Is it now? I've found myself a nice little source of income, and I'm not letting go of it that easily. My cousin Ben can afford to pay up, knowingly or not. I've been watching him, and he's doing very nicely at the gambling tables, winning a packet at all the gaming houses in town lately.'

Morwen's heart leapt. So that was where Ben went, and where he had got all that money. No wonder there were so many used bank-notes. Ben never used to keep so much money at home… her thoughts began to scramble again, and she needed to keep a clear head. Whatever she thought of Ben's gambling had nothing to do with this confrontation with Jude Pascoe.

'You won't get another penny from me,' Morwen said in a tight, deliberate voice. 'If you threaten me again, I shall go to the constables with certain evidence.'

The sound of a sea-bird screeching high above was the only sound in the next seconds, and then he had moved across the sands to her, his hand digging cruelly into her arm.

'What evidence?' he snarled. 'Did that poxy brother tell you of the seaman who drowned the night of the wrecking? It was an accident, but we knew nobody would ever believe us, and decided to leave the country fast—'

'I know nothing of any seaman drowning,' Morwen's lips shook and she was sure they were drained of colour from the faintness washing over her again. Nor could she remember the night of one wrecking among many along the Cornish coast, but it explained so many things, and how her sweet gullible brother would have been swept along under the influence of this man. That, and his dream of America suddenly beckoning…

Jude let her go so violently she almost fell in the soft sand. She forced back the involuntary tears at the pain in her flesh from his rough handling.

'Then what the hell are you talking about, shit-bag?'

The tears dried, and her voice was as vicious as his.

'My friend Celia. The girl you murdered, along with her unborn baby. *Your* baby, though God knows I blessed the day when that died too, thinking it had come from your stinking flesh—'

He gaped at her in disbelief.

'What baby?' he blustered. 'And how could I have murdered her? She was well enough when I left for America. I'd forgotten her—'

'But I don't forget,' Morwen whipped out. 'Nor does the doctor who examined her after she was found floating in a claypit. Nothing was said of her condition then, but it would only need a word from me and the body could be exhumed and there would be clear evidence of a child being conceived. The constables would take a very keen interest in the person responsible, I promise you, and I'd be more than willing to give evidence. So would Ben!'

She finished wildly. She didn't know if the doctor would even remember anything. At the time, Morwen was sure he suspected, although Celia had put about her fear of a growth in her stomach and had walked into the claypool to her death. If they dug her up from Penwithick churchyard, would anything but bones remain after all these years? Morwen couldn't even guess, but she stared unblinkingly into the eyes of the man she had hated for so long, and prayed that he would believe it all.

'The girl on the moors—' he muttered.

'That's right. The girl on the moors. Don't you remember her screams, Jude Pascoe? They're still in my head, and I pray they're still in yours.'

He laughed uneasily.

'Who'd take notice of anything Morwen Tremayne said?'

For the first time in her life, she felt the power of her position, and straightened her back.

'Probably nobody. But everyone would take notice of Morwen Killigrew, wife of the owner of Killigrew Clay, daughter of the Works Manager, and someone who's considered a lady in St Austell.'

Jude's eyes were dark slits.

'So what's your price for not telling Ben about your fancy-man?' He still bluffed, but his voice was less sure now, and Morwen felt the sweet triumph of revenge at last.

'My price is never to see or hear of you again as long as I live. Never to contact me or my family, and to go back to America or anywhere else on earth, as long as it's away from England.' It was no longer enough just to say Cornwall. He had to be away from these shores for ever. 'If I get one hint that you don't do as I say, I shall take my evidence to the constables, and also to *The Informer*, in Truro. I promise you that even if your part in Celia's death couldn't be proved and the law didn't get you, the clayworkers would.'

She stood very still now. Jude knew the character of the clayworkers. He knew well enough that he would be lynched and strung up without a trial or a hearing. Morwen Killigrew might be a lady in the eyes of the town, but to the clayworkers she would always be Morwen Tremayne, one of their own, and one whom they trusted and believed. And Jude's fate would be assured.

He scowled furiously. 'All right. It seems that you've won, dear cousin. I've had enough of this narrow-minded country, anyway. And with this to buy me a passage and a new start, I'll get back to where a man can breathe without feeling stifled. You'll see no more of me.'

He patted his jacket, and any hope Morwen had of retrieving the five hundred pounds faded. He would never give it back, and she had been stupid and reckless in bringing it. But it was too late now, and she must be thankful for what she had.

She turned blindly, unable to look at him a moment longer, slipping and sliding up the winding sandy steps to the cliff-top and rushing towards Sheba. The mare whinnied in protest as Morwen twisted the reins sharply, and galloped as fast as she dared away from the shore and towards the moors.

She couldn't return to the house yet. She needed time alone. She needed to free her mind of the painful memories Jude Pascoe revived. She needed to talk to Celia…

–

It was a long while since she had visited Penwithick churchyard, to the quiet corner where the simple granite stone recorded Celia's name, the dates of her birth and death and nothing more, as her father had wanted. Celia Penry, 1834–1850. Morwen stroked the marbled surface, wishing she had some flowers to arrange. She looked around. There were early wild daffodils already blooming along the grassy banks. Quickly, Morwen picked some, and lay them by the headstone.

'It's over, Celia,' she murmured softly. 'I'd have paid a king's ransom to see the look on his face when he realized what it would cost him if he dared show his face here again. I've done what had to be done, so sleep easy now.'

A soft, sighing breeze was all the answer she got, but her eyes were calmer when she finally rose from her knees. In some small way, Celia's death had been avenged. It wasn't the worst that could happen to Jude Pascoe, but it was the worst that Morwen could do, short of betraying Celia's shame, and the public knowledge of which her friend had been so terrified.

She remounted her mare and trotted gently now, past Clay One, where the throb of the beam-engine was the heartbeat of Killigrew Clay. Past the hordes of clayworkers, gouging and firing, trundling and tipping. Past the groups of bal maidens, their distinctive white bonnets bobbing as they scraped the clay blocks and chattered incessantly. Past the milky-green clay pool where Celia had drowned, and past the peaked, white sky-tips, where the impurities of the clay waste glinted in the watery January sun.

She had just cast out the biggest impurity of her life, and she could swear with that strange Cornish intuition of hers, that Celia knew and approved. She could feel it in the nodding sway of bracken and sense it in the clear golden blossoming of gorse that welcomed another year, another beginning.

-

Such serenity of mind was dashed as soon as she returned to Killigrew House late that afternoon. Ben was home from his meeting with the accountant, and it obviously hadn't gone well. The children were home from school, and Morwen could hear raised voices the minute she stepped inside the house.

'I didn't take it,' she heard Justin scream. 'Why do you always think the worst of me?'

'I bet you did, you little sneak. You pinched my pencil yesterday—' Primmy said maliciously.

'Nobody's talking about bloody pencils,' Ben roared. 'I'm talking about a great deal of money that's missing from my study, and none of you is getting anything to eat until I find the culprit. You can starve for a month, but I'll have an answer.'

Outside the drawing-room door, Morwen froze for a moment, as if willing the scene inside to go away. She knew it wouldn't. She could imagine the children, frightened and upset, each knowing they weren't to blame, each wondering which of the others had done this terrible thing. Charlotte was crying noisily, and Walter and Albert were fighting.

'I never go to Daddy's study,' Albert shouted. 'It's not allowed—'

'You're a pompous pig, Albert,' Walter bawled back.

'Have you been in there without my permission, Walter?' Ben snapped.

'No, I haven't!' Walter began howling at once, all his hurt pride evident in his voice. 'Are you accusing me now?'

'I am not. I'm waiting for the guilty person to do the honourable thing and own up.'

'It might have been one of the servants,' Primmy defended her brothers hotly.

'It might,' Ben retorted. 'But they've all been in my employ a long time, and none of them would be so stupid as to think they could steal hundreds of pounds and get away with it.'

'Hundreds of pounds!' Justin said in a strangled voice. 'What would we do with hundreds of pounds?'

'That's what I'm bloody well trying to find out, you nincompoop!' Ben yelled at him.

Morwen couldn't bear it any longer. She opened the drawing-room door and went inside. All the children looked terrified, and Charlotte rushed to her mother at once, burying her face in Morwen's skirts. Ben was puce with rage.

Morwen looked at him over the top of the child's dark head. She didn't need to be a medical expert to know that such anger was bad for him. The long scar was a livid red lightning slash in his cheek.

'Please don't censure them any more,' she said quietly to Ben. He rounded on her at once.

'This is nothing to do with you, Morwen. One of these little charmers is a thief, and I'll know which one if I have to take a strap to them all.'

'You'll take no strap to any of my children,' she said furiously, and at the sudden sneer on his face, she guessed he was on the brink of disclaiming parentage of three of them. She knew she must act quickly to prevent the damage it would do to them to hear the truth this way.

'You seem to have lost your senses to think the children could have taken your money, and I know more of this matter than you think. We'll discuss it in private, Ben.'

His face registered complete outrage at her words, and she shooed the children out of the room, saying they could go to the nursery and have their tea sent up, and everything was going to be all right. She stood stiffly, facing her husband.

'So we've got petticoat rule in this house now, have we? You'll please remember that I give the orders here, Morwen!' He oozed sarcasm.

'Since when did Ben Killigrew give his wife orders? Please sit down, dar, and calm yourself. I fear for you—'

'I'm perfectly all right. Don't fuss, woman,' he snapped, the ghost of his father at that moment. But he sat down heavily, glowering up at her, and told her sarcastically to explain herself, if she could.

Chapter Eleven

She hadn't thought this far ahead. She had taken the money in a panic, fearing what Jude Pascoe might do, and seizing on the chance to challenge him with the truth about Celia, and be rid of him for ever. Now she saw that the only way out of this was to be scrupulously honest. As Ben waited, hard-eyed, she rummaged for the letter Jude Pascoe had sent to the house that morning, and handed it to him silently.

'Good God!' Ben's rage was directed at Morwen now as he skimmed the words. 'Do you mean to tell me you stole from me to pay off a common blackmailer?'

And never a word about whether there was a grain of truth in the letter. Never a care about his wife having a lover… just concern for his precious money… at the realization, something in her died at that moment.

'I did it for one reason only!' she said fiercely, praying that her voice wouldn't break. 'And not the one I might have expected you to show concern about! You obviously don't care whether I'm enamoured of Ran Wainwright or not. But I'll put your mind at rest, in case you should be interested: nothing happened between us at his house. I'll admit I panicked when I got this letter, as any wife would, but I decided to pay the man for a very different reason.'

'There's no bloody reason for associating with scum. You should have torn the thing up, or come to me, and I'd soon have gone to the authorities and got the man locked away—' Ben was incensed now.

'You don't listen to me or talk to me lately, Ben. Besides which, I was positive I knew the identity of the blackmailer, and now he's gone—' she began to feel hysterical at the look of derision in his eyes.

'My God, you're more of a simpleton than I thought,' Ben said savagely. 'Blackmailers never give up.'

'This one will. He's gone for good. If not, he knows I'll expose him for the murderer that he is.'

At last she had got his attention, she thought bitterly. Until now, his total concern had been for his money. He was obsessed with it, and she had never realized it until now. 'Murderer? And who is this choice person, may I ask?'

'Your cousin. Jude Pascoe.'

Ben leapt out of the chair. '*What?* Have you lost your mind? He's in America, and good riddance to him—'

'No, he's not, Ben. Although I hope he'll be on his way back there very soon. He's been in Cornwall for some time. I thought I saw him at Truro Fair, and I assume that he followed Ran and me to Ran's house, and got completely the wrong idea.'

Ben's eyes narrowed at the small quaver in her voice. 'What the hell did you tell him that makes you think he'll go away again?'

'I told him about Celia,' she said. 'I told him the doctor had evidence of her losing a baby, and that she drowned herself because of the shame. I said I'd ask the doctor to dig up Celia's body, and that I'd send the whole story to the newspaper so that everyone would know, and that if he didn't get lawful justice, he'd get it from the clayworkers. You know as well as I do that they'd tear him to pieces and no one would ever know the truth of it.'

Ben stared at her in silence for a minute or two. 'Christ, but you never let go, do you?' Ben said in grudging admiration. 'Your bluff wouldn't have held up, of course, because the body would be decomposed by now, but the thought of a mob of clayworkers lynching the bastard would have done the trick. You're cleverer than I gave you credit for.'

He never noticed how she flinched at his callous reference to Celia.

'I didn't do it to be clever,' she said hoarsely, wilting now. 'I did it for Celia. Five hundred pounds was a small price to pay for revenge.'

Ben's eyes flashed again. 'It doesn't alter the fact that you stole it from me, but we'll ignore that for the moment. What's important is that I need that money, and I need it *now.*'

'What on earth for? The boxes were stuffed with money! I've never seen so much.' She was suddenly shame-faced. 'Ben, I'm sorry. I had no right to take it. I didn't think—'

'I said we'll forget it.' She could tell that his nerves were on a knife-edge once more. 'I've just had a blistering afternoon with Daniel Gorran. Thank God the American's no longer working with him. I wouldn't have cared for him to hear us wrangling like fish-wives.'

'What's happened?' she said in fright.

He looked at her coldly, moving to the sideboard to pour himself a large brandy. He wasn't supposed to drink heavily and he knew it, but his eyes dared her to question him as he spoke mockingly. Morwen knew him well enough to know it hid real alarm.

'What's happened, my dear, is that the price for china-clay is plunging, and we've had outstanding debts to pay for months. It didn't matter too much. Businesses are always run like that, and Killigrew Clay's name was enough to put the debtors off while the bank interest accumulated. Only there's not much money in the bank now, and with the rapidly falling prices for clay, the debtors have decided they won't wait, and I was counting on the money in the study to pay the bills.'

Morwen ran her tongue around her dry lips. 'But Ben, there must have been several thousand pounds in there—'

'And it might just have been enough to keep them quiet for the time being. As it is, I shall just have to get more from somewhere.'

'You're in debt for over two thousand pounds?' she whispered. Such money was a fortune. She belonged to a family who would have scratched for pennies to keep themselves honourably out of debt, and now her husband owed thousands. It all made a mockery out of gentle-folk and their morals.

He laughed without humour, speaking now with false bravado. 'Oh, a bit more than that, my love, but I dare say I'll find the money, providing you keep your fingers out of my affairs in future.'

'How? Oh Ben, you won't try to gamble for it, will you? 'Tis such a mug's game!'

He scowled at her. 'Then I must be a mug, but it's nothing you need worry your head about, and you'll keep this conversation to yourself. Especially from our colonial cousin.'

She flushed at his keen gaze, praying that he wasn't storing away the information on Jude's obnoxious letter for some future reckoning.

That night, her fears were proved right. She heard the click of her door handle when she had lain sleepless for an hour, and turned her head swiftly. In the half-light from the window, she saw Ben standing inside the door. He threw off his dressing-robe, and climbed into her bed before she could utter a word. His arms imprisoned her, and she could hardly breathe as she was pinned beneath his weight. He made no attempt to move or to force himself on her, he just lay heavily on her body like a block of iron. His voice was cold.

'I've been having second thoughts about our blackmailer's note. Perhaps there was some truth in it. You and cousin Ran. Have I been too blind to see what's right under my nose?'

'Please, Ben, I told you the truth. Nothing happened at Ran's house—'

She prayed he wouldn't dig any deeper. It was bending the truth, for the wonder and glory of sharing Ran's love had been in London, in the place where she had never wanted to go, to which circumstances had forced her.

'But you've shown no interest in coming back to my bed, have you?' he said ruthlessly.

'You know why! It was out of concern for you, Ben, since your attack in London—'

'Ah yes, my attack,' he spoke softly now. He held one of her hands and forced her fingers to gently touch the tender line of the scar even while it hurt him, knowing it repulsed her, and goading the shuddering response from her.

'Did you never wonder who my attackers were, Morwen?'

His words startled her, but at least it seemed to have diverted any idea he might have had of ravishing her. She could feel none of the once-welcome hardening of his body against her flesh. He lay limp and heavy.

'You *knew* them?' she echoed.

He gave a harsh laugh.

'I'm sure you haven't forgotten the name of Neville Peterson! Yes, my lovely wife, Captain Neville Peterson,' he said, at her muffled exclamation. 'That man you thought so charming, and championed against all my advice, until you realized he was the scum of the earth. It seems we've both had dealings with our personal devils of late.'

'Is that why you wouldn't report it to the authorities?' Morwen said, shaking. 'Because of what it might do to me – and Freddie?'

'Full marks, my dear. You see, your husband still has some finer feelings.'

'Ben, please stop this.' Tears began to slide down her cheeks. 'I hate to see you so full of self-condemnation. What you did was worthy of the Ben that I married, and I want – I want us to be like we were. I want us to be friends—'

'Friends! Is that what marriage is all about? It's supposed to mean more than just friendship, or have you completely forgotten your duties?'

There was sudden urgency in his voice, and she trembled to respond. But it was unnecessary. After several minutes, Morwen realized that nothing was happening. Ben, her virile Ben, was unable to perform the very act that made him a man, and Morwen knew what the realization would do to him. Impotence would wound him deeper than all the knife-cuts from Neville Peterson. Ben moved away from her, his voice gravelly.

'So that's that. I wish you joy of your virginal bed, but be very sure that if I can't have you, no one else will. I shall watch you like a hawk from now on.'

In seconds he was gone, and she lay as if carved in stone. What had happened to make them like this with each other? How could two people, who had once been so close, change into the strangers that they were now? And then, once the bitterness of his words had faded, she was left with an unutterable sadness for Ben, and for their bright love that was dying as surely as a summer rose in autumn.

-

A few weeks later, when the dull month of January was past, and the February mornings were spangled with frost and dew, Bess Tremayne didn't bother waiting for Mrs Horn to show her into her daughter's drawing-room. She had come to Killigrew House with all speed in the little trap, her blue eyes alive, her rosy cheeks like ripe apples. Her excitement bubbled over, and Morwen hadn't seen her mother so animated in a very long time.

'What's happened to you, Mammie?' she exclaimed. 'I know it must be something extra-good, so don't make me wait while you take off your bonnet—'

Bess laughed. 'I can't waste time wi' bonnets and the like! Our Matt's coming home! He sent a letter to your Daddy and me, and he's coming on a visit wi' his wife and boy, and they'll be here in April! What do 'ee think of that, our Morwen?'

Morwen couldn't speak for a moment. She saw the shine of tears on her mother's lashes, mingling with the joy, and it all matched her own feelings. Matt – her darling, dearest Matt, was coming home at last – and it was almost too much, too much… after the terrible weeks just past, when she thought she would go mad if Ben didn't stop watching her, his edginess with the children, and Ran's more-frequent absences from the house, she was badly in need of good news. But she had never imagined that it would be this! This was the best news of all.

'Oh, Mammie—'

Then they were in each others' arms, laughing and crying and making plans… Matt would want to see everyone, of course. He'd want to admire Ben's railways, and visit Ran's clay-stone works; he'd meet all the children and compare their looks with Cresswell's; Morwen would learn to love Louisa and the American nephew; they would meet Annie, and Jack's twins, and see how fine a man young Freddie had turned out, with his own business and all… so many plans, tumbling out all at once, and when they heard Mrs Horn's dry voice asking if they wanted some tea to give their throats a rest, they laughed some more.

'Yes please, Mrs Horn, and some champagne as well,' Morwen said recklessly.

'In the morning?' the woman said incredulously.

'Right now,' Morwen said imperiously. What was the point of being mistress of Killigrew House if you couldn't order champagne when you wanted it! She caught her mother's glance as Mrs Horn went out muttering, and giggled. It was so long since she had laughed so much. So long since the world had felt a happy place to live in, and she was savouring every moment.

'Does Daddy know yet?' Morwen asked next.

Bess shook her head. 'The letter's just come, and I decided it was quicker to come here than to toil up to the moors. Besides, I know how much you miss our Matt, and it seemed right that you should know first.'

'After you, Mammie. We both loved him best, didn't we?' she said softly.

Bess gave a small snort. 'Mothers don't have favourites, Morwen. You should know that.'

'I know it,' Morwen nodded, and each gave the other a satisfied smile.

They drank tea and champagne, and both were in high spirits when Ben came in from the stables. Where he went these mornings Morwen didn't know and never asked, but he stopped dead when he saw the two of them.

'What's all this? Has my wife turned into a secret drinker now?' he said unpleasantly.

Morwen ran to him, her eyes glowing. 'Oh Ben, we've had such marvellous news. Matt's bringing his family for a visit in April. They can stay here, can't they? And we must throw a party for everyone. It will be so wonderful to be all together again! I shall be so proud of my prosperous brother, and want to show him off to the whole town!'

He couldn't resist the look on her face. She didn't just glow, she radiated happiness. Despite the fact that the Killigrew luck had turned against him, and instead of winning at cards he had begun losing badly, he couldn't dash the joy in Morwen's face by being less than generous.

'Of course they can stay here, and of course we'll give a party. Why not? If it takes every penny we have, we'll make Matt Tremayne's homecoming one to remember.'

Morwen hugged him, pressing her warm lips to his, regardless of her mother's presence, and hardly realizing it was the first time she had voluntarily kissed him in months. Neither of the Tremayne women realized either, that there was reckless desperation in Ben's words.

'It's hardly going to take every penny, Ben,' Bess laughed, easy with her son-in-law now that the years had forged the relationship between them.

'We'll have to forget that holiday in France though, if Matt's to be here in the spring. He'll want to stay a month or so to make the long journey worthwhile. I hope you won't be too disappointed, Morwen, but we can't do both.'

He kept his eyes on hers as he spoke, and saw the flush deepen. The foreign holiday had been forgotten for many months now, and to her shame, Morwen knew it was the last thing she wanted, to be abroad in the sole company of her husband. It was an appalling realization, but it was one she had to accept.

'I must admit it's more important for me to see Matt,' she said. 'And we can make plans to go abroad another time.'

'Yes, we can,' Ben agreed, but at that instant Morwen had the strangest presentiment that it would never happen. 'So I suppose we must let everyone know about this great event. I've decided to go up to the works this afternoon. It's time I saw what was going on up there. I'll tell Hal your news – unless you want to tell him yourself, Bess?'

'No – tell him, please! 'Twill gladden his heart, and perhaps Morwen and me can ride over to Truro and let the other boys know? And Ran, of course! He'll be pleased to see Matt and Louisa as well. I was forgetting Louisa is his cousin. Such a mish-mash of folk we are!'

'Ah yes, Ran,' Ben said thoughtfully. 'Isn't that house of his going to be ready for him to move in soon, Morwen? Perhaps Louisa would prefer to stay there, or to take turns between us. We must consider her needs as well as ours, my dear.'

Morwen flashed him an annoyed look, seeing Bess's sudden crestfallen look.

'It's Matt who's coming home, Ben, and he'll want to stay with his family,' she said coldly. 'And Mammie, if we're going to get to Truro and back today, we had better start right away.'

She turned her back on her husband and began fussing over her mother. The small house Bess and Hal shared would be too small and too modest for the grand Tremaynes of California, and Killigrew House would naturally be the focal point for their visit. How dare Ben put such doubts into her mother's head. And although Ran was hoping to move into the new house in a month's time, there would still be a lot of work to do there.

He wouldn't be able to cope with visitors, as well as being so dedicated and enthusiastic about his new business.

For his house, he had staff to hire yet, a housekeeper and maids, and men for the outside work. What Ran needed too was a wife, Morwen thought suddenly, ignoring the pain of the thought. Ran was young and handsome and virile, and she had actually heard women in St Austell market-place sigh wistfully when they saw him walk by. It must only be a matter of time before some pretty young lady took his eye, and there wasn't a thing Morwen could do to stop it.

Ben let her pass without another word as she went to fetch her cloak, and called for a maid to inform a driver that he was to take them to Truro. How smoothly she slipped into the role of the lady, Ben thought, a small sneer marring the handsome features already split by the scar, and how soon she was going to learn that the Killigrew coffers were emptying rapidly.

-

Jack and Freddie were overjoyed at the news. Jack had been an adolescent when Matt went away, but the two of them had been close companions before Matt began to feel restless and had taken up with Jude Pascoe. And Freddie, young and impressionable then, had looked up to his brother, and through all the passing years, had seen him as a kind of romantic adventurer.

'What was he really like, your Matt, whom everyone seems to idolize?' Annie Tremayne asked her husband curiously, when the two St Austell women had finally taken their leave, exhausted with all the chattering and reminiscences.

Jack leaned back in his own armchair, comfortable and self-satisfied that at least his brother wouldn't find him a pauper, or still scratching in the clay for the Killigrews. His children had gone to bed, excited and awed at the thought of a family from across the ocean coming to visit them, and Annie was in her favourite position, sitting on the rug in front of the fire and leaning against him, where he could stroke her fine-spun hair.

'Our Matt?' Jack's voice was indolent with memory. 'The best-looking of all the Tremaynes, I'd say—'

'I doubt that, my love! Not as far as I'm concerned, anyway—'

Jack laughed. 'You're prejudiced in my favour, and that's as it should be. But there was something special about Matt. He was always dreaming, yet you always thought Matt's dreams might come true. Daddy used to get mad with 'un sometimes, saying he had dreams in his head where other folk had clay in theirs.'

'You make it sound as though everyone for miles around St Austell was bound in some way to the clayworks—'

'So they were, most on 'em,' Jack said seriously. 'Over here in Truro, you don't know the half of it, Annie. You live in a different world from that of the clayworkers and their families. I'm not belittling it, just saying 'tis different.'

'Why, Jack Tremayne, I do believe you miss it!' Annie said softly, twisting her face to look up at him.

He laughed self-consciously. 'That I don't! Not when I remember the hardships and the misery of working long hours in stinging rain, with feet so constantly wet they came near to being webbed like the ducks. Nor when I remember how we were all crushed into that small cottage, where you could see the stars through the slates afore summat was done about it.'

'But?' Annie prompted him as he stopped, his eyes faraway.

He leaned down and kissed her willing lips. 'You see too much. You're like our Morwen, Annie. You can always see when there's more to tell.'

'So why don't you tell me?'

'Oh, 'tis nothing worth telling. Just that sometimes I get a feeling for the moors, and for the smell of the clay. It don't make sense to me, when I wanted to get away from it so badly. But I suppose it was born in me, just like the boat-building was born in your Daddy, and it's something that'll never really leave me. It's part of me, I suppose, and of our Freddie and Morwen as well.'

'And Matt? How do you think he'll feel, after all these years? Will he want to stay, like his American cousin?'

Jack was thoughtful. 'I doubt that. Matt's found all he wants in America. He's got his wife and a son and he's a wealthy man. Randell Wainwright's still looking for what he wants, and 'tis not in California or New York, that's for sure.'

'You think he wants Morwen, don't you, Jack?'

'Don't you?'

She didn't answer. She turned to watch the leaping flames in the firelight. She loved Morwen like a sister, and she didn't want to see her hurt. Certainly today, there had been dancing lights in Morwen's eyes, reflected in her mother's. The news that Matt Tremayne was coming home was the best for both of them. But there were other times when Annie had glimpsed shadows beneath Morwen's lovely eyes, and the closeness that she and Jack shared seemed to be eluding Morwen and Ben lately. And the thought of another man intruding into their marriage could only mean heartache for everyone.

Annie lived by simple rules. One man, one woman, and anyone else meant trouble. But she agreed with Jack that there were undercurrents in the family. Ran had called to see them on several occasions now that he had a smart new office in Truro, and it was easy to see how he could turn any woman's head. If Morwen was keeping secrets from Ben, Annie prayed they would soon be resolved.

She turned away guiltily, leaning back against Jack's knee. She too had a secret. One that she would eventually have to share with her husband, if what she suspected was true. Without realizing what she did, she softly patted her abdomen, and wondered how he would take the news, if it were true.

It wasn't that the doctor's device had failed. It was just that she knew they had been careless because their love was always so spontaneous. It was far too soon to tell, of course, and a few days late with her monthly flows was really no reason for her to suspect. This had happened before and it had meant nothing...

but she hadn't needed logic or a doctor's examination to know when she was expecting the twins.

It was more than missing the flow of blood. More than counting the days, and wondering and thinking that it might be so. The certainty was borne out of something deep and fundamental inside her, and she desperately longed for another baby. It was her right as a woman, and no amount of medical warnings was going to make her agree to any surgical interference if God had decided to give her one more of His greatest gifts.

'Annie?' She heard Jack's voice, suddenly questioning, as she sat so still, her palm just gently caressing her stomach. He had seen such an action before, seen her like this before, somehow remote and beautiful, and it wasn't just pleasure on account of his brother Matt coming home…

Lulled by the firelight, she felt as though she turned to look up at him in slow motion. She didn't want to move too quickly, in case she broke the spell of these perfect moments together. And in that instant, everything there was to know was in her face for him to see. He gave a low groan.

'Annie, you're not—'

She had moved in one fluid movement and was in his arms. He held her close as though she was a child.

'Jack, it was meant to be. If God didn't want us to have another baby, He wouldn't have allowed it. Trust Him, Jack!'

Her simple faith embarrassed him. He wasn't a churchgoing man, but Annie's faith was absolute. He buried his face in the softness of her hair.

'But if I was to lose you—'

'That would be God's will too, my darling,' she whispered, and Jack was thankful she couldn't read his thoughts then, for they were nothing short of blasphemous.

Chapter Twelve

Freddie Tremayne didn't remember his brother Matt in the same way as the rest of his family. To his sister and older brothers, Matt had been frequently in scrapes, sometimes in disgrace, and never more so than when he took up with Jude Pascoe and ran off to America. Yet for all that, Freddie was very much aware that Matt held a special place in all their hearts. Freddie only vaguely remembered all the upset, but he remembered very well his Mammie's red eyes, and the way his father refused to mention Matt for a long time, as if he was dead… in fact, at eight years old, Freddie had fearfully believed that Matt was dead, and that everyone was hiding the truth from him.

In time, the fear had diminished, especially when the letters began to arrive from America, and they learned to their amazement that Matt was married with a baby son, and making his fortune. More than once, the idea of going to America to join him had intrigued Freddie. America, where the streets were paved with gold, and you could kick around in the earth and find nuggets of the precious stuff right beneath your feet.

He had settled for a far more mundane existence. And proprietor of his own chandlery shop suddenly seemed insignificant compared with all that his brother Matt had achieved. There could still be time, of course… Freddie let the thought mull around in his head, and as quickly dismissed it. What would he do in America! He would be even more alone.

The thought startled him. He had friends and neighbours and a loving family… but he realized how alone he really was. He had no one of his own, and that was what really counted. Matt had his own family; Jack had Annie and the twins; Morwen had her own children, and Sam's; his parents had each other. But Freddie had no one to call his own.

The jingle of his shop doorbell jerked him out of his sudden apathy. He smiled at the two seamen who entered, bringing a whiff of the sea with them, and ready to banter awhile with the obliging chandler about the places they had been, and the exotic sights they had seen. And the thought lingered in Freddie's head that perhaps the lure of the sea wasn't just one Tremayne brother's dream after all.

–

Bess went off happily to her own home, eager to welcome Hal home from the works, and to share in their momentous news together. Morwen waved from the door until her mother left Killigrew House, and turned back to her own excited brood. Young Charlotte was already clambering over Ran Wainwright and begging him to tell them more about their new American cousin that they would see in a few months' time.

'He's not new,' Justin scoffed. 'He's ten years old, same as me!'

'He'll be new to you, Justin, and that's what your sister means,' Ran said patiently. 'Don't be so pernickety, young man.'

Justin looked suspicious, uncertain what the word meant, while the older three hooted with laughter.

'Justin Killigrew's pernickety, pernickety. Justin Killigrew's pernickety, pernickety!' They chanted, while he punched imaginary blows at their dodging bodies, his face red with fury.

'Calm down, all of you!' Morwen had to shout to make herself heard. They were noisy and boisterous, and the end of the afternoon was turning into something of a pantomime. Ben should be enjoying this, she thought with a pang. But Ben was nowhere to be seen, and Mrs Horn informed her he hadn't been home since the morning, leaving shortly after Morwen and Bess had left for Truro.

'Why don't you tell us a bit more about Matt's family, Ran?' she said to him above the children's heads. His eyes met hers. In them she saw all the love he hid so quickly. It was not for public display. Nor private indulgence either, and each found ways of keeping carefully apart unless there were others present.

'If these young hooligans will sit still, I just might do that,' he teased, his tone keeping the sting out of the words, but exacting obedience from them all the same.

They sat round him in a circle on the floor in front of the drawing-room fire, while Morwen sat on an opposite chair from his, to listen. And to watch the changing planes and contours of his face as he spoke. And to love him.

'Your Uncle Matt is tall and handsome, and very much like your other uncles in appearance. But you know all that. You've heard it many times before. Your Aunt Louisa is pretty and dark-haired, and her eyes are deep brown, and as soft as velvet.'

Morwen felt a shoot of jealousy at his words. It was quite illogical, for Ran spoke with nothing more than affection for his cousin Louisa, and the jealousy that was part of her nature was a wicked thing that she constantly tried to conquer. But it was odd that Ran's description of Louisa's eyes should match the way she always thought of Ran's eyes. Deep brown, and as soft as velvet…

'And Cresswell?' Albert said eagerly, less interested in the grown-ups than the intriguing new cousin. Ran laughed.

'Cresswell is a very precocious child,' he said deliberately. 'But then, many American children are. It comes of being treated far more like junior men and women than children over here. That's not a criticism of either method, just an observation.'

'What's precoc – what you said, Uncle Ran?' Charlotte asked curiously.

He scooped her up into his lap, where her fingers tickled his sideburns and then played with his expensive lapel pin, made out of Matt's gold, he had once told Morwen, to her amazement.

'It means he sometimes says things before he thinks. His mouth works before his brain at times, but you'd better not tell him I told you so,' Ran chuckled. 'I'm sure you'll all get on well together, and he'll be able to tell you lots of things about America.'

'We can tell him things about Cornwall as well,' Justin said belligerently.

'Well, of course you can.' Ran glanced at Morwen, raising one eyebrow. She frowned. Sometimes Justin could put on too many airs, and if Cresswell was of a similar type, there could be clashes of personality ahead. But she was probably seeing things that weren't there. And she was looking forward immensely to meeting her new sister-in-law and nephew. And nothing in the world could dim the joy of seeing Matt again.

–

Ben finally came home to find a very cosy domestic scene, with his youngest daughter sleepily sitting on Ran's lap, her arms around his neck, and the rest of the children poring over a map spread out on the floor. Morwen spoke quickly.

'I hope you don't mind, Ben. I brought it from the study for them to see. They're keen to follow the progress of Matt's journey from California.'

Ben went unsteadily across the room to pour himself some brandy. Morwen didn't need telling that he had been drinking already, and heavily at that.

'Ben, why don't you wait until dinner's ready to have a drink?' she said hesitantly.

His answer was to tip the contents of the glass down his throat before pouring another.

'When I need your advice, my dear, I'll ask for it,' he snapped. 'And why should you think I'd mind that you brought the map from my study? I rather thought you considered anything in there was fair game.'

She flushed, praying that he wouldn't blab about the money she had taken and what she had done with it.

'Isn't it time these children went to the nursery for their tea?' He growled. 'I want to talk to you, Morwen, and Ran may as well hear it too, but it's not for children's ears.'

'If it's about the clayworks, can't I stay?' Walter said daringly. 'You know how interested I am in it, Father—'

'No, you can't bloody well stay!' Ben roared. 'When I say get your tea, I mean get out of here and get your tea!'

'You treat me like a baby!' Walter shouted. 'I'm old enough to work, and you make me stay at school—'

'And you act more like a clayworker's son than a gentleman's,' Ben bawled back.

'No, Ben, please, *don't*!' Morwen's heart pounded, seeing where this was leading. She leapt up at once, pushing the children towards the door. 'Walter, darling, don't be upset. Daddy's out of sorts. Please do as he says and take the others upstairs. I'm relying on you.'

He looked at her, hurt and vulnerable, and her heart ached for him. She dearly wanted to take him in her arms, to kiss away all the uncertainties, but she daren't for fear of Ben's scoffing that it was Morwen who was treating him like a baby.

'All right, Mother,' Walter said, choked. 'I'll do it because *you* ask me to.'

He threw a look of pure hatred at Ben, but he was too taken up with his own thoughts to notice or care. Morwen closed the door behind the children, staring at it for a long moment, and wondering how long she could go on like this, in an atmosphere so full of tensions. She turned to face her husband.

'Must you humiliate him so?' Her voice was tight with controlled anger. 'He's not a child, and boys far younger than him are doing a man's job at Killigrew Clay—'

'Not for much longer,' Ben said savagely. 'I'm having to let all the kiddley-boys go, and some of the older clayworkers as well. The rest will have to double up on the jobs.'

Morwen's jaw dropped open, and Ran looked at him sharply.

'Things aren't that bad, are they, Ben? Surely you don't need to sack kiddley-boys. Their wages will hardly make much difference—'

'Because they're only paid a pittance, you mean? My father always said it was pennies that made pounds, and if you need to cut costs, then start cutting where it will hurt least. Would you rather I sacked all the prime workers with families to keep? Young boys and old men must go first.'

'But Ben, why? And you surely can't include my father in all this!' Morwen felt rising hysteria. Bad times for the clay were always ominous.

He gave a short laugh. 'Naturally I don't include your father. Use your head, woman.'

She deeply resented his tone, humiliating her as he had humiliated Walter. But of course he couldn't sack Hal Tremayne, who was his partner, unknown to the rest of the men. It was one small crumb of comfort. As to the rest of it…

'Are you going to tell us why, or do we have to guess?' she said quietly. 'And if you can't talk civilly to me, Ben, you can talk to yourself.'

She lifted her head defiantly. How dare he make her feel so gauche and unimportant? Was that how he saw her now, after all the good years? Her throat was thick, tears not far below the surface. She had been so happy, so full of plans for when Matt came home, and she had so wanted Ben to share in that happiness.

'We're not making money,' he said harshly. 'Not only that, we've debts to pay that can't be met. Only a fool would keep on workers that aren't necessary, and it's time some of them were weeded out, especially those I suspect of scaggying.'

'Scaggies, yes, but not men who have worked at Killigrew Clay since your father's time!'

Her silent censure was evident to him. Charles Killigrew would never be so disloyal to men who had given him a lifetime's service, whether in the damp of the clay pit or the hot stench of the fire-hole.

'If things are so bad, Ben, perhaps I can help financially,' Ran offered quietly. Ben glared at him.

'I'm not begging for hand-outs,' he snapped. 'I'm just telling you what's happening. I'll sort out this mess in my own way, and I don't want a hue and cry from my own wife when Hal comes storming up here with the news. And there's more ways of finding money than borrowing—'

'Gambling, you mean? Is that your fine way o' handling things now?' Morwen flashed at him in fury. 'You shame us all, Ben.'

'Really?' he sneered. 'It comes to something when a clay-worker's daughter tells a gentleman he shames her—'

One minute he was looking her up and down contemptuously. The next he was on the floor, rubbing his sore chin, and looking up in disbelief at Ran Wainwright's furious face. Ran hauled him to his feet.

'Go and stick your head beneath a cold tap and sober up, and then apologize to the lady.'

Ben spluttered furiously, 'Who in God's name do you think you're talking to? This is my house, and nobody tells me what to do in it—'

'Please stop it, Ben!' Morwen heard her own shrill voice, appalled at the sight of them wrangling.

Ben jerked his head to look at her. 'Afraid I might take a swing back at him, are you? Perhaps you care more about him than your husband after all, is that it?' He made a choking sound as Ran grasped him by the lapels.

'I'm warning you, Killigrew. Act like a lout and you can expect to be treated like one. As for this being your house, I'm well aware of that fact. You treat everyone in it like servants, including your wife and family. It will be my pleasure to move out of it tomorrow.'

'Ran, no!' Morwen was hot with embarrassment. 'Your house isn't ready yet—'

'I shall go to an hotel,' he told her.

'I'm sure my parents would be happy to have you stay with them – if you didn't think their house too small,' she spoke quickly to cover the shame she felt at Ben's words, then immediately had doubts.

'I would be more than honoured to stay with them, but it will be more sensible if I go to an hotel in Truro nearer my own office and business.'

And farther away from all that he loved best in the world. Leaving her to this shambling man who was once such a proud young clay boss. What had made him sink this low, Ran couldn't guess. He hated the thought of leaving her, but if Ben suspected the two of them had been more than friends, Morwen's life would be made a misery. Ben still had some pride, he conceded. He would never accept outside help. Instead, he intended to risk everything on the throw of a dice or a turn of the cards. In Ran's opinion all gamblers were fools, and this one, with so much to lose, was the biggest fool of all.

'I have to go out for a while, Morwen,' he spoke to her directly, ignoring her husband. 'Will you be all right?'

'Why shouldn't she be all right?' slurred Ben.

'I'll be fine,' Morwen nodded. There might have been only the two of them in the room. His eyes told her how much he loved her, and hers sent a silent message back to him.

'I'll pack my things when I get back, and leave right away. I'll let your brothers know where I'm staying, and of course you know where my office is, any time you want to get in touch with me.'

He squeezed her shoulder for a second, then turned and went swiftly out of the house. He would give the world to take her with him, to make her his for ever, but there was more to consider than the love and desire he felt for her. There were the children, and her family, and the scandal that would follow.

And even though Ran knew in his soul that he could persuade her, it cost him more to walk away than to beg her to go with him.

But before it was too late, there was something he had to do. He saddled a horse, and rode through the gathering dusk into the town of St Austell. The lamplighter was doing his rounds, and the bow-fronted shop windows were lighted and welcoming, throwing a silvery sheen on to the cobbled streets. Ran found the street he wanted and tied his horse to the iron ring of a mounting-block. He took the stone steps two at a time and went inside a sombre brown door. A few minutes later he entered the accounting chambers.

'My dear Ran, it's good to see you,' Daniel Gorran said with real pleasure. In the few months he had known the American, he had grown to like and respect him. He had been sorry to lose Ran's services to the claystone works, but was glad of the man's success and appreciative of his keen business sense.

'Will you take a drop of brandy to keep out the cold?' Gorran asked.

'Thank you, no, but don't let me stop you,' Ran said drily. He'd seen enough of brandy drinking that afternoon, but didn't begrudge this man his drop of comfort. When Gorran had poured his drop, he turned to his visitor with a smile.

'Now then, what brings you here? You just caught me. I was about to shut up shop and go home.'

'It's rather a delicate matter, and you can tell me to go away and mind my own business—'

'I doubt that I shall do that, my dear young Sir.'

'You may do so, when you hear that I'm prying into another man's business affairs.'

'I see. And that man would be?'

Ran looked at him steadily. 'I think you must guess that it's Ben Killigrew, Daniel. And I don't pry out of idle curiosity, but because I'm damnably worried about the state of the man, and what I suspect the state of his business to be.'

'You're not alone in that, Ran, but you know that I can't divulge my client's affairs to you.'

'I do know it, and I respect you for that. But if you were to leave the file on the desk for ten minutes or so while you are out of your chambers, I could look after the place for you until you came back.' He looked at the older man steadily. 'Daniel, I can't help him if he doesn't want to be helped, but neither can I know how deep a mess he's got into unless I know facts and figures. The information will remain strictly confidential, naturally.'

After a few seconds, Gorran nodded slightly.

'I know I can trust you, Ran. Well then. I do have to see someone which will take about ten minutes, so if you wouldn't mind holding the fort, I'd be obliged.'

He opened a drawer in a wall cabinet and took out the bulky file that Ran recognized immediately, even if it hadn't been stamped with Ben's name and that of Killigrew Clay underneath. He waited until Gorran's footsteps had gone and then opened the file and began to read quickly, taking notes as he did so.

'Dear God!'

He muttered the words time and again as he read. Debts had mounted alarmingly. Ben owed money for just about everything. He owed the coal suppliers for six months' fuel to stoke the fire-holes in all four pits, and for running his railway. He owed payment on the fine new beam engine he'd had to replace the old one at Clay One. He owed various shipping accounts. There were debts on the household accounts, from the simplest things like candles and kitchen supplies, to stabling bills and overdue payment for school fees.

There had been renewal work done on the settling pits and linhays that hadn't been paid for. The cottages on top of the moor had had repairs done to them, and masons, tilers and timber merchants were all demanding payment. The lists were endless, the amounts horrifying. How could Ben possibly owe so much? When Ran arrived in Cornwall, the debts were modest, as he had discovered on his brief working time in Gorran's chambers, but since then the price for clay had plummeted, and Ben had become careless, taking more out of the business than was going in.

By the time Daniel came back, Ran had seen enough and the file was safely back in its drawer. Ran was grim-faced. The older man shrugged his shoulders expressively.

'Not even the best of friends can help a man who won't help himself, Ran, and I fear that's the condition Ben is in at this moment. The man has everything to live for, yet he's throwing it all away as though there's no tomorrow.'

Ran gave a start. Was that what this was all about? Was Ben so uncaring, knowing his future was uncertain, that he had lost interest in everything but self-indulgence? Ran had no pity for him if it was so. What of those who were left? What of Morwen, and the children? Gorran knew nothing of Ben's precarious state of health, so couldn't guess at the turmoil he must be suffering. Even so, it didn't excuse this, and Ran hardened his heart against the small burst of pity.

'I appreciate your trust in me, Daniel,' he shook the man's hand as he made to leave.

'If you think it's of any use, then I'm glad. But I fear old Charles Killigrew will be resting uneasily in his grave at the present fortunes of his clayworks,' Gorran said sadly.

Ran stepped out into the darkness of the February evening, slid easily on to his horse and headed back to Killigrew House, far more disturbed than before he came. The man was a fool to allow things to happen like this, and short of a hefty loan or gift of money, it seemed as if Killigrew Clay was doomed. Ran had tentatively offered both and been refused, and in a short while, Ben Killigrew would have no choice but to sell up.

Ran couldn't imagine what the shame of it would do to Morwen. For a high-born lady to fall on hard times was bad enough. Such people seemed to face lowered standards with a special inborn dignity. Morwen, born of humble beginnings, would have to accept charity all over again, and he wasn't sure she would be able to cope. He acknowledged that all his worries were for her. For her husband, he had nothing but contempt. Ben had it all, and he was throwing it all away.

He arrived at Killigrew House to collect his belongings and told a tearful group of children that he wasn't going away for ever, and that he needed to be nearer to his work. Morwen was white-faced, and he could hardly bear to look at her. But he couldn't prolong the parting. He kissed them all, and held Morwen to his heart for a precious moment.

'I'll see you all again soon,' he promised. 'And when my house is ready, you shall all come to stay with me if your parents agree.'

'Of course they may,' Morwen said through parched lips. She felt as though she was losing her only ally, and it was a terrible admission to make. But after their fight, it was obviously impossible for Ran to stay here, even if Ben would allow it. And he had made it very clear by his rantings when Ran had gone out, that the American cousin was no longer welcome.

They were both relieved that Ben had gone out again, but neither would have felt so easy had they known where he had gone and for what purpose.

–

The smoke-filled room was filled with gentlemen, and one particular gentleman was very interested in the one who had just arrived. Wild-eyed, with an ugly scar still lovid on his handsome face, and looking less like the prosperous clay boss he was supposed to be, observed Jervis Penhaligan. He didn't often visit the gaming-houses in St Austell, living on the far side of Truro, but this new haunt was an attraction he had recently discovered. And he remembered the young Killigrew very well, even though it was years since the boy had taken a packet off him with one throw of the dice. He was a very astute opponent, Penhaligan recalled. But from the look of him, tonight was a night for revenge. Penhaligan mentally rubbed his hands together.

'We've met before, I believe, Sir,' he called across the table. 'Are you planning to put your clayworks up for offer again? Or your house, maybe?'

Ben looked at him with open dislike as a few cat-calls went around the table.

'I didn't come here to bet goods and chattels, Sir,' he said stiffly. 'If you care to make a wager, I shall be pleased to meet it.'

Penhaligan taunted him. 'You're sure of that, are you? I hear the clay industry's meeting hard times. It's a dishonourable man who can't meet his debts.'

'Be careful, Killigrew,' an acquaintance whispered behind Ben's back. 'The man's been having phenomenal luck lately. He'll wipe you out if he gets a chance.'

'I know what I'm doing,' Ben growled.

He'd had a bellyful of ale before he came, still incensed at the way Ran Wainwright had got the better of him, and finding solace in a pint pot. His nerves were steady enough, even if his hands were not, but he was still canny enough to beat any man. He forgot all the losing times. In his head there was only the desire to win, and to win from this bastard who thought himself so superior.

'Come on, Killigrew.' Penhaligan still mocked him. 'Your business against a few thousand? It sounds about right to me.'

'You must be raving mad! Have you no idea of the worth of a clayworks—?'

'I know the worth of a dying concern,' the man said drily, to more guffaws from his supporters.

Ben knew he was being a fool. He knew he was being goaded into this just as he was goaded into it by Desmond Hartley-Hogg in London. But his own pride wouldn't let him back out now.

'All right, I'll make it easy on you,' Penhaligan said with false kindness. 'Never mind one turn of a card or throw of a dice. We'll start modestly, doubling the stakes until the most cowardly one of us cries stop, and then the loser buys brandy for the whole company, so be sure to leave enough in the coffers for your round, Killigrew.'

Ben was pushed forward by the cheering crowd who sensed a confrontation and wanted to be in at the kill. There was no getting away, and Ben knew now exactly how it felt to be a rat caught in a trap.

Three hours later, he staggered out into the cold February night. He was ruined. The word hammered in his brain. Jervis Penhaligan had all the remaining money from the boxes in the study and a pile of IOUs that would keep all his other debtors waiting for months, even if the clay profits held as good as they were now. And all the signs were that things would get worse…

He was soaked in sweat as he fell across his horse and headed for home. He tried to think coherently, trying to find some comfort in what he still had. He'd kept the works and the house, the horses and vehicles, and his precious railway. But for how long? For how long?

Chapter Thirteen

There was only one person that Morwen could speak to on the subject.

'Daddy, will you please find out what's wrong with Ben?' she begged her father. 'I just can't talk to him, and he snaps everyone's head off as soon as he comes into the house. It – it's not doing his digestion any good to be so cantankerous.'

It was all she dared say about Ben's real medical condition. Not even to her beloved parents would she betray him, knowing how he hated to be pitied by anyone. Her father frowned.

'He's changed, for sure,' Hal agreed. 'Even to the way he comes to the works so often, as if he's driven to be there like some kind o' penance. There's no need for a boss to have his finger in every pie, though the men are givin' 'un grudging respect, for all that he sacked some of the young 'uns and old 'uns like he warned.'

'How did they take it?'

Hal shrugged. 'Up in arms at first, but your man has a way wi' words, Morwen, that I needn't tell 'ee. He made 'em see it had to be done, to keep jobs for those that needed 'em most – the young men with families. Oh ah, Ben's got a way wi' words.'

Morwen thought bitterly that he had developed a fine way of wounding with words too.

''Tis a pity he can't be such a champion to his children then,' she burst out. 'They almost fear his footsteps lately, knowing he's going to find fault with everything they do. 'Tis no wonder they find such pleasure in going to Ran's house, for there's precious little at home.'

Hal looked into the beautiful hurt eyes of his daughter, and sighed. Time was when she would have given the earth for Ben Killigrew, but the boy was throwing it all away.

'Is the house nearly ready?' Hal turned the conversation, and Morwen nodded, still troubled.

'He'll be moving in very soon, before Matt comes home.'

Even saying those words failed to give her the usual thrill at that moment.

'Daddy, I so want Matt and his family to stay with us, but what Louisa will think of my husband's manners, I can't think. He makes me ashamed.'

'I'll talk to 'un, my love,' Hal promised. 'Somebody'll have to, I can see that.'

Morwen was relieved. She was ostensibly taking a ride up to the moors, knowing just when to catch her father on his way down from Clay One. She leaned forward from her mare and kissed him, and then she was gone. Hal Tremayne watched her for a long while, until her lithe young shape and flying dark hair were lost in the mist, before continuing home. Yes, something had to be done. Morwen and Ben had been such spectacular lovers, so wrapped up in one another, and it pained him deeply to see them drift so far apart. It didn't do to interfere into somebody else's marriage, and he knew he'd get more than tongue pie from Ben Killigrew. But if anyone had to interfere, it was better to be someone who loved them both.

He resolved to do it right away. Bess had gone over to Truro to have tea with Jack and Annie, and for once, wouldn't be there to welcome him home. And Ben was due down from the works soon after himself. He screwed himself round in the trap, and strained his eyes for the first sight of Ben's steaming horse. The boy never did anything by halves these days, Hal thought.

It was only a short while later that he saw the mud flying from beneath the horse's hooves. Hal hid a small smile. Here was he, Works Manager, but still a clayworker at heart, riding grandly home in a trap, the one-time gift of old Charles Killigrew, and here was the young boss, careering about on the back of a horse. The irony wasn't lost on him.

'What's to do, Hal?' Ben reined in at once. 'You're not ill, are you?'

Hal grinned. 'Not ill at all, just wanting a few words wi' you, Ben. Can you spare some time at the house?'

Ben shrugged. 'Why not?'

They rode together, awkward in the unfamiliar setting. At work there was plenty to say. At Killigrew House or Hal's small home there was the family to draw them together. Now, jogging along in silence, they were in a kind of limbo. Hal felt a sense of satisfaction at his reply to Ben's curt query. No, he wasn't ill. There was a time when he'd thought he might be, but that had passed, and he felt as fit as ever. More so than this young man, who looked suddenly drawn and care-worn, and to his alarm, Hal realised he hadn't even noticed it until now. The ugly scar on his face didn't help, but it was more than that. There was more to know, and after his daughter's plea, Hal Tremayne meant to find out just what it was.

'Will you take a jug of ale, Ben?' he asked, once they were inside the house.

'If you're offering, I'm drinking,' Ben said in a lazy voice. The house was warm, and it was good to stretch out, arms behind his head, hands clasped. He could forget his troubles for half an hour or so, and he'd always had a healthy respect for his father-in-law, whatever his background.

'What was it you wanted to see me about?'

''Tis our Morwen, and the way you'm treating her.' There was no guile in Hal Tremayne. If he had a grievance, he came straight out with it. If things needed to be settled it was best to get them out in the open and sorted. It was his only philosophy, though he himself wouldn't have credited it with so grand a name.

Ben looked at him over the jug of foaming ale. He drank deeply, curling his tongue around the froth on his upper lip. His eyes were cold.

'Really. And just how am I treating her?'

'Now before you think our Morwen's been telling tales to me, let me tell 'ee you're wrong, Ben. She's worried sick about 'ee, Ben, and about the way you don't have much time for her and the children any more.'

'My family affairs are no concern of yours.'

'You're wrong. What affects Morwen affects me and her mother. And when I hear of the children being unhappy, it affects me on their account as well. I'm their Granddaddy, Ben, and I've seen how Walter aches to work wi' the clay, rather than going to that fancy school of his, and he's only one example—'

'Where I send Walter is my business,' Ben was cold as ice now. 'He's got a brain, and he needs to use it, not let it stagnate—'

'Like my boys' brains stagnated? Have a care, Ben. 'Tis the Tremaynes and others like 'em who helped to make Killigrew Clay the concern that it is.'

'Not for much longer!'

Hal felt his heart lurch. He'd expected a bit of retaliation, then he could go on to say how stubborn Justin was becoming, and how Ben needed to handle the boy with more gentleness, and how Primmy was growing up and he'd seen the way the young boys looked at her... but all that was lost on hearing Ben's flat voice.

'What did you say?' Hal said carefully.

Ben gave a short laugh. He knew he was about to dispel a dream. He was about to send this fine man's world crashing about his ears, and he was unable to stop it. The stab of remorse was momentary. Hal Tremayne must fall like Killigrew Clay.

'You want to know why I'm such a bastard to my own family, Hal? Then I'll tell you. It's because I'm in so much debt I doubt that Killigrew Clay can last out another year. Another few months will be more like it. If we get the spring despatches away before the bailiffs come in and break up the railway and commandeer the pits for the highest bidder, we might be able to hold our heads above water until the autumn. And I don't even know if I'll be alive to see it. Do you want more reasons?'

He drained his ale, holding out the jug for a refill. Hal saw how his hands shook and complied without question.

'What are you saying?' Hal said harshly, white-faced. 'You still pay the dividends to me. We still operate—'

'Hal, you're an ignorant man, and I don't mean that in any derogatory sense. You simply don't understand business. Your dividends have been paid, and that's the one saving grace that might earn me a place in Heaven. I've let everybody else down, but not my partner.' His voice was heavy with sarcasm against himself.

'I want to know more about this,' Hal said grimly. 'But what's all this talk of dying and places in Heaven? I don't like to hear you tempt fate like that, Ben.'

Ben's laugh was coarse. 'Oh, I'm not tempting fate, Hal. I've already had my warning. Morwen obviously hadn't told you that bit of news. My ticker's like a bomb set to go off at any minute, only I don't know the exact time it's set for. Would you care to live under those circumstances? For two pins I'd finish it off now, and there's plenty who'll be saying good riddance in a few month's time.'

Hal was still reeling under the shock. It was true that Ben looked terrible lately. He was clearly drinking hard and living hard, and the attack in London had left more scars than the one on his face. But this…

'Is it true, Ben?'

'It's true. You don't lie about a death sentence. It would be tempting fate,' he threw back Hal's own words with a grimace of humour.

'And Morwen knows?'

'Morwen knows, and Randell Wainwright, and now you. Apart from that, there's only the doctors in London, and Doctor Pender. I'd prefer to keep it that way.'

'I've never kept secrets from Bess. She needs to know. Our Morwen should know where there's a shoulder to cry on when she needs it. Women are different creatures to men. They need other women to blab to about their troubles.' He looked at Ben steadily. 'Or would you rather she cried on Ran Wainwright's shoulder?'

Ben's eyes flashed. 'So you've seen the way he looks at her, have you?'

'Do you blame him? Morwen's a beautiful woman, but she's loved you since she was a girl. Don't throw it all away, Ben.'

'I don't want to talk about my marriage or my health. It bores me,' Ben said crudely, and Hal pursed his lips.

'All right. We've other things to talk about. How bad is it for Killigrew Clay? Your father built it up from nothing, and I can't believe that things can be as bad as you say. Where have all the assets gone, Ben?'

'The *money*, you mean. Money for bills, for new equipment, for repairs, and wages.'

'Yes the money. I've a right to know, and I'll know it all before you leave here.' Hal was steely now, as Ben raised his eyebrows over Hal's suddenly harsh tone.

'You already know the circumstances by which I got control of the business,' he snapped. 'Put two and two together.'

'Good God, man, you're a bigger fool than I took you for if you've been gambling with Killigrew Clay's money!' Hal was incensed now, seeing ruination staring him in the face, and all because of this young fool's weakness.

'You've had your dividends regularly, haven't you?' Ben was shouting now, blustering at the look of disgust on the other's face. 'You've just said you had no wind of anything wrong. You didn't want to be concerned with the business side of it, did you—'

'I didn't want to be anything more than Pit Captain, ever,' Hal bellowed back. ''Twas you and your fancy talking who talked me into being Works Manager and setting clayworkers against me I'd known for years, until they calmed down and saw that nobody was changing Hal Tremayne. 'Twas you who persuaded me into being a partner, when all I wanted for me and my Bess was to live quietly—'

'And it was your Matt's money that bought you in, so don't forget that. You Tremaynes have entwined yourselves around Killigrew Clay as surely as if you'd chained yourselves to it. You can't escape that easily.'

Hal wasn't too sure where this conversation was going, but now he saw everything with sudden clarity.

'Our Matt got you out of a hole once before, and now 'tis my turn. 'Tis my duty, so don't you dare refuse me.'

'What in God's name are you talking about?' Ben said irritably. Pennies would do nothing to help his fortunes.

Hal strode across to a small bureau and drew out a large envelope. Inside were various papers and documents, and a slim official-looking book. He handed it to Ben without a word.

'Go on. Take it. 'Tis yours, and I'll be glad to be rid of the millstone it's been round my neck. The children would get it when I'm gone, so you might as well make use of it now.'

Ben opened up the book, a banking account from a bank in Bodmin. He remembered advising Hal to put his dividends into an out of town bank for added security, since Hal was so adamant about his partnership being kept a secret. Ben glanced at the entries in the book, and the figures danced before his eyes. Christ, but the man was worth a fortune and didn't seem to realize it.

'Haven't you spent any of the money that was due to you?' he said hoarsely.

'Of course, but only what we needed. Our needs are small. Bess and me don't aspire to anything grand. 'Tis not our way.'

God, but it was tempting. Ben realized he could clear everything in a single swoop. The money was here. It was his for the taking. He could rob this simple man of everything, including his pride, and leave him with nothing. Nothing for his children and grandchildren after he was gone. And someday the truth of the partnership would come out. Someday when both Ben and Hal were dead. How would it look then, to the rest of them? How would they ever cope with the shame of it all, knowing Ben had used all his partner's money to pay off gambling debts? He couldn't do it, not even for Killigrew Clay. He snapped the book shut and handed it back to Hal.

'This is yours. I won't touch it, but I thank you from my heart for offering it. I'll thank you even more never to mention it again.'

Their eyes clashed, and what Hal saw in Ben's made him put the book back in the envelope and close the bureau.

'What will you do?' he grunted.

'Pay off a bit at a time, as best I can. And Hal – this is our business, and nobody else's.'

'Just so long as you go easy on Morwen and the children,' Hal bargained with him. ''Tis you who has to pay. Don't make all of them pay as well.'

'I'll do my best. But it's not always easy for a dying man to cope with the trivia of daily life. My father discovered that,' Ben said, the lightness of his voice betraying how deeply affected he really was by his condition.

'If ever you need somebody to confide in, come to me, Ben. 'Tis not only women who can use a strong shoulder.'

Whatever Ben would have said to that was lost, as Bess came in through the door, bringing a sting of light rain with her. She smiled in pleased surprise at the sight of the two men, apparently jawing over a jug or two of ale in front of the fire. Ben rarely called in for a casual visit.

'Ben, I'm so glad to see you! It gives me a chance to ask about the welcome home party for Matt. If you want any extra help at the house, I'd be only too happy to help Mrs Horn. Will 'ee tell her so?'

He looked at her round, beaming face, and the incongruous thought flashed through his mind that Hal Tremayne was a lucky man. He had contentment, a loving wife, and the years ahead to share with her. He heard Hal gently chiding her.

'What are you thinking of, woman? You'll be an honoured guest, not a skivvy!' he forestalled Ben.

'I think it would be a splendid idea,' Ben was surprised to hear himself say. He made an effort to sound hearty. 'It would give Matt special pleasure to know his mother prepared some of his old favourite dishes. I'll certainly tell Mrs Horn, and the two of you can get your heads together before the big day.'

He wouldn't stay any longer, and when he'd gone Bess smiled in delight at her husband.

'You see, dar? Ben can be as homely as the next 'un when he's given the right lead. I thought you said he was a bit tetchy lately, but he seemed quite like his old self to me. Trust a woman's nose to know about these things!'

She spoke gaily, and went quite pink when Hal suddenly moved across to her and held her very tightly in his arms without speaking. As though he needed to feel the warmth and the strength of her, and to be glad that they still had each other. Hal could feel the beat of his own heart against hers, and each was steady and strong. He felt a fleeting pity for Ben Killigrew and his uncertain future. They had lost Sam irrevocably, but through it all, it seemed that the Tremaynes were the survivors.

-

Jack looked at his wife with a sense of hurtling doom.

'It can't be true! Annie, we've been so careful. It's not true, is it? Can 'ee be sure yet? Have 'ee seen the doctor?'

He gripped her slender shoulders and felt them tremble, even though she gave a nervous laugh.

'I don't need doctors to tell me when I'm having a baby, Jack. I feel it here, under my heart. I know what was said, but I'm still *glad*. Be glad as well, darling. Say that you're glad!'

He folded her in his arms. How could he say what he really felt? That if he lost Annie he would no longer want to live? That he knew just how Dora must have felt after losing Sam. Without the will to live, even for the children that were left… Jack squared his shoulders. He wasn't a woman, to succumb to the first ailment that took him, as Dora had. He didn't blame her. She was weak… but Jack Tremayne was strong, and if strength were ever needed, it was now.

'We'll see Doctor Vestey straight away,' he said huskily. 'We'll see about taking you to a specialist, to check that everything's all right. If it's not – perhaps we should see about—'

She put her fingers over his mouth. 'No, my love. I won't kill our baby.'

'It wouldn't be killing, Annie,' he said desperately. ''Tis hardly a baby yet, just a speck.'

'It's a speck made from our love, Jack, and we could never live with ourselves if we did anything to harm it. You know it, don't you?'

'I do,' he agreed grudgingly, knowing it was the truth. Any baby had a right to life, and one that they created was doubly precious. But if it cost Annie her life… Jack swallowed painfully.

'But you'll do as I say, now. We go to see Doctor Vestey tomorrow, and ask 'un to make arrangements to see a top man.'

Annie smiled indulgently. 'And what can he do, my love? Tell me to stop eating sweetmeats so I don't put on too much weight? Or to stop enjoying my husband's attentions?'

He looked at her. They were in their bedroom, cosy for the night. They hadn't yet turned down the gas-light, and her eyes were large and luminous and inviting. She saw the dawn of pleasure in his answering look, and pulled him closer.

'Nobody's told us yet, darling. And we don't have anything to worry about for the next seven months—'

He groaned, holding her slim body and feeling himself rise at her teasing. Nothing to worry about… their carelessness might be their disaster… but for tonight it would be farthest from their thoughts. Jack kissed the parted mouth awaiting him, and made love to his wife with the abandonment of desperation.

They were taken to task at the doctor's office the next day, and Jack was angry and upset at being made to feel like a naughty schoolboy.

'What d'you expect folks to do wi' their natural urges?' he said sharply, less concerned with Annie's blushes than this elderly man censuring them.

'Jack, I thought we'd discussed all this, and found the solution—'

'Ah well, 'tis all right for medical men to give the instructions. 'Tis summat else for two red-blooded folk to remember to carry 'em out,' he muttered.

'We did try, Doctor,' Annie's soft voice was pleading for him to understand. 'I'm sure 'twas only once that we forgot.'

'It only takes once, young lady,' the doctor said drily. 'However, the thing's done, and you have to make a decision.'

Jack felt his temper quicken at the doctor's choice of words. The 'thing' was their child, his and Annie's, and it was made out of love. In that instant he felt a fierce surge of love for it, speck or no speck… fatalistically, he knew he was totally in tune with her wishes. Life was sacred, and there could be no question of being rid of what had begun.

Annie spoke up before the doctor could clear his throat, shuffle his papers, and construct a sentence about advisable termination that wouldn't horrify them both.

'I won't have my baby taken away, Doctor. 'Tis blasphemous to do so. If it's God's will to take it from me, I shall accept it, but I'll do nothing to help Satan.'

He stared at her. He hadn't taken Annie Tremayne for a religious woman, nor her husband. He saw their fingers meet and entwine, and knew that they shared a special kind of faith. He sighed. He was a practical man who believed in science, not mystical beings, and knew that faith alone wouldn't deliver this woman of a healthy child.

'Can we see a specialist in these matters, Doctor Vestey? 'Tis not that we doubt your abilities—' Jack said, his voice awkward lest the doctor should think their faith in him was quickly waning.

'I was going to suggest it.' The doctor spoke with some relief. Of course he would continue to keep an eye on Annie, she was his patient. But he much preferred to pass the case on to some other man, should the worst happen. He took a notepad stamped with his name and credentials, and wrote quickly, sealed the letter in an envelope and handed it to Jack.

'I want you to take Annie to the Truro Hospital and ask to see Mr Shiner. He's the gynaecologist I'm referring you to. He'll be there tomorrow and Friday, but I suggest you see him as soon as possible. He'll want to examine you, Annie, and he may want to do some tests. It's nothing to be afraid of, but I do urge you to do exactly as I say if you want this child.'

The fright in Annie's eyes gave way to hope. 'Then you do think there's a chance for the baby?'

'I think there's a chance for the baby. It's the mother I'm concerned about.'

He showed them out, thinking there were no fools like young folk, yet aware of a brief sigh of envy before the next patient came hobbling in, stiff with arthritis and grumbling incessantly at his lot for the next half hour.

–

Morwen was surprised to see her brother and his wife turn up at Killigrew House the next afternoon. Jack wasn't one for visiting, but after she had welcomed them inside, it struck Morwen at once that Annie looked pale and on edge.

'We've come from Truro Hospital,' Jack said at once. 'Annie didn't feel like going straight home, and the twins are being taken care of, so we decided to take a ride—'

'Why were you at Truro Hospital? You're not ill, are you, Annie?' Morwen couldn't wait for all these fancy explanations, which merely told her how edgy Jack was too.

Annie gave a shaky laugh. 'I'm not ill. Just pregnant.'

Morwen's face broke into a delighted smile. 'But that's marvellous – isn't it?'

Jack took up the tale as Annie bit her lips, and Morwen saw how they were shaking.

'It will be if Annie's all right. We had to see some gynee-summat-or-other fellow, and he says Annie ought really to go into hospital and have a termination. He means we should kill our babby, and if you'd heard the callous way he said it, you'd be as upset as we, our Morwen. Killing a babby's wicked, whatever the reason. Everybody knows that.'

Morwen felt her face blanch. She had helped her friend Celia to kill a baby, and as she heard the condemnation in her brother Jack's voice, she felt almost as if he knew. That he was accusing her on account of Celia, and blaming her in some obscure way for Annie's troubles.

'Jack, love, don't take on so.' Annie's placid voice calmed him, and Morwen blinked rapidly. Jack knew nothing about that night on the moors that had led to Celia drowning herself in the clay pool, and his sole concern was for his wife.

'Did the man say it has to happen, Annie?'

'No. He said it was our choice, but that he couldn't be responsible for the consequences if we didn't heed his advice.'

'And what do you intend to do?' Morwen asked carefully.

The two of them clasped hands, their fingers interlacing as if to close out the rest of the world.

'Have our baby, of course. What else does a woman do when she's pregnant?'

In the small silence, Annie began to giggle, her blue eyes shining like stars. 'His name's Mr Shiner, Morwen. Did you ever hear anything so daft? And he's got dark shadows under his eyes that look as if somebody's punched him, and left him with two real shiners!'

'He's got dark shadows from looking up too many womens' clouts,' Jack grunted. 'It probably drives him batty—'

'Jack, for heaven's sake!' Annie went scarlet with embarrassment, but his sister knew he only spoke with such crudity when he was totally at a loss for anything else to say.

She spoke quickly. 'Well, I think we should celebrate. A baby is always good news. Can you take a drink of something, Annie?'

'Only hot chocolate from now on,' she gave a mock groan. 'I'm to follow a strict diet, to rest every afternoon, and to see Mr Shiner once a month.' She repeated the words parrot-fashion.

'And at the end of it, there'll be another little Tremayne!' Morwen tried to revive her brother's gloomy spirits. 'I wonder if it will be a boy this time.'

'I pray for it,' Annie said softly. 'I want a boy for Jack, and I've already picked out his name. We'll call him Sam.'

At that, Jack's eyes seemed to be more moist than before, and Morwen knew that within seconds they were going to be in each others' arms and sharing the love and the fear and the resolution they had made. She tip-toed out of the room, knowing they wouldn't even notice her go. She mumbled that she'd get them both a hot drink, but in reality she went because she couldn't bear to see such perfect harmony between them, when it contrasted so vividly and so heartbreakingly with what was between her and Ben.

Chapter Fourteen

If there was anything guaranteed to make Morwen more restless than before, it was the news of Jack and Annie's baby. She was happy for them, of course, but their closeness emphasized more sharply how far apart she and Ben had become. So many times she saw him come home drunkenly and was helpless to do anything about it. He was no longer the old Ben. He was some new and frightening person who reminded her more and more of his odious cousin, Jude. How *could* he let that happen?

When she tried delicately to offer advice about business affairs, he shouted that business affairs were none of her concern. He'd see to it. When a man couldn't sort out his own problems, he was no longer a man. Since Hal had reported back to her all their conversation, it was on the tip of Morwen's tongue to beg him to think again and accept her father's help. But she knew that his pride would never let that happen. A Killigrew begging from a Tremayne…?

Ben told her harshly what he had told Hal. He'd pay off his debtors a bit at a time, and hope to satisfy them until the dues from the spring despatches came in. There was still money owing to him from the autumn despatches, he scowled, and ordered Daniel Gorran to send off demanding letters, without heeding the effect they were having on associates who had once been pleased to call Ben Killigrew friend. But, with typical Killigrew luck, it seemed to be working, at least for the moment. The gambling episode with Jervis Penhaligon had put the frighteners into him, and he kept strictly away from the gaming-houses now.

And some semblance of sanity made him thankful that he hadn't gambled away the house and the clayworks. He would never admit how dangerously close he'd come to doing just that. The shame of making his family homeless would have made him suicidal. He was already so muddleheaded from excessive drinking and health worries that he was just thankful to put the business dealings in Gorran's hands and let him do the sorting. What was the use of having an accountant if he couldn't deal with awkward customers? Ben blundered on, alienating everyone around him.

–

Ran Wainwright was moving into his splendid new house. He had named it New World, which made Ben scoff, and charmed Morwen and all the children, linking his old country with his adopted one. They had been to see it many times now, and knew every nook and cranny. In particular they loved the little round room, hidden away from the bigger rooms, and overlooking the sea, where Ran swore there must be a friendly ghost, a fact that nonetheless sent them shiveringly to bed.

'You shouldn't tease them, Ran,' Morwen laughed, when Charlotte had asked curiously if he had ever seen the ghost and he had to admit that he had not, to her great disappointment. 'They'll be wanting one at Killigrew House next!'

'I thought there were already enough ghosts there,' Ran said lightly, as they went on a tour of the house now that all the furniture had been delivered, and it began to look like a home.

'Do we have ghosts, Mother?' Albert said at once, and she shook her head quickly.

'No, we don't, love. Uncle Ran's just being facetious.'

'What's that?' Charlotte pouted, hating words that she didn't understand.

'It means "funny", silly. Uncle Ran's always funny. Not like Daddy. He's miserable all the time,' Primmy added for good measure.

'Daddy's got a lot of business worries—'

'Killigrew Clay's not in trouble, is it, Mother?' Walter was too sharp, too keen on his heritage to ignore any such comment, and Morwen wished she had never made it.

She would have fobbed him off, but she looked into his clear anxious blue eyes and knew that he deserved more. He was growing up so fast. He was going on for fifteen, tall and muscular like Sam had been, and already a young man to make girls' heads turn. Ben was wrong to treat him like a child the way he did.

'Prices have fallen, and folk aren't so keen to pay their bills, which stretches us to pay the wages and other things,' she said as honestly as possible without giving too much away. 'But you know the clay prices go up and down, darling. 'Tis nothing to worry about.'

'We're not worrying today,' Ran said heartily. 'I thought you were all having tea with me, and I want no glum faces around my table.'

Walter looked at him steadily. 'You're all right, aren't you, Uncle Ran? The clay-stone's doing well. I read it in *The Informer.*'

'Did you? I thought your father discouraged you from reading newspapers at home,' Ran said mildly.

'I don't read them at home. We get a selection of papers from all over the country at school. If Father wants me to be educated, he must expect a private school to provide such literary masterpieces along with Dickens and Shakespeare.'

He spoke with studied irony. He was going to be clever with words, Morwen thought suddenly. Her clever, clever son – Sam's son – who still wanted to work with the clay, despite all his learning. Just as Ben had done, once long ago. She felt a glow of pride for Walter. Sometimes she felt that he was more her child than all the others, even her own two that she had wanted so much. The thought made guilt stab at her, and she gave Charlotte a hug, and Justin an extra-warm smile.

After tea, the children asked if they could run down to the sea, excited that the grounds of the house ran right down to a small cove.

'Just be careful,' Ran warned. 'The cliffs look as if they might crumble, so don't go climbing on them, and you boys take care of the girls.'

They watched them go from the tall dining-room windows, scampering down the slope in the lovely March afternoon, a little troupe in descending heights, and it was Albert who waited for Charlotte's short legs to catch up. Morwen felt the curl of Ran's fingers in her own. They felt comforting and warm. It wasn't often they touched, as if by an unspoken vow. She didn't move away. She wanted to hold this moment. She had felt this way many times in her life, wishing there was some way a moment could be captured and savoured, to bring out on the miserable days when nothing went right.

'We could never destroy that innocence,' Ran said softly.

'No.'

'It doesn't mean that I don't think of you, and want you, and love you, every waking moment of my life, and in every dream.' He spoke intimately, without looking at her. She could feel the restrained passion through his fingertips, more powerfully than if he had crushed her in his arms.

'And I you,' Morwen whispered, and the surge of love inside her was a tightening in her chest and a thickening in her throat. She trembled involuntarily, and Ran felt that too. He released her hand and turned to her.

'Shall we walk in the gardens?' he said quietly. 'If we stay here alone, I fear I might even yet carry you away upstairs, and do what my heart tells me to do.'

'Then we had best go outside,' she said unsteadily. 'For if you ask, I shall be unable to say no.'

So formal, when all they wanted to do was forget the proprieties and be themselves, two lovers who loved and ached to be part of each other. But it was necessary to play these games, to give so much and no more, to know that each still yearned for the other, and it was a talisman they each cherished. Morwen still feared that one day Ran would tire of having so little, and would want something of his own, but she refused to think of it. If she didn't give the words space in her head, they didn't exist. She clung to her own simple logic.

They strolled in the grounds and New World looked very beautiful in the afternoon sunlight. For a second, Morwen imagined herself as the mistress here, with children who were not hers and Ben's, or theirs and Sam's and Dora's, but children born of a new love...

'I thought we'd wait for the house-warming party until Matt and Louisa are here,' Ran said. 'It will be my pleasure to entertain you all, and my housekeeper was undaunted when I mentioned the fact.'

'It sounds a lovely idea, Ran.' It was best to keep away from personal topics and plan ahead. 'You were very fortunate in finding such a good housekeeper. Mrs Enders seems like a treasure.'

'And very well recommended. She brought references with her, you know.' Ran smiled, as if all this talk of housekeeping was of vital importance to them both. 'Her sister works for Richard Carrick, the solicitor, and his wife. Didn't you say you knew them?'

'Oh yes, I know them—' and have been snubbed by them, and despised by them, and been insanely jealous of their beautiful daughter, when Mrs Carrick was determined to make her Jane Ben Killigrew's bride...

'Well, they were gracious enough to give Mrs Enders a character reference too, which made me more than happy to employ her, and I've been well rewarded.' He glanced down at her, aware that she was suddenly quiet. 'Morwen? Honey, is anything wrong?'

Her eyes glinted with tears. She adored the American form of endearment that Ran used rarely, and only to her.

'Just a goose walking over my grave, that's all. Forget it, Ran. Let's talk about Matt instead. We're all going to travel to Falmouth to meet him, and I hope you'll come as well.'

'Of course. You'll need an extra carriage,' he said. 'I'll come over to St Austell and pick up your parents, if you like. You and Ben will have enough to do with the children, and I daresay Freddie will go with Jack and his family. Will he shut up shop for the day?'

'Of course. There'll be no work done by any of the Tremaynes on that day. And Ben's promised not to go to the works.'

She forgot the tussle she'd had with Ben. He'd been surly and said Matt wouldn't care whether Ben Killigrew went to the port to greet him or not, but Morwen insisted on it and eventually got her way, angry that Ben had thought Matt's homecoming of so little importance. To the Tremaynes it was the most important day of their lives, and Freddie would certainly shut up shop! She murmured that it might be a good idea to call and surprise him when the children got back from the cove. She made the suggestion because Ran's house was beginning to feel too desirable to her, too much a place where she wanted to stay.

–

Freddie Tremayne was having second thoughts about going to America. It had been a whim, a moment's thought, but now there was something more alluring here in Truro. It had been here all the time, but he had only just found it. He stopped thinking of the object of his attentions as "it", and into his mind came the picture of a silky blue gown that fitted lusciously over curves of soft white flesh. The breathtaking vision was transformed by the face of an angel with a rosebud mouth and gentle grey eyes, surmounted by a cloud of titian hair that could have come straight from an artist's palette. Freddie Tremayne was in love, hopelessly and unbelievably in love, and he had danced with his love and felt as though he floated on a cloud.

He forced himself to stop daydreaming and serve the rough seamen who came into his shop for ropes and candles, and to admit that his life was far more aligned to such as these, than the elite of Truro society, to which the Honourable Venetia Hocking belonged. He felt a shiver of excitement just thinking of her name. It was such a beautiful name, but then to Freddie, everything about her was beautiful…

'Our Freddie, get that bemused look off your face, and say hello.'

He heard his sister Morwen's teasing voice with a start. How long he'd been gazing into space he didn't know. But the seamen had been replaced by a whole shopful of people, Morwen and the American cousin, and the five jostling children. He forced a smile to his face.

'Well, what brings you all here? You're a long way from home.'

'Not from Ran's home. We've been visiting, and seeing how the other folk live,' she laughed. 'You must see it soon, Freddie, and Ran's bringing an invitation.'

He thought that she and Ran seemed on very good terms, and wouldn't blame them if they were. Freddie had less and less time for Ben these days, seeing what a mess he was making of his life, and he liked and admired the American cousin.

'It's hardly an invitation, since we're all family. It's a house-warming for when Matt and Louisa are here. You'll come, of course, Freddie – and bring a friend if you like.'

He said it carelessly, a friendly gesture without guile. But Morwen saw the way her youngest brother coloured up, his hands fidgeting with some brochures on the glass counter, and was instantly reminded of a time years ago when she and Ben had taken Freddie on a picnic to the beach. The boy had begged to go for a swim, and had come out of the water happy and shivering in his under-drawers, and Morwen had first been aware of the tender finger of manhood in her baby brother, and had been suffused with love for his growing-up.

Why she should think of that now, she couldn't imagine, and it sent a wave of embarrassment through her. To be instantly dismissed as a new thought struck her, confirmed at once by Freddie's words.

'I will if she'll agree to it.'

'She?' Morwen echoed at once. 'Freddie, you've been keeping things from us. Who is this "she"?'

He laughed. 'You were allus a nosey one, our Morwen. I don't even know if she'll remember me.'

But he remembered her, Morwen thought. It was written in his face, all the wonder of falling in love, the agony and the joy.

'Are you going to tell us her name, or do we have to guess?' She went on relentlessly. She was aware of Ran's amused look, and the children's disinterest. The chandlery shop was infinitely more exciting, with its hotchpotch of knick-knacks and the pungent smells of candles and soap and wax and varnish. She ignored them all. This was family talk, and the Tremaynes had always been intensely interested in each other's doings.

'All right, then. 'Tis Venetia.' Just saying it made Freddie glow in a way he found pleasurable and new. He had been telling himself ever since he met his lady that there was nothing wrong with him after all. He was a man with a man's healthy appetites and responses, and just meeting Venetia had restored his confidence in himself.

'Venetia!' Morwen echoed. ''Tis a fancy name. Where did 'ee meet a body wi' a name like that, our Freddie? Is she the daughter of a Lord or summat?'

Only two sorts of women had names like that. Daughters of the gentry, or moonlighters who gave themselves airs to attract their gentleman callers. She hardly thought it could be either! But she lapsed into the old patois so that Freddie wouldn't think she was being too serious. To her horror she saw him nod.

'The Honourable Venetia Hocking. What do 'ee think of that, then?'

Morwen couldn't think of anything at all for a moment. The fatuous smile on her brother's face made her so fiercely protective that she wanted to hug him close. He was destined for heartbreak… but how could she tell him that? Any more than she could say baldly that a Lord would never hand over his daughter to a young man with a modest chandlery shop, however well-up he considered himself in the social scale. Compared with Lords and Honourables, the Tremaynes were still nothing. Her eyes stung with tears, but it was Ran who spoke.

'Good for you, boy. So we'll expect to see you and your Lady Venetia at the party. I haven't fixed the date yet, but I'll let you know in good time.'

'Where did you meet her, Freddie?' Morwen said quickly. She wasn't even aware that her brother was doing the social rounds in Truro. She had become introverted in many ways. Since Ben had stopped entertaining and accepting invitations, she had been obliged to do the same. The Killigrews were practically recluses and outcasts from St Austell society, she realized with a little shock, where they had once been coveted guests.

'Lord Hocking's Chairman of the Small Businesses Club,' Freddie said with as much pride as if he had helped the gentleman attain the honour. 'He inherited his title from a distant cousin, but still maintains his roots, our Morwen, so you needn't be afeared that I'm leaping out of my class just yet. He ran some stables and a riding school for other folk's daughters and still keeps his finger in the commercial pie.'

'Well, I don't know what to say to it then.'

'Don't say anything, just wish me luck.' Freddie grinned, the brief defensiveness gone, and the cheeky look of the young kiddley-boy back on his face.

Morwen leaned across the counter and kissed him.

'You know that I do,' she said softly. 'And I just can't wait to meet this Venetia of yours. Do we have to call her "my lady", by the way?' She still couldn't resist teasing him.

'You do and I'll clock you,' Freddie reverted even more to the old Freddie. 'Now get out of here, the lot of you, so I can serve some real paying customers.'

They moved hastily, still smiling as the door opened and a salt breeze wafted in with the burly clients. Morwen was somewhat easier at Freddie's revelations about Lord Hocking, but it still seemed a far cry from the aspirations of a one-time kiddley-boy at Killigrew Clay. She was suddenly ashamed. What of herself? Who would have thought that a bal maiden would be the wife of a clay boss? She saw Ran watching her, and knew he could read her thoughts.

'All right, so I'm anxious about him,' she murmured. 'Why shouldn't I be? He's still my little brother, and any woman should be proud to be loved by him. He's handsome and open, and he's done well for himself—'

'You don't need to defend him to me, Morwen,' Ran said mildly. 'I told you once before. In my country, we take a person for what they are, not for what their parents made them.'

'I think I'd like to see your country.' She spoke without thinking.

'Perhaps one day you will.'

She didn't answer. They both knew there was only one way Morwen would ever go to America. Ben had no interest in the country. But if there was no Ben, and the way was clear for her and Ran... Morwen smothered such thoughts immediately. They were bad thoughts, and she had never wished another harm in all her life... except for one person, and she had successfully dealt with him, she remembered.

The thought suddenly chilled her. She mustn't, for one moment, wish Ben ill. She may or may not have the power... old Zillah had once hinted that she did. Charles Killigrew had been convinced that there was healing in her hands. But she didn't want it. Not if she could unconsciously use it to wish Ben ill. She would never do that. She loved him. She did. She did. She repeated the phrase over and over like a talisman.

'If Uncle Freddie's going to marry a Lady, will that make him a Lord?' Primmy asked, the thought clearly enchanting her.

Ben spluttered over his glass of brandy. He had come home from Clay One to find his entire family poring over the atlas again, tracing how many miles Matt Tremayne would have travelled so far, and for some reason the whole scene irritated him. It only needed the American cousin to be here, and he might as well be ousted from his own hearth, he thought disagreeably. But this remark of Primmy's was ludicrous enough to make him guffaw loudly.

'Freddie Tremayne marrying a Lady and becoming a Lord? Have you lost your reason, girl?'

His tone made Primmy burn with embarrassment, and Morwen could have shaken her husband. Not least because of the scathing dismissal of such a possibility. She hadn't been aware that the children had taken any interest in the conversation at the shop, but it soon become obvious that they had.

'Why shouldn't Uncle Freddie marry a Lady?' Walter said stoutly, still resentful of Ben's blocking of his wishes to leave private school and start work.

He wasn't stupid. He knew that money was beginning to be a problem. He had inherited the Tremayne logic, and thought that a saving of school fees would prove more useful to Ben than keeping a frustrated son in a place he didn't want to be.

'Because, my dear boy, his father's hardly likely to want his daughter to marry somebody who lives in a few rooms above a shop, is he? Use your brains, if you have any.'

'What's wrong with Uncle Freddie? He's nice,' Primmy was bitterly resentful of Ben's attitude to them both. 'Uncle Ran says it's what a man is that counts, not what his father gives him.'

Ben's eyes narrowed. 'Really? Uncle Ran seems to figure very frequently in your thinking these days, but an American is hardly in a position to discuss our social system.'

'You don't like anybody, do you, Daddy?' Primmy stated. 'Not Uncle Ran, or Uncle Freddie, or Mother – or us.'

Ben drained his glass and poured another. 'You're talking rubbish. When you're older you'll understand—'

'We understand now.' Walter moved close to her, and Morwen looked at the two of them in astonishment and alarm. They seemed to have grown in stature. She had seen that Walter was growing up fast. She hadn't realized that Primmy was beginning to use all her woman's intuition too. Albert wasn't anxious to leave childhood behind, and Justin and Charlotte seemed like babies compared with these two.

'Well then, my braves,' Ben's voice was heavy with sarcasm. 'Do you think a Lord would want an ex-kiddley-boy for a son-in-law?'

If he hoped to shock them, he failed utterly. How thankful Morwen was now that she had already told the children about the Tremayne background. Walter and Primmy stared back at Ben unblinkingly.

'Why not?' Primmy said. 'Mother married you, and we know what she was. She's still more of a lady than you're a gentleman.'

'Primmy – darling—' Morwen gasped, but she was too late.

Ben was across the room in a few strides. He hit Primmy so hard that she staggered and fell against the piano. The keys reverberated around the room. He looked fit to do murder, but before he could move, he was suddenly leapt upon from behind. Walter caught him off-balance and knocked him to the ground beside the sobbing Primmy. The boy had him by the throat, twisting the neck-cloth and making Ben's eyes bulge.

'If you ever touch my sister again, I'll kill you,' Walter snarled. 'You may be our father, but it doesn't give you the right to behave like an animal when somebody tells you the truth for a change.'

Ben spluttered furiously, but no words came out of his mouth, and Morwen felt a sudden alarm. In those terrible seconds she could see old Charles Killigrew suffering from the stroke, unable to speak and turning from a bull of a man to a pathetic bedridden lump.

'Walter, that's enough!' she shouted, seeing that the boy hardly knew when to stop. Later, he would probably be appalled at himself, and if anything should happen to Ben after this... She pulled Walter away, and the children all crowded together. The family ties were as strong as steel, and, even through the holocaust, Morwen couldn't help being aware of it.

And it was only Ben's pride that was hurt. He got to his feet with an effort, seeing Morwen in front of the group, her arms outstretched. Primmy was still weeping, and Morwen spoke hoarsely.

'Get out of here, Ben, until you're sober. You stink of brandy and God knows what else. And I'll repeat what Walter said. If you ever touch Primmy again – or any of the children – I shall leave this house and take them with me, and you can live with the scandal of it.'

Their eyes met and held. He was strong, but she was stronger. She looked at him unflinchingly out of her blue Tremayne eyes, and in the end he growled something unintelligible, and then went storming out of the room, bellowing back that they'd all have to leave here if their fortunes didn't change direction soon, and if he had to go on the streets, it would be his pleasure to take them with him.

Morwen closed her eyes for a long moment after he had gone. She stood rigidly, before her arms fell to her sides, and she suddenly felt old and beaten. The girls were snivelling behind her now, the younger boys muttering that they hated Ben, and then Walter put his arms around her.

He was taller than she was now, and she hadn't even noticed it happening. He held her like a man comforting a woman, and for a moment she leaned against him, drawing from his strength.

'Don't let him frighten you, Mother.' His voice was thick with emotion. He had surprised himself by his reaction, but he didn't regret it for an instant. 'I'll always take care of you, and he's only taunting us with his threats.'

'We wouldn't really have to go on the streets would we, Mama?' Justin said in a fright. 'We belong here, don't we? Nobody could take Killigrew House away from us, could they?'

'Of course they couldn't, you little snob,' Walter said roughly, before Morwen could reply. 'And if they did, we could always go and live with Uncle Ran, so stop that grizzling.'

Morwen felt the weak tears squeeze out from behind her eyelids at his show of bravado, which proved to her that he wasn't yet a man after all. If he was, he would have understood the sweet impossibility of his own words…

Chapter Fifteen

Strangers weren't usually accepted as readily into local activities as Ran Wainwright had been. There were still a few who spoke of the American suspiciously, but for the most part Ran was well liked for his open manners and genuine interest in the clay-stone quarrying. This was no fly-by-night from up-country England out to make a quick shilling and then disappear. This was an intelligent fellow who listened when they aired their grievances and agreed that their pay should be raised to provide a decent standard of living. This was a man who didn't mind getting his hands dirty in order to understand what went on at the works, and was less temperamental than that Killigrew cousin of his over at St Austell, the old wags said dourly.

And of course, if the Wainwrights and the Killigrews were cousins, then their new boss couldn't be called a total stranger, despite the strange quick accent they couldn't always follow. But family ties created instant bonds between them all.

Ran discovered to his satisfaction that china-stone fetched a consistently high price. While profits from china-clay ebbed and flowed, china-stone remained steady, and companies that produced both had the best of it, using the china-stone reserves as a buffer when times were bad for the clay.

Prosper Barrows should have been in its heyday when Ran took it over from an ailing owner, but the huge deep quarry and the grinding mills had been slowing down merely because the owner's lack of interest had been transferred to the men.

Now, there was a new injection of enthusiasm, and the American owner was not averse to putting advertisements in newspapers and periodicals to advertise the finest Cornish china-stone for sale to genuine clients at competitive rates. The quarry-workers preened themselves on seeing their works displayed so prominently in local advertising and gave Ran of their best because of it.

It was the American way, Ran smilingly told Morwen, when she first exclaimed at seeing the name of Prosper Barrows splashed all over *The Informer.*

'I've seen advertising before, but not quite on this scale,' she commented.

Ran laughed. 'If you've got something to sell, you need to make people aware of it, honey.'

'You also need money to put into the advertising,' she said wryly, and he knew she was thinking of the fortunes of Killigrew Clay.

It would be disastrous for Ben to start speculating at the present time, when it was all he could do to pay off a few debts at a time. The news seemed to be common knowledge in St Austell and Truro now, and Ran could only admire Morwen for the way she held her head high whenever she walked in either town. Her husband's circumstances might be in an appalling state, but no one would ever guess it from Morwen Killigrew's calm features. The more he knew her, the more he loved her, and nothing could change that fact.

'I suppose you're counting the days until Matt comes home now?' he said quickly, and saw her face light up. She had come to Truro to visit Annie, and called in at Ran's fine town office to admire it. The width of his oak desk separated them. He was the elegant successful businessman, she the beautiful wife of a clay boss. They were cousins, but the ties between them went far deeper than that.

'Of course! Only three weeks, and Ben will be so busy right up until then with the spring despatches to get away to Charlestown port.'

She hesitated, then said the real reason she had come to his office. 'Ran – there will be two parties: ours to welcome them to Cornwall, and yours as your housewarming.'

'And you want to keep the distinction between them, do you? Perhaps we should have special cards printed—' he smiled, not understanding.

'No. It's not that. We want ours to be just the family,' she said in a low voice. 'At least – it's what Ben wants.'

His smile faded. 'You mean he doesn't want me in his house? I thought I was family too. What of Louisa? What's she going to think if your husband cuts me so obviously? Believe me, I've no wish to socialize with Ben any more than I have to, but this is being childish and ridiculous.'

'I know it!' Morwen said in misery.

'And am I supposed to leave him out of my invitations as well? Because I shan't. He's welcome at my hearth, Morwen, and I didn't come to Cornwall to make enemies.'

Nor to make love, nor to make this beautiful woman's eyes fill up...

'Ran, I'm just passing on what he said last night. He was in a strange mood. He may change his mind. He's always tense until the clay's safely on board the ships—'

'He's always tense lately,' Ran said drily. 'But I shan't leave it there. It will be an insult to Louisa if she doesn't see me at your house, and Ben must realize that! I shall speak to him. He's no right to make you his go-between.'

'He doesn't know I'm here. He wouldn't like that either.'

For a moment she looked so abject, so lacking in the fiery spirit that made her so uniquely desirable to him, that Ran moved swiftly around to the front of his desk. He caught her hands in his.

'Dearest, I can't bear to see you look so unhappy.'

She pulled her hands away. Not because she didn't want him holding her, but because she wanted it too much.

She wanted *him* too much, and the knowledge of it was suddenly unbearable.

'I must go, Ran. If you leave it until the spring despatches have gone, I'm sure Ben will be more reasonable.'

She turned and went out of the office, suddenly unable to look at him. If she stayed a moment more, she would have been in his arms, and it must not happen. She prayed that Ran would understand, and not think that her feelings had changed because she was so abrupt. If he thought that, he might easily turn to someone else, and Morwen would have lost him as well as Ben. She couldn't have them both, but with Ben the way he was, she sometimes felt already that she had neither.

–

Two weeks later Ben was feeling more expansive than he'd done in months. Some of his debts were paid off, and he was just scraping by. And today, the last of the clay blocks were being loaded on to his railway trucks and being sent to Charlestown port. Clayworkers and bal maidens and kiddley-boys grouped round to watch the last load being hoisted, cheering and dancing and welcoming the spring in their own special way.

''Tis a good load, Ben,' Hal said with quiet pride. 'For all that you had to employ some scaggies to help get it down to the port.'

Ben grunted. It was the only sour note. He'd let off so many men that there weren't enough hands for the final hectic days' work, and he'd agreed to some scaggies coming in and helping out. He despised them all. They were drifters, picking up pennies here and there for whatever work they could find, and fights among them were everyday occurrences. They disrupted settled men and turned the heads of the bal maidens by their bohemian ways.

For once, Ben had allowed the children to come and watch the clay loads leave the works, and saw the way young Albert laughed with the scaggies when they made their raucous jokes. He didn't understand half of it, but the atmosphere had clearly caught hold of him. The scaggies played up to him, and Ben disliked the way Albert responded.

'You children can go home now,' he said sharply. 'Walter, I'm trusting you to take them straight back. Don't dawdle, but you can call into your Grandmother's for a drink, since Hal says she's expecting you.'

He could hardly refuse them that. Walter had barely spoken to his father since the scene at home, and Ben seethed over it. The boy was no longer a child, although he persistently treated him like one. Inside was the fear that Walter would be stronger than himself one day, and there was no charm in that thought.

But he wasn't going to bother with all that now. His clay was on its way to the ship, and his white-dusted workers could be pleased at their efforts. He called out to the children again.

'If you stay at Hal's until I arrive, you can come to the port with me and see the clay being loaded on the ship.'

'I don't want to,' Primmy said sullenly. 'I shall go straight home when I've seen Grandma.'

'So shall I,' Justin said.

'And me,' Charlotte echoed.

Ben scowled. 'What of you two?' he asked Sam's sons.

'We'll come to the port with you, Daddy,' Albert said eagerly. Ben looked enquiringly at Walter, guessing rightly that Walter would be unable to resist seeing the final destination of the clay before it went off for refining for the manufacture of fine tableware.

Ben's rail tracks ended at Charlestown port, from there the clay was loaded into chutes that took it directly into the holds of the waiting tall-masted ships. Some went north to Staffordshire to the potteries. The rest went to more distant destinations, to France and Spain.

The negotiations between Killigrew Clay and these countries were coveted by Ben, having gained the concession in fierce competition with Bultimore & Vine's clayworks several years back. It was a French ship awaiting the last load of blocks in early April, a good load from which Ben expected to make a fair profit once the blocks were safely delivered. And a few more debts could be paid off.

The scaggies accompanied the rail trucks on their journey, sitting astride the blocks like lords of the manor. Ben rode alongside, hoping that Walter and Albert wouldn't loiter with Bess. It was a fine sight to see the end product of sweat and toil, and the eight long months drying of the clay in the winter damp.

He remembered his father once saying it was like giving birth. All the hard work was done, and the child was about to be safely delivered… and while the scaggies were unloading, Ben intended paying a visit to Daniel Gorran to report the good tonnage of the spring despatches. It was a satisfying showing, the news of it might stop Daniel looking so all-fired gloomy the minute he saw Ben Killigrew, and could only do good for his precarious reputation.

–

'Why don't you come to the port, Justin?' Walter asked the youngest boy when they had had their fill of Bess's seed cake and lemonade and were back in the cart.

'Because it's messy and horrible and the seamen push you about,' Justin said belligerently.

Walter laughed contemptuously, knowing he'd goad him into some such reply.

'You're a soft egg, Justin. You're better off with the girls. I'm surprised you don't wear their skirts.'

'Don't be beastly, Walter,' Primmy defended her younger brother angrily. 'If Justin doesn't want to go to the port, he needn't. You can leave us at the gates of the house and we'll walk the rest of the way, thank you.'

She was cool and distant to him, though she was fonder of him than she ever let on, and she would never forget how he had championed her with their father. But Primmy kept her feelings very private. If she didn't, she'd reveal how much she agreed with Walter. Justin was a softie, and she really didn't like him much. But that was so wicked, that she never let on about that either, and made up for it by being especially nice to him.

The older boys left the others at the gates of Killigrew House and Walter jerked the reins of the horse to take them the short distance to the port. He was adept at controlling any horse now, whether he was on horseback or in this small cart, or even one of the carriages, when he could persuade Ben or one of the drivers to let him take the reins. Walter wanted to be best at everything. It was a compulsion he couldn't explain, but one that he knew was important to him. He needed to prove himself.

He felt a personal pride in watching the clay blocks hurtle down the chutes into the waiting ship. The clay was part of him. He felt it as surely as he breathed, and not just from an owner's stance. Ben was the owner, but Walter felt much nearer to the heart of the clay, like his grandfather Hal. He would never dare try to explain such a feeling to Ben, who would think he was going queer in the head.

'Hey there, young Killigrews,' one of the scaggies called out jeeringly. 'Want to try your hands at shoving some o' these blocks down the chute?'

'I wish we could,' Walter muttered. 'But Father would have our hides—'

'Why can't we?' Albert said at once. 'It would get the job finished sooner.'

'All right.' Walter became reckless as the scaggies continued to throw ribald remarks their way. 'Father's not about, so let's do it.'

They tied up the horse and scrambled over the piles of ropes and rubbish at the quay. The scaggies cheered, showing the boys where to heave the blocks and tip them into the dark hold, where the clouds of clay dust rose to gag their throats and sting their eyes. The scaggies whistled while they worked, muscles straining and bodies reeking of sweat, and the seamen joined in the bawdy laughter at the sight of the two young gentlemen dirtying their hands and clothes and seeming to enjoy it all.

The load was almost complete when Albert leaned forward too far in order to see how the black hole was filling up with clay blocks. One minute he was shouting to Walter to come and see how far down the ship sat in the water now with all the extra weight. The next minute the shout turned to a scream of terror as he lost his balance and plunged head first down the chute.

'*Albert!*' Walter screamed back. He scrabbled to the edge of the quay, peering downwards. He could see nothing in the chute, and he could hear only an ominous silence. He turned blindly to be held fast by the nearest seaman.

'Steady, *mon brave*,' the man spoke in a strange, halting accent. He stunk of garlic as his arms strove to stop Walter struggling out of them.

'My brother's down there! He'll be suffocated,' he screamed. 'We've got to him out!'

'Not you, *mon petit*. The others will find him, but don't worry. He'll be black and blue, but not dead.'

Walter shuddered. Putting such thoughts into words made them terrifyingly real. And what if Albert *were* dead? Their father would blame him for not looking after him. He was the eldest, and would take all the blame. He felt a cold sweat run down his back and into his groin.

'What's happening here?'

Walter heard Ben's bellowing voice. He had been so stunned for the last few minutes he'd been unaware of all the commotion around him; the scaggies shouting, and the French seamen on board the ship getting access to the hold. With Ben's arrival, everybody seemed to shout at once, and Walter felt himself cringe with fear at the look on his father's face.

'If the boy's hurt badly, I'll hold you responsible,' Ben ground out, just as Walter had known he would.

They brought him out carefully. By then, Doctor Pender had been sent for, and Ben wondered if he would have need of his services himself. For the first time, he was aware of a searing pain in his chest, and knew that the London doctor's warning wasn't an idle one. Until now, he had ignored it. He hadn't visited Doctor Pender, nor made the slightest concession to ill-health. But now, as he saw them bring out Albert's limp form, he knew he was only mortal after all. He waited, hushed with all the rest, while the doctor leaned over his son, trying not to listen to Walter's ragged beathing beside him.

'He's not dead,' the doctor pronounced at last. 'He's concussed, and he'll have bruises the size of oranges tomorrow. I can't find anything broken, but he'll be badly shocked when he comes round, and he'll need complete rest for a week.'

The groups of men cheered, and Walter felt as though he had just run up a mountain and back as he let out his breath.

'Can I take him home?' Ben asked sharply.

Doctor Pender glanced at him. 'Are you all right?'

'Of course I am. It's Albert who's the patient, not me,' he snapped.

They lifted Albert gently into the cart, and Ben took the reins to take him home. He told Walter to ride on ahead on Ben's horse and prepare Morwen, and to see that hot water bottles were put into Albert's bed. After that, he looked stonily away from his eldest son, and Walter knew that the reckoning was still to come.

-

When the girls had done their crying and Morwen had been assured a dozen times that concussion wasn't anything to worry about, and Albert had finally come round and weakly demanded food, Ben ordered Walter to the study. When they came out later, there were weals on Walter's back and his eyes were red-rimmed but he had stoically refused to cry. It was the first and last time his father would take a strap to him, he vowed.

And later, in his own room, when he undressed and tenderly touched the raw patches on his back, the tears flowed. He knew it was unmanly, but he wasn't yet a man, and the one thing he wanted out of life was the thing that was seemingly unattainable. He needed his father's love and approval, and for some reason it seemed the last thing that Ben Killigrew was able to give him.

–

They took it in turns to sit with Albert. He recovered quickly, and was soon acting the little hero, and it was Walter who took longer to recover from the beating, physically and mentally. But none of the others knew the truth of that. They could only guess why Walter winced and moved so stiffly, and was more silent than usual.

Ben was surprisingly gentle with Albert, not blaming him for the accident, and the boy took every advantage of it.

'Can I have anything I want, Father?' Albert said on the fourth day.

'Nobody can have everything they want, Albert,' Ben reproved him. Morwen was sitting quietly by the window, and paused over her sewing at the odd request. 'But in moderation, perhaps. What is it that's so necessary to you?'

Albert drew a deep breath.

'I want to see Uncle Ran. Why hasn't he come to visit me, Daddy? Walter said it's because of all the fuss, but I miss him. He'll be coming to the party for Uncle Matt, won't he? Walter says he doesn't know about that either—' He prattled on and on, making things worse, digging deeper and deeper.

'Walter seems to do a great deal of talking out of turn,' Ben retorted.

'He means no harm,' Morwen spoke up in defence. 'And 'tis such a little thing for Albert to ask, and such a big gesture for you to make, Ben. 'Twill put things right, and save any unpleasantness. Families shouldn't be split like this.'

Ben looked at her for a long moment. She wanted to go to him and put her arms around him, and beg him not to be so hard, so unlike her Ben… but the moment passed and she remained exactly where she was as he nodded grudgingly.

'Then we'd best not spoil a family reunion, had we? All right, he can come and visit and come to the party, but you needn't expect me to be civil to him.'

'Ben, you *must*—'

He looked at Morwen with open hostility. 'No woman tells me what I must do. All the same, I may reconsider that remark. Nobody accuses Ben Killigrew of being uncouth either.'

She was thankful when he left the bedroom. She didn't press it further nor refer to it again. It was enough that he'd unbent far enough to allow Ran to visit. Albert missed him. All the children missed him. And oh, she missed him too… so much…

–

He came to Killigrew House as soon as he received word that Albert was eager to see him. Ben greeted him cautiously, but Ran was streets ahead of him in gentility, and conversed with him as if there had never been bad feeling between them. It was Ran who soothed the way, and Morwen was immensely grateful for his tact. She took him up to Albert's room and was touched by the way the boy's eyes lit up at the sight of the handsome American.

'I can't wait for my new cousin to come, Uncle Ran,' Albert said excitedly. 'I shall take Cresswell and show him the stables and the beach, and everything!' He waved his hands about expansively, wincing a little where the bruises still hurt, and Ran spoke with mild reproof.

'Just as long as you don't go showing him any clay chutes. You know you were very lucky, don't you, Albie?'

The boy pulled a face. 'I know Daddy's never stopped telling me what an idiot I was! How long do you think it'll be before he stops being so angry with me?'

'He's only angry because he's concerned for you.'

'Do you think so?' Albert said doubtfully. 'It seems a funny way to care for anybody, to be angry with them all the time. You never get angry with me, do you?'

Ran laughed. 'I might, if I lived with you all the time and you did crazy things.'

'No, you wouldn't,' Albert said positively. 'You're different. Sometimes I wish you were my Daddy.'

Ran got up from the bed. 'Now, you musn't say things like that, Albert. It's not right. Your father does what's best for you, and you must remember that.'

'All right, Uncle Ran,' he replied meekly.

Morwen cleared her throat. 'I'm taking Uncle Ran downstairs to have some tea now. He must be parched after riding over here and coming straight up to see you. He can come back upstairs later,' she forestalled the question.

Outside the bedroom, she closed the door and leaned against it for a moment, her eyes distressed as she looked into Ran's eyes.

'Some day they'll have to be told that Ben's not their father,' she murmured. 'I can't face the telling, Ran, yet I feel strongly that we shouldn't hold it off for much longer. I dread the outcome of it.'

He longed to hold her close and kiss away all the uncertainty, but there were people downstairs, and there was only the width of a door between them and Albert.

'I'm sure you'll have nothing to worry about if you tell it calmly, my dearest.' He spoke quietly so that no one would hear. 'You coped with telling them half the story, and the rest needn't be so terrible if you choose your moment well.'

She wasn't convinced. Something deep inside told her the children should be told now, before they heard the truth from outside. There were people in the town who knew… but so far no news of it had reached the children's ears. And they never came into contact with the clayworkers, none of whom would have forgotten the disaster that resulted in Sam Tremayne's death, his wife's untimely death a few weeks later, and the adoption of the three orphaned children by Ben Killigrew and his wife.

She had to admit that St Austell didn't particularly concern itself with the doings of moorland folk, and that by now the circumstances would have been forgotten by most. And although only a few miles separated the town from the clay-workings, they might have been oceans apart.

Morwen consoled herself uneasily with the thought that Ran was right. She must choose her time well, but it must be soon. Perhaps when Matt and his family had been for their visit, and they were all feeling relaxed and happy. And hopefully, Ben would join in the excitement, and the telling would be made that much easier with his support.

She gave up worrying and enjoyed the rest of the day with Ran's company and tried not to compare the atmosphere in the house with the way it was when Ben was prowling about in one of his foul moods. She tried to make allowances. She couldn't blame him for being on edge all the time after the doctor's pronouncement, and she was half-beginning to wonder if it was all nonsense after all. Ben seemed perfectly well, if she discounted his recent gambling fever and the bouts of drinking that frequently left him sprawling on his bed in a stupor.

Doctors could be wrong. Hadn't Jack and Annie proved? With great care, Annie was going to survive this pregnancy. Ben could survive too, given reasonable luck, and when he realized he wasn't about to die, perhaps he would relax and be her old Ben once more. Morwen tried desperately to recapture the glow of such a thought, and knew with a great sadness that it would never come again. They had already lost too much, and she was already too much in love with Randell Wainwright.

All she could give Ben now was loyalty, and she owed him that. She had been unfaithful once, and perhaps she continued to be unfaithful in spirit, but that was something Ben must never know. And when Matt came home, things would surely be better for everyone. Perhaps it was foolish to set such a store by Matt's homecoming, but foolish or not, she undoubtedly saw Matt as the catalyst to make everything come right again.

Chapter Sixteen

Morwen awoke early on a fine mid-April morning, and in her first sleep-hazed moments, she couldn't quite remember what it was that was so stupendous. She experienced the delicious, not-quite-aware feeling that she hadn't felt for years. It was a feeling that didn't happen too often, and therefore made it all the more special.

Like the day after Ben Killigrew had told her he loved her, and she had still found it almost impossible to believe.

Like her wedding-day, knowing that this day was going to change the rest of her life and she had gone to meet Ben at Penwithick church with flowers in her hair and love in her heart.

Like the day their son was born… and she had given Ben what he wanted most in the world, after her.

And now the feeling was here again, tingling through her veins as she stretched into wakefulness and remembered joyfully that this was the day Matt was coming home. She tried to imagine just how her mother must be feeling this morning. Bess, who loved all her children equally… but loved her wayward Matt just a little bit more…

Before Morwen could wallow too deeply in nostalgia, the girls had come bursting through into her bedroom.

'Primmy says I can't wear my new dress yet, Mama,' Charlotte howled. 'Uncle Ran says I look as pretty as a flower in it. *Why* can't I wear it, Mama?'

'I only said she had to keep it for the party, that's all,' Primmy said, affronted, as Charlotte climbed on the bed and was immediately wrapped in Morwen's comforting arms. Charlotte still smelled of sleep, and at six years old, hadn't yet lost the chubby softness of childhood.

'Primmy's right, darling,' Morwen said gently. 'We'll all want to look our best at the party, won't we? And it's only one more day to wait. We must give Uncle Matt time to get over the journey, and tomorrow evening we'll all be dressed in our finery, and you'll both be my prettiest girls in your new dresses.'

She was careful to include Primmy. Bess had insisted on making new dresses for all her girls, and had been working diligently on them ever since the news of Matt's homecoming was announced. Dresses for Morwen and Primmy and Charlotte, and for Annie, whose dress had to be let out even before it was finished, and the twins, Sarah and Tessa. At the last minute, at Morwen's insistence, Bess had found time to make herself a new dress.

She was such an accomplished seamstress that they would all do credit to Killigrew House. The image flashed into Morwen's head of another time when her family had all been gauche guests in this very house, the first time she had set foot inside it.

It had been her seventeenth birthday, and the humble Tremaynes had been included in one of Charles Killigrew's evening occasions after the last of the spring despatches had been sent careering through the steep streets of St Austell in the loaded clay waggons, long before Ben's railway was built. And Morwen had been so excited over the second-hand muslin dress that her Mammie had decorated with silk ribbons.

And later she had been mortified to discover she was among a company dressed in fine silks and satins, not the least among them the beautiful golden girl she was convinced Ben Killigrew was going to marry, Jane Carrick, who had eventually run away to marry the newspaperman, Tom Askhew.

It was all a long time ago, but the memory was as sharp as ever. And tomorrow it was her birthday again, and there was to be another party at Killigrew House. And Morwen Tremayne was no longer the humble girl dressed in muslin, but the mistress of the house who would be wearing a beautiful blue satin gown to match her eyes. And she wouldn't be seventeen years old, blushing at birthday kisses, but a wife and mother of thirty-two. The thought gave her a small shock.

'Mama, aren't you ever getting up?' Charlotte wailed, now that she had been mollified. 'The boys are already downstairs, and I'm hungry, and isn't it time to go soon?'

Morwen laughed, shaking off the little silent ghosts that plagued her.

'All right. Let's go and have some breakfast. I don't know how long we may have to wait for the ship to arrive at Falmouth, and we can't have you starving, can we?'

She was smiling now, for this was no day to be sad or regretful. This was the best day of her life so far…

-

By the middle of the morning, the entire family was gathered on the quayside at Falmouth, straining their eyes for the first glimpse of the ship that would bring Matt Tremayne home to Cornwall. Ben and Morwen had brought the three older children with them. Hal and Bess came in their modest trap after all, bringing the younger ones, for Ran would need his transport to take the American Tremaynes and their luggage to Killigrew House. It had taken some sorting out, but it all added to the heady excitement of the planning that had culminated in this wonderful day.

And Ben had at last shaken off the irritability of recent months. He seemed to be enjoying all this as much as anyone, and Morwen gave a silent prayer of thankfulness. They had been joined by Jack and Annie and the twins, and Freddie, handsome and elegant, with a young lady stepping out of his trap and clinging to his arm. This then, was the Honourable Venetia Hocking.

Morwen felt swift sympathy for Freddie, knowing her youngest brother so well. This was the least embarrassing way of introducing Venetia to his family. Without formality, when all of them were too taken up with the day's important happening to be too over-awed at the lady's status.

But from the moment Freddie made the swift introductions, Morwen realized that what he said about Venetia's father being only recently made a Lord through an accident of kinship, was obviously true. The girl had a soft accent like her own, and seemed more nervous of meeting this large family than the rest of them were of meeting her.

The tables had turned, Morwen thought. Venetia was the odd one out for the moment, like Morwen had once been. She was very secure now in her place among the Tremaynes and the Killigrews, and she spoke with a special warmth to the titian-haired girl.

'We've heard a lot about you, Venetia.' She addressed her simply. 'Has Freddie asked you to come to the party tomorrow night? You'll be very welcome.'

'I would like to,' the girl said shyly. 'But are you sure I won't be intruding on a family occasion, Mrs Killigrew?'

'Of course not. And my name is Morwen.'

Again that little echo from the past. Jane Carrick, splendid and serene compared with the awkward bal maiden, and telling her quietly that her name was Jane. Morwen seemed beset by echoes of the past today, but perhaps it was only to be expected. The past had a habit of overlapping into the present, and especially on days like these... she gave a small smile. As if such spectacular days happened that often! This was one to savour, and to cry over a little, if need be...

'I saw someone you used to know the other day, Ben,' Freddie remarked later. By now, the children had begun to tire of waiting for a ship that was dependent on winds and tides and seemed as if it would never come, and were now racing about, to the despair of the grown-ups.

'Oh? Who was that?' he said carelessly.

'Jane Carrick – Askhew, I should say now, of course. Her husband's gone on some foreign jaunt for his newspaper, so she's in Cornwall on a prolonged visit with her daughter.'

Hearts didn't really leap, Morwen told herself furiously. It was just an expression. They stayed firmly in one place inside the rib-cage. And if they didn't actually leap, then did this searing jealousy running through her at the idle mention of her old rival's name, mean that she was still in love with her husband after all? How could Freddie have chosen this very day to bring such irritating news!

But of course Freddie had been too young to know how certain Morwen had been that Ben couldn't really be in love with a clayworker's daughter. That his destiny had been with Jane Carrick of Truro, and Morwen Tremayne was going to be merely a dalliance… Freddie had never known of the jealousy that had tormented her on Jane Carrick's account…

'Perhaps we'll see something of her then,' Ben was casual, as if the news meant little to him. 'You must invite her to tea one afternoon, Morwen.'

'Yes, of course.'

Just don't suggest that she comes to tomorrow night's party, she thought heatedly. The moments passed, and Ben didn't mention it. She sighed with relief, knowing how foolish she was to let old feuds cast a cloud on today.

At last there were excited shouts from the children, and they were carried forward with the rest of the expectant people on the quay as the long-awaited ship was sighted.

They pressed towards the big basin of the harbour. The ship gradually edged nearer to the mooring awaiting its arrival, and they could see the decks crowded with passengers. They couldn't make out anyone yet, and the sun was blinding their eyes, or perhaps it was pent-up emotion that was making some of them smart a little. Morwen saw her mother grope for a handkerchief, and her own throat was thick. They had waited so long for this moment, and it was almost here.

'I can see our Matt. Look there, by the railings!' Hal shouted, once the ship was tied up, and the passengers began to emerge on to solid ground. At least, it was meant to be a shout.

To his own ears, his voice was thick and hoarse, and at last, at long last, Hal admitted how very much this moment meant to him too. He had been the strong one for too many years, keeping silent over his own sadness at Matt's hasty departure from Cornwall. All the amends the boy had made in later years, sending gifts of money and making his peace with his family, hadn't changed the agony Hal felt at Matt's leaving. The sense of betrayal, of loss… but somehow it was all wiped out in a single moment, and, for one instant, it seemed that there was no one else there but the two of them. He looked at his boy, whom he had never thought to see again, and the moment of recognition was charged with emotion and forgiveness and love.

Morwen felt shock ripple through her. It was Matt. Oh, it was undoubtedly Matt, her dearest one… and of course she had expected a change in him. He had gone away a boy, and was coming home a man. But she had never tried to picture him changed. To her, Matt was always the handsomest of the Tremayne boys, with dreaming blue eyes and a way of listening attentively when anyone talked, as if intensely interested in all that was being said.

He was still handsome. God, but he was, too! What she hadn't expected was that he would be so like Sam. It was uncanny. Jack and Freddie had developed their own characteristics over the years, but Matt… Morwen swallowed dryly. The sea breeze ruffled Matt's dark hair in the old unruly way of the Tremayne boys.

And it was as if time had stood still, and the Sam who had died in the railway accident had suddenly come to life again, more elegant and clearly well-to-do, but unmistakably *Sam*…

'Are you all right, Morwen?' It was Ran who murmured beside her, holding her elbow and bringing warmth back to her skin. Ben was trying to control the younger children.

'Yes. It's just ghosts,' she said quickly. She glanced at her mother. How must Bess feel, seeing the reincarnation of Sam… and her father, to whom Sam had always been the echo of himself…?

There was none of Morwen's reaction on the faces of her parents. No horror, no signs of collapse or weeping, other than happy tears. Was she the only one who saw it, then? Morwen felt faint, finally accepting the inescapable.

But there was no time to ponder on things that she couldn't explain, and the small terror passed as soon as Matt was thrusting forward, hugging and kissing every one of his family, those he knew and those he didn't, but who were all a part of him. He held Morwen away from him for just an instant, and there was only love between them. No ghosts, no past regrets, nothing but Matt coming home.

'You've grown so beautiful!' he said, in the new accent that was half Ran's, half clinging to his roots. 'I always knew you would, and I didn't need Ran's letters to assure me of the fact. Ever since he came here, I've wanted to come too. I was so jealous of his being here with you all.'

'Oh, Matt, 'tis so wonderful to see you. I just can't believe 'tis really you—' the words bubbled out, and the tears turned to laughter as she thought how foolish they must all look, holding one another and laughing and crying, and taking so much time to be reacquainted that folk must wonder if they were arriving or leaving.

There were so many introductions to be made with all the new members of the family. And there was Louisa, whom Morwen loved at once, and Cresswell, whom the children hated on sight.

–

They finally got away from Falmouth for the joyous journey home. They pointed out Ran's house on the way, stopping the carriages for a few minutes before returning in triumph to Killigrew House. At least, that was how Morwen saw it. The prodigal son had returned, and was more deeply loved by everyone. Bess seemed totally content now, and the lines of age seemed to have dropped from Hal's face. The American Tremaynes were to stay for a month, and it seemed an endless time stretching ahead of them, with the mellow golden days of a Cornish spring beckoning.

Morwen showed the visitors their rooms while the rest of the family were relaxing and chattering excitedly below, and Mrs Horn and the maids bustled about with refreshments.

'It's all just darling, Morwen,' Louisa said happily. 'I can't tell you how happy I am to be here. I've wanted to meet you for so long, and Ran's told us so much about you I feel that I already know my sister.'

Morwen warmed to her at once. She was pretty and vivacious and given to plumpness, but it was clear that she and Matt simply adored each other. She gave her a quick hug.

'I'm so happy that you've come,' she said with a catch in her throat. 'All of you.' She included Matt's wife and son in the welcome. Louisa smiled, understanding.

'Come, Cresswell, and help Mother unpack the presents. I think the valise will be in your room by now.'

The two of them went out, with Cresswell scowling. He'd much rather have stayed in California where his friends were, than come to this miserable little country full of people who talked so strangely, and children who had seemed to herd together when he looked at them, as though he were an alien. He didn't like travel. His stomach was infuriatingly delicate, which he knew was unmanly, and he was still queasy from the long journey and felt anything but sociable. He also knew very well he was about to get a lecture from his mother on the subject...

–

The two people left behind in the best guest-room knew or cared nothing of this. Matt held Morwen at arm's length, his eyes smiling down at her.

'Let me look at you, Morwen. You have no idea how often I've pictured this moment.'

'I too,' she murmured. 'And Mammie never even dared to dream that you'd come home again. It's been a long time, Matt.'

'Too long,' he admitted. 'I know it, and I intend to make up for it by spending as much time as possible with her, and with all of you.' The smile broke through the seriousness again. 'You've all changed, of course. Older, and yet still the same. Freddie's the surprising one, but of course, he was just a sprig when I left. He's like Sam.'

'Yes,' she said softly, her face betraying none of the emotion at realizing it was Matt who was and yet wasn't Sam, but who was essentially himself. It was an illusion, no more…

'Are you happy, our Morwen?' The voice was suddenly the old Matt's, softer than his brother's, speaking in the old way, the Cornish dialect as rich as cream.

'Happy?' she said huskily. 'Why shouldn't I be happy? I've got everything I ever wanted.'

It wasn't a direct answer and it seemed as though he looked into her eyes, through them and into her soul, knowing everything. She had never been able to keep secrets from Matt.

She gave him a quick hug as she heard Louisa and Cresswell coming back with the large bag full of packages. Brother and sister broke apart as awkwardly as if they were lovers, and Morwen knew there were secrets that not even Matt must know to spoil his visit. No one else must know of the intimate troubles between her and Ben, nor of the business worries, and especially not of Ben's uncertain health.

'We had a wonderful time shopping for all of you, Morwen,' Louisa said now. 'I just hope you'll like the gifts we've brought.'

Morwen gave her sister-in-law a hug as well.

'The best gift is just all of you being here. But I know the children will be excited at the thought of presents when it's nobody's birthday, so shall we go down, if you're ready? There will be tea and cake waiting downstairs.'

'It's your birthday soon, isn't it, Morwen?' Matt said.

'Tomorrow,' she smiled. 'I wasn't going to embarrass you by mentioning it, but I see how daft that was, when everybody else will know it! We're having a party tomorrow night, but it's for you more than me, to celebrate your visit.'

'We came here once before to a party, remember?' Matt said. 'Ben kissed you when his father teased him into it, and his awful aunt was trying to get the better of you, as I recall. I could have told her then that nobody gets the better of Morwen Tremayne!'

'And you were so thick with Jude Pascoe, and I was all fingers and thumbs because Jane Carrick made me feel out of place.' The words came quickly, without thinking, and suddenly none of it mattered, because the Tremaynes had found their place after all, and today Morwen and Matt could laugh together over the memories.

'Can we go downstairs, Mother?' Cresswell said petulantly. 'I'd like some tea for my stomach.'

'Of course, honey,' she said at once. She looked at Morwen. 'He needs something to settle it. You understand.'

'Of course. Can Mrs Horn mix you a powder or something, Cresswell?'

'There's no need, thank you, Aunt Morwen,' he said. 'Some weak tea will be most acceptable, though.'

Morwen almost smiled at the exaggerated good manners, and then she saw that he wasn't being clever or precocious just to impress her. It was the way he was. Far older, in ways, than Justin, who seemed such a child beside him, yet they were the same age. Already Morwen sensed that he was an oddly remote boy. It was probably due to his being an only child, Morwen thought generously, meaning to make him doubly welcome and able to fit into this large and loving family.

Louisa put her hand on Morwen's arm as they all went downstairs, Matt carrying the heavy valise.

'This means so much to Matt, Morwen,' she whispered. 'He's talked of his family so often that it was obvious how much he missed you all.'

'Yet he never came home before.' She tried not to make it sound like a censure.

Louisa shook her head. 'Somehow the time was never right. We had the business to build up, and then my parents needed us in their later years. Cresswell's schooling was important too. Well, you're a woman, Morwen, you know how these things take up time, until before you know it a whole decade has gone.'

Morwen supposed these things were important. Of course she knew about them, being the wife of a businessman… but she had been a clayworker's daughter before she was a lady, and family ties had always been the most important of all, and Matt was part of them. Losing him had been like losing a limb. She caught herself up short. Was she being totally selfish? Louisa had been talking about her family too, and her ties were just as strong. The small antagonism passed, and she gave the other girl an answering squeeze around the waist.

'I know exactly what you mean,' she said, and walked downstairs with her arm still around her new sister-in-law, to be absorbed into the family.

–

Charlotte was bouncing on her bed again early the next morning. Morwen felt as though it was still yesterday, and half-wished that it was, because the expectation of something wonderful was almost as exciting as the real thing, and this morning her head felt as if it had been put through the mangle.

'Everybody's awake, and we all want to get up,' Charlotte shouted. 'You have to come down right now, Mama.'

Morwen groaned. 'Must I?' she said, wanting to snuggle down beneath the bedcovers for a few more precious minutes.

Primmy came rushing in as well.

'Please, Mother!' she was using the grown-up term more and more now. It was a little thing, but it pushed her further away from the dependence of childhood. They were all growing up, Morwen thought with a little pang… she sat up carefully.

She had drunk too much wine last night while they all sat and gossiped until the last of the family went home in the early hours of the morning, and her head spun. There was something she should remember about today, but for the moment it escaped her. The girls were giggling together like two small conspirators. She threw off the covers, knowing she would get no more peace. She pulled a dressing-robe over her nightgown and followed them down to the dining-room.

She was halfway down the curving staircase when she remembered. It was her birthday and neither of the girls had come in singing their usual greeting. They must have forgotten in the excitement of last night. It didn't matter.

They reached the dining-room door and threw it open. And Morwen saw immediately that no one had forgotten. A chorus of greetings welcomed her, and the room was filled with laughter at the astonishment on her face. The five children, and Matt and Louisa and Cresswell, and Ben, smiling more naturally than she had seen him in weeks… and in the middle of the table an enormous facsimile of a birthday cake that she knew would be there tonight. A 'cake' of piled high breakfast muffins and toast, and in the centre, 'candles' of softened and rolled porridge oats stuck into waxed paper holders.

'We did it all ourselves,' Charlotte shouted. 'The boys made the cake, and Primmy and me made the candles, Mama. It's an early present. Do you like it?'

Morwen ignored Cresswell's continuing incredulous smile at the extraordinarily naïve efforts of these exuberant Cornish children.

'It's the best birthday cake I've ever had,' she said, unbearably touched, and kissed each one of them.

'You thought we'd forgotten, didn't you, Mother?' Justin said gleefully. 'I told Charlotte we'd all sit on her if she dared to let you guess.'

'He would have done it too,' Ben put in, giving his son a playful cuff around the head.

This was the best gift of all, Morwen thought. Ben was behaving like any other husband and father, indulging his children's secrets to please their mother. He even kissed Morwen lightly on the forehead and wished her a happy birthday. No one watching them would have thought that they were more usually virtual strangers in the same house.

She knew it was all a charade, or a kind of truce for Matt's benefit, but she didn't care. It was enough that he was considerate enough to do this, to give her the dignity of feeling loved and a part of her husband's life. Guiltily, she knew it didn't change her feelings for him.

She could never recapture that old heady feeling of magic that had existed between her and Ben, and for the moment, this tolerance between them was all she asked.

–

And tonight they were having a party. Earlier, Morwen had heard the boys arguing over who was going to show Cresswell around the town of St Austell, but in the end it didn't matter, because Cresswell had decided to spend the morning in bed, reading. Morwen suspected that his weak stomach was a perfect excuse for anything he didn't want to do.

'I don't think I like him very much, Mother,' Primmy confided after lunch. They had gone upstairs together to catch the hem of Primmy's dress where she had caught her heel in it.

'You mustn't say that, darling. You don't know him. He'll be feeling very excluded being on his own, and we must do our best to make him feel welcome.'

Primmy frowned. 'But he doesn't want to feel welcome. He won't agree to any suggestion we make. And he's so pompous and superior.'

Morwen sighed. She felt that too. It seemed so difficult for Cresswell to unbend. He wasn't at all like Matt in his ways, who had always been so easy-going. It seemed that Cresswell's strict and exclusive boarding-school had succeeded in making a man of him long before he was ready, and he didn't quite know how to deal with it in the company of other children.

'I'm sure he'll start to relax soon,' Morwen said helplessly. 'Meanwhile, you must try to like him—'

'Why?'

'Well, because he's your cousin. He's part of the family. Don't be silly, Primmy.'

She looked resentful. 'It's not silly. I don't see why we have to like people just because they're family. They can still be stupid and horrid, and I think Cresswell Tremayne is a spiteful little prig, if you must know.'

'Primmy!' Morwen was annoyed now at the vindictiveness in her voice. 'You've no reason to talk like that—'

'Yes I have. He was arguing with Walter about the clayworks when we were in the nursery, and said that clay was poor stuff compared with the gold company his father owned. And *his* family were far superior to ours, because they could eat off gold plates if they wanted to.' She snorted. 'What rubbish he talks. I hate him, Mother.'

She had said it now, and she didn't care. Morwen had finished mending the tear in the girl's dress, and bit off the cotton thread with growing anger. Her voice wasn't raised, but Primmy was quite aware of the warning in every deliberate word.

'Primmy, you will never let me hear you say anything like that again. While your cousin is our guest you will be polite at all times, and considerate of the fact that he's a stranger in this country. Do you understand me?'

'Yes, Mother,' Primmy said sullenly.

'And you will go immediately, and convey what I've said to your brothers and sister.' Morwen's voice was icy now at the sarcasm in the girl's tone. 'Nothing must be allowed to disrupt the happiness of this visit, and I demand that you all remember it. Is that quite clear?'

Primmy flounced off without answering, and Morwen was tempted to call her back and box her ears. But that would make her all the more resentful against Cresswell, and this was a situation she had never anticipated. She hoped fervently that it was only temporary.

Chapter Seventeen

Primmy had evidently reported Morwen's words to the others and they all realized she meant them. Morwen heard the repeated attempts to draw Cresswell into their activities, and his constant rebuffs. She felt a swift sympathy for her own, reluctantly agreeing that Cresswell was really a most difficult child to like. But she would never reveal her feelings. It would be too awful if Matt and Louisa ever guessed, and certainly Jack and Annie seemed to find the boy interesting enough at the party that evening when they were listening to his tales about California and the excitement of a gold-mining town.

'I once thought about going to America,' Freddie murmured to the girl by his side on the large sofa. He was merely testing her reaction, and her reply was eminently satisfying.

'Oh, no Freddie. Oh, I do hope you're not serious. I'd never see you again!'

He smiled teasingly into Venetia's grey eyes.

'And would that matter to you?'

'You know it would.' She blushed, the soft swell of her breasts relaxing a little inside the creamy silk dress she wore.

Freddie spoke softly. 'That's all I wanted to know. Do you think I'd go anywhere now, where I couldn't take 'ee with me?'

He was suddenly feeling ten feet tall. Venetia Hocking was the most beautiful girl he had ever seen, and she was as much head over heels in love with him as he was with her. He knew her father for a plain man, for all his new status, and he'd be perfectly happy to give his daughter in marriage to a decent man with a good living.

There was only one thing preventing Freddie asking her right away, sweeping her off her feet and making her his bride before spring was out. He still didn't know if he was capable of doing what he should. He respected Venetia too much to anticipate the marriage bed, but he went cold every time he thought of failure. The humiliation would be too great, but he was as innocent as any of the Killigrew boys when it came to lying with a woman. He knew the mechanics, but not the reality.

And the more he thought of performing well on his wedding night, the more there seemed to him only one way to perfect the art. He must get tuition from an expert.

'Come on, you two love-birds, and join in the games,' Morwen called across to them. 'Our Freddie, you're all red in the face. Have you been drinking too much champagne already?'

'I daresay,' he agreed laughingly, wondering what they would all think if they knew he'd just been picturing himself lying with a whore to learn the rudiments of fornicating.

He allowed Venetia and himself to be pulled into the centre of the circle where they were all about to play charades. He loved all his big-hearted family, but now he loved Venetia more than any of them. Not more, perhaps, but differently... He caught his mother looking speculatively at him, and wondered if she could tell what his thoughts had been. No, Freddie dismissed the idea. If anybody could tell, it would be Morwen, and she was too busy entertaining Matt and Louisa and Cresswell, and Ran as well, who was livelier than of late, with his own kin around him.

Did Ran Wainwright never feel the need of a woman? Freddie's thoughts kept going off at tangents. He felt the familiar stirring in his loins that never seemed to come to anything, and decided desperately that his tuition had best be soon if he wanted to make Venetia his bride without feeling as futile as a eunuch.

There were whorehouses to be found along every waterfront. Freddie Tremayne picked his with care. Not in Truro, where he was well-known, nor even in St Austell, where the family likeness might be recognized. A week later, he locked up his chandlery shop and rode off towards Falmouth. Nobody knew him there, and in such a busy port, with seamen arriving and departing all the time, there was bound to be everything he required.

He was doing all this for Venetia, he reminded himself. For the girl he loved… though some might think it a peculiar mission to be frequenting a house of ill-repute in order to prove to himself that he was capable of a man's most important act. Peculiar or not, it was perfectly logical to Freddie, and that was all that counted.

The horror of years past could still haunt him. He had been innocent of the lewdness of sexuality that was unnatural and frightening to a vulnerable child.

For a long while it hadn't mattered physically. He was still a boy then, and had years of growing-up ahead of him. But now he was a man with a man's needs, and he had to know that everything was all right in the marriage department. He didn't dare to risk Venetia's disappointment in him.

It only took a few coppers to get a waterfront scruff to give him the address he wanted. His pockets jingled with silver for the right instruction. Whatever it took, Freddie was willing to pay. He saw the house, knocked on the door discreetly labelled Madame Tania, and was admitted at once.

He blinked at the softly lit interior. He had expected something tawdry and sleazy, but this was subdued elegance in furnishings and drapery. He felt mildly reassured, and then a well-corseted woman of uncertain age came towards him.

'Can I help you, Sir?' she asked, as though she had vegetables to sell.

Freddie felt a sudden wild urge to laugh. It was so incongruous. Himself on the brink of marriage; this woman, selling other women's bodies… at least, he hoped so. He didn't fancy lying with this old hag, however well-preserved…

The tingle in his loins began again. He was here, and he may as well get what he'd come for. He cleared his throat.

'A young lady—' he began diffidently.

'Of course,' the woman said smoothly. 'Perhaps you will just tell me your preference. We cater for all tastes here.'

He looked totally blank. Was there anything more than the simple act of which he had no knowledge whatsoever? Madame Tania shrewdly read his expression.

'Are we perhaps wanting a first experience, sir?' she spoke gently and tactfully. 'If so, if you will allow me, I will choose one of my young ladies who will give you every assistance in making this a momentous and memorable occasion.'

'Thank you,' Freddie murmured. With every second that passed, it all became more and more dream-like. He was glad of that; it put less emphasis on the thing he was about to do. It made it totally impersonal.

He was shown into a small room. There was nothing in it but a bed and a small table. The covers and sheets on the bed were of red silk, the wall lights making it warm and inviting. All around the room, the walls were lined with mirrors, making the room seem larger than it really was. Everywhere Freddie looked, there was a reflection of himself, and he realized that the mirrors were angled to give infinite reflections of what went on on the bed.

For a minute he was tempted to change his mind and leave quickly. But it was too late. The door opened quietly and a beautiful dark-skinned girl came inside. He was too surprised to say anything for a moment. Whatever he had expected, it wasn't someone like this. Her hair was as black as Morwen's, but it reached to her waist in rippling silken waves, and even as Freddie gaped at her, she slid out of the white satin negligee she wore, and she was completely naked.

Freddie gulped. The image of the girl was reflected a score of times in the mirrors. Everywhere he looked there were breasts and thighs, and tufts of black pubic hair between long supple legs. He panicked, suffocated by the images.

The girl smiled, moving softly towards him on the carpeted floor. She lifted his hand to touch one of her breasts, sensuously rotating it so that he felt the nipple stiffen beneath his palm.

'You like?' she asked. 'My gentleman would like more? My gentleman wishes to learn how to please a woman?'

'Yes,' Freddie croaked. The heady scents in the room were enveloping him. He was drowning in them. He wanted to drown in her. He felt aroused, even though nothing seemed to be happening down below. He nodded stupidly, and felt the girl's fingers begin to unfasten his clothing.

'But first I pleasure you,' she said softly.

She appeared to expect him to stand impassively, allowing her lips to touch each exposed place on his body as she worked. It was extremely pleasurable. Her mouth was soft and warm. It covered each of his male nipples until they were little erect peaks, commanded to stand up by her circling tongue.

His shirt was pushed away from his shoulders now, and the girl sighed with pleasure, murmuring words in a language he couldn't follow, smoothing his strong young flesh. Her hands ran down his chest, kneading and caressing, and Freddie ached with new and wonderful sensations. The girl continued to remove his clothing. He lost the restriction of his trousers, and then his underpants, and caught sight of himself.

For a second, the girl stood beside him, smiling at both their reflections with satisfaction. They were Adam and Eve, Freddie thought incoherently, and the great stalk of his manhood proved to him that the girl's administrations had already done what he hoped.

But she had hardly begun. As he watched, he saw her hand slide down his belly and grasp him. He saw her fingers start to smooth and caress, and the shooting sensations he began to experience were akin to exquisite pain.

'Not yet, my proud one,' the girl murmured. 'Now you must learn to do your part.'

She lay down swiftly on the bed, her legs slightly parted in invitation. She patted the space beside her, and feeling as though his legs would hardly hold him up any more, Freddie sank down beside her. The mirror images followed them. He couldn't keep his eyes off them, off her, off the ebony breasts that so tantalized him, off the silken chasm that was his for the taking… when the time was right. There was evidently more to learn yet…

'You want to please your lady?' she whispered. 'Then you touch her here, you kiss her here, you stroke and caress and make her glad that she is a woman, with a woman's special places to please a man.'

She guided his hands and his lips, and he was bemused by the expertise with which the girl performed. His mouth was on those beautiful breasts. One by one he drew the nipples into his mouth and felt them awaken, and glowed at his own ability. He followed the softly spoken instructions, finding the trail to the triangle of darkness below the soft belly.

His fingers found and explored and aroused in this new world of pleasure, and small cries of ecstasy came from the girl's mouth. Then his tongue, on an exciting voyage of discovery, while her fingers groped for him, and she told him at last that the time was right. The mirror images magnified Freddie's clumsy movements as he raised himself above her, preparing to follow her instructions.

She guided him. She was ready, and so was he… until the moment when his erect flesh touched hers. And as if someone had doused him with cold water, he felt himself dwindle into a pathetic lump of flabby flesh. The girl gave an impatient sigh.

'It seems we have more work to do here, sir.' She spoke politely. 'You will pay for the extra time?'

Freddie gawped down at her, speechless for a moment. But even if his mouth refused to work, his brain whirled with the truth of it all. She was flawlessly beautiful, and totally cold. The cries of pleasure had all been false, the erotic pantings well-rehearsed, and to her this was no more than an hour's work. He hauled himself away from her, fumbling for his clothes, feeling the need to cover himself, to stop looking at her, to resist the awful reflections of his inadequacy…

'I'm sorry. I've no more time.' He spoke jerkily.

'I understand. You will pay Madame Tania, sir, and thank you for your company.'

The fact that she didn't even care doubled Freddie's humiliation. He couldn't get out quickly enough. But the scent of her seemed to linger on him, no matter how many times he scrubbed himself the minute he got home. And he was just as tormented as ever after this failure, if not more so. Any man could succeed with a whore, he thought agonizingly. It was human nature, and had been so throughout the ages. What was wrong with him? And what was worse, could it ever be put right? Did he have the right to ask a lovely girl like Venetia Hocking to marry him, if he was impotent? The word burned into his brain, and he couldn't rid himself of that either.

–

'You call this a beach?' Cresswell Tremayne said mockingly. The children had been allowed the use of the trap, after Walter had insisted that he was old enough to drive it. They had all piled in, eager to show the new boy some of their favourite places, more relaxed away from the house, where Cresswell acted more like one of the grown-ups than one of them.

'What's wrong with it?' Albert stared around the beautiful little cove. This was his particular favourite, almost closed in by the cliffs, and studded with small caves. The cove was golden, washed by the sea that rippled towards them now.

Cresswell sneered, scuffing the virginal sand into little flurries that stung Charlotte's eyes and made her howl with rage.

'It's so small! Everything here is small. It's nothing like America—'

'Thank God for that,' Walter muttered.

'Walter, you know you're not to say that,' Primmy said automatically, but her blue eyes flashed furiously. 'How dare you come here, Cresswell, and belittle everything about us. Your mother crows about your good manners, but it's a pity she can't hear you when you're with us!'

'My mother never crows,' he snapped. 'I shall be sure and tell her that you said so.'

She went scarlet. 'I hope you won't. I like Aunt Louisa very much, and I'd hate her to think differently—'

'Then you shouldn't say things you don't mean,' Cresswell said nastily. 'Anyway, I didn't ask to come here. I'd much rather have stayed at home.'

'I wish you had,' Justin was just as aggressive. 'We can't do the things we want to do because you're here. We have to take you around with us all the time.'

'I can't see that there's anything much to do around here. It's the most boring place I ever saw. Nothing ever happens, and the people are all simpletons.'

Walter cuffed him on the side of his head.

'You'd better not let my family hear you say that,' he shouted. 'Just because you're a visitor it doesn't give you the right to insult us.'

'Don't you dare hit me, you pig!' Cresswell broke in furiously. He punched Walter in the stomach, and Albert joined in the fight at once. Primmy screamed at them to stop, but the next minute Cresswell was stumbling backwards, losing his footing, and rolling about in the sand with the two older boys on top of him.

They were too near the water's edge, and the tide was coming in fast, but none of them noticed the chill of it as they rolled about, locked in rage. They were egged on by the others now, screeching and yelling, until they were suddenly dragged to their feet. All three had bloody noses, their clothes sodden and covered in sand, and they looked up into the furious face of Ben Killigrew.

'What the hell do you all think you're doing? You're like rag-tags, the lot of you! If you can't behave in a more civilized way, you'll all be confined to the house, do you understand me?'

'He started it, Uncle Ben!' Cresswell whined, pointing savagely at Walter.

Ben looked at him with poorly disguised dislike. Cresswell was no kin of his, and he had despised him from the start. He'd kept his opinion to himself, but privately, he loathed children who were old before their time, and antagonized everyone else around them.

'I didn't start it!' Walter bellowed. 'He insulted us, and I gave him what he deserved.'

'He did, Daddy, he did!' Charlotte shrieked.

Ben shook them all off. 'I don't give a damn who started it, but I'm finishing it here and now,' he said coldly. 'You will all go home at once, and I want to hear no more fairy tales. How did you get here?'

'Mother said we could use the trap,' Walter said sullenly, and before Ben could rant at him about that, he added swiftly, 'she treats me fairly. I'm not a baby any more, and I'm perfectly capable of driving a horse and cart.'

'You should be,' Cresswell muttered. 'In a farmyard, preferably.'

'That's enough.' Ben looked at him sharply. All three boys looked a sorry mess, glowering at one another like miniature prize-fighters, and if he wasn't in such a state about the news he'd just received, he might have found the situation faintly amusing. 'You will all get in the trap, and I shall ride alongside you to see that there's no more trouble, since you obviously can't be trusted to be by yourselves.'

It was galling to Walter to know that Ben's eyes were on him every minute of the journey, watching the way he handled the reins, and ready to criticize the instant he did anything wrong. But he never faltered. He was very capable, and it was time Ben realized he was nearly a man, he thought resentfully.

When they reached home, Ben ordered them into the drawing-room with him, no matter how they looked. They must face everyone and see just how upset everyone would be by their bad behaviour. Primmy tried to object, but Ben shouted her down. She ached for her two brothers, whose stubborn faces told her that they weren't going to forget any of this, not the insults from Cresswell, or Ben's harsh treatment because of him.

When the drawing-room door opened, Morwen stood up with some relief. It was lovely to have had time alone with Matt and Louisa, and they had spent a happy gossiping hour before Jane Askhew and her daughter Cathy had arrived unannounced. They were still there, and Morwen had been conscious of the growing constraint between them all. For once, she longed for Ben to come, to make the conversation easier.

She started to smile, and then the smile changed to a gasp of horror as Ben stood aside after the briefest of greetings to Jane and Cathy, and ushered in the five dishevelled children. Everyone seemed to speak at once.

'What on earth's happened?' Morwen gasped. 'Who's done this to you?'

'My poor baby!' Louisa said, rushing to hold Cresswell and examine his cut face.

'Did you know who it was?' Matt snapped. 'Louisa, leave him. You know how he hates babying—'

'Perhaps we should go—' Jane began in embarrassment.

Cathy looked on, wide-eyed, a younger version of her mother, all the concern in her face focused on the oldest boy, about the same age as herself. The one they called Walter…

Ben spoke sarcastically.

'Nobody set on the fine young specimens. I found them fighting among themselves, rolling about in the sea like the abominable wreckers greedy for their spoils.'

He never noticed how Matt flinched, nor recalled the old suspicions that Matt and Ben's cousin Jude had once been over-charmed by the excitement of the wreckers.

'It seems they've had punishment enough,' Morwen said through stiff lips. 'The three boys look bruised, and the others shaken, and I've no doubt you've already dealt with them, Ben.'

He nodded curtly. 'They can all go to their rooms, and the maids can attend to them, unless you wish for special attention for your son, Louisa?'

'Ben, really!' Morwen hated him at that moment, but Louisa covered the insult magnificently.

'Not at all. He probably got what he deserved, the same as the others. Let the maids take care of them, by all means.'

The children escaped thankfully, and Ben bawled instructions to the maids before coming back to the room and slumping in an armchair. Morwen handed him some tea, tight-lipped and appalled at his insensitivity. The thought flitted through her head that Jane must be glad she didn't marry this oaf of a man after all. Her newspaperman, brash though he was, had always been infinitely better-behaved than this in public.

'So, Jane,' he made an effort to be sociable at least. 'And how are you liking it back in Cornwall?'

She gave a wry smile. 'I seem to have lost my feeling for it,' she admitted. 'I've lived in Yorkshire for so long now, I feel it's where I belong.'

'I love it here,' Cathy said. She spoke like her father, with the quick, flat accent of the north, but somehow it suited the girl. 'I'd like to stay, but Mother wants to get home as soon as Daddy finishes his present assignment.'

'That's understandable, Cathy,' Louisa said gently, still ruffled at the fight between the boys, and trying not to show it.

'Yes, I know, but I want to stay with Grandma, and I'm still trying to persuade everyone to let me.' Whenever she gave that quick smile, her face glowed with prettiness. She was like her mother, but with all her father's astuteness. Whatever Cathy Askhew wanted, Morwen had a shrewd idea she would get it.

'Well, if you do get your wish, you can come and visit us as often as you like, Cathy,' she said, mildly astonished at her own generosity. But Cathy wasn't Jane, and she hadn't missed the looks that passed between her and Walter. How odd, how very odd it would be… They were children… yet not children. Fifteen was old enough to fall in love, however immature that love might be.

She stopped her thoughts immediately, as Jane said she thought they must go home.

'By the way, I met your cousin in Truro, Louisa,' she remembered to say just as they were leaving. 'He's such a charming man, isn't he? I was passing the time of day with Annie Tremayne and she introduced me to Mr Wainwright. It's so nice for you all to be here at the same time.'

It was polite conversation, no more. It didn't mean a thing. It certainly didn't warrant the old familiar jealousy to stab at Morwen, just hearing Jane Askhew mention Ran, and to see the smile playing at the sides of her mouth as she remembered their meeting. First Ben, now Ran…

'Are you coming to see Jane and Cathy out, Morwen?' Ben said pointedly. He was already on his feet, waiting for her to act the hostess, and she flushed at her own tardiness. She followed them to the door, and waved until the Askhew carriage was out of sight.

'And now we'd better have a discussion about our children,' Ben said grimly. 'I don't imagine Matt and Louisa are too pleased at seeing their ewe-lamb come home bloodied.'

Morwen frowned. The easy-going Matt who had gone away would probably have laughed it all off, saying that the children could sort out their own problems. But this was a different Matt, an older and keener Matt, and she wasn't sure how much he was offended by the fight. As soon as she and Ben went back to the drawing-room, she could see that her brother was very angered by what had happened, and that he and Louisa had been discussing it.

'We shall have to do something about this,' he said at once. 'I don't like family tensions, and if they can't get along together, then they'll be best kept apart. Your children don't go back to school yet, do they?'

'No,' Ben said shortly. 'Their holidays coincided with your visit. Unless you're suggesting that we pack them off somewhere, so that Cresswell can have the run of the house?'

'Ben, don't be ridiculous,' Morwen muttered.

'I didn't mean any such thing. I was going to suggest that Cresswell spends a few days with his grandparents, if my mother's agreeable, and then perhaps he could stay a short time at Ran's house. We must obviously keep the children apart for a time, until their tempers have cooled. I shall speak to Cresswell, of course.'

He was very much in control, and Ben nodded curtly. He too, could see that this was no dreaming Matt Tremayne, but a man whose business demanded a cool brain and clear thinking. And Ben's own thinking was becoming more muddled by the hour.

Louisa suddenly leaned forward, her face full of concern.

'Please don't let us quarrel about this,' she pleaded. 'We've looked forward for so long to this visit, and if I've any excuse to offer for Cresswell, it's that he's so rarely among other children. Even his school is progressive in making them grow up as early as possible, and at home we've always included him in adult conversations and discussions.'

Morwen's warm heart went out to her.

'Please don't distress yourself, Louisa. These things happen, and nothing changes the feelings we have for one another. It will all blow over, I'm sure, but I do think Matt's idea is sensible. Keep them apart for a week—'

'I think we should go to Ran's as well,' Matt decided. 'He's Louisa's cousin, after all, and it would give us all a breathing space. Cress can go to Mammie's on his own, then we'll pick him up and take him on to Ran's. The invitation's there.'

'All right. If that's what you think is best,' Morwen said slowly. She wished she could go too. How easy it was for Louisa to be installed in Ran's house as his cousin, when all Morwen wanted was to be there as his lover. Even more so as his wife…

This day was turning out all topsy-turvy, she thought miserably. But she would see Ran this evening. Since the visitors had been here, he had started coming to Killigrew House most evenings for dinner. Ben had reluctantly agreed to Morwen's insistence that it was only good manners to include him.

Ben was thinking of Ran too. Good riddance to his visitors for a few days, and it was only right that Ran should have a share of them. Not that he was indisposed to Matt and Louisa, who were likeable enough, just their snot of a son. And he might not have felt so irritable with him if he hadn't just had the most appalling news from Charlestown port.

Chapter Eighteen

He kept it bottled up inside himself for half the evening. The children had been allowed down for a short while, cleaned up and looking abject and strained, and having to explain it all to Ran when he arrived. After dinner they had been sent to their separate rooms again to ponder on their rudeness, and when the adults were all moderately relaxed, considering the trauma of the day, Ben told them.

Morwen gasped, and even though it meant little to Louisa, she couldn't fail to see how serious it was, by the reactions of the others. Morwen was the first to speak.

'The ship turned back before it got anywhere near France? But I thought you expected to hear that it had arrived safely long before this.'

'So I had,' Ben said harshly. 'That's why I was at the port, to check with the harbour-master on the delay, and I was actually there when the ship was sighted and eventually came limping back. She was holed on a rock, and since she was still nearer to England than France, the captain had no choice but to throw some of the cargo overboard to ease the weight of her in the water, and bring her back to Charlestown for repairs.'

'And the cargo was your clay blocks?' Louisa asked.

'The cargo was my clay blocks.'

'How much was lost?' Ran said.

'Enough to make a difference on the price paid for what's left. Not quite enough to ruin me, but with the time wasted while the repairs are being made, and then the delay in getting the blocks to France, and the money coming through—' He shrugged, wishing he hadn't run on quite so eloquently.

'But this won't be the only ship taking spring despatches away, surely, Ben?' Matt put in.

Ben saw that he hadn't forgotten how the clay business operated. He hadn't seemed so keen to stay in it as a young man, but the interest was still there, all the same. It wasn't so surprising, when his family had been so much concerned with it.

Morwen gave her husband a warning look. Don't spoil this visit, the look said. Let Matt and Louisa go away unaware of the problems looming ahead… Ben ignored the warning.

'Maybe it's time you all knew what's been happening lately. We're in a bit of trouble, financially.' He stopped, and then gave a twisted grin, his voice still harsh. 'I'll rephrase that more honestly. Killigrew Clay is in the devil of a lot of trouble, and the loss of half a shipload of clay and a delay in payment could mean disaster. I just thank God that the ship didn't sink, or I'd have sunk with it. It's a damnable situation.'

Matt spoke up at once. 'But good God, man, couldn't you ask someone for help? A gentleman's agreement, rather than going to a loan-shark. You could have gone to Ran here, or come to me. I can still help. Tell me exactly what's involved—'

'Matt's right. You should have told me, Ben. Whatever's needed, we could have sorted something out—' Ran intervened in annoyance.

'No!' Ben's voice was brittle. This was more humiliation. Matt Tremayne was a fine man now, but he'd once been a clayworker in Ben's father's employ, and Ben would never beg from him. It was also why he could never accept such help from Hal. If these people couldn't see why, then it only marked the differences between them. And he didn't want a foreigner interfering in his business affairs…

'Ben, please don't upset yourself,' Morwen said quickly, seeing the pulse beating in his throat, and the reddened veins standing out on his forehead.

'Your father's already offered me money, Matt, and I refused to take it. I'll never accept charity.'

'I hardly think Daddy's in a position to help much,' Matt commented. 'But I could, and so could Ran. We're all family, Ben, and we don't offer charity.'

'Look, I don't want to discuss it any more!' This time, he did take notice of Morwen's look. Nobody else knew of Hal Tremayne's true situation. Nobody knew he was a partner in Killigrew Clay, and that apart from this house and its contents, that he had more assets than Ben Killigrew himself.

Louisa spoke nervously. 'Ben, I do understand that this is all embarrassing to you, but Matt doesn't mean to offend you, and I'm sure Ran doesn't either.'

'I'm not embarrassed. But the subject is closed.'

For a few seconds nobody spoke. Then Louisa turned quickly to her cousin.

'Ran, it was so sweet of you to agree to our coming to stay at the end of next week. Are you sure it's not putting you out? Matt thinks his mother will love to have Cress for a few days first, and we mean to go see her tomorrow.'

'Of course you're not putting me out. I can take some time off and show you around Truro. It'll be my pleasure.'

'Actually, I'm keen to take Cresswell up to the clayworks. We haven't been there yet,' Matt said suddenly. 'Perhaps we could go on up to the moors after we've called to see Mammie tomorrow. Will you come too, Louisa, or will it be too boring for you?'

'Of course I'll come. I want to see it, and especially the cottage where you lived and all.'

'You know all about that, do you, Louisa?' Morwen said, smiling. The other girl laughed.

'I should just say I do. When I first met Matt, he was so homesick for Cornwall and all of you that I was quite jealous. But then when he began talking about it in that poetic way he used to have, I felt I knew it all, and I began to love it too, even though I'd never seen it.'

Matt moved across to her and put an arm loosely around her shoulders in a gesture of real affection.

'You've never had anything to be jealous of, honey,' he said softly. He looked at his brother-in-law. 'How about it then, Ben? Is it all right if we come up to the works tomorrow?'

'Suit yourself. Hal will be there if I'm not. He'll show you around – but of course, you won't have any need for a guide.'

'It'll have changed a bit, though.' There was an odd nostalgia in Matt's voice now. 'You've a railway instead of the old clay waggons, and there'll be less excitement than in the old days. And a lot of the people I knew will have gone.'

He looked at Morwen, and she sensed that they were both thinking of two particular people at that moment: of Celia, whom Matt had found drowned in the claypool and brought to the Tremayne cottage, frightening Morwen out of her wits; and Sam, their brother, the only fatality in the collapse of Ben's first rail tracks.

'We'll go on to Penwithick church as well,' Matt said, confirming her thoughts. 'I want to see where Sam's buried.'

'We'll take some flowers,' Louisa nodded. 'I want to see that too.'

Ran broke into the sudden air of gloom.

'I was wondering about postponing the party at my house until just before you all leave. Sort of a house-warming and farewell party in one,' he said. 'What do you say, Louisa? And how about inviting that nice Mrs Askhew and her daughter, since all Matt's family knows them?'

'That would be a lovely idea, Ran,' Louisa said warmly. 'Jane came here to visit with us today, and I liked her enormously. Yes, why don't we do that?'

Morwen kept her eyes down. Suddenly, it seemed as if Ran's party was none of her business. It involved him and his cousin Louisa, and they could invite whom they liked. Including Jane Askhew. It was a neighbourly thing to do, and since Morwen had already seen the attraction between Walter and Cathy, it would be nice for the young people… but deep down, she knew she didn't really want them to meet. She didn't want Jane Carrick Askhew having any connection with her family, and she especially didn't want her at Randell Wainwright's party.

But she didn't have any say in it, and everyone else was smiling and saying how nice it would be. And Ben was looking at her in that mocking way as if he guessed how she was feeling, and remembered her one-time frustration at trying to learn the pianoforte in order to compete with the accomplished Miss Finelady Jane… and now she was seething all over at knowing it had been Ran who suggested this party invitation. It was Ran who wanted Jane inside his house…

–

The children were all busy the next day, thankful to be free of Cresswell, who had gone off with his parents to visit Bess, and then to go to the clayworks. Ben was away to Charlestown port again, hoping desperately that the repairs to the French ship wouldn't take too long. Morwen had the day to herself for once, and decided she would do some calling too. Ostensibly to visit Annie in Truro, but mainly to go to Ran's office. He had once said if she needed him, she only had to go there. And she did need him. She had never needed him more.

He looked up in pleased surprise when she was shown in by his clerk. One look at her face, and he told the young man that he could take the rest of the day off. He turned the key in the lock and she moved into his arms.

There was no constraint between them. No false modesty or preliminary flirtatious remarks. There was only love. She saw it in his face and felt it as his body pressed close to hers. They didn't kiss at first, merely held each other close, as if to draw strength from one another. And she leaned against him, feeling the steady beat of his heart, and wanting him.

'Ran, I had to come. I miss you so much,' she whispered tremulously.

He lifted her face to his, his hands cupping her cheeks. She saw the longing in his eyes, matching her own.

'Do you think I don't miss you too, my darling? Do you know how it torments me to sit there so politely in your husband's house, making small-talk when all I want to do is ravish you?'

'Oh, Ran—'

'Have I shocked you, honey?' he said softly. 'Don't you know that love and lust go hand in hand? One without the other is either pure or hateful, but both together make the best loving of all.'

'I'm not shocked,' she said huskily. 'I remember how it was in London—'

'So do I. And I want it again. I want *you* again. All the time I want you, but I dare not let it overwhelm my life.'

'Just as long as I know that you still feel the same—'

He looked down at her flushed face.

'Why should you ever doubt it, darling?'

'I thought – I thought you showed an interest in Jane Askhew. 'Tis foolish of me, I know—'

'It's foolish, and impossible, when my heart already belongs elsewhere. I've no interest in Mrs Askhew apart from showing friendship, honey,' he said gently. 'Besides, she's a married lady.'

'So am I, my love.'

He said nothing for a moment, and then he gave a small sigh. 'Morwen, if you were free, I would marry you tomorrow. It's what I want most in all the world. But I can't shut myself up in a tower until that day happens. I like people, and that includes women. It doesn't mean I've stopped loving you, or ever will.'

'And if you find someone else to love before – I'm free?' She hated herself for even saying it, as though she willed Ben's death to free her.

'I'm not looking for anyone else to love. I can't guarantee that it will never happen, but I can't imagine it, because you're everything I want. Do you have any more questions, or are you going to stop talking and let me make love to you?'

She drew in her breath. The offer was there, and she only had to say yes. She ached for it to happen, to renew the feelings that had been born in a hotel room in London. All the love she ever wanted was in Ran's eyes, in his arms… She swayed towards him, hiding her face against his chest.

'No, my love,' she said in a muffled voice. 'Not until I'm free to love you.'

She moved away blindly and turned the key in the door with shaking fingers. It would have been so easy. It could have started a precedent. Stolen afternoons, secret meetings, a haven of love… but it would be wrong. She decided in those sweet moments of indecision that being unfaithful in spirit was not the same as being physically unfaithful. The one was so much the lesser evil after all. It had to be, because otherwise God wouldn't let her suffer so because of it.

Ran let her go, but at her final look back, there was understanding in his face. He didn't love her any the less for her refusal. And if Jane Askhew accepted his invitation, which of course she would, then that was something Morwen must accept as well. If God intended her to conquer her jealousy, it was only right that He gave her something significant to be jealous about. She applied her own logic to the situation, and felt oddly reassured by it.

She hurried through the busy Truro streets to pay her visit to her sister-in-law. Annie was obeying the doctor's orders very stricdy, and was resting in bed for her afternoon hour when Morwen arrived. The twins had been sent off to stay with Annie's friend for the afternoon.

'How lovely to see you, Morwen,' Annie said in delight. 'You don't often come over here. Where are your visitors today?'

Morwen explained quickly.

'You're probably glad of a bit of time to yourself,' Annie remarked. 'However much we want visitors to come, it's always nice when they've gone, and we can relax, isn't it?'

'I never really thought of it before, but you're right,' Morwen said slowly. 'I was feeling quite guilty at the relief I felt when they all went off this morning, but now I don't feel so bad. And how are you?'

'I'm fine,' Annie said cheerfully. 'Jack's wonderful and helps with the girls, and I know this baby is going to be all right, Morwen. I just know it.'

Morwen felt a tug of envy. She looked fulfilled and happy, even though the swell of her pregnancy made hardly a bump beneath the covers yet.

'I know it too,' she said suddenly. 'As long as you take care and do as you're told, I know you'll be all right, Annie.'

'I want this babby so much, Morwen,' Annie said, with a catch in her throat. 'Jack was supposed to keep away from me, but how can you expect a man to lie with his wife and not want her? I know I can talk freely to you, because you'll know what I mean.'

Morwen felt the colour stain her cheeks. What would this simple girl say if she knew how long it had been since Morwen slept in the same room with her husband? Even worse, that this very afternoon, she had been sorely tempted to spend the hours in the arms of her lover instead of coming here?

'I understand, Annie,' she murmured, hardly knowing what to say. 'And I know Jack wants what's best for you.'

'He's what's best for me,' she said softly.

Morwen cleared her throat. 'Can I get you some tea, Annie?'

'Oh, I should have thought of it sooner, and offered you some! Will you pull the bell cord, Morwen, and the maid will bring it up. I'm due to get up soon, but I might as well laze here awhile longer, if you don't mind. It's so nice to look out of the window and see the river.'

The house was on the edge of the town, and the busy river wound past the gardens, taking the ships and sailors to the sea. The sight of it reminded Morwen of Ben's new anxiety, and she prayed fervently that the cargo would soon get safely to France. She stayed long enough for some tea, and then got back in the trap for home. She passed Ran's New World, and deliberately kept her eyes ahead, and tried not to imagine how wonderful it would be to be its mistress. The tang of the low moors was in her nostrils, and she wondered how Matt was faring, back in his old world high above St Austell.

–

Louisa was fascinated with everything she saw. There were plenty of folk at Killigrew Clay who remembered Matthew, the Tremayne boy who'd run off to America. There were few who would have recognized him for the same scallywag, and muttered in some surprise at the fine man he'd become. Hal escorted Matt around Clay One, proud to be showing him off with his comely young wife and son.

Cresswell was bored. He didn't understand the way these people spoke, and although the milky-green claypool was interesting enough, and the white mounds of clay waste glinting in the spring sunlight were unusual, he'd far rather be doing something else. He trailed through the various parts of the clayworks, listening as his grandfather Hal explained it all to his mother, and wondered how anybody could work here day in and day out, and not go crazy with boredom.

'So this is the linhay,' Louisa murmured, eyeing the open dries with the thatched roofs, beneath which the white-bonneted bal maidens laid out the clay blocks to dry in the wind and sun. 'I could never quite understand what Matt meant by it, but now I see. And the kiln – where's that, Father? It always sounded such a fearsome place to me.'

Hal liked the way she called him Father so naturally. He pointed out the kiln, where the strongest men worked stripped to the waist, bodies glistening with sweat, as they spread the semi-solid clay with long spades to distribute it evenly as it began the long process of drying. It was blisteringly hot and humid, and Louisa felt her clothes begin to stick to her, and was glad to spend the shortest time possible there.

Outside, everyone seemed to be dusted white from the dust and clinging particles of clay. And she remembered how Matt had once told her how the men would often scoop up a mouthful of the clay slurry to swallow, being a finer cure for dyspeptic stomach than all the doctor's medicines.

'Have you seen enough, honey?' Matt said smiling, when he had been hailed by so many old acquaintances that his head ached with trying to recall all the names. They were part of his past, like forgotten ghosts coming to greet him, and he was both touched and somewhat embarrassed, because his station had changed so much while theirs was still the same.

'I'm ready,' Cresswell said instantly. Louisa laughed, ruffling his dark hair.

'Cress doesn't find all this very entertaining, do you, honey? All right, let's go see the cottage and then we'll visit the church. I don't want the flowers we brought to wilt before we get them there.'

Hal watched them go with a slight sadness. He had longed for Matt to come home. He had missed his son all through the years, but Hal was nothing if not a practical man. And it was obvious that Matt didn't belong here any more. They had all moved on, and found their own places. Matt's was in America now, and if Hal felt strangely content, it was because he had been able to see it for himself.

–

'You mean you once lived here, Father, in this awful little house?' Cresswell said incredulously.

Matt laughed, but there was an edge of steel in his voice when he answered.

'This was the happiest cottage on the moors, son. We didn't have much money, but we had so much love between us that we always thought ourselves rich compared with other folk. Morwen told me that old Charles Killigrew, Ben's father, once said as much too.'

Louisa curled her fingers around his.

'I think that's the loveliest thing I've heard, Matt,' she said softly.

'Well, I should hate to live here,' Cresswell said, irritated because his parents seemed so charmed by this miserable hovel, and were as good as shutting him out by the way they were looking at each other in that soppy way.

'Then just be glad you don't have to,' Matt said smartly. 'But if we hadn't all lived in such a crush, I might never have felt the need to be free and gone to America. I'd never have met your mother, and there would have been no you. So be grateful to this cottage and your grandfather Hal and the rest of them!'

'But where did you all sleep?'

Matt laughed. 'Your Aunt Morwen had a corner downstairs behind a curtain, because she was a girl and needed some space for herself,' he told him. 'My Mammie and Daddy had their own bedroom, and we four boys had the other. We were lucky to have two bedrooms. Most of these cottages have only got one. Shall we knock at the door and ask if we can see inside?'

'Oh, Matt, honey, we can't. It would seem like we were condescending,' Louisa said quickly. 'Really, I don't think it's such a good idea—'

'Nor do I,' Cresswell grumbled. 'I want to go back and collect my things for the move. Granddad Hal is going to show me how to fly a kite. Can't we go now?'

'We're going to the church first,' Matt said shortly. Some day soon he was going to get to grips with Cresswell. It didn't need his sister Morwen, or any of his Cornish relatives to tell him what an unbearable little snob his son was becoming. It was partly the teachings of that exclusive school, of course, but in Matt's opinion it needed a father's influence to knock some humanity into the boy.

He jerked the horse into action and the trap took them across the few miles to Penwithick church. Memories rushed back at Matt now. He hadn't been here when they brought Sam to rest.

He hadn't even known his brother was dead until long after the tragedy. But he'd been one of the mourners when they brought Celia Penry's coffin to the churchyard. He'd supported the Penry family, as had all the Tremaynes, walking behind the coffin with the great company of clayworkers, and ached for his sister Morwen who had lost her dearest friend.

He hadn't been here for the happier occasion either, when Morwen had married Ben Killigrew. News of that too had been one of the gaps to be filled when he finally made contact with his family again.

'It's such a beautiful little church,' Louisa murmured. 'I'd like to go inside for a minute or two. Cress, if you like, you can stay here in the trap.'

'It's too cold. I'll wander around the churchyard looking at the names,' he said.

'See if you can find your uncle's grave, then,' Matt suggested. 'We'll be with you very soon.'

He went inside the cool church with Louisa. It smelt musty and old, but to Matt it was still part of his life. The Tremaynes had never been great church-goers, except for the three necessities of giving thanks for a birth, for marrying and burying, but it didn't mean they didn't have a simple faith, or the need to know that there was a Divine Being somewhere in the universe. He and his wife knelt in silent prayer for a few minutes, each concerned with private memories, and then went out into the sunlight again.

Their son was pottering about among the granite stones, peering into one faded inscription after another.

'It's over here,' Cresswell called. 'It says Samuel Tremayne, beloved husband and father, 1830–1855.'

They threaded their way through the crumbling headstones and humble crosses until they found the one with the stone that Ben and Morwen had erected to Sam's memory. Beneath his name was his wife Dora's, who simply hadn't wanted to live without him, and had died barely weeks after Sam's accident.

There was a well in the churchyard, and several jars left nearby for flowers. Louisa filled one of them with water and arranged the posy she had brought. She had never known Sam, but she could feel the great sorrow of Matt's emotion, and shared it with him.

'It says he was a father. If he had children, what happened to them?' Cresswell was suddenly curious.

Matt gave a small smile. 'You've been fighting with them practically ever since you got here, Cress. Don't you remember me telling you all about it a long time ago?'

'No, I don't think so. You mean Walter and Albert?'

'And Primmy too,' Matt nodded. 'They were Sam and Dora's children, and after they died, Ben and Morwen adopted them and brought them up as their own. It was a fine thing to do, but no more than I'd have expected of our Morwen. She always had the warmest heart.'

Louisa gave a shiver. 'Matt, I think it's time we left,' she said gently. 'We've to go back to Killigrew House and collect our belongings yet, and your mother won't want us descending on her after dark. Have you seen enough for one day?'

He took a last glance to the far corner of the churchyard, where the wild flowers grew in such golden profusion over Celia Penry's grave, and guessed accurately that his sister Morwen had carefully planted them there.

Matt gave his wife a sudden hug. 'More than enough. There's a limit to how many old ghosts you can be comfortable with. It's time for the living now, and I can promise you that until you've tasted Mammie's Cornish pasties, you haven't tasted anything!'

Chapter Nineteen

Morwen suddenly felt free. With the new arrangements, she had a whole week to herself! She faced the fact that, as much as she loved Matt, their lives had changed, and they no longer had quite the same empathy towards each other as the young Tremaynes who had run barefooted over the moors.

It would be impossible to be the same, but at last she no longer thought of it with guilt and regret. Just as the pain of Celia's death had left her overwhelmed with guilt, and had finally passed, this was passing too. Matt was her loving and much-loved brother and would always be so. But their lives no longer ran the same course, and she accepted that too.

Ben's feeling about the visitors' temporary departure was much the same as Morwen's, though his aggression was directed to only one of them. It seemed a long time since she and Ben had been alone in the evening, and Morwen realized what an effort it was to try and behave normally with her husband as they discussed everyday affairs. But the tension between them doubled as Cresswell's name was mentioned.

'Thank God that little ponce has gone. I tell you, Morwen, one more day with him in the house and I'd have been unable to keep my hands to myself. He upset everybody—'

'Well, he's gone now, so let's forget him for a while, Ben,' she soothed. 'I'm more concerned with what's happening at Charlestown. Have they done the repairs to the ship yet?'

He scowled, and the ugly scar on his cheek seemed to swell and redden as he raged.

'It's hopeless to try and get anything done quickly these days. They keep promising tomorrow and then the next day, as if they don't realize that every hour that passes is costing me money. I'd get your Jack to come and look at it, but the French captain's got a contract with the boatyard at Charlestown, and won't break it.'

'Is it really as bad as you said?'

He looked at her with an expression bordering on dislike. She knew that superior look, and hated it.

'Don't you *ever* listen? We're nearing disaster. Is that bad enough for you?'

'But Ben, why won't you be sensible and accept help from the family?' she said, appalled at the venom in his tone.

'Because they're your family, not mine, and I'll see hell freeze over before a Killigrew accepts help from his own clayworkers,' he snarled.

Morwen felt the blood rush to her cheeks. 'How dare you humiliate me so?' Her voice shook with fury. 'My family *is* your family or so I thought. Marriage is meant to be a partnership, but there's precious little appearance of it in this house!'

She went to push past him, but his hand reached out and grasped her wrist. He hurt her, twisting the flesh until she almost cried out. But she wouldn't give him the satisfaction. He pulled her close to him. The children had long gone to bed, and from the strong smell of spirits on his breath, she guessed he had had his fill of drink throughout the day and evening.

'Marriage?' he slurred the word. 'I seem to recall that marriage means a wife sharing her husband's bed, and when you come back to mine, I might feel more charitable towards you. Or do you have someone else on your mind these nights? I doubt that dreaming of him will keep you warm, so when you feel the need of a real man, you might try knocking at my door again. And I just might let you in, if I'm feeling generous.'

She shook herself free. 'I've no wish to sleep with you, or to feel your hands on me, ever again. I loved you so much,

Ben—' her voice broke a little. 'So much that I would have died for you, but you've managed to chip away at my love with your hatefulness over the years until there's nothing left.'

He stared at her resentfully. 'Well, that's fine talk from a clayworker's daughter to the man who puts a roof over her head and provides for her and her children – *and* her brother's children—'

'You see?' she said hopelessly. 'You can't forget, can you? You'll never let it be. What happened, Ben?'

His eyes narrowed. He looked at her, seeing the way her breasts rose and fell inside her gown. She was as alluring as ever. She had always been unconsciously sensual with those flashing blue eyes and that voluptuous mouth. He had always wanted her. But not any more.

Not when lying with her might mean the death of him. It wasn't something he could tell her, no matter how much he taunted her with sharing his bed, guessing that she'd never agree. For the first time, he admitted to himself that he was scared. Scared of dying, of pain, of becoming the hulk that his father had been. He'd rather have a clean cut than linger for years like old Charles Killigrew. Still, she deserved to know some of it. Why shouldn't she suffer, like he was suffering, with the threat of death constantly by his side like an extra shadow?

He spoke caustically. 'What happened was that I was told I'm going to die. The hellish part is not knowing when. It's like hovering over a pot of boiling oil, and never knowing when you're going to fall in. It's slow death by inches. Are you satisfied, my lovely wife?'

'Oh Ben,' she murmured, weeping inside for him.

And wishing desperately that there wasn't this barrier between them that was impossible to cross. But was she failing so badly in her duty? Should she make amends by sleeping in his bed, giving him comfort in the most basic way she could? The terrible thing was, if she slept with her own husband, she felt that she betrayed Ran, and that thought was the most shaming of all.

She went upstairs before him, and after an agony of indecision, she finally slid into the bed they had once shared, quaking as though she were a bride. She had no idea what his reaction would be when he saw her, but she didn't have long to wait. He came upstairs, stopping short as soon as he saw her.

'What's this? Pity for the poor patient, or are you trying to hasten the end?' he said sarcastically.

'Ben, don't be so full of hate,' she whispered. 'Please – can't we give ourselves another chance?'

He was silent for a moment, then he spoke coldly. 'No, I don't think we can. It's best that we carry on as we've been doing for the last few months. I've discovered that a life of celibacy suits me.'

'And what of me? Or aren't women supposed to have needs and feelings?'

The fact that he didn't want her spurred her to anger. She was as good as sacrificing herself, and he was tossing her aside.

'My love, if you've such need of a man, then I suggest you go and find one. I'm sure there would be plenty willing to oblige,' he taunted.

She leapt out of bed and struck him hard across the face. If she opened up the scar, she wouldn't care. If she killed him, she wouldn't care… he pulled her into his arms and kissed her cruelly on the mouth, and the passion he had once shown her was all hate. There was nothing else.

Morwen gave a dry sob and rushed from the room. All she wanted was to be alone, to bury her head beneath her own bedcovers and try to forget the utter humiliation of Ben's rejection. She tasted salt in her mouth as bitter tears stung her bruised lips, and if it was the wickedest thing she did in her life, she prayed that this situation wouldn't go on for much longer. She couldn't bear it. She simply couldn't bear it.

–

Another Tremayne echoed the same words the following day, but for a different reason. Venetia had agreed to come to Freddie's rooms for afternoon tea that day, and he had been drinking to give himself courage.

He was trying to put the memory of his visit to Madame Tania's out of his mind, while wrestling with another problem that was allied to it. He knew now how stupid he had been. Some men might be able to find relief in the arms of a whore, but it hadn't been relief he sought. It was merely knowledge, so that he wouldn't disgrace himself with his beloved Venetia.

And now that it had failed, he was wondering how he could possibly ask her to marry him, unless he confessed everything. The shock of his first glimpses of sexuality, the brutal insults of Neville Peterson, his fear of impotence over the intervening years; the desperation that had led him to Madame Tania's.

He couldn't bear to live with the knowledge that physical love might never be possible for him. But Freddie was too honest a man to go into marriage with this lovely girl without hinting to her of the risks, at the very least. It could all be a farce, and if it was, their future life would be unbearable.

In Freddie's large family, his own parents had set warm and loving standards. In the nature of things, he expected, like the rest of them, that in time he would marry and be the father of children. He went cold all over, wondering if he was to be denied such a basic pleasure.

Venetia was made of the same stuff as his sister, Freddie thought, as he made clumsy attempts to make his table as elegant as anyone's. She was strong and spirited, and quite ready to defy convention whenever necessary, as long as it didn't affect anyone else. Otherwise, she would never have dreamed of coming here today without a chaperone. But she was coming very soon, and Freddie knew he owed her the truth, whatever the outcome.

He heard her light step on the stairs leading up from the rear entrance to his rooms, and dried his damp palms on the sides of his trousers as he went to open the door for her.

'Freddie, how lovely!' she exclaimed at once as she saw the neatly-laid table, with small cakes and slices of bread and preserves, and a pot ready for the tea. 'A bachelor's lone existence is obviously a useful background for a married man!'

She teased him, her grey eyes sparkling as she removed her bonnet and cape and allowed him to span her waist with his hands. There was no guile about her. This was the man she loved and wanted to marry, and it enchanted her to know that his feelings matched hers exactly.

But after a very satisfactory kiss, she looked searchingly into his eyes. It was a look that instantly reminded Freddie of Morwen. She too, sensed things with uncanny accuracy, and was just as perceptive.

'What is it, my love? Is something troubling you? Are you regretting inviting me here for our little tête-à-tête? I promise you, I shan't tell, if you don't, and I'm sure that my reputation will be quite intact!'

His hands tightened on her waist. For a moment his voice was bitter. 'Yes, sweetheart, I'm very much afraid it will.'

She looked at him in astonishment. She had expected a deliciously flirtatious afternoon, perhaps more daring than previous meetings with this tall handsome man. They considered themselves already unofficially betrothed, and even if the ultimate happened, it would make no difference to her respect for him. It was hardly something a young lady could tell a gendeman in words, of course, but surely Freddie must know... didn't men instinctively know these things?

'Are you going to tell me what's wrong, or are we going to play guessing games all afternoon?' she said lightly. 'Let me see! Your brother Matt has insulted you by not wanting to stay here with you; or young Cresswell's looked down his nose at your being a mere shopkeeper, odious little wretch; or it's none of those things, and something far more personal.' She paused for breath, still in the circle of his arms, her last words seductive and inviting. Freddie heard her breath quicken and felt her heartbeat against his, and ached for her.

'It's far more personal,' he said slowly.

She caught her breath. 'You haven't fallen out of love with me, have you?' She gave a shaky laugh.

He didn't laugh back. He merely held her closer, as if the words wouldn't come immediately. And she saw that this was something very serious after all. Not some fatal illness, she thought fearfully. Or a previous attachment that meant they could never marry. Or some close family relationship between the Hockings and the Tremaynes that had come to light, preventing their marriage...

Venetia moved out of his arms and sat down on the sofa, looking up at him.

'Why don't you just tell me, Freddie? I can't do anything to help unless I know what the problem is.'

He sat heavily beside her, not touching her.

'I never wanted to tell you. It's too embarrassing to tell anyone. But I can't marry you unless you know—'

Her stomach churned. It must be some ghastly affliction to make him so agitated. She couldn't bear to see him like this. She loved him so much... she took his hand in hers.

'Whatever it is, Freddie, the worry will be halved if you share it with me. And who better to share it with than someone who loves you? Please, darling, don't make me think it's something terrible. Please tell me.'

'Just promise me one thing. That you'll listen until the end.'

'I promise I'll sit still without interrupting – if you'll only *begin.*'

He gave a short laugh. 'I'm not going to shock 'ee with words, my dearest, just wi' my inadequacy.'

She twisted her face to look at him. She wasn't stupid, and knew instantly what he meant. That bitterness alone would have told her, even more than the words.

'I don't believe it,' she said, but his embarrassment was becoming hers too, and she found it difficult to explain. 'I mean, I've had proof, Freddie. When we've been close – I know you've been – I've experienced—'

Even Venetia's outspokenness deserted her now. How could she say that she had felt his body harden against hers? How could she say she knew what it meant for a man to be aroused by a woman, and had been thrilled by the knowledge that she could do this for Freddie?

'You mean you know that I've frequently had an erection?'

Without warning, the crudeness of the word was there between them, and she nodded dumbly. Did he think such a natural bodily function was so wrong? She was blindly aware now that whatever his imagined shame, it was fundamental to both their lives, and that the time for teasing was long past.

'You've been around horses, Venetia. You know that even animals can get erections that never get past that stage.'

'Freddie—' she said faintly.

He was suddenly furious with the whole rotten business. He was furious with himself for going to a whore and proving the worst. He was furious with Venetia for being the catalyst that shamed his very masculinity. He'd have been better to remain celibate – which was undoubtedly what he was destined to be – without ever half-discovering the delights of a woman…

'Look, you want to know what's wrong, so I'll tell you,' he said savagely. 'I warn you, it's not pretty telling. It started when I was a very impressionable thirteen-year-old, and hoping to go away to a posh London college on a scholarship, since my teachers thought I was so bright—'

'Really? How exciting. And did you go?' Venetia said. He glared at her.

'You promised not to interrupt. No, I didn't go. They couldn't have dragged me there.'

He expected a comment then, but she said nothing. Her thoughts were spinning, trying to anticipate what he was going to tell her, so that she wouldn't appear too shocked after all… she could see that Freddie's nerves were very fragile at the moment, and she tried to keep her face expressionless. Inside, she wept as the tale unfolded, and she could see that Freddie lived through it again in the telling.

'I assumed the memory of him and his insults would go in time,' the words were flooding out now. 'It never did. Even then I thought it would make no difference to me. It seemed only a matter of time before I found a woman to love, and then marriage and children would follow.'

He looked directly into her eyes now, and Venetia was filled with pain at the agony she saw there.

'But?' she whispered, when he seemed unable to continue.

'But then I had more doubts,' the harshness was back in his voice again. 'I love you more than life, and I want you physically. God knows how I want you. But I fear failure so much. I'm not sure if I can take the risk of marrying you and not be a proper husband to you.' Christ, but it sounded so weak, and Freddie hated himself even more.

Venetia rested her head on his shoulder. He could smell the flowery scent of her hair and the musky warmth of her body.

'I would have taken that chance, Freddie—'

'I know. But I wouldn't. That's why I had to know – to find out—'

This was the moment when she would really despise him, he thought fatalistically. But she had to know all of it, and he had to tell it. He said it as clinically as possible, leave nothing out. He told her of the excitement as well as the shame, and the final humiliation…

Her face was white when he had finished, and then she took his hand and cradled it against her cheek. Her voice was muffled, and passionate with emotion, and he could only just make out the words.

'I'm glad you told me. I'm even glad you went to a whore and discovered that you're not the kind of man who does no more than the beasts in the field can do. You're a finer man than that, my love.'

He gave a bitter laugh. 'There's nothing fine about me!'

'I won't hear you say such things. I've no intention of marrying a weakling, and I have every intention of marrying *you*, Freddie Tremayne.'

Something inside him seemed to relax at her words. It was as though he had been constricted for half of his life by a band of steel that suddenly gave way, releasing him from all the tensions that were crushing him. And there was a new kind of exultation coursing through his veins.

'You still want to marry me, even after hearing all this?' he said huskily. 'You're willing to take that chance?'

Venetia swallowed. Very gently she moved Freddie's hand from her cheek to cover her breast. He felt its softness beneath his palm, and the flickering response of the inexperienced nipple. There was no brashness of the prostitute in her innocent movement, no crudity of over-intimate surroundings. Venetia's voice was breathy, her whole body an invitation.

'Freddie darling, I don't know anything about making love either. But I do know that the most important thing is that we should learn together. I don't want a man who's had a string of lovers showing him the way, and nor do we need any instruction. We just need love.'

The room was warm with the heat of the fire. The carpet was soft, and the tea things waited. And Freddie Tremayne proved beyond doubt to himself and his beloved, that he was a man after all.

–

Lord Cyril Hocking was still getting used to his new title. It was inherited from a distant cousin, but if the truth were told, he'd still rather be running his humble riding school for the children of the gentry, than living in this fine house and being obliged to entertain them. Still, he owed it to his girl to take up residence at Hocking Hall and give her every advantage of the new status that had come their way.

Though if she'd fallen for one of these chinless wonders who called themselves the huntin', shootin' and fishin' set, he'd have had serious doubts about agreeing to it. His girl was a normal, healthy young woman, and she needed a real man, not a rich

Daddy's puppet, which was what Lord Cyril considered most of the ones he'd seen.

To his relief, Venetia had met up with this sparky young fellow, Freddie Tremayne, at one of his house bashes for the local dignitaries and tradespeople. Mixing them all together had become one of Cyril's new delights, and seeing how the bigwigs were obliged to make polite conversation with the rest. He still chuckled at the memory. And he'd also made it his business to learn a lot about Freddie Tremayne during that evening.

It didn't matter a jot to him that some of them looked down their noses at the Tremaynes and their upward progress in the world. He admired them for that. It made more sense of a man's own ability than having grandeur thrust on him the way it had happened to himself. And if Freddie Tremayne was the man of his girl's choice, then he'd be only too happy to hand her over to his marital keeping.

Besides, Lord Hocking had his own eye on a nice little woman who kept a needlecraft shop in the town, and if that was going to throw a few more hens in the pond if he decided to make her his Lady, he'd have a chuckle over that as well.

He hadn't expected to see Freddie today. His daughter had gone into Truro on some errands, and said she'd probably have tea in a tea-room. Cyril considered himself a shrewd old boy, and if Venetia's heightened colour meant an assignation with the young man at the chandlery, then good luck to her. Everybody had a right to their secrets in his opinion.

But now here they were, whirling into the drawing-room of this barn of a place, with Venetia glowing, and Freddie looking as though he'd just won a fortune. And it wasn't all that hard to guess why...

'Daddy, Freddie wants to ask you something,' Venetia burst out at once. 'Perhaps I should go and leave you two alone for a few minutes—'

'There's no need, my dear,' Cyril said dryly. 'Not if it's what I think it is. And good afternoon to you, Mr Tremayne.'

'Good afternoon, my Lord,' Freddie said, praying that he wouldn't go all tongue-tied now that the moment was here, and this spectacular girl was as eager to marry him as he was to have her. There was just this little hurdle of her father, and the uneasy thought that Lord Hocking might well want someone better-connected for his daughter...

'Let's have it, then. What's this great question you're about to ask me?'

Freddie squared his shoulders. He had overcome one great hurdle today. Two, really. The telling, and the doing. This was the third, and he wasn't balking at it.

'I want to marry Venetia, Sir. I know I'm not a rich man, and we haven't known each other long, but we love each other very much, and we both think that's more important than material things. I'm not a pauper, but we shall obviously need a proper family home if you agree to our marriage, and it will be my first priority to find us a suitable house.'

He dried up, but the thought was in his mind that no splendid surroundings could ever be more dear to him that the warmth of a small room above his shop, where Venetia had become part of him. And a family home had a special meaning for him now.

'Daddy, you will agree, won't you?' Venetia broke in. 'If you don't, you'll have me around your neck for the rest of your life, because I shall never marry anyone else if I can't have Freddie!'

Lord Hocking laughed. He walked briskly to a side table and poured three glasses of porter and handed them around before he said anything.

'Then you'd better have him, my love. And you, young man, I hope you realize what a bossy young woman you're taking on. Do you think you can handle her?'

Freddie looked over the top of his glass into his beloved's eyes, and the love that flowed between them shut out everything else for a few blissful moments of remembering.

'I know I can,' he said softly. Venetia put down her glass after one sip, and flew into her father's arms.

'Oh Daddy, thank you for being so marvellous. We want to get married very soon. I do so want a June wedding, and if we haven't found our house by then, we'll live in Freddie's rooms above the shop. Say you'll agree to it all, please!'

'I wouldn't dare disagree.' Cyril laughed at her excitement. 'As for the house – choose it at your leisure, but it will be my wedding present to you.'

Freddie bristled at once. 'Oh, no. It's too much. We can't accept a house—'

Cyril sighed. 'I'm not going to have a struggle with you over this, am I? What else am I going to spend my money on if not my daughter and son-in-law? Anyway, you can't have one without the other, Freddie. Take Venetia and a house or nothing at all.'

Venetia looked at him pleadingly, willing him not to let stupid pride come into this. At last, she saw his muscles relax again, and gave up her silent thanks.

'In that case, I've no choice but to accept, since nothing will keep me from making Venetia my wife,' Freddie said, more easily than he would have believed. 'And may I have a drop more of that porter before my knees give way? You'll appreciate that it's not every afternoon that ends up like this.'

He had to keep being jocular to cover the emotion he felt, unknowingly reacting in exactly the right way to the blunt-speaking man. Venetia knew though, and rejoiced in the friendship already growing between them.

They were two of a kind, she thought gladly, and the future blossomed before her, beautiful and golden, like the best of a Cornish summer.

Chapter Twenty

April merged into May and still Ben's clay blocks hadn't left Charlestown port. His temper was so precarious that neither Morwen nor the children hardly dared speak to him. He had no patience with anyone and when Matt and his family returned to Killigrew House for the final week of their visit, he was away from the house more often than he was in it.

None of them was sorry. Matt wasn't wild about Ben Killigrew, if the truth was told. When Matt and Jude Pascoe had left for America, Ben had still been an upstart from his London college, and he'd had no time for him then. He couldn't see that there was much difference in the Ben of those days and the man he had become. The years in between may have softened him in Morwen's eyes, but there was no evidence of it to Matt.

He was suddenly hungry to be back in the land that was now his own. He had missed his family, and longed to see them again. But he had put down roots in his chosen country, and wouldn't be sorry to leave Cornwall after all, even though the days were mellow with approaching summer, and Freddie's wedding was arranged for the end of June.

Matt was regretful that he couldn't stay for that, but in any case another two months away from his own business was more than he could spare. His arrangements must be unchanged, but he could be glad that there was something lovely for the Killigrews and Tremaynes to look forward to.

He echoed his sister's hopes that the last week of the visit would be uneventful as she shooed the children out into the garden to play hide-and-seek on the Sunday afternoon. They headed for the shrubbery, well away from the house. Cresswell was still smarting from a rebuke he'd had from that Ben that morning.

'Why is your father always so cross?' he asked Primmy.

'He's not always cross,' she came to Ben's defence at once. 'He has a lot of business worries. I heard him telling Mother about the clay blocks still not leaving Cornwall. They should be in France by now. Our clay goes to lots of different countries,' she added for good measure.

'So does my father's gold.' Cresswell immediately pooh-poohed her words. 'Our gold is far more precious than a lot of old clay. It's made into jewellery and important things, not just cups and saucers and plates.'

'Everybody needs cups and saucers and plates,' Walter said testily. 'People can get along without jewellery and stuff, so don't talk rubbish. Clay is just as important as gold.'

'That's silly. Anybody knows gold is the best—'

'Don't call Walter silly,' Albert said threateningly.

Charlotte looked from one to the other, while Justin folded his arms and glared as belligerently as the older boys.

'Are you going to have another fight?'

Walter ignored his little sister, speaking loftily to all of them. 'Cresswell's the idiot, for not understanding about all the things that depend on Cornish china-clay. It's not found just anywhere, and our clayworks are among the biggest around here.'

'Your clayworks!' Cresswell was still scoffing.

Walter suddenly saw red at the sneering little squirt. He didn't normally boast, but there was a time and a place for everything.

'Yes, *mine*,' he bragged. 'When I'm old enough to take over from Daddy, I shall run Killigrew Clay the way I want to. Even if I wanted to export clay blocks to America, I should do that too,' he added wildly.

Cresswell let out a shriek of laughter.

'You'll have to wait a long time for that, Walter *Tremayne*! Killigrew Clay's never going to belong to *you*. You're not even

Uncle Ben's eldest son. You're not even a *Killigrew*, so how is it ever going to belong to you?'

Walter had got him by the scruff of the neck before he finished talking. Albert piled on top of him, and the three of them went down on the grass. This time, Justin pummelled his small fists against the American cousin as well.

'What the hell are you talking about, you boring little bastard?' Walter grated, uncaring of his language.

Cresswell furiously panted out the words, nearly suffocated by three bodies smothering him, and half a dozen hands squeezing his throat.

'It's true! If you don't believe me, ask my Daddy. You can't ask your own, because he's dead, in the churchyard at Penwithick. I saw the name on the stone. Sam Tremayne. That's who your Daddy is. Yours and Albert's and Primmy's.'

Walter wrenched him to his feet. The blue of the sky seemed to dazzle in front of his eyes and he couldn't think straight for a minute. He could hardly breathe.

'You're a bloody liar!' he shouted. 'I'm not Sam Tremayne's son. He's our uncle who died years ago—'

'He's not!' Cresswell shrieked. 'He's your Daddy, not your uncle. And Aunt Morwen's not your mother, neither. It's only Justin and Charlotte who belong here, and it'll be Justin who owns Killigrew Clay one day, not you.'

For a few seconds the only sounds to be heard were the harsh breathing of the older children, and Charlotte's noisy sobbing. Walter felt as though time were suspended. Then gradually all the soft sounds of summer, the humming of bees, the soaring birdsongs, the busily scratching crickets, penetrated his senses once more. Normal everyday sounds, that were in such contrast to this sudden nightmare of a day.

'You're coming with me.' He yanked Cresswell's arm and held it cruelly, not heeding the boy's yelp of pain. 'You'll tell my mother exactly what you've told us, and then we'll see what a little liar you are!'

Albert grabbed his other arm, and they frog-marched Cresswell to the open French windows of the drawing-room, with the rest of the children forming the rear-guard.

–

Morwen saw them coming. Dimly, she had been aware of some commotion, and had laughed ruefully with Matt and Louisa over it. It seemed that their children were always destined to be at odds with each other, no matter how fond the regard of their elders. Now, she half-rose at the white, set faces of her boys, and the obvious distress of the girls.

She could see that Cresswell was furious and humiliated by their treatment of him, and she might have found it secretly laughable, had she not sensed that something awful had happened.

Walter thrust his cousin forward, so that he stumbled into the room, and Matt jumped up, exclaiming angrily. Before he could demand to know the reason for it, Walter was shouting.

'Do you know what lies this little shit has been telling about us, Mother?'

Morwen gasped. She'd never heard Walter speak that way before. She could suddenly hear Sam in him, defending to the death what he thought to be right.

'It's not lies!' Cresswell bellowed. 'It's the truth. My Daddy told me. Ask him if you don't believe me.'

For a second, the room blurred in front of Morwen. Even before Walter spilled out the words, she knew what they were going to be. She had never thought to warn Matt that the children didn't know the facts of their birth. She had always intended to tell them gently, and now it was too late for that… too late…

'He says we're not Killigrews. He says Sam Tremayne was our Daddy instead of our uncle. He says Killigrew Clay's not my inheritance, but *Justin*'s—'

Walter stopped as suddenly as if he had been punched in the stomach. The full pain of that statement had only just penetrated. Ben rarely allowed him to go to the clayworks, even though he wanted to work there so badly. When he was fully grown, he had every intention of doing so. The clay was in his blood. He wanted it as fiercely as any man born to be a clayworker and not a boss… the full impact hit him anew of what he had always felt, and he almost staggered and fell. If the other children hadn't been right behind him, grabbing him, he probably would have done.

Matt spoke up hoarsely. 'My God, Morwen, have you never told them?'

'Oh, Cresswell, how could you do such a thing?' Louisa's eyes were filled with tears as she saw the shock still rippling across the three older children's faces.

'Cresswell, what did you tell them?' Matt thundered.

For the first time, the boy looked uncertainly at the faces of the adults in the room. His Aunt Morwen, whom he liked quite well, looked as though she was about to faint, and his parents were angrier than he had ever seen them. He began to shake all over, his voice hoarse with fear.

'How was I to know they didn't know? Nobody told me it was a secret. I thought Walter was just showing off about owning the clayworks, and I told him it would be Justin's not his, because he wasn't really a Killigrew.'

'He said our Daddy was Sam Tremayne,' Primmy said shrilly. 'He said we don't belong here, only Justin and Charlotte. *Mother*—'

She looked beseechingly at Morwen.

Dear God, Morwen thought frantically, where was Ben? Why wasn't he here to help her with all of this? She swallowed painfully, then looked at Matt and Louisa.

'Would you please take Cresswell for a walk or something? I have to be alone with my children for a while.'

There was nothing Matt could say to ease the painful telling, except to murmur that if she wished, they would go around the rest of the family and tell them what had happened. Morwen agreed at once. As soon as he and his family had gone, she faced the five wounded young faces, suffering along with them.

'Come and sit down, all of you—'

'I'd rather stand,' Walter said stiffly.

Morwen put her arms around his unbending young body, knowing that Walter's hurt would be the worst of all.

'Please sit down, darling. 'Twill make no difference to the telling whether you stand or sit.'

'I can't see that there's anything else to say,' he burst out. 'It's obviously true, and you've been letting us live a lie all these years.'

Morwen refused to speak until he sat down, and after a minute or two, he sat with his legs sprawled out in front of him. It was the way Sam used to sit. Morwen's heart turned over, wishing such images wouldn't keep coming to haunt her right now. She didn't know where to begin, and there was no one to help her.

'Walter, do you know the cottages on the moors?' she said finally.

He fidgeted. 'The ones where the clayworkers live? Of course I do,' he grunted.

'And you remember I told you that Granddad Hal and Grandma Bess and all my family once lived there, when we all worked for Killigrew Clay?' She looked at them all steadily, daring any of them to ridicule it now.

'When you and Grandma Bess were bal maidens,' Primmy muttered.

'That's right. When Granddad Hal moved to his house, Sam and Dora moved into the cottage. When you were very young, you lived there as well. Walter was only three years old, Albert was two, and Primmy was six months old when we brought you away from there to Killigrew House.'

She saw a spark of memory in Walter's eyes.

'I do remember something. A woman with soft hair, and a man who looked like Uncle Matt.'

'They were your parents, Walter,' Morwen said quietly. 'My brother Sam, and Dora, as pretty as Primmy is now. You've heard about the accident on – Ben's rail tracks where Sam was killed? When that happened, your mother lost the will to live, and when she got the measles she died a few weeks after your Daddy. It was a terrible time for all of us, and you three were just babies, and Ben and I brought you here to love you and care for you, and that is the truth of it—'

She realized that she was speaking wildly now, that Primmy's eyes were filling with tears at the sweet romantic tragedy of it all, and that Walter and Albert were still too upset to accept it all so easily.

'You should have told us,' Walter's voice shook with anger. 'We had a right to know.'

'Of course you did, and we always meant to tell you, darling. The time never seemed to be right—'

'Today wasn't right either!' Walter leapt to his feet, the enormity of it all still washing over him. 'To hear it from that crowing little sod wasn't right Mother – or do I have to call you Aunt Morwen from now on?'

Anger blazed up in her. 'You do not! You're my son and always will be. I may not have given birth to you, but Ben and I legally adopted all three of you, so there's no question of your not being Killigrews, and Cresswell doesn't know what he's talking about.'

'And what about me?' Justin said resentfully.

They all looked at him. He was Ben in miniature at that moment, arrogantly good-looking, temperamental, the well-bred claimant to his rights.

'Walter's always kept on about his inheritance and owning Killigrew Clay one day, and what he's going to do with it when it belongs to him. But if he's not Daddy's oldest son, it really belongs to me. Doesn't it Mother?' Morwen heard Walter's cry of outrage, and felt like strangling Justin at that moment. She spoke icily.

'Killigrew Clay belongs to your father, Justin. If anything should happen to him, it will belong to me. I assure you he's made provision for all his children, just as I shall do when the time comes. Unless of course, there is continued wrangling about it by then, when I promise you I shall have no hesitation in selling out.'

And long before that, if and when Ben died before her, another reckoning would have to come. Hal Tremayne must be recognized as half-owner of Killigrew Clay, and under the terms of his will, the Tremayne brothers would get equal shares along with Morwen. It was too much of a tangle to explain to these children, and anyway, Hal's intentions were private ones. Even Morwen wasn't supposed to know, and wouldn't have, except that her mother had felt the need to confide in her.

She hoped desperately that she had done as good a job as she was able in explaining everything to the children. Charlotte was too young to understand all the implications, and Primmy seemed to find it all reasonable enough, with reservations. The three boys were the aggressive ones, with poor Albert torn between loyalty to the other two.

'Anyway, Father had better let me leave school now,' Walter said belligerently. 'I'm not going into any stupid office when my place is obviously in the clayworks.'

'There was no disgrace in Sam's work, Walter,' Morwen said sharply. 'Don't belittle it—'

'I'm not!' he howled. 'I just want to work there, that's all! I've told you a hundred times.'

Ben's voice startled them all. He'd followed the raised voices around the side of the house, ready to snarl at them for behaving like fishwives. He reached the open French windows in time to hear Walter's last remark.

'Are you still snivelling on about being a clayworker, Walter? I haven't paid out expensive school fees all these years for you to spend your time grovelling in filth, and it's high time you recognized your position in life.'

Morwen gaped at him. If only she could have warned him, but it was too late for that too. Walter whirled on him, all the frustration inside him a match for Ben's at that moment.

'That's just what I am doing, *Father*! Or should I call you Uncle Ben, since my real father was no more than one of your wretched clayworkers, which is clearly what I was destined to be. How does it feel, to know that you can't rid your *son* of his true blood after all?'

For a second Morwen saw Ben lift his hand to strike him for his insolence. She quickly put herself between them.

'No!' she said sharply. 'This time you'll leave well alone. Can't you see the shock he's had? He knows, Ben. They all know, and we owe it to them to sit down and talk quietly and sensibly about it all.'

It took a few minutes for her meaning to sink in. He found it hard to concentrate on anything these days but his own troubles. His clay blocks and his heart. The rhythm of the words were a constant drumming in his head, like the rattle of his railway trucks.

'So they know,' he muttered. 'It had to be told sometime. You decided to go ahead without consulting me, did you?'

His anger was redirected to Morwen, and without thinking, Walter defended her.

'Don't blame Mother,' he said bitterly. 'She's the only one who seems to care enough about us to try and make sense of it all. It was that little shit Cresswell who told us.'

The faint surprise at his son's fearless language in front of him passed unheeded. He was more concerned with the other thing.

'So the Americans haven't made a perfect visit after all,' he sneered.

'Is that really all you can say?' Morwen was weary, of him, of the whole clay business, of everything.

Even of Matt's visit, which was becoming more of a strain than she would ever have dreamed. She longed for Ran's good sense, for him to take her in his arms and gentle away the pain, remembering how he had been the one to smooth over telling the children about the family background on the way to Truro Fair.

'I want to know about me,' Justin said.

Ben looked at him, standing ramrod straight in the middle of the room, bottom lip stuck out, brows drawn together.

'What about you?'

Morwen had been so taken up with Sam's children, she had overlooked just how all this was affecting Justin. She and Ben had done what was right by the children. They had legally adopted Walter and Albert and Primmy, and in the eyes of the law and in Ben's will, Justin was their fourth child. It would need gentle handling now... She heard Ben give a raucous laugh.

'Ah, I see! You think you're to be done out of your pound of flesh, do you, my pretty boy?'

Justin went brilliant red. 'Why do you always belittle me?' he almost wept. 'Why do you hate me so much?'

'Don't be ridiculous, Justin,' Ben said coldly. 'I don't hate you. You're my son.'

He stopped, the realization of all that was happening finally sinking into his fuddled brain. Again, he turned on Morwen.

'You can deal with this. It's your family at the root of it all, so you sort it out. I wash my hands of it—'

'Ben, you can't!' she said, incredulous.

'Why not? They'll all get the money when I'm dead, and I've no intention of standing here wrangling about it now. That's what it's all about, isn't it? They each want their portion of silver, but I'm not dead yet, and until I am, you'd all better remember just who holds the purse-strings.'

'Even if there's nothing in it? Even if the head of the household is feckless enough to gamble it all away?' She whipped out the words without thinking, and he rushed at her so fast she had no chance to avoid the blow to the side of her face. She reeled backwards in shock and pain, and the next second she saw Walter at Ben's throat. The boy was strong, and Ben was unprepared. He staggered as Walter all but throttled him, shouting into his mottled face.

'You touch my mother again and I'll kill you, you bastard! Get out of here before I forget my upbringing and revert to my common roots! *Get out*, you hear?'

He let him go, and Ben choked, clutching at his throat. The children crowded together, circling Morwen, more in fright than anger, but to Ben they formed a solid barrier. And since his head spun so much and his chest sawed with knifing pains, he blundered out of the room, shouting back abuse that could be heard all over the house, and would surely be repeated by the servants all over town.

'Walter—' Morwen said faintly.

Should she go to Ben to see that he was all right? He had looked so alarmingly awful... but the children needed her more, and she put her arms around the girls.

'You needn't worry about him,' Walter said bitterly. 'If he tries to hurt you again, come to me. I've no intention of returning to school and he can say what he likes about that.'

There was no sign of love in his manner, it was merely the voice of a young man defending a woman. There was no hesitancy about the school, either. He stated his decision, and she knew he meant it. If she had ever thought Walter immature, Morwen knew that the last hour had changed everything. Walter was a man.

'I hate him,' Justin said unnecessarily.

'Please don't,' Morwen said swiftly, at which Albert and Primmy spoke at once.

'How can you say that after what he did to you?'

'How can you defend a man like that?'

Morwen tried to explain. 'He wasn't always like that, my darlings. When I met him he was young, strong and handsome, and very much like—' she had been about to say like Walter, until she caught Justin's eye. She gave a small sigh. Every word would have to be used carefully now, if she wasn't to divide the children. 'He was like a god to me,' she amended. 'Things change people, and he's under a lot of strain.'

'It doesn't mean he can hit a woman,' Walter was still stoical, and Morwen saw that his schooling had done him some good after all.

'What are we going to do, anyway?' Primmy muttered.

Morwen stared at her. 'Do? Why should we do anything? We're still the same people, Primmy—'

'No, we're not. I'm not your daughter any more. I'm somebody else, and I don't even know who I am.'

She began to cry. She had held in all the emotion all this time, but now it came flooding out, and when Morwen tried to hold her close, the girl flung herself away and lay face down on the sofa. Charlotte looked frightened, and the boys uncertain. Primmy so rarely cried.

Hal and Bess found them all like that when they came into the house after Matt had delivered his message and gone on to Truro. The revelation was too important to all of them to keep to themselves now. Jack and Freddie must be told, and so must Ran.

'Our Matt says they'll stay at Ran's for tonight,' Hal told his daughter. 'They'll come back sometime tomorrow unless you send word to change their plans.'

Morwen's eyes filled with tears. What Matt meant was that if he wasn't welcome any more, he would stay away.

'Matt will never be turned away from my house, Daddy,' she choked, and then she was in his arms, while Bess seemed to encompass all the children at once, talking to them in her calming voice. Bess had never lost her homely Cornish accent, or tried to.

'We'll go up to the nursery and try to sort things through,' Bess soothed them. 'Nothing was ever so bad that talking it through didn't make it better. Will 'ee all come with your Grandma, me dears?'

They didn't move for a minute, and then Charlotte put her hand in the old pin-pricked one.

'You'll always be our Grandma, won't you, Grandma Bess?' she said waveringly.

'Of course I will, my lamb. Allus was and allus will be.'

Morwen watched them go, trailing behind her comfortable shape, until at last she and Hal were alone. She looked at her father wordlessly. He held her close to him, and she could smell the rugged outdoors on him. The clay and the moors and the dear familiar essence of him.

'Your Mammie will sort this, my darling girl,' Hal said huskily. 'She'll find the right words, never you fear.'

It was ironic. Her uneducated mother would find the words… when all the explanations in the world couldn't put this right, not really. She leaned against Hal, wanting his strength, his solid sense of immortality in a world that was frightening in its changing patterns. She was an adult, but suddenly she longed for the simplicity of childhood, when decisions were made for her, and she had none of life's responsibilities.

'Oh, Daddy, how I wish—' she whispered against the dark woollen cloth of his coat. 'I wish everything could be like it was before. All of us cosy at the cottage, with Sam and Matt and Jack working with the clay, and Freddie running wild on the moors with the kiddley-boys, and me and Mammie and you—'

'We can't ever go back, Morwen love,' he said quietly. 'You know that. All we can do is go on the best we can. 'Tis all any of us can ever do.'

He kissed her fevered cheek, his girl-child who was so very special to him, and he longed to give her the comfort she sought. Knowing that he couldn't, not this time. But he believed implicitly in his own words. Bess would sort things, as she had always done for all his family.

–

Whatever her mother said to the children, they came downstairs subdued but clearer-eyed. Sam's children spoke in whispers about being chosen ones, which made it all sound a bit irreverent, and clearly irritated Justin. But they had stopped resenting Morwen so much, and were trying very hard to understand that she and Ben had only wanted the very best for them.

Walter still thought darkly that the real villain was Cresswell for being so snotty, however unintentional. But since it was unlikely they would see him again after next week, Grandma Bess had made it plain that it would upset her and Hal very much if they didn't all try to get along together for these last few days. And the children had reluctantly agreed.

Hal and Bess stayed until after the children went to bed. There was no sign of Ben, and Morwen guessed he would be drinking again to put the afternoon into oblivion. He would never think that she needed him, that this was something they should be sharing, and she had never felt so lonely.

She had been in bed a long while when she heard her door open, and remembered too late that she had forgotten to lock it. She turned quickly, seeing Ben's swaying figure silhouetted in the light from the window. For a moment she felt real fear.

And then she heard him. Deep, wrenching sobs were coming from his throat, as if they came from his soul. She had never heard him cry like this before. Her heart ached for him. He stumbled to her bed, and almost fell on to it, scrabbling to get beneath the covers to hold her.

Her fear dissolved. There was nothing sexual in his embrace. There was only the need to be with another human being, and she recognized that need and met it generously. She held him, rocking him in her arms as if he was a child, and his muffled words throbbed through her body.

'Dear God, Morwen, what a mess we've made of our lives. What a bloody terrible mess.'

There was no thought of recrimination in her. No accusations, no hate, just pity for this poor wreck of a man who had once been so strong and so loving, and everything she had ever wanted.

She held him until he felt heavy against her and she knew he was asleep. And when she awoke in the morning she was alone.

Chapter Twenty-One

It was an uneasy, nervous week. Cresswell had been given a very strong talking-to, and had apologized to everyone in sight, scared out of his wits by his father's anger. No matter how much Louisa pleaded that the boy hadn't known the truth, Matt had been increasingly aware of his son's vindictive nature, and this seemed as good an opportunity as any to assure him in no uncertain terms that it must stop.

On the evening after all the upset had occurred, Freddie and Venetia arrived at the house. She proudly displayed a gleaming new betrothal ring on her third finger, the heavy gold circlet enclosing four beautiful garnets.

'We haven't come merely to show off Venetia's ring, though,' Freddie smiled, when everyone had duly admired it. 'We want to ask the children a special favour.'

Venetia broke in. 'I specially want Primmy and Charlotte to be my flower-girls at the wedding, and since the boys are too old to be pages, we wondered if Walter and Albert and Justin would be ushers at the church door. It's a very responsible job, showing people to their seats and handing out the hymn books. Do you think you can do it, boys?'

Morwen held her breath. How thoughtful they were to think of this. Drawing the children together in a common task. And of course, there was no question of including Cresswell, since he would be back in California with his parents long before then.

Primmy's smile was almost back to normal, and Charlotte squealed with delight.

'Will Grandma Bess make us each another new dress, do you think?' Primmy enquired eagerly.

'Of course,' Freddie grinned. 'You and Venetia can choose the colour you want, and what flowers you'll wear in your hair and strew about the church.'

It would be a grander wedding than her own, Morwen thought reminiscently, since Venetia's father was now a Lord. But it had been Morwen and Ben's own choice to be married at Penwithick church, so that Celia could be a part of it all…

'Mother, can we?' Primmy asked, and Morwen nodded at once.

'Of course. I think it's a wonderful idea.' She looked at the boys, waiting.

Walter was still edgy. He had stolidly refused to leave the house that morning and go to school, no matter how Ben had raged at him. Morwen had supported the boy's wishes, and in the end Ben had stumped off, defeated. She hated to see him like that. She still remembered last night, when he had cried in her arms. But Walter was still the vulnerable one, and he was the one who needed her now.

Ran had brought Matt and his family back during the day, but they were never alone together. He couldn't say the things he wanted to, but to Morwen his strength and love were almost tangible. She could see it in his eyes, and wondered that no one else could see it too.

'We won't have to dress up in frills, will we?' Walter hedged, before agreeing to this new suggestion.

'Good Lord, no,' Freddie said quickly. 'You'll wear proper suits like the rest of the men. As the oldest, Walter, we shall expect you to keep the other boys in order.' He gave a small wink as if they shared a secret, and Walter suddenly smiled.

'Can I come and stay with you for a while when Uncle Matt's gone home? It will be very dull around here with the others at school, and Granddad Hal thinks it's best if I don't start at Clay One yet. The men are getting angry because of the delay with the French ship, and he thinks my presence will annoy them even more.'

Freddie laughed.

'Is this your price for being chief usher at my wedding?'

Walter laughed back, and the camaraderie between them was the best thing Morwen had seen in two days.

'If you like.'

'Then, if your mother agrees, of course you can come and stay. You can help me in the shop.'

Morwen wondered fleetingly if Walter's presence would disturb any little têtes-à-têtes between the newly engaged couple. But Freddie and Venetia had made their own decision about that. They had all the rest of their lives to be together, and they could wait now until their wedding-day.

It wasn't until later, at Ran's house-warming-cum-farewell party for the American Tremaynes, in fact, that Morwen realized there was another attraction in Truro, apart from Walter's sudden affinity for her brother Freddie. There was also Cathy Askhew.

–

Ran was determined to make this party a happy occasion. There were to be no upsets, no favourites, no undercurrents. Louisa was his cousin, and if this visit hadn't been all that she might have wished, he meant to make this last day the happiest since her arrival. Tomorrow the whole family would be taking the journey back to Falmouth to see them safely on the ship to America. Tomorrow there would be time enough for tears.

Tonight they were all going to enjoy themselves. There was food and drink in plenty, and games, and he had hired some musicians to play for dancing. The young ones as well as the older ones were encouraged to join in. Hal declined, and Annie had gone upstairs to rest for an hour during the party. Ben said valiantly that it was bad manners to leave someone sitting alone, and volunteered to sit out with him. He flashed Morwen a quick glance, daring her to comment, but they both knew well enough that such exertions would be bad for him.

When Morwen was out of breath with circling in Matt's arms, she begged to be allowed to rest awhile, and watched instead as Walter manfully cavorted around the large drawing-room with Cathy Askhew held at arm's length. This was something neither she nor any of her brothers had done at so young an age. She was filled with tenderness at the concentration on Walter's face, obviously wanting to make a good showing in front of his lady.

She caught her thoughts up short – his lady? Cathy Askhew was still a child, the same as he was… but Walter had proved of late that he was far from being a child, and Morwen noted with surprise the way Cathy lowered her eyes in an unconsciously flirtatious manner, and the way her small breasts rose and fell in the silky dress she wore. Her ringlets were golden, like her mother's had been, and Morwen saw Jane's knowing smile as she passed Morwen and Ben in the arms of the gallant Jack Tremayne.

'History repeating itself, would you say, my love?' Ben mocked her. 'Worried by it, are you? And no doubt dubbing the delicious little Cathy as the next Miss Finelady!'

'Don't be ridiculous, Ben. And please don't drink too much,' she hissed beneath her breath.

Despite her own feelings, she hated to hear him demean Cathy by his words. She was a nice girl. She too would be leaving Cornwall soon, which might be just as well, Morwen thought with sudden anxiety, as the dance ended. She didn't miss the way Walter followed the girl's every movement and accompanied her to the cold table to help her load her plate with meats and vegetables, and carried the food for her.

The music started up again, and she saw Ben lurch through the dancers until he reached Jane.

'Will you dance with me, my Lady?' he said in a voice loud enough for Morwen to hear.

Morwen turned away as she heard Jane's friendly laugh. He did this to torment her and she knew it. But while she still burned with mortification, Ran held out his arms to her, and she went into them, dream-like, and everything in her world was the right way up once more.

'I've missed you,' he said, under cover of the music.

'And I you,' she whispered back. 'So much.'

Only by the tightening of his fingers around hers would anyone with sharp eyes have noted the intimacy between them. They were isolated in the midst of their family and friends, and for poignant moments Morwen could pretend that this was a dance without end.

'How is he?'

'The same. I wonder how long he can go on like this. He drinks incessantly. He – he revolts me.' She said it quickly, knowing that she betrayed Ben by her words, but unable to be anything but honest with this man who gave her hope that someday life could still be beautiful.

'He doesn't attempt—'

'Oh no.'

They shouldn't be having this conversation. It was farcical and endearing to feel Ran's indignation that her husband might be sharing her bed, which he had every right to do. They could only speak in short snatches, as they whirled around the room with the others. But she was very aware of his caring, and was cheered by it.

None of them was going back to St Austell that night, since Matt and his family had to reach Falmouth by mid-day. There was plenty of room at Ran's house for Hal and Bess, and for Ben and Morwen and the children, though it had been necessary to suggest that Ben shared a room with the three boys, and Morwen with the girls, for which she was eternally grateful.

The others would go home to Truro, and they would all be together again tomorrow. Except for Jane and her daughter, of course. But Walter had something to say about that.

'Mother, Cathy's never seen the harbour at Falmouth. Couldn't she come along as well, to see them off?'

'I don't know what her mother would say about that,' Morwen began, but Jane smiled at once.

'I don't mind, if you agree, Morwen.'

Freddie suggested, 'Cathy can come with Venetia and me, and we'll deliver her home safely later in the day.'

It was all arranged. Jane didn't suggest coming as well, to Morwen's relief. It would be enough of a strain saying good-bye to Matt, and now that the time they had together was hours rather than days, all the things she meant to say to him came crowding back. All the regrets, and the confidences, and the lovely times they should have had, that were somehow marred and not quite as any of them had expected.

Sadly, Morwen wondered if it was always like this. The anticipation of something was often so much more enjoyable than the actual event.

'I think it's time we went to bed,' Bess said at last, finding it hard to keep awake. Jack and Annie and the twins had gone long ago, and the four younger Killigrew children had also gone to their beds. Walter was still outside somewhere, seeing Jane and Cathy Askhew into their waiting carriage and checking that their driver wouldn't fall asleep on the way home.

When he came back inside the house, Morwen thought in amusement that he was as attentive as a lover. And realized that that wasn't quite as foolish as it seemed. But not yet… Walter was barely fifteen years old. It was too soon to be thinking of such things, and it made Morwen feel far too old to contemplate it!

'We should all go to bed,' she agreed quickly, thinking that the sooner Ben went up, the sooner he would finish with the brandy bottle.

She said good-night, glad that the party was breaking up. It had been more successful than anyone could have hoped, after the previous week. And, at last, the French ship had left Cornish shores, and was on its way to France with the clay blocks, so they could all breathe easier again.

It was hard to sleep. She was in Ran's house, sleeping in one of Ran's beds, and although the girls were snuffling noisily alongside her, Morwen was very conscious that they were under the same roof. The last time that had happened, they had shared a small hotel room in London… she kept her thoughts rigidly away, refusing to remember the pleasure and the pain of that time. If it hadn't been for Ben's attackers, she might never have found solace in her lover's arms… and there would always be guilt mingled with the joy of it.

–

They were all up early. The day was here, and Bess was very pale as she picked at her breakfast. It was worse for her, Morwen thought. In all probability Bess would never see Matt again. But each of them seemed to have decided not to cry for the sake of the others. Amid all the hugs and kisses when the moment of embarkation came, throats were thick and voices choked, but they managed to hold back the tears until the last of the waving hands could be seen no more, and the ship glided majestically into the wide basin of Falmouth harbour.

'Good-bye, our Matt,' Morwen heard her mother whisper. She put her arm around Bess, who suddenly seemed to have shrunk.

'Come on, Mammie. Let's go home. We've still got a wedding to plan, and Jack's babby to be born before the end of the year.'

Bess gave her a watery smile. 'You were allus a good girl, Morwen. A wedding and a birthing are the two best things.'

Morwen felt a chill run through her. She wished she hadn't mentioned the two together. It left a great question mark over the third. There was always a third, and the third was a dying.

She heard Cathy Askhew thanking Bess politely for letting her come to Falmouth with them.

'You'm welcome, my lamb,' Bess said warmly now. ''Tis nice to see young folk getting along so well.'

Cathy blushed, and Morwen realized that Walter was hovering right beside her. He would be staying in Truro with Freddie now, and impulsively she gave him a hug too.

'Take care, darling,' she said. 'And come home when you're ready.'

He nodded, knowing the implication in her words. The other children had found their own kind of acceptance now that the initial shock of their true identity was over, but Walter was still unsure, and needed time away from them to see things clearly. Morwen understood that.

In the same way, she had always needed to be on the moors away from people, the child of nature that old Zillah used to call her. She smiled ruefully; Walter's needs weren't quite the same. All he needed right now was to get away from her and Ben.

She prayed that they were all going to be less troubled now. Matt's visit had been as traumatic as it had been wonderful, and what they all needed now was a return to normal living.

She helped her parents into the trap with Primmy and Charlotte, who begged to ride with them. She and Ben would take the younger boys and all meet at Killigrew House. She looked around for Ben. Where was he…?

She heard him before she saw him, and her heart lurched. Dear God, not more arguments…

'I saw the way you were behaving with the Askhew girl, Walter, and I'm just warning you to behave yourself. Jane is an old friend of mine, and if I hear of any trouble being brought to my door because of young Cathy, you'll answer to me for it. Do you understand?'

Morwen could have wept for his insensitivity. Walter's love for Cathy, if love it was, was so new and so fragile, and Ben's harsh words were destroying it. She heard Walter's angry reply.

'I've no intention of bringing trouble anywhere. And certainly not to your door. You do that well enough for yourself.'

'You young devil. How dare you speak to your father like that?' Ben was incensed, his face puce.

'But you're not my father, are you? And I'd say my real father would despise you just as much as I do for the way you trample all over everyone around you. Is there anything more, or can I go now?' He oozed sarcasm, and Morwen knew it was time she intervened.

'Walter, please apologize at once.'

'Not this time, Mother. He got what he deserved for once, and I hope my opinion chokes him.'

He stalked off to join Freddie and Venetia and Cathy, too far away to hear what was happening with the general harbour commotion going on all around them. Cathy could obviously see that something was wrong. She threw a puzzled glance their way, and then slipped her arm through Walter's for a moment, before dropping it just as quickly.

'Did you see that?' Ben spluttered. 'There's something going on there, Morwen. And did you hear the insolence of the boy?'

'Ben, for pity's sake. You'll make yourself ill, and people are beginning to stare—'

'Let them,' he snarled. 'Is that all you care about? Your son? What people will think?'

'I care about you, Ben,' she said steadily.

He stared at her stonily, and at last he seemed to slump and to let her lead the way to the carriage. The boys were already inside it, and as they left Falmouth, Morwen felt as though all the close family ties she cherished were beginning to unravel. It was a terrible, empty feeling, and at the heart of it was losing Matt all over again.

–

Two days later a messenger came rushing to Killigrew House.

'Mr Killigrew, Sir, you'm wanted at Charlestown port. Summat terrible's happened, Sir, and the harbour-master wants 'ee there right away.'

'What's happened?' Ben said at once.

The man snorted. 'I dunno the ins and outs on it, but 'tis summat awful bad about your clay blocks, so he said. He just said to get 'ee there quicker'n yesterday.'

Ben was out of the house without even calling Morwen. His gut was filled with a sick dread. He leapt on the back of his horse, leaving the man running behind him, and cursing about the ingratitude of gentlemen. Ben raced his horse towards the port and slithered off its back, not noticing how it lathered and laboured, nor how its movements matched his own labouring heart.

'What's happened?' he gasped out when he saw the harbour-master's grey face.

'Mr Killigrew, calm yourself—'

'The devil take you! I've no time to be calm!' Ben roared. 'Is the ship sunk?'

He saw the man nod. 'It had almost reached France, but I fear all the cargo has been lost. Everything was over in minutes. A vessel on its way back here saw it happen. The repairs may not have been sturdy enough, or the ship may have been holed again. There were dangerous rocks in the area, but the ship was old, and her timbers were in need of renewal. By some miracle a few of the crew were saved and were picked up by the other ship—'

Ben heard his voice meandering on. At least, it seemed that way to him. The voice seemed to float somewhere between him and the sea, where his precious cargo of clay blocks was absorbing salt water and slowly sinking to the bottom. It was crazy and ironic that all the months of drying the stuff at his clayworks had resulted in the clay becoming swollen and bloated, like old men distorted after drowning…

It was so ironic it was laughable. Ben suddenly heard himself laughing, laughing and screeching, because it was all so hilariously funny. His clay blocks had been lost too far out for even the wreckers to take an interest in them, unless the French had wreckers too. That would be a laugh. They'd probably serve them up as some new French delicacy and cure the stomach-ache at the same time. Somebody should market that.

The agonizing pain in his chest was funny too. Everything was a huge joke, and this was the biggest joke of all, because Ben Killigrew was never going to be able to pay off his debts now, and it didn't matter a damn, because he wouldn't be around to see the fury of his debtors…

'Mr Killigrew, should I call a doctor?' he heard the harbour-master's voice again, hazy, alarmed, and he grimaced as the pain clenched him in a death-hold.

'No. An undertaker,' he managed to choke.

–

There was nothing they could say that would pacify Walter. He was totally convinced that it was all his fault that Ben had died so unexpectedly. He had goaded his father. He had been so bitter and not tried to understand. The other children went around like silent little ghosts, whispering and worrying, but Walter wept openly, and to Morwen, it was the worst thing of all.

'Will you please listen to me, darling?' she tried yet again. 'It was not your fault. Doctor Pender's already told you of your father's heart condition. He's shown you the report from the London Hospital. This was going to happen some day, and both your father and I knew it.'

'Another secret you decided to keep from me?' Walter said bitterly.

'Would you rather I had told you so that you watched him every minute like a hawk? Do you think Ben would have wanted that? He was strong and proud, Walter, and so are you.

You may not have his blood in you, but you have his strength and his pride, and I need you to be strong now. I need it for myself.'

She tried not to tremble over the words. She ached for him and loved him, and knew that he was going through a private wilderness.

'I blame myself. If I hadn't been such a bastard—'

He glanced at her, and she gave a tiny smile. 'It's all right. Swear if it makes you feel any better. But don't go on hurting yourself so needlessly.'

He didn't answer, and she knew she wasn't reaching him yet. He had come rushing here from Truro as soon as Morwen had sent word to everyone, and had been white-faced and devastated ever since. He had spent hours in the room upstairs, where Ben was now laid out in readiness for the burying. Morwen prayed for the day to come and be over, and then perhaps Walter could find some sort of peace with himself.

Killigrew House had become a kind of focal point. All the family were there at different times, except for Annie who needed daily rest and not too many shocks. Hal and Bess were as supportive as always, and there was always Ran, at her side whenever she needed him. But Morwen felt oddly constrained with him. Her husband lay upstairs, not yet buried, and yet she felt as though her heart was encased in a block of ice.

She had made her own peace with Ben. She had wept in unexpected agony when they brought him home. He was more relaxed in death than in many years of life, and she saw in him no longer the hard, brittle, and unpredictable man of recent years, but the young, virile Ben Killigrew she had loved so madly. She wept for all that they had shared, and all they had been to each other, and when she had finished weeping, it seemed there were no tears left for herself.

She made polite replies to all those who called to pay their respects, and who went away awed at the dignity of Ben Killigrew's widow, still beautiful in her mourning, still a desirable young woman, whether the words were said aloud or not.

And amid all the misery, there was something else that needed to be made clear. There was supposed to be a wedding in the family…

'I see no reason why it shouldn't still go on,' Hal said evenly, when they were all together a few days later. ''Tis up to Morwen to say if she thinks it fitting, of course, but we've allus been clayfolk, and weddings and birthings and buryings are all part of life, and have to be accommodated.'

'Daddy's right,' Jack added just as gently. 'Mourning never did any good to anyone, and we won't remember Ben any the less by going on with Freddie's wedding. 'Twill do us all good, in my opinion.'

They were all beginning to treat her as if she was made of the finest porcelain fired from their own china-clay, Morwen thought, and said her piece.

'It's not my say-so, but Freddie's and Venetia's. If they think it's too soon, then we'll wait, but if they want to go ahead, I'd have no objection.'

'We don't want to wait.'

Freddie sat with Venetia's hand in his, and Morwen could see the faint relief on both their faces. Her small feeling of resentment died. Why should they wait, when all they wanted was to be together? And it wasn't going to hurt Ben.

'That's settled then,' she said briskly. 'There's no need to change any of the arrangements. And after the – the funeral, Walter wants to come back with you again, Freddie. Is it all right? I'd like it too, if he's no trouble.'

'He's a help in the shop. Of course he can come.'

He hesitated, then decided it was wisest not to tell any of them about the nights he heard the boy crying. It may have been his sleep, but awake or not, it was obvious to Freddie that Walter was still going through torment. And if he wanted to ask that nice Cathy Askhew to tea, Freddie't wouldn't object. In fact, it was probably the best thing, to take his mind off everything else. He would definitely suggest it.

It was easy enough to settle things, Morwen thought. Everything in neat little compartments, and Ben in his box upstairs. Freddie and Venetia would be married, and Annie would have her baby. Matt wouldn't know about Ben until he reached America and her letter caught up with him, but she doubted it would cause more than a ripple, other than his concern for herself. In time, the children would cope with the new way of life, and she…

Morwen knew that even this terrible time was only a little respite. Ben's business affairs were nagging to be dealt with, and she couldn't put it off for long. Once the funeral was over, she must turn her attention to them. The will must be read, and then she intended going to Killigrew Clay, with Hal at her side, to tell the clayworkers exactly what the situation was. Just how bad it really was, she still had to find out from Daniel Gorran, and that too, was a meeting she dreaded.

There was one more compartment in her life that as yet she dare not open. She had been born an optimist, with a zest for life that surrounded her like an aura. But for now, the bright future for which she yearned beckoned from a far distance as if through a Cornish mist, elusive and unattainable.

Chapter Twenty-Two

It was the biggest funeral St Austell had seen for a long time. All the town wags said so, even if the bulk of the walking congregation were those extraordinary clayworkers. Not that they could fault them for their deference to a fair boss. They were all agreed on that. Their garb may be strange… the men in their tidied working clobber, because most of them had nothing else… the young kiddley-boys mostly in bare feet… the bal maidens in their brightest and best clothes and bonnets, because this was still an occasion, and they loved an occasion, whether it was a wedding or a burying…

They all shuffled behind the black-plumed horses of the hearse, lending dignity and spectacle to what was still essentially a family affair.

'The poor young woman,' some muttered, seeing Morwen's set face, white and cold as if frozen in stone.

'And all those debts that Ben Killigrew was rumoured to have left. How will she cope wi' those—?'

''Tis no time to be speaking such ill of the dead,' the speaker was shushed at once as the cortège began to pass them.

For Morwen, it was still a nightmare. She walked behind the black-draped coffin, finding it unbelievable that Ben was inside it. No matter how prepared you were, she had discovered that the shock of death was always the same. And for all his faults, Ben had been so vital, so alive… and now he was dead. She choked back a sob, and felt the arms supporting hers tighten.

Her two strong brothers, Jack and Freddie, were at her side, while close behind them came the three young boys in a small scuffling group of misery. Then came Hal and Bess, and behind them Ran, with Venetia. No one expected Annie to attend in her condition, but everyone else was in more or less their proper order, with friends, business acquaintances, and the heartbeat of Killigrew Clay in the background. Only the two girls, Primmy and Charlotte, stayed behind at the house, at Morwen's insistence and their own relief.

The ceremony was long and dismal, which was as it should be. They were here to bury Ben Killigrew, and it was the end of an era. They laid him to rest in a fine part of the churchyard with a view of the sea, and Morwen suddenly thought how ludicrous it was.

As if Ben cared now whether he was in sight of land or sea. They had once shared a lot of laughter, over big things and small. Ben would laugh at the incongruity of all this…

To her horror, she felt the appalling laughter begin to bubble up inside her and managed to crush it with an enormous effort. And the saddest and most terrible thing of all, was that the one person she wanted to turn to and say how funny it all was, was Ben…

People were shaking her hand and murmuring condolences, and she was answering them with the usual platitudes in use on these occasions, to be brought out and dusted and then put away until the next time. It was all meaningless. The only thing that counted was that Ben was dead and she was alone. Even among all these crowds, all wishing her well, their waves of sympathy almost smothering her, she was alone.

She felt Walter's hand reach for hers and heard his voice telling her it was time to come away from the graveside. His young, heartbroken voice… Morwen drew in a small breath.

'Mother, we should get back to the house. The carriages have arrived, and the lawyer will be expecting us.'

How did he manage to say such sensible words when all the pain in him was so obvious to her? But apparently his real pain was clear only to her. She heard someone say what a fine support the eldest Killigrew boy was going to be, so like his father... Walter heard it too, and she saw his jaw clench.

They had had a bad time with Walter this last week, who still blamed himself totally for his father's death. No matter how often Morwen told him the truth, that it was going to happen sooner rather than later, Walter blamed himself for hastening the end. She just prayed that time would lessen the unwarranted guilt he felt. Time, and love.

Two hours later the family arranged themselves in a tableau for the reading of the will. They had invited no one back to the house, and when they were fortified with whatever they needed, the lawyer cleared his throat and broke the seal on the bulky envelope.

He need hardly have bothered, Morwen thought later. Everything was clear-cut, exactly as she had explained it to Walter. There were no surprises. Everything was left to her, with no mention that her father was a partner in Killigrew Clay. Hal had always insisted on that. Not until he chose to reveal it, would that bit of truth come out. And the final statement said that on Morwen's death, all that part of Cornwall known as Killigrew Clay should be shared equally between their five children, Walter Killigrew, Albert Killigrew, Primrose Killigrew, Justin Killigrew and Charlotte Killigrew. There were no special tributes, no tokens, everything was equal.

The children were snuffling as the lawyer gathered up the papers with a slight feeling of disappointment. It would have been so much more dramatic if there had been some family histrionics, but Ben Killigrew had always been clear in his mind about his will. As he shook the hand of the lovely young widow, the lawyer thought dryly that it was probably the only thing he had been clear about in recent months.

They all relaxed when the man had gone, but there was little left to say. Freddie and Venetia wanted to leave as soon as possible, and Walter was thankful to get away with them. It seemed as though he couldn't bear to be in this house a moment longer than necessary.

The others lingered, but were obviously anxious to get away as well. There was suddenly a great need to pull back the curtains, to let fresh air into houses that had been dark with mourning, to feel part of the world once more. Bess hugged her daughter as she and Hal got ready to depart.

'I'll come and see 'ee tomorrow, my lamb,' Bess said.

Morwen gave her a tight smile. 'Yes. We must discuss the girls' dresses for the wedding, Mammie. Time's getting short, and Venetia will be anxious to have everything ready.'

If Bess thought it odd for her daughter to be thinking ahead to a wedding when she had just buried her husband, she didn't say so.

They were all leaving. The younger boys begged to be allowed to go to the beach, and Morwen didn't have the heart to refuse them. The girls wanted to play in the nursery, and Morwen knew so well that need to do normal, ordinary things, to allay the fear and horror of death. She let them all go, and finally there was only one person left with her.

Ran took her in his arms, and they were the arms of a friend. They couldn't have been otherwise at this time. He knew that she was as fragile as glass, that if he made the wrong approaches to her, she would splinter and break. And she had been so brave, so beautiful and brave through it all.

She leaned her head against him, closing her eyes. She was so tired. She wasn't sleeping properly, and it was comforting just to stand here like this, knowing that he was willing to give all that she needed and no more.

'I want to make you an offer, Morwen,' she heard his voice against her cheek, and her eyes opened like a startled fawn's. He took her cold hands in his and led her to the sofa. Mrs Horn had lit a fire. Not because there was any chill in the May afternoon, but because spirits were low on such a day, and the warmth of a fire gave some kind of cheer.

'Morwen, I'm well aware of the state of Ben's finances,' he said abruptly. 'I know about his gambling disasters, and because

Daniel Gorran and I became good friends, I persuaded him to let me see the Killigrew ledgers.'

He saw her eyes flash with anger. Her pride was bruised at his words, and he was glad to see it. It was preferable to the awful blankness that had made him so afraid for her sanity.

'It was none of your business—'

'I made it my business. I did it because of my attachment to the family, and because of what you and I might one day become to one another.'

He felt her flinch, and knew he must tread carefully.

'I'm not speaking of such things now, Morwen. I know the time isn't right—'

'No, it's not right,' she whispered. 'None of what we've done is right. Ben is dead, and I betrayed him, and now it's too late to make amends. It's too late for me to ever tell him again how much I once loved him—'

Deep, racking sobs shook her whole body as he held her silently. He had seen grief before. He knew the guilt and self-condemnation of the bereaved. He knew it would pass, and that it was a transition period Morwen had to go through. He could only wait, and suffer with her.

When the paroxysm had passed, he spoke unemotionally.

'What I'm offering is financial help, Morwen. Not as a gift or a loan, or anything that will insult you. I want to buy into Killigrew Clay, to be your business partner. Prosper Barrows is living up to its name, and we could easily expand to include china-clay in our assets. Together you and I would own the biggest company in Cornwall.'

His words dazzled her. She hadn't expected this. Ran must have thought hard and carefully about it. It was so very tempting. His money would pay off all the debts, even give the clayworkers a small wage rise, perhaps. She had never been in charge of anything in her life, except five children… Her thoughts whirled. She knew that her father, too, was very uneasy with his new status. He had never wanted to be a boss, and now the position was thrust on him. With Ran, there would be another man to turn to…

And there lay more problems. Ran assumed, like everyone else, that Ben's widow was now the sole owner of Killigrew Clay. No one but a lawyer and a bank manager in Bodmin, knew that there was a silent partner. That Hal Tremayne, one-time clayworker, Pit Captain, and more lately Works Manager, was in reality now the equal partner of the new owner, Morwen Killigrew.

She sat up slowly. Tears streaked her cheeks, but where she had been so pale, there was a flush of colour on her face.

'I can't make any such decision yet, Ran. I'll have to think about it. But I thank you from the bottom of my heart for your offer.'

He could see that she was nearly at breaking point. She needed a breathing-space, from business worries, from her family, from him. She was like a delicate flower, dormant after the winter, needing to be renewed by the summer. But it seemed he didn't know her well enough yet…

'I shall go to the works in a day or two,' she said. 'The men need to know that nothing will change because there's a woman in control. I'm not the first woman clay boss in Cornwall, and I have to let them see that I'm not weak and flighty and about to let the business collapse. There are matters I must discuss with my father, and we both think it's best to let the clayworkers know exactly what's happening. It will be the new policy.'

He nodded approvingly at her small show of determination. Anything that made her look to the future, whatever that future might be for Killigrew Clay, was better than wallowing in the past, and Ran greatly admired her strength of character. She saw a challange, and she met it head-on. He was just as determined. They were a match, and some day soon, she would come to him, and theirs would be a true and full partnership, in both the physical and the business sense of the word. But he was wise enough to say no more for the present. He loved her too much to risk her fragile hold on sanity. He had dangled the bait, and he was a patient man. He would wait until she was ready.

–

Morwen faced her father in the small house. Bess stayed silently in the background. Her daughter was stronger than she herself had ever been, even now, with her husband's death so recent. Black suited Morwen, but Bess sensed that she wouldn't stay in deep mourning for long. The conventions of the town wouldn't trouble her one jot, and she would need to feel less oppressed by the bleak colour. She murmured something about bringing in tea and fruit cake, but the others hardly heard her as she escaped to the scullery.

'Daddy, you have to let everyone know now,' Morwen said passionately. 'I'll not take on this burden alone. 'Tis not fair of you to ask it of me—'

'I still don't see the need.' He was as dogged, as stubborn as ever. 'The men have a fondness for 'ee, Morwen, knowing of your roots, and they'll be loyal to 'ee now that you'm the boss—'

'But I don't want to be the boss. I want the partnership to be out in the open! I've never cared for secrets—'

She stopped, biting her lip as it wavered uncontrollably. Secrets! Suddenly it seemed that her whole life had been bound up with them. Seeking the help of a witch to see her true love… and again to help Celia be rid of a child… the guilt of burying the so-called 'waste' that had been the result of the abortion… the horror of Celia's death and pretending that her friend had been so afraid of a growth that she drowned herself… her own dealings with Jude Pascoe… wicked secrets…

'Morwen, love, don't take on so. Do it really mean so much to 'ee?' She heard her father's troubled voice now, and realized that she was sobbing quietly. She, who never resorted to women's tears, and she dashed them away angrily.

'I respect your views, Daddy, and if you want to wait awhile before telling the men, then we'll see how it goes. But I can't wait for ever. And there's another matter.'

She took a deep breath. Bess came into the room in time to hear what she was saying.

'Ran has offered to buy into Killigrew Clay. He knows nothing of your share in it, and merely thinks he's doing me a favour. Or both of us. He says that if Prosper Barrows and Killigrew Clay combined, we'd be a powerful force in Cornwall.'

'Ran suggested such a thing? When was this, our Morwen?' Bess said sharply.

Morwen gave a half-smile. She could read her mother's thoughts at that moment.

'It was all very proper, Mammie. It was after you had all left the house on the day of the funeral—'

'I'm not sure I call that a proper time. Were the two of 'ee alone then?'

Suddenly it all seemed too much bother to continue fencing. Morwen looked squarely into her mother's eyes, and spoke with a mature dignity.

'Mammie, Ran and I have had a fondness for one another for a long time. But no one could ever have accused that meeting of being anything but proper. Ran made the offer as a good friend, nothing more. If ever the attachment becomes more serious, 'twill be when time has softened the pain of these last months. I promise 'ee that.'

She carefully avoided any reference to times past when she and Ran might have shared other moments, other pleasures.

''Tis not the point at issue now, Bess,' Hal put in gently, 'We'll need to consider Ran's offer, and obviously my thoughts must come into it, but our main concern now is to assure the clayworkers that nothing's going to be changed because of the new ownership.'

'That's right. There are still debts to be paid, and wages to be kept low, and the disaster of losing a good proportion of the spring clay despatches,' Morwen said bitterly.

The breath caught in her throat for an instant. 'I hadn't really thought hard enough about it, Daddy, and my immediate reaction to Ran's offer was to reject it and to think defiantly that we could manage perfectly well. But I'm not sure that we can. I'm not sure that we don't need him desperately.'

None of them spoke for a few minutes, and Morwen felt a cup of tea thrust into her hands. It was her mother's panacea for all ailments, and obediently she drank deeply of the hot strong brew. For a fleeting moment she thought how idyllic it would be to be a child again, even a ragged child of the moors, running barefoot, and never having to rely on herself for anything. Slowly she put down the cup and looked at Hal; there was no going back.

'Shall we go to the works today, Daddy?' She kept her voice rock-still. 'We can't put it off, and I know the men will be getting anxious the longer we put it off.'

'Aye, love, we'll go today,' he said heavily. 'There's always anxiety until they're assured that things will continue the same as before. Though 'twon't be easy to make 'em see it.'

-

They left Bess at the small house and rode up to Clay One together. Ironically to Morwen, it had never looked more beautiful than today in the May sunlight. Some might find the clayworks a scar on the moors. She had always found them beautiful. The milky-green claypools, with their mysterious depths, and the glittering sky-tips of waste, sparkling with mineral deposits, and the throb and hum of energy and power.

That energy was all concentrated now in the mass of clayworkers awaiting them. Morwen knew of old that the kiddley-boys would have reported the first sighting of her and her father, and news of their arrival would have spread like flames from a grass-fire. The clayworkers stood ten-deep, arms crossed against their chests, like ancient stalwarts in their thigh-length boots and clay-dusted clobber.

The bal maidens fussed around like white butterflies, their bonnets bobbing as they muttered between themselves, clearly wondering how Morwen Killigrew, lately Tremayne, was going to handle this new situation of being boss.

The kiddley-boys drove everyone mad as usual, darting between the rest and bantering irreverently, despite the fact that their late boss, Ben Killigrew, was so recently buried. To them death was all part of life, and if today's appearance by Morwen Killigrew meant a respite in the daily working, it was their lucky day.

'You'll know why we've come,' Hal said loudly, when the raucous noise had died down. ''Tis not my place to speak for the new boss, but I'll say my piece afore Morwen says hers. You all know my daughter. You've known her since she were knee-high to a sparrow, and you all know that she knows the workings of Killigrew Clay as well as any of 'ee. 'Tis not a bad thing for a boss to have worked with the clay, and I'll ask 'ee to remember that when she talks to 'ee.'

He stopped abruptly, more conscious of his own position with every word he said. He was describing himself, as well as Morwen, and he wasn't sure what these simple folk might say if the truth were told. That their Works Manager, once their Pit Captain, had been part-owner for many years, and was still part-owner with his daughter. If you ignored the fact of a change of name through marriage, it was a twist of fate that Killigrew Clay was now in the control of the Tremaynes.

Even years into the future, when Walter and Albert and Primmy, and Justin and Charlotte became owners, it would still be more Tremayne than Killigrew. It was a queer thought to a man.

He was aware of a sudden hush among them all, and realized that Morwen was standing up in the trap now.

They respected her. They knew her. Hal hoped to God it was going to be enough.

He heard her soft, husky voice, not raised in anger or superiority, but strong all the same.

'You're all my friends here, as well as my husband's employees,' she said. 'As my father just said, you know why we've come. This is a sad time for me and my family. But I know you'll be concerned about the future of Killigrew Clay—'

'As well we might be,' a lone voice came from somewhere at the back of the crowd, and Hal gave a small sigh. It was too much to hope that this meeting would continue in this same dignified manner. It wasn't the clayworkers' way. If they had a grievance, it must come out, however bad the timing. He saw Morwen's face flush.

'You all knew my husband for a fair and just man.' Her voice was raised higher now. 'He was devoted to Killigrew Clay, just as all my family have always been. I trust none here will deny that!' This was greeted by shuffling feet and mutters of agreement all around.

'I want to assure you that everything will continue as before. I don't mean to sell out, nor to change the name of Killigrew Clay. Our production will continue the same, and I hope we'll all enjoy a good relationship for years to come.'

'I 'ouldn't mind a good relationship with 'ee, Morwen Tremayne,' a voice sniggered from the middle of the crowd. 'Tell us when 'ee be looking for a new husband—'

'That's enough of that kind of talk, you buggers!' Hal roared out. 'Mrs Killigrew's here to reassure you all, not to invite comments from scum.'

He knew his mistake before he'd finished speaking.

'Scum, is it?' The man's workmate shouted back. 'Billy Paddon's given good service to Killigrew Clay all his life, and if scum is all 'ee think of 'un—'

'And since when did we have to call Morwen Mrs Killigrew?' One of the older bal maidens screeched. 'Since when did she become so all-fired uppity?'

'Since she married Ben Killigrew, and especially now, since she's your boss and 'tis her say-so whether you get your dues at the end of the week to put food into your babbies' bellies,' Hal bellowed back.

Morwen listened, appalled. One minute they were an orderly crowd. The next, they were a belligerent mob. She felt her hands clench on the rail of the trap, and her knuckles were white, the skin stretched taut.

'Will you listen to me?' she almost screamed the words to make them quiet. Some were prepared to listen, but she had to yell above the mutterings that were never going to die down.

'I've said what I came to say. You have jobs to come to every day, and there'll be wage packets for you every week. What more do you want?'

'We want to know who's paying off Ben Killigrew's debts, and what effect the loss of the spring despatches is going to have on we, Morwen Killigrew, that's what.'

The words were taken up again and again, and threaded between them was a new and insidious message.

'A woman ain't the proper person for being in charge of a clayworks. 'Tis a man's job. We don't want no tales of some other woman boss's success. Killigrew Clay's allus been run by a man, and 'tis a man we want now.'

'Do you want me to change my sex or wear trousers or work in the fire-hole?' Morwen screamed back at them. 'I can't change the fact that my husband's dead. I apologize for his death. It was unthinking of him to leave you all like this!'

She was desperately near to tears. She swallowed the great lump in her throat, frustration and despair almost overcoming her. She felt Hal's large calloused hand close over hers and looked at him through brimming eyes.

''Tis time,' he said quietly, close to her ear. He put his arm around her shoulder, and she wanted to lean there, to melt into his strength, to let him take all the burden away from her. But this was a sharing, a partnership, and she kept her weight firmly on her own feet as Hal roared out for silence. The shock of his voice stilled them for a moment, but it was long enough.

'You want a man at the head of Killigrew Clay, you buggers? You want the truth of it? You've had a two-man partnership at the head of Killigrew Clay for years now, ever since the rail tracks disaster.'

The crowd was church-hushed now, uncertain, disbelieving, as Hal continued in a voice as unyielding as the granite cliffs.

'You all remember my son, Matthew, come home lately on a visit from America. You all know how he went away poor and came home rich from the gold pickings in California. What you don't know is the gift he made my Bess and me in those early days, wealth enough to help save Killigrew Clay when all seemed lost. Without our Matt's money, you'd all have been scratching for pennies years back.'

'What in hell be 'ee saying, Hal Tremayne?'

'What I'm saying, you shit-bagging buggers,' he went on in their own free language, 'is that Hal Tremayne's been more'n your Works Manager these past ten years. I've been in partnership wi' Ben Killigrew all that time, and now that he's dead, I'm in partnership wi' Morwen. Killigrew Clay belongs to the two of us, and 'ee can all like it or lump it, but that's the way 'tis going to be.'

The silence was like a shock wave running through them. Too traumatic to draw breath for a second, and then explosive in its violence.

'You'm a lying bastard, Hal Tremayne, and if 'tis your way of gaining control, we'll not stand for it. You and your daughter have cooked this up atween 'ee—'

'We have not!' Morwen yelled. ''Tis all perfectly true, and my Daddy has papers to prove it. We'll have a deputation of you to come to the Killigrew offices in St Austell in a few days from now to show you—'

'Oh ah! To give yourselves time to fix up the papers, I s'pose—?'

'No, you ignorant fools!' Morwen was appalled to hear herself shout so witheringly, but she couldn't seem to stop. 'To get the documents from the lawyers and the Bodmin bank, so you'll see for yourselves that it was all done legally ten years ago. Do you think I'd be daft enough to say my Daddy was part-owner if it wasn't true? It could all be proved otherwise easily enough. And if none of you likes the present ownership, you can all try for jobs elsewhere. There'll always be men eager to work for Killigrew Clay, whoever's in charge.'

She saw the heads begin to nod reluctantly. Inside, all her nerves were like jelly, but she'd be damned if she would let them see it. She was Morwen Killigrew, and never more conscious of old Charles Killigrew's trust in her. She owed this to him, and to Ben, and she kept her head held high until the angry mutterings were distilled into a single voice from one spokesman, the recently-appointed Pit Captain of Clay One.

'All right, Mrs Killigrew,' he growled in what might or might not have been a sarcastic tone. 'We ain't pleased with the way Hal Tremayne's deceived us all these years, but none of us wants to be out on our backsides. Give us the day of the meeting, and a deputation will be there.'

She nodded briskly. They had won. The papers were all legally solid, and her father would take his rightful place in the order of things at last. Hal may not have wanted this, but she did. Oh, *she* did. The responsibility of it all was too much, but it wasn't until she and Hal were on their way down the moors towards St Austell again that the tears finally began to fall, and when they did, they came in a torrent.

Chapter Twenty-Three

'We have to discuss Ran's offer, Morwen, if only because he'll not be satisfied until he gets a proper reply,' Hal said eventually. 'I can't make up my mind about it. The money's in the bank account to settle a lot of the bills, and I'm not sure we need another partner.'

Was she just contrary, or was it just Tremayne pride that made her react in the same way Ben had done?

'It's your money, Daddy, and you and Mammie might need it one day—'

'What should we need it for?'

'To visit Matt, maybe—'

'Your Mammie don't need that, my love. Matt's come home, and she's content to have seen 'un once more. Money means nothing to us, but it means a lot to Killigrew Clay. Dammit, girl, 'tis as much my business as yours, and if I say we put the money to good use, then that's what we'll do.'

He was as unbending as she, and she could see that his temper, slow to rise, was beginning to come to the boil again, so soon after the confrontation at Clay One.

''Tis something we must sort out with Daniel Gorran, Daddy. In a few days, when we've got over all this.'

She kept saying the same words. In a few days. Later… Yet it wasn't her nature to put things off. Once trouble was imminent, she had always preferred to get it out in the open and thrash it out. But where business was concerned, Morwen was already learning that impetuosity didn't always pay. She soon learned something else too.

Once the news of Hal Tremayne's long-time partnership with Ben Killigrew was out, the whole town seemed to be talking about it. Tales were garbled and often ludicrous, and through them all, Hal Tremayne and his daughter behaved with dignified control. If the maids at Killigrew House wondered, and street acquaintances whispered and stared, they could all be ignored.

What couldn't be ignored was the reaction of the children. Walter was still away in Truro, but the others were agog with the sudden interest in their family. They trailed into the drawing-room together, and Albert was the new leader in Walter's absence.

'Is it true, Mother?' Albert demanded. 'A woman stopped me in the street and asked if my grandfather was the real owner of Killigrew Clay. What's happening, Mother?'

Morwen looked at him with a little shock. She had always thought Walter was growing up too fast, but now that he wasn't here, Albert was taking charge. He seemed taller, less in Walter's shadow… the sensation of the new generation taking the place of the old made Morwen give a sudden shiver.

'He's not the sole owner, darling, but he's a partner with me. He was in partnership with your father for many years, but he never wanted it known. You know Grandfather Hal. He never liked any fuss.'

She kept calm and brisk as she spoke, seeing the frown on Albert's face. She quickly realized she had underestimated him in many ways. With barely a pause, he echoed her own thoughts of a few days ago when she and Hal had faced the clayworkers. Since then, Hal had obtained the necessary documents, and together with Morwen and the lawyer to explain things properly, they had satisfied the deputation of clayworkers at the town offices that Hal's claims were as he had stated. And then the town had buzzed with the revelation. As Ben's wife, Morwen had known of the partnership from the start, and now Hal himself had gone to Truro to let Jack and Freddie in on the best-kept Killigrew secret, before they heard it from outsiders. It was yet another secret…

'Will it be called Tremayne Clay now then, Mother?'

She gave a small laugh. 'Of course not. Why should it be changed?'

'Granddad Hal's a Tremayne, and so were you, and me and Walter and Primmy will inherit, along with Justin and Charlotte, and we're all half-Tremaynes.'

His blue eyes challenged hers.

'Nothing will change, Albert,' she said firmly, catching the look of alarm in Justin's face.

'I don't want to be a Tremayne,' he muttered.

'You're not,' Morwen snapped. 'Don't be ridiculous, Justin, and don't make difficulties where there aren't any. And if any more people stop you in the street, you're to say, it's family business and nothing more. Do you understand?'

'Yes, Mother,' they said in unison.

Charlotte began to pout, tired of the others looking so cross at matters she didn't understand.

'When are we going to see Uncle Ran again? He said we were going to have a party at his house.'

'Darling, we can't have parties just yet,' Morwen told her gently.

'Why not?'

Justin suddenly shouted at her. 'Because our father's just died, that's why not, you ninny. People can't sing and dance for years and years afterwards—'

'Not years, idiot,' Primmy said nervously. 'It's not years, is it, Mother?'

Morwen looked at the four bleak faces and felt a stab of compassion for them.

'No, my loves. Your father wouldn't have wanted that. It will be weeks, not years—'

'Can't I even play the piano?' Primmy was mournful. 'I'll play the saddest songs I can, Mother. That will be all right, won't it?'

'I'm sure it will. And we'll see Uncle Ran soon, I promise, even if it won't be for a party. We could ask him for Sunday tea, though. You boys can ride over to New World this evening and invite him, if you like.'

They cheered up at once.

She left them to their own devices, hearing the strains of Primmy's tortured piano playing drift out of doors as she took a stroll around the garden in the afternoon sunshine. It was already a few weeks since Ben's death, and she was lonely without him. With his death, she forgot all the bad times, the hateful times, and remembered only the love. It was as though distance from him had totally changed her feelings.

There were times when she ached for Ben with an almost physical pain. There were others when she hated herself because of her disloyalty to him, remembering how she had betrayed him with Ran. There were times when she panicked, wondering if she would ever be able to love again, or if she was trapped now with her own guilt. She felt truly as though she was in some kind of wilderness, and it was an effort to suggest doing anything, even inviting Randell Wainwright to tea. *Especially* inviting Ran to tea, because she was no longer sure of her own feelings.

-

Before that happened, there were uninvited visitors to the house. The children had gone to the beach, and Mrs Horn came into the drawing-room with a sniff and a snort.

'Mrs Killigrew, are you at home to Mr and Mrs Askhew from Truro? If 'ee don't feel like seeing folks, 'ee only has to say the word and I'll send 'em packing!'

Morwen was startled. 'The lady *and* her husband?'

Mrs Horn nodded. 'That's what I said. Shall I tell 'em you'm not up to seeing visitors yet?'

'No. No, don't do that, Mrs Horn. Send them in, and make us some tea in a little while, please. We'll take it in the summer-house.'

The housekeeper sniffed all the way out, and Morwen guessed rightly that it would be the hard-voiced newspaperman that she didn't like. Miss Finelady Jane Carrick – Mrs Tom Askhew – was liked by everyone.

Jane came in like a refreshing breath of spring, moving to take Morwen's hands in hers for a moment. Naturally Jane and her parents had been at the funeral, but this was the first time she had called to pay her respects.

'Morwen, darling, how are you?' Jane said softly.

Morwen retreated at once. How dare this girl call her darling, as if they were friends? They had never been friends. Rivals, yes, and uneasy acquaintances, but never friends.

'I'm well,' she said coolly. 'But what a surprise to see your husband in Cornwall again. Does this mean you'll all be going back to Yorkshire again soon?'

Tom spoke in his gravelly voice.

'Quite soon, Mrs Killigrew. 'Tis a place of little attraction for me, except for finding my wife here, of course. And Cathy seems to have found some amusements of her own in Truro.'

'How nice,' Morwen said politely, and turned away from him. 'Jane, it's very warm indoors. I've asked Mrs Horn to bring us tea to the summer-house. Shall we go and sit there?'

'That will be lovely.' The warmth in Jane's voice made up for the coolness in the other's. For the life of her, Morwen couldn't take to this girl. That devilish jealousy she had experienced on their first meeting still plagued her, and it irritated her still more to know that it was for no possible reason.

'It's good of you to call, Jane.' She made an effort to be sociable when they were seated in the wicker chairs in the summer-house.

'I would have come sooner, but I wasn't sure when Tom was arriving, and he wanted to see you too.'

Morwen looked at him in surprise. 'Did he?'

She couldn't think why. They had never had much to say to one another before he whisked Jane off to Yorkshire years ago. In fact, she had never really trusted the newspaperman, despite the fact that he'd helped Ben further his cause for his rail tracks by his hard-hitting and sensible features in the Truro newspaper, *The Informer.* Apparently, now he was a leading light in *The Northern Informer* in his home town.

He said nothing as Mrs Horn brought out a tray of tea and Morwen acted the hostess, and then he leaned back, stirring the cup with unnecessary force.

'I won't beat about the bush, Mrs Killigrew.'

Why did his use of her full name irk her so? Yet, if he'd been familiar and called her Morwen, she knew very well that would have irked her just as much. She just didn't like him, and had always found it hard to resist showing her dislike. She looked at him impassively.

'Everyone knows by now that your father's been in partnership with your husband for some years.'

She hated his flat nasal voice. She made no comment, but waited for him to go on.

'It's no secret, either, that the clayworks business has been falling off lately, and your own losses when the ship sank must have been a real disaster to you. What I'm interested in doing for my northern paper, Mrs Killigrew, is a feature on these events, as seen through the eyes of an owner's wife; namely, you. Naturally, my paper would pay you handsomely for any personal details you may care to offer.'

Morwen's mouth had fallen open at his gall. She heard Jane murmur something to her husband, and then he spoke more quickly.

'I don't mean to offend you, Mrs Killigrew, but my readers would find it enormously interesting, and since we're doing a series of articles on the potteries, the story of your lives here would complement these. Starting from the humble clayfolk and going on to the gracious tables of the rich, so to speak.'

With every word, he dug himself in deeper. He was bloody irritated by her. She sat there as if carved out of ice, her beautiful face glaring at him and making him feel less than dirt. And who the devil was she, anyway? Nowt but a clayworker's daughter, if the truth be told.

Morwen found her voice. 'Get out of here, Tom Askhew,' she said in a deep, vibrant voice. 'How dare you come here so soon after my husband's death and try to make me bare my emotions for your miserable little readers?'

'Morwen, Tom didn't mean it like that—' Jane said, distressed. Morwen rounded on her at once.

'How else did he mean it? Does he hope I'll say that Killigrew Clay will come a cropper now? I'm sure he knows all about Ben's little difficulties. Everyone else seems to know. Why doesn't he just make up a tale and be done with it?'

'Now then, Mrs Killigrew, don't jump to conclusions,' Tom patronized her. And oh, how she hated that emphasis on the first syllable in conclusion. Con man was more to the point, she thought furiously. Conning his way in here and playing on her vulnerability…

'What I want to show my readers is that the business will undoubtedly survive, despite having a woman at its head. Your father will see to that, I've no doubt, knowing the clayworks so well. You Tremaynes seem to be a strong-willed class of folk. What are the chances of changing the name to Tremayne Clay instead of Killigrew Clay? I confess it'll not have the same ring to it—'

When Albert said it, Morwen could shrug it off. When this condescending lout said it, she could have strangled him.

'Get out of my house, and don't come here again, either of you. You're not welcome here, and now that the Killigrew men are gone, I don't have to pretend an acquaintance with you that I don't want and certainly don't need.'

She could see that Jane's pretty eyes were filled with tears, but she hardened her heart against her. Jane may have toyed with

Ben's youthful love, but *Morwen* was the bereaved widow, and how dare they come here with their insulting offers of money for a newspaper story!

Jane pulled her husband away without another word, though he still looked as though he would argue. When they had gone, Morwen sank down on the summer-house floor in a rustle of skirts, feeling more lost than before. Ben was gone, and in a month from now, Freddie would be marrying Venetia. Another cycle would begin, yet for Morwen life seemed to stand still. She no longer knew who she was. She had been so proud to be called Killigrew's lady, but now she wasn't even that. She was nothing. Without Ben, she was nothing. She leaned her head in her lap and wept.

–

Ran found her there. Without a word he gathered her up in his arms and held her close. His warmth comforted her. His need for her was subdued, yet she wasn't unaware of it. He was a haven to her right then, and she needed someone so badly. Without knowing it, her arms reached for him, and he felt a small shiver of relief that she was turning to him at last. When he was able to ask her what had happened, she told him in gasping words.

'The insensitive swine,' Ran said savagely. 'You did the right thing, dearest, in sending him packing.'

'Did I? Or should I have settled for the money? It would have paid off some of our debts.' The bitterness seeped into her again, and he shook her gently.

'I've told you what to do about that. Let me buy into the business. Let me discuss it with your father, Morwen. Oh yes, I've heard the gossip, darling, and I presume it must be true.'

She had looked at him sharply. Of course, he would know by now. The news would have spread beyond St Austell.

'I can't,' she whispered. 'It would be letting Ben down.'

'Ben didn't object to taking a partner, so why should you mind taking a third? Or is it just because it's me? Does the thought of tying yourself to me in a business sense bother you, Morwen? Perhaps you think I'm becoming too close for comfort.'

There was a new note in his voice. He thought she was rejecting him in every way, and it wasn't that at all. It was just all happening too soon, and she was too muddle-headed to give a sensible answer.

'If that's what you think, I can't stop you, Ran,' she said wearily. 'Have you seen the boys this afternoon? They were going to ride over and ask you to Sunday tea, but now you're here, I can ask you instead—'

'I think not,' he said, to her shocked surprise. 'I think it's best that we stay apart for a week or so. We'll meet at the wedding, if not before, but by all means, let the children come over at the weekend.'

'Ran, don't be like this, please—'

'I can't be any other way. And I love you too much to watch you killing yourself out of useless remorse and delusions of keeping faith with Ben. He was a rotten husband to you in the months that I knew him, and the sooner you face the fact that you're better off without him, the better.'

He gave her a hard kiss on the mouth before he let her go, and she watched him go striding off, just in time to catch the children returning from the beach, who greeted him with ecstatic shouts. If only she could be that uninhibited, that free of guilt… she knew that everything he said was true, and her little burst of anger at him dwindled away.

At least the children were united in their inheritance, she kept thinking, trying to hold on to some kind of security. Ben had done that for them, and she was grateful. Walter was still unsettled, though she had had reports from Freddie that he was more relaxed in Truro, and going out and about more instead of brooding. Morwen let him be. If he missed school, she didn't care. None of the children had begun school again since Ben's death, and she didn't care about that either.

And what was she doing, pushing Ran out of her life? She tried desperately to recapture the feelings they had shared, and found it as elusive as the mist on the moors. She knew the love was there, but she just couldn't grasp it. If she lost him too…

–

A week later, there was an excursion to Venetia's home for a dress-fitting. It would have been far easier for Venetia and Bess to go to Killigrew House, but, wisely, Bess had suggested this visit. The shadows beneath Morwen's lovely eyes had begun to alarm her mother, and Venetia's jovial father was happy to show the little Killigrew girls, their mother and grandmother, around his newly-acquired stately home.

The boys had begged to go to Ran's house, and had been left there on the way. Morwen missed him so. As good as his word, he had left her strictly alone while she recovered herself, but these glimpses of him were bittersweet.

Later, when Lord Hocking had gone back to his beloved horses, Venetia, Morwen and the girls tried on the dresses Bess had made. They all gasped at the sight of one another, and of Venetia in particular, lovely and ethereal in cream taffeta and lace, and Morwen caught her breath, remembering how beautiful she had wanted to look for Ben, all those years ago.

She realized suddenly how good it was to be out of gloomy clothes and into something light and normal again, and from that moment, Morwen vowed to take the children out of mourning, and to dress herself in soft greys and browns. There was nothing to be gained in looking miserable, and it didn't make them remember Ben any more than they did already.

'I do love my dress, Mrs Tremayne,' Venetia hugged her future mother-in-law. 'I can't thank you enough for making it so well.'

Bess went pink with pleasure.

‘’Tis my only skill,’ she said modestly, and Venetia laughed indulgently.

‘Oh, I think not,’ she said softly. ‘Your real skill is in producing your wonderful family, and I’m so happy to think I shall soon be a part of it.’

‘Well, if ’ee don’t want me to blub all over that fine dress, you’d best take it off before ’tis marked,’ Bess said, suddenly busy with the little girls to hide her moist eyes. ‘Are you coming with us to see Freddie this afternoon?’

‘No. Daddy’s got some horsey people coming in for dinner, and wants me to be here, so give him my love and tell him I’ll see him tomorrow.’

It was mid-afternoon when they left. Ran had said he would take the boys home when they were ready, so there was no need to rush away from Freddie’s. They were to call in on Jack too, to see the children and to check on Annie’s welfare. Jack had reported that the gynaecologist was cautiously pleased with her, and their family doctor was frankly astounded that the pregnancy was progressing well so far. Annie herself was frustrated and often bored with spending part of every day in bed, but in her heart she knew it would be worth it, especially if she gave Jack the son they both longed for.

Freddie greeted them with pleasure, and a hint of annoyance in his voice.

‘I’m afraid that son of yours has gone off again. He knew you were coming, but he seems to be absent-minded these days—’

‘He’s not ill, is he, Freddie?’ Morwen said quickly. ‘He was so distraught after Ben’s death. I was worried about him—’

‘He’s not ill,’ Freddie assured her. ‘In fact, I suspect he’s growing into a very normal young man, from the way he preens himself sometimes. ’Tis probably thinking about girls.’

He grinned, intending to bring a smile to his sister’s lips. But at his words, a sudden shiver ran through Morwen’s body, the kind of shiver that came more from premonition than from being chilled.

It wasn't cold, anyway. It was a lovely May afternoon, and her girls were chattering like magpies about Venetia's lovely wedding-dress while her Mammie was shushing them and telling them it was bad luck to let the bridegroom know what his bride would be wearing. And all the time, the vague shadow that Morwen couldn't quite dispel hovered nearby…

They took tea with Freddie, and time and again, Morwen's eyes turned to the window in search of Walter. It was bad of him not to be there when he knew they were coming. She was hurt by his absence, feeling that he slighted her.

'What the devil's that?' Freddie jumped up at the loud hammering on his shop door. He had closed up, but that was never enough to stop customers banging for assistance if they needed it, knowing him for an obliging chandler.

He went down the stairs from the rooms above, and minutes later came running back up again. He wasn't alone, and for Morwen, the premonition of disaster was very strong…

Jane Askhew's blotched and tearful face was the first one she saw behind Freddie, and then the furious countenance of her husband, waving a letter about like a flag.

'Dear God, what's happened?' Bess breathed.

'These people have found a note left by their daughter, saying she's run off with Walter,' Freddie said tersely.

Morwen felt the room sway. All these years she had known jealousy on this woman's account, because of her supposed feelings for Ben. The jealousy had been unworthy and unnecessary, it was wicked and a sin, and in her jumbled thoughts at that moment she saw this liaison between Walter and Cathy as a punishment for her own inadequacy… God had found a way to entwine her family with Miss Finelady Jane's…

The room steadied a little as she heard Tom Askhew's penetrating voice.

'You clayfolk have no control over your lad!' he shouted. 'God knows what he's done wi' my Cathy, but I'll tan his hide when I catch up with him!'

Morwen felt her nerve-ends bristle with rage. How dare this lout demean her by calling her and her family clayfolk in that common way. She was Mrs Ben Killigrew, and he had best remember that. Her anger fizzled out in shock as Jane suddenly rushed to her and put her arms around her.

'Oh Morwen, I'm so sorry to bring this trouble to you now, when you're still grieving over Ben. Walter came to the house several times, and he and Cathy seemed to find such pleasure in one another's company, and I thought I was helping him get over Ben's death by letting them be together. There was no hint of this, you must believe that, or I would have tried to stop it. Tom's time away from the newspaper is over, and we're all going back to Yorkshire the day after tomorrow. We only decided last night, and Cathy threw such a tantrum, screaming that she didn't want to leave Cornwall, but I never guessed that Walter was the reason for it!'

She was sobbing the words incoherently, and by the end of them, Morwen was comforting her and holding her close, and it was all so unbelievable to Morwen that this was happening… that she and Jane Askhew should be united in a common fear… whatever Tom Askhew might think of Walter, there was no animosity between the two women. They were both mothers, anxious for their children. In those moments, Morwen felt all the years of jealousy diminish and die, and it was like the releasing of a heavy burden.

'What exactly did the note say, Jane?' She heard Freddie say brusquely, having no patience with the rough-speaking Yorkshireman. Tom thrust it into his hands.

'You can read, I take it?' he said, insultingly. Freddie ignored him and scanned the note quickly, handing it to Morwen.

'Walter and I want to be together,' she read Cathy's large, childish scrawl aloud. 'He knows a place where we can stay, so don't try to find us. Try to understand, Mother. We truly love each other. Goodbye. Your loving Cathy.'

Jane gave a shuddering sob. Primmy and Charlotte were both crying noisily into Bess's skirts, and for a second Morwen felt a burning anger against Walter that this day that had started out so well, should be ending in such a nightmare.

'Well? Have you any ideas on this wonderful place where your lad's taken my lass? We've not seen Cathy since early this morning.' Tom glowered at them all. 'I warn you, if he's harmed her—'

'Why don't you stop your bloody useless surmising, and go and look for them?' Freddie snapped.

'*Where*, dunderhead?'

'I know where they might be,' Morwen said quietly.

They all gaped at her: Jane tearful; Tom still incensed; Freddie red-faced; Bess astonished at the certainty in her daughter's voice.

'There's a secret room at Ran's house. A round, turreted room that Ran showed me and the children. They were all intrigued with it. Walter may have taken Cathy there. They probably intend creeping out at night to get food and water from Ran's kitchen.'

It all sounded delightfully adventurous and romantic and unlikely, and yet the more she thought about it, the more certain Morwen was that Walter and Cathy would be there.

'A secret room, be buggered!' Tom was past caring that there were ladies present. 'I'll give the little bastard secret rooms with my lass—'

Before he could get down the stairs, shouting at Freddie to come with them to show him the way, there was the sound of more people downstairs. When Freddie opened the door to them, it was to find Ran Wainwright and the two younger Killigrew boys outside. With them, shame-faced and scarlet, were Walter and Cathy Askhew.

Chapter Twenty-Four

Morwen learned later that her intuition about the turreted room had been right. Walter had taken Cathy to Ran's New World, and they had planned, immature and confused, to stay for a while in the secret room. They had chosen a bad day, unaware that the other boys were visiting the house. And forgetting that a good hiding place for a game of hide-and-seek was the turreted room…

As Tom leapt at Walter, Freddie and Ran pulled him off the boy. Walter was stiff with fear, and Cathy was crying, running straight to her mother's arms.

'I'm sorry for all the worry we've caused, Mother. Walter's Uncle Ran gave us a terrible talking-to, but I don't want to go home. I really don't. Please let me stay behind with Grandma!'

'You'll come home with us the day after tomorrow, my lass, and the sooner the better,' Tom said explosively. He glared at Walter keenly. 'Have you touched her? You know damn well what I mean. You're not a child by the looks of you—'

Walter's fear dissolved as he glared back.

'No, I haven't touched her. I respect her too much for that, which is something you wouldn't understand.'

Bess hustled the other four children into a back room while the wrangling went on. Morwen went to her son and looked deep into his eyes. She ached for him. His pain was so obvious to her. He was about to lose his love, and he was slowly dying inside because of it. She knew she had to deal with his emotions very carefully.

'Walter, you know what you did was wrong. Cathy's parents have every right to be angry and upset—'

'I just wanted to be with Cathy, and she with me,' he said, awash with misery. The two of them still held hands tightly. Not even facing Tom Askhew had been enough to make them break their hold on one another.

'I'm all right, Mother, really I am,' Cathy whispered, her pale face flushing.

'That's as may be, but you'll not stay in this God-forsaken part of the world a day longer than I say,' Tom snapped. 'I'll have no arguments, Cathy.'

'But Walter will forget me,' she wailed.

'You know I won't. I'll never forget you,' his young voice was vibrant with unrealized passion. There might have been no one else in the room but the two of them.

Ran had stayed silent all this time, but now he spoke up, the one calm and sensible voice amongst them all.

'There's nothing to stop you writing to one another, is there? Letters can bring people close. Ask your mother, Walter. For many years she never saw your Uncle Matt, but he wrote to her, and she read you his letters, and you knew plenty about the Californian gold-fields, long before Matt came home. You know that's so. It's a special privilege to get letters from the people you love. They can often say things in letters they find difficult to say out loud.'

Morwen listened to his voice, the sharp American accent so dear to her now, and prayed that Walter and Cathy would be as enchanted by the idea of writing to one another as Ran suggested. She saw the look of uncertainty in Cathy's eyes, and swiftly added her own thoughts.

'And you're not going to be parted for ever, Cathy. I'm sure there will be other times when you'll be visiting your grandparents.' Her eyes dared Tom to spoil this fragile moment, and Cathy flashed a look at Jane.

'Mother?' she said hesitantly.

'I think it's the best idea, and of course you can write to Walter, darling, as often as you like. And perhaps he could come to Yorkshire to visit us sometime.'

Tom threw up his hands at the flare of hope in Walter's face at her words.

'God help me from women's interference!'

'Just be glad that your daughter's come to no harm,' Jane said sharply. 'First love can be a painful business, and perhaps you've forgotten just how much you wanted me to be with you, Tom! You can hardly blame your daughter for taking after her father.'

To Morwen's relief, there was the glimmer of a smile on Tom's face now. He would be remembering, as Morwen was too, of the times Ben Killigrew had come to Truro, supposedly courting Jane Carrick, when all the time Jane and her newspaperman were meeting secretly in Tom's rooms. And there was nothing very innocent about those meetings either. At last he gave a decisive nod, and spoke as though the whole idea was his.

'That's setttled then. Cathy comes home with us, but there's no objection to the two of you writing to one another. And if Walter's mother allows him to come on a visit north in due course, well, we'll think about that too. I'm not saying I'm pleased at today's little escapade, but as long as no harm's come of it, maybe it's best forgotten.'

By the time Ran had escorted the family back to St Austell, Morwen felt utterly drained. They hadn't even been to see Jack and Annie, but Freddie was going to let them know all that had happened. Walter was allowed to stay on at Freddie's, providing he gave his word that there would be no more dramatics, and he would be able to see Cathy, properly chaperoned, until she left for Yorkshire.

The boy was even more crushed than he had been at Ben's death, and Morwen was fearful for him. But she knew she was helpless to do anything. It was something Walter had to get over by himself.

Ran took Bess home when he had left them all at Killigrew House. Morwen watched him go with tears stinging her eyes. Was she being such a fool to reject him when she needed him so much? All the love was still there, yet it seemed somehow as if it was held in a block of ice. She couldn't touch it, couldn't reach it.

The children needed hardly any persuading to go to bed. They were all exhausted too, in their ways. And then she leaned back on the sofa, wondering if life was ever going to feel normal again.

She hadn't expected Ran to come back to the house after seeing her mother safely home. She was alone, and lonely. She missed Ben. She missed Ran. She heard someone open the drawing-room door and murmured tiredly to Mrs Horn that she would love a cup of something hot.

'Will you settle for me, instead?' Ran's deep voice said.

The tears that welled up in her eyes seemed to come from the heart and soul of her. She held out her arms to Ran and was being rocked within them as if she was a child needing the comfort that only this man could give her. She wept uncontrollably against his chest, while he murmured soft words that she barely heard, and yet somehow they melted all the ice inside her.

'Do you know what I think, Morwen?' Ran whispered eventually, when she was sensible enough to listen.

'No. Tell me what you think,' she whispered back, their voices as hushed as if they were in church, even though there was no one else to hear.

'I think it's time for all this crying to stop before we're drowned in tears.'

For a second she wondered if she had heard aright. If he was laughing at her, it was a very bad time for it… and then she felt her own laughter begin, deep down, tremblingly at first, because it was a sound she wasn't used to, and suddenly they were laughing and crying together, and all the unbearable tension was leaving her.

'Oh Ran, you're so good for me,' she gave a long, sighing breath at last, leaning her head against him. 'And I know we shouldn't be here like this—'

He put a finger against her mouth to still her words.

'Why not? How can it be wrong for a man to be with the woman he's going to marry? Is it wrong for me to tell you how much I love you and how I've suffered with you these past weeks?'

'It's wrong because of Ben—' she said sadly.

'Ben's gone. Nothing we do or say can ever bring him back, Morwen. Nothing we do is going to change our feelings, whether we stay apart for a hundred years of mourning to salve your conscience. And I don't have a hundred years to spare.'

She gave a small smile. 'What about your conscience? Don't you have one?'

'I consider it logically. We're both free now, so there's no point in letting my conscience get in the way of my love for you. And you do know that I want to marry you, don't you, Morwen?'

For the first time in a long while, she felt the ripples of desire wash over her.

'I know it. And I want it too,' she said huskily. 'But it must wait awhile, my love. You must see that.'

'Just as long as I know you'll be mine before too long.'

She drew in her breath, loving him so much. 'I'm yours already. Don't you remember?'

She felt his hand, warm on her breast, and held it there with her own. She wanted him with a fierce need, but she could only go so far and no farther. She was still Ben's widow, and this was still Ben's house. It was the Killigrew House, and it would always belong to them, no matter how many brides and interlopers came along to inhabit it. She had never felt that so strongly as she did right then. Old Charles Killigrew had built this house for his bride, and their ghosts still lingered.

She looked at Ran with mute appeal, and, as if understanding more than she realized, Ran spoke less emotionally.

'Have you thought what to do about Walter?'

'I thought you'd seen to that. I can't thank you enough, Ran. Thank God you knew how to handle the situation—'

'I don't mean the letter writing. I mean his future.'

She looked blank. 'He'll go back to school, I suppose,' she said slowly. 'He'll have to, sometime.'

'Don't you think he's had all the education he needs? He's a young man now, and his heart isn't in it, Morwen. Besides, there's something he wants far more. You're the only one who can give it to him.'

'I can't give him Cathy Askhew!' she began with a small laugh, and then she knew exactly what he meant. 'You mean I should let him work at Killigrew Clay! But Ben hated the idea, Ran—'

'Like I said before, Ben's gone. The decisions are yours now. Just consider what it would mean to the boy, Morwen. Working with his grandfather and doing the work he's always wanted to do. It might make all the difference to his feelings right now.'

'A sort of consolation prize for losing Cathy, you mean?'

'Perhaps. But I think you should do this for him. Or does it hurt your pride to have a son working at Killigrew Clay?'

She moved away from him indignantly.

'No, it does not! My parents worked there, and so did I and all my family, and there's nothing lowering in working with the clay—'

At his soft laughter, she saw the trap he had set her, and smiled sheepishly. She hardly needed to consider.

'I know you're right, Ran. You always are, aren't you? You see things for me before I see them myself—'

'And I thought you were meant to be the fey one.'

He could tease her and coax her so effortlessly, and make her feel so comfortable with him. He was the other half of herself… and she felt the sweet exquisite longing for him that was going to be denied until they were man and wife. And that day musn't be too far away… once the mourning time was over…

'I'll ride over to Freddie's on the day Cathy goes home to Yorkshire,' she said decisively. 'Walter will be feeling very low, and this news will be the best he can hear. Perhaps he'll come home then. I miss him, Ran.'

Her eyes misted with tears. Until that moment she hadn't realized just how much she missed her eldest. He had been her son since he was three years old, and although he wasn't born of her flesh, he was more dear to her than any of the others.

'No more tears, my darling,' Ran said gently, kissing them away from her eyes, and she gave a tremulous nod. The time for tears was past. He saw her chin lift in the old, spirited way, and was infinitely relieved.

–

Walter's eyes were dark with unshed tears when Morwen arrived at her brother's house two days later. She had told no one she was coming. The other children had all gone back to school, glad to be back to everyday activities. They were resilient, and must be allowed to develop and grow, without the spectre of death shadowing their days. But Walter was different. Walter was older, and had two griefs to bear.

She asked Freddie to leave them alone upstairs while she had a little talk with her son.

'You haven't come to lecture me, have you, Mother?' he asked wearily. 'I haven't the stomach for it today.'

At his tone, she felt a little shock. He wasn't an abject child, submissively waiting for his punishment. He was a man who was suffering, and taking it for granted that as a woman, Morwen understood his suffering. In that moment, they lost the tie of mother and child, and found a newer tie that was more valuable.

'I wouldn't presume to lecture you, darling,' she said quietly. 'I know how it feels when someone you love seems beyond your reach. I felt that way about your father – about Ben – for a long time. But we came together because our love was strong enough, and if yours and Cathy's is as strong, then you'll be together again too. Try to believe that.'

His face was still steeped in misery. 'I'll try, but no matter how young people think we are, Cathy and I are sure that our feelings won't change.'

'I know, love—'

'And I don't know how I'm going to face every day without seeing her, Mother. Ever since Father died, I've felt adrift from the rest of you. You all had each other, and I had no one but Cathy. And now she's gone.'

The agony in his voice might have been almost comic if it hadn't been so tragic to him. There was no point in telling him his family had been there all the time, loving him and wanting him home, because he simply wasn't seeing things that way. There was no point in feeling hurt at his words, because he never realized for a moment that they could hurt.

'I'll tell you how you're going to get through the days, Walter,' Morwen spoke with as little emotion in her voice as possible. 'You're going to live each one as if it's important, because every one you waste is one less of your life.'

'I have no life without Cathy—'

'You have Killigrew Clay.'

For a moment, it was obvious that her words didn't register, and then he shrugged.

'So I have Killigrew Clay. I'm part of a family business and that gives me a certain prestige. It means nothing to me, Mother. Can't you understand?'

'Would it mean more to you if you worked there every day with Granddad Hal? If you were part of it all, instead of going back to school for another year?'

At last she had got his full attention. At last the bleakness began to leave his eyes, and a spark of excitement replaced it.

'Do you mean it? I can work with the clay?'

Morwen laughed. 'I never heard anyone so eager to get his hands dirty! Yes, darling, if it's what you want, you can work with the clay. Your Granddad will be glad to have you there. It's time some of the family went back to their roots.'

Suddenly he was hugging her. There was no embarrassment, nothing but the delight of a young man who had got what he always wanted, and Morwen silently blessed Randell Wainright for putting this idea into her head.

'We'd better go and tell Uncle Freddie,' Walter went on joyfully. 'I'll be leaving with you today, of course, Mother.'

'Of course!' She found it hard to keep a straight face now, and her veins were singing with the glory of this day. 'But you'll have things to pack, and I want to go and see Jack and Annie, so I'll come back for you in an hour.'

As she reached the door, he called her. His voice was cracked, and she knew he wasn't far off tears of mingled joy and regret that he wouldn't want her to see.

'I do love you, Mother.'

She stumbled down the stairs, hardly able to see, just because her best-beloved had called her by that name.

-

Hal was delighted, though he warned Walter that the men might not take too kindly to a young whipper-snapper coming in and thinking he could take over.

'I don't want to take over,' Walter said indignantly. 'I want to learn everything. Uncle Freddie said he was once a kiddley-boy, but I'm too old to fetch and carry and make tea, but I can start with the middling jobs, can't I, Granddad, and work up? I can wheel the little trucks with the waste to the sky-tips or help in the fire-hole—'

'Hold on, boy,' Hal laughed. 'You'll do as I say and not try for everything at once. And you'll be answerable to your Pit Captain for a start—'

'I aim to be a Pit Captain one day,' Walter said confidently.

Hal's eyes were moist. 'You'll work up, I have no doubt. And you'll be a Pit Captain, like I was once. And just like Sam.'

They smiled at one another in satisfaction. They had suddenly discovered a great rapport with one another, and not the least of it was the ease with which they could use Sam's name. Hal's son, and Walter's true father. It was a bonus neither had expected, and tied the family bonds still tighter.

–

The weeks moved on, sliding from May into June, and the bad memories were beginning to recede. Consultations between Morwen, her father and Daniel Gorran had resulted in Hal's money being put to good use and settling a good proportion of the debts and dues that had accumulated. Killigrew Clay was just holding its head above water, but there was no margin to spare.

Walter was happier in his new job than Morwen had believed possible, and the men had accepted the new cheerful young Killigrew boy with an unexpected readiness. He wanted to learn, to know all there was to know for the days far into the future when he would take a share in the running of the business, and they respected him for that.

He was no toff, like his father and grandfather had been, they said sagely, he was more like one of their own. And those who knew the truth of it said it was only to be expected, with Hal Tremayne and his brood in his background. Walter was a born clayworker and revelled in it.

And every week there was a long letter from Cathy Askhew, to which he replied with an eagerness that made Morwen envy him a little. She never asked to see the letters, but the contents put an extra smile on Walter's mouth for days after they came.

Morwen decided the time had come to confide in Bess about her feelings for Randell Wainwright. Sitting comfortably in the garden of her mother's small house, it was easy to say the words, and when she did she caught her breath, because just saying them brought his image near to her.

'Mammie, would you think it wrong if I were to marry again someday?' she said softly.

Bess was startled by the question, not expecting it after the mundane discussion they had been having about the children and Walter's new outlook.

'No, I wouldn't think it wrong, my lamb. You're still a young and lovely woman, and t'ain't right for you to bury yourself in memories. Later on, when you find the right man—'

'I've already found him, Mammie.' She spoke in a rush, seeing the little look of shock come into Bess's eyes now. Morwen took her mother's pin-pricked hands in her own.

'Oh, can't you guess who it is? He's been my strength for many months now, and I can't keep it to myself any longer—'

'Not Ran!' Bess echoed. 'But he's family—'

'No, he's not,' Morwen laughed gently. 'He's no blood relation, Mammie, and that makes it all right for us to marry.'

'Does he want to marry 'ee then?'

'Oh, yes. We both want it, very much.'

She felt her face grow hot, and it was just as though her mother could see into her thoughts, and know that she was remembering all the times they had shared. The few precious kisses since Ben's death, and all the clandestine meetings before that, and the one magical night in a London hotel room when they had truly belonged…

'Then that's what 'ee should do, Morwen. There's no sense in two people living apart when both of 'em want to be together. Even young Walter knew that, but thank the Lord he's found his feet in the clayworks. The boy's not ready for marrying, but I'd say you'm more'n ready for it again by the looks of 'ee.'

Her face was hot as fire now, and she knew she had betrayed her feelings on it.

'But not yet, Mammie. I'm still in mourning for Ben. We have to wait a while, of course. I was just telling you so you wouldn't be too surprised.'

'Mourning's a waste of living time,' Bess said practically. 'What do it matter if a few townsfolk raise their eyebrows and look scandalized for a week or two? 'Tis your life, and if you and Ran want to be married, that's all that counts.'

For some inexplicable reason, Morwen hadn't wanted her mother to react like this. She couldn't explain it, but she'd wanted Bess to look indignant and demand that her daughter waited a decent interval before walking down the church aisle a second time. For Bess to give her blessing so freely was disconcerting, even though she knew the sense of it.

Her mother's reasoning was still that of the clayworkers, for whom life and death could be a swift cycle, and moorland folk took no notice of the conventions of townsfolk. Morwen had become so used to town ways, and to Ben's ways in particular, that her own mother's ready acceptance of the new situation made her recoil from rushing into a hasty marriage, as though there were a shotgun at her bridegroom's head.

'I'd rather you didn't tell anyone about this, Mammie,' she said awkwardly. 'Ran and I aren't ready to do anything yet, and besides, there's Freddie's wedding to be thinking of in a couple of weeks. Let folk get used to one Tremayne getting married, before they start gossiping about another.'

Why had she called herself a Tremayne, when she had been a Killigrew for fifteen years! Sometimes there was no difference between them, she thought faintly. Their lives had intertwined and mingled and all merged into one, so that she hardly knew who she was any more.

'All right, if that's what 'ee wants, my lamb.' Bess was comfortable, whatever was decided. She was just thankful that her girl had someone to turn to, and that the children were settling after Ben's death, and that she and Hal were still muddling on like they had always done…

'Your Daddy were telling me about Ran's offer to buy into Killigrew Clay,' Bess commented. 'We don't have no secrets from one another, Morwen, as well you know, and 'twas beyond me to give 'un any ideas on it. 'Twill all be solved easily now though, won't it?'

'Will it?' Morwen stared, not understanding yet.

Bess gathered up the sewing that was her constant companion, indoors or out, and arranged it more comfortably on her ample lap.

'Well, when you and Ran are married, I suppose he'll be taking control of Killigrew Clay instead of you, won't he? You won't want to be bothered with all that business nonsense, 'specially if more babbies come along, and you ain't too old for that yet, Morwen, nor will 'ee need to watch the pennies.'

She hardly noticed how set her daughter's face had become as she rambled on, happily making plans and looking into an imaginary future.

'Thirty-two's no age at all to be thinking of having more babbies, and with a new husband 'twill possibly be easier than with the last, God rest Ben's soul. No, you'll be nicely set up, Morwen, with money coming in from two sources, and good luck to 'ee both. 'Tis summat I never dreamed of seeing for 'ee, and that makes it all the more deserved. You've always been a good girl to your father and me, love, and I'm happy for 'ee.'

Morwen stood up, almost knocking over the garden chair. Her voice was surprisingly calm, considering how much her stomach churned so sickeningly.

'It's time I went, Mammie. I didn't realize how late it was getting, but I'll see you again soon.'

She left Bess in the garden, blissfully unaware of saying anything amiss. And Morwen climbed into the little trap and jerked the reins, her heart like stone, with the insidious thought drumming in her head that Ran might only want to marry her to gain control of Killigrew Clay.

Chapter Twenty-Five

A wedding had been arranged for the end of the month. June was the traditional Cornish bride-month, so it was only fitting that half of Truro should turn out to watch this one, between Freddie Tremayne, the well-liked chandler along the waterfront, and the pretty young woman with the unusual name, Lady Venetia Hocking.

Venetia's father had decided to do things in style. What was the use of having money if you didn't enjoy it? He'd put the question to Hal in his thick, booming voice, insisting on having an outdoors reception at his new country estate, catered by the best chefs in the County, so that the servants of the house could become honoured guests for the day, and the rest of them could like it or lump it.

Families and friends were invited, together with the elegant acquaintances that formed Truro's social set, and if it was a stranger mixture than usual at a wedding, nobody seemed to mind or to notice overmuch.

There was a time, Morwen marvelled, when her family would have felt miserably out of place amidst all this grandeur. Time had changed all that. Even her Mammie and Daddy seemed to be enjoying themselves, slightly swished on Lord Hocking's champagne, but confident that they looked as good as anybody in their new wedding clothes.

Venetia, of course, looked dream-like in her cream silk and lace, and Freddie could hardly take his eyes away from her. All through the service, Morwen too had been misty-eyed as the couple repeated their vows. Primmy and Charlotte had stood, ramrod-stiff in their flower-girls' roles behind the bride, and on either side of Morwen, the two younger boys had tried not to fidget. Walter had sat slightly apart from them, next to Hal and Bess, but flashing his mother a slight smile now and then, and never far from her heart.

Ran had joined Jack and Annie and the small girls in the pew behind them, and while the ancient words were being said and the rings exchanged, Morwen could feel him watching the back of her head. She didn't want to look at him. She still felt brittle inside, wondering if the doubt her mother had so innocently put into her head could possibly be true. It would break her heart if it were… and there was no way she could tell for sure.

For the first time in her life, she hated Killigrew Clay. It had brought her and Ben together, but it could just as easily split her and Ran apart.

–

'Why have you been avoiding me?'

She heard Ran's voice with a little start, and took the glass of champagne he was holding out to her without thinking. She took a large swallow, feeling her head spin at its fire as it slipped down her throat.

'I have not,' she said in a low voice. Wedding guests were laughing and chattering, and the smaller children were rushing about the lawns in delight, knowing that none of the grown-ups would reprimand them on such a day.

'You know that's not true. When did you start telling lies as well?' he said insolently.

She looked into his face, flushing at the brutal words, and felt a stab of anger.

'When I met you, I suspect!'

They were standing on the edge of the lawns, and to any onlookers they must look like any two guests holding a normal conversation. Only between themselves was the feeling that the air was as brittle as glass, the tension almost unbearable.

Ran stared at her, seeing the shadows beneath her lovely eyes. He had thought they were dispersed for ever since they had made their own private avowal to one another several weeks ago.

'Are you going to tell me what's troubling you, Morwen?' he said at last.

'Nothing's troubling me—'

'Good God, don't go all little-womanly on me!' He seethed with impatience. 'It's perfectly obvious that something's happened to make you so frigid towards me, and I demand that you tell me what it is.'

'Demand?' she said sarcastically. 'What right do you have to demand anything of me?'

'I thought love gave me the right. Tell me what's wrong before I wring it out of you.'

She wanted to, desperately. She wanted to scream out at him to say it wasn't true – that it couldn't possibly be true – that his reason for marrying her was to gain power. To be in control of Killigrew Clay as well as Prosper Barrows. He had wanted power. He had seized the opportunity to stay in Cornwall when he had seen the growing prosperity in the clay-stone works…

She wanted to scream at him and pummel him and beg him to deny it… because she hated deceit and lies, and despised herself for every lie she had ever told in her life… but how could she ask him? If he denied it, she still couldn't be sure… he might be so shocked by her question that he would leave her anyway and the heartbreak would begin…

Had she already hurled all the accusations at him? In her mind, she was already screaming… she blinked against the sunlight, as though she had been momentarily in the grip of an hallucination, yet all around her the wedding guests still smiled and gossiped, and the children still screeched with laughter…

'Well, Morwen?' Ran's voice had hardened, wondering if he was ever going to get through the mask on that lovely frozen face. He cursed this wedding of Freddie's, thinking it had probably brought back that damnable conscience of hers, remembering Ben, remembering too much of the past.

He burned to take all the troubles away from her, to restore her to the beautiful serenity that had so charmed him on that first meeting with her. He had fallen in love with her then, and was even more in love with her now, but for some reason she was treating him like a stranger, and it tore at his gut.

'I'm still in mourning for my husband,' she said stiffly. 'You should remember that, Ran. I can't forget it, even though everyone seems able to.' She met his eyes and then had to look away.

'It's more than that, and we both know it. When you're ready to tell me, perhaps I'll be ready to listen.'

To her disbelief, he turned away from her, to be triumphantly captured by one of the Truro dames, anxious to introduce her two daughters to him. And why not? Randell E Wainwright would be quite a catch. He was handsome, successful, and extremely attractive to women. It didn't need a clairvoyant to know that. It was obvious from the way some of the unmarried girls had been eyeing him, wondering who he was.

Her father's gentle voice spoke right beside her. 'Are you in some kind of a dream, my love? You'll be missing Ben on such a day, and 'tis only to be expected.'

She hugged his arm, loving his simple conclusion. Never in a hundred years would Hal Tremayne think that his daughter was at that moment eaten up with jealousy on account of Randell Wainwright smiling into the provocative eyes of another girl!

'I was just thinking, Daddy,' she said huskily.

He tucked her hand in his arm and held it there. 'Aye, love. Weddings make the best of folk look to their own lives in some peculiar way. Weddings and buryings both. You'll be all right, I have no doubt of it.'

She smiled wanly. 'Of course I will. I was just being silly. And Daddy, while we're on our own for a minute, I want to say something.'

'What is it?'

She said it quickly, before she could change her mind. Hal had been half-swayed already by Daniel Gorran's words, and it only needed Morwen's agreement to tip the balance.

'I think we should accept Ran's offer. It will put Killigrew Clay back on its feet again, and will save us the worry of dealing with things I don't really understand – and no more do you, I suspect!'

'That's true enough. But you're quite sure on it, Morwen? You've given it enough thought?'

'Oh, I've given it more than enough thought.' She tried to keep the bitterness out of her voice, not wanting to blight this lovely day. 'But let's leave it a few more weeks before we tell Ran of our decision. Ben always said it didn't do to appear too eager to accept a business offer, and it won't hurt Ran to think we're managing well enough and don't need him.'

Hal laughed, not seeing the irony in her words. God knew that she needed him. Out of the corner of her eyes she could see him flirting with the two Pendewy girls, and it hurt. If he was doing this merely to spite her, he was succeeding. If he did it because he enjoyed it, that only deepened the hurt.

'You're right, love. No one need know of it but we two for the present. No more'n a month though, before we bring him in. We'll be due for payment to the shipping company by then, despite the loss of the clay, so 'twill be a good time – so long as he hasn't backed out in that time.'

Morwen felt a burst of fright. 'You don't think he will, do you, Daddy?'

He remembered Bess telling him that Ran and Morwen were thinking of getting wed, and if he thought it odd that the man should be sporting with two other young women at the present, he assumed it was with Morwen's blessing, for propriety's sake.

'I'm sure he won't,' Hal said confidently. 'When a man's made up his mind he wants summat badly enough, he'll stick to it, no matter what.'

He was meaning his daughter, but all she saw in his words was Ran's desire for Killigrew Clay. And if he got what he wanted, would there still be any reason for him to marry the widow of Ben Killigrew? It was a thought that only occurred to her as her father moved away to rejoin Bess, and Morwen felt suddenly afraid and alone. But surely it would prove something? If he still wanted to marry her, then she must believe that what he felt for her was love.

-

A wedding had an effect on people. It made soft-centres of those who didn't normally have a romantic bone in their bodies. It sent the children wild with excitement, because the older ones seemed more indulgent for the day.

It made Walter Tremayne long for something out of reach. He knew he was far too young to be thinking of marriage, but there was a bond between him and Cathy Askhew that was too precious to discuss with anyone. Fifteen wasn't too young to be in love, and he and Cathy had made a secret vow to be faithful, and to tell each other the truth if their feelings should ever change. Their letters constantly reassured each other that such a happening was an impossibility.

But he was growing up. He knew that people's feelings did change, through no faults of their own, just as their bodies changed. Walter was discovering himself in ways that were almost frightening. He knew the power that was in a man's body, and was aware of new and pleasant sensations within him that made him curious about a woman's.

One day, he kept reminding himself, when he and Cathy were old enough to defy their parents' wishes, they would be together, as they were always meant to be.

Unwittingly, he echoed Morwen's own philosophy. Things that were meant to be, would be, however long the waiting.

Hal and Bess were more than content that their youngest had found himself a good wife. There had been a money gift from Matt and Louisa that would help them with furnishings, once they had found the house they wanted, and for now, Venetia was happy enough to move into Freddie's rooms above the shop and to blazes with what folk thought.

Jack wished his Annie wasn't so hugely pregnant that there was hardly room for both of them in the bed, let alone make love to her. They had seen the gynaecologist just before today's wedding, confirming that Annie was well enough to stand the excitement, and he strongly believed now that the baby was due in August, a month earlier than they had thought.

'A month less to wait until I can get my arms around 'ee again,' Jack had teased her, when they were all done up in their wedding finery.

'You'll just have to curb your impatience, Jack,' she had said, blushing.

'I know, but 'tis not the easiest of things to do when a man loves his wife the way I love mine.' He spoke lightly, because such words didn't always come easy to him.

Knowing it, Annie hugged him tightly. Between them they both felt the baby stir, and smiled at each other as if they guarded a royal treasure.

Freddie was in a high old state of jubilation by the time he and Venetia made a move to leave the celebrations. They were to spend a few days in the small fishing village of St Ives, where the sands were golden and the sea would be warm, and they might even risk dipping in a toe or two, as reckless as two children on a spree.

But there was nothing of the child about either of them as he took his wife in his arms on that first night of their new life, and felt the desire in him rise up and meet hers. Neither felt the need to prolong the sweet preliminaries, and Venetia pulled her husband into her as Freddie covered her body with his own, and each knew that fulfilment was theirs for the taking, for all the rest of their lives.

–

Lord Hocking urged his guests to remain as long as they liked once the newly-wedded couple had gone. He was red-faced and amiable. He liked his daughter's new in-laws, and saw no reason for them to rush off. Hal and Bess weren't so anxious to stay, and since Charlotte was almost dropping with sleep by now, they decided to take her home with them for the night.

'Uncle Ran said we can stay at his house if we like, Mother, instead of going all the way home,' Justin shouted joyfully. 'Say that it's all right, please!'

'Oh no, I don't think that's such a good idea—'

'Why not?' Ran's voice said. 'The children are tired, and you'll all be fresher tomorrow for not having to go all the way to St Austell.'

His eyes clashed with hers. *You know why not*, she wanted to shout at him. *You know I don't want to sleep under the same roof as you*… How could she bear it, knowing they were just doors away from each other, when her feelings about him were so disturbed?

'Haven't you other business to attend to, rather than bother with us?' she spoke freezingly, her meaning obvious to him, if not to the children. She saw a tiny smile pull at the corners of his sensual mouth, and was immediately angry with herself for letting her jealousy show.

'Not tonight.' He spoke with careless unconcern. 'I've told Mr Pendewy I'll call and see him in his offices tomorrow when I've tried to sort out a few things in my mind.'

Morwen caught her breath, feeling the ground sway beneath her feet. He couldn't mean what he was implying.

He surely didn't intend asking George Pendewy's permission to court one of his prissy daughters! They were a colourless family. Pendewy owned a modest little clayworks to the west of Killigrew Clay. Ben had always referred to it scathingly as a piddling little business, and not worth the moorland it covered.

'It's of no interest to me what you do tomorrow,' she retorted.

'In that case, stop being so obstinate and stay the night at New World. The children have enjoyed this day, and it's good to see them happy again. Don't spoil it for them, Morwen.'

She looked at their beaming, hopeful faces. It was true. All of them were happier than she had seen them in a long time, even Walter, who seemed to have come to terms with being parted from Cathy Askhew.

As for the others, Ran was right. It was more than good. It was almost miraculous to see them behaving like children again, instead of looking so lost and afraid since Ben's death.

'All right. We accept, and we thank you.'

Why did she have to sound so stilted, as though she had never lain in his arms and known the glory of his love? What devil held her in such a grip that she couldn't unbend towards him and beg him to tell her that what she suspected wasn't true?

As the children hooted with delight all around her at this unexpected treat, Morwen saw the Pendewy family approaching them to make their goodbyes to Ran, and as he was momentarily surrounded by them, she was drowning in misery.

'Mother, it will be all right,' Walter said quietly. 'There's nothing to rush home for, and the morning will do just as well. I know you must be missing Father, but if it helps at all – well, I do understand.'

Tears pricked at her eyes. He took on a man's role so effortlessly. He was strong for her, thinking she needed his strength. He was ready to shoulder any burden she put on him. And it only added to her guilt to know that it wasn't him that she needed, nor Ben. She nodded quickly, blinking away the tears.

'I know, my love. I'm just being foolish. Weddings sometimes make people act in a silly way.'

'You're not silly, Mother. You're special.'

He turned away quickly, choked at his own impulsive words, and from his brilliant colour Morwen knew at once that Walter had been drinking a little champagne too. She pretended not to notice, and fussed around, telling the children they must make their proper goodbyes to Lord Hocking for providing them with such a splendid day.

Several hours later, she was saying goodnight to all four of them as they settled down for the night in Ran's lovely new home. Then at last there were only the two of them, Randell Wainwright and herself, and she felt an acute embarrassment at being here with him, where once she would have felt so relaxed and welcome. He leaned against the mantelpiece, tall and elegant, and very much in control of himself. So much so that it added to Morwen's nervousness.

'I think perhaps I should go to bed too.' She put down the glass of wine he had poured for her.

'I think not, until we've talked,' Ran said evenly.

'There's nothing to talk about—'

He gave a heavy sigh. 'Morwen, give me credit for knowing when a woman's avoiding me—'

'I wonder you know how to recognize such a thing,' she was stung into answering. 'It can hardly be a frequent occurrence. From the way the Pendewy girls were fawning over you, I should think you'd had your fill of adulation for one day.'

'Do you think I give a damn about the Pendewy girls?'

'It certainly looked as if you were interested from the way you were being so attentive to them.'

'And that bothered you, did it?'

She gave him an angry look. 'It's not the sort of behaviour I'd expect from the man I'm supposed to be marrying.'

She bit her lip, wishing she hadn't spoken so recklessly, especially as Ran said nothing for a few minutes, and continued to lean against the mantel, studying her.

'Forgive me, Morwen.' The sarcasm in his voice belied the words. 'I'd begun to overlook that little fact. I'd always thought the lady that I expect to marry was warm and loving, and not a firebrand.'

'*Firebrand?*'

Ran gave a short laugh. 'You're right. It's hardly the word to use in the present circumstances. Iceberg might be more to the point. Are you going to tell me what I'm supposed to have done to produce this freeze between us? I don't care for guessing games, Morwen, and this childishness is unworthy of you.'

The words brimmed on her lips …*Is it me you want, or Killigrew Clay?* Or is it just the power? Bess had said it in all innocence. If he married Morwen, he would control it anyway. So why make this offer to buy into it, unless the desire for power was so strong that he had to have it all legal in his name, before a wedding ever took place. Her thoughts surged on. When – if – they married, he would then own two-thirds of Killigrew Clay, and he could overrule her father's wishes any time he chose.

She hadn't realized he was striding across the room towards her nor that her breath was so tortured in her throat as all the possibilities presented themselves to her in a horrifying kaleidoscope. She didn't realize it until she felt his large hands gripping her arms, hurting her, and she gasped out as his face seemed to blot out everything in front of her.

'Morwen, darling, for God's sake, stop tormenting me like this, and tell me what's wrong,' he said hoarsely. 'I thought we were over the bad times, but clearly I was wrong. And if you can't share your worst fears with me, what hope is there for us?'

'What hope is there for us, anyway?' she choked out. 'Everything we are is based on lies and shame, and I don't know who to trust any more.'

He held her close, feeling the rapid beat of her heart against his. In his arms, she wanted to twist and flee, but he held her too tightly, and she was trapped.

'Trust?' Ran said huskily. 'Who else should you trust but me, my dearest girl?'

'Who but you can I trust the least?'

Her voice quavered, and slowly he put her away from him, looking incredulously into the lustrous blue eyes that could become even more beautiful when softened by love. Eyes that looked up at him now with nothing but accusation in them. He sat her down on the sofa, still keeping his hold on her arms, and feeling the trembling in her body.

'I think you'd better explain that remark,' he said at last. 'When did you stop trusting me, Morwen, and why?'

If it was painful to speculate on the possibility of his power-lust, it was even more painful to speak of it. It was sordid, and made a mockery of all they had been to one another. But they had come too far for her to back down now. And the only way to find the answer to a question was to ask it.

'Is it me you want, Ran, or the clayworks?'

For a minute, he didn't speak. She was conscious of many things in that instant. The tick of the clock in the corner of the room. The soft movement of the curtains in the salt breeze through the open window. The drumming of Ran's heartbeat. The sudden look of disgust and disbelief in his eyes.

'Dear God! What miserable bastard put that idea into your head? You'll tell me, Morwen, and I'll see him swing for it.'

He rarely swore in front of her, and she knew by his savage tone how much he was affected.

'It wasn't a man—' she said through dry lips.

He stared at her.

'What does it matter who it was?' she said shrilly. 'What matters is whether 'tis true or not!'

'What matters to me is whether you believe it's true,' he raged, 'and I don't need any more answers on that.'

He got up from the sofa, looking down at her, his hands clenched by his sides.

'Are you going to tell me who it was?' he demanded.

'*No!* It doesn't matter. Don't try to make me, because I'll never tell.'

His mouth twisted. 'Your loyalty to the lying bastard is touching. Obviously, you prefer to believe him to me. Unless you've managed to dream all this up by yourself, which seems more likely. In any case, there's nothing more to be said, and you may as well go to bed. I promise you I shan't bother you with my company during the night, in case you were wondering. You know where to find your bedroom.'

She felt totally destroyed by his manner, knowing she couldn't expect anything else. And nothing was solved. He hadn't told her anything, and now it had become impossible to ask.

'We'll be leaving early tomorrow morning, Ran,' she mumbled as she got unsteadily to her feet. 'We won't bother you any longer than necessary.'

'Good,' he said curtly. 'I have that casual appointment with Mr Pendewy that I may as well attend. He's asked if I'm interested in buying into his clayworks business. I hadn't taken him seriously, but since I intend to stay in Cornwall with or without you as my wife, I'll see what he's got to offer, if only out of politeness.'

Morwen reeled with shock. She couldn't fathom out the meaning behind his words. He could just mean he was still genuinely intrigued with the idea of combining a clay-stone business with china-clay. Or it could be that one of the Pendewy girls had caught his eye after all, and if Ben Killigrew's widow wasn't ready to marry him, he was quite prepared to set his cap in another direction.

Or it could just mean that he was so stunned by Morwen's lack of trust in him that he wanted to get as far away from her as possible, just as quickly as he could… but she couldn't take the risk…

'Ran, Daddy and me want you to come in with us. We want you to buy into Killigrew Clay,' she stuttered, forgetting everything about waiting a few weeks.

Forgetting everything but the fact that she was losing him, and she just couldn't bear it.

For a second, she thought he was going to turn her down flat. She wouldn't blame him. She deserved it.

'Then I accept,' he said coldly. 'If only as a business arrangement. I have every respect for your father, and I'll go to see him tomorrow, after I've seen Pendewy.'

'You won't still go through with that?' she said in disbelief.

'I haven't decided yet. When I do, I'll let you know.'

He strode from the room without saying goodnight, while Morwen stood there, feeling like a wrung-out rag. She wasn't sure who had won, except that the future of Killigrew Clay was presumably saved. But if this was how it felt to be a victor, then she would hate to be a loser at Randell Wainwright's hands.

What was certain was that she had sold out. Ran had his partnership, and there had been no more mention of marriage, which was hardly likely with such bitterness between them. To Morwen at that moment, whether the question would come up again in the future seemed as remote as the stars.

Chapter Twenty-Six

By the end of July there were many changes at Killigrew Clay. Walter had found his own place there, and was happy to take his Pit Captain's instructions as well as Hal's.

There had been several formal meetings with Daniel Gorran and the three prospective new partners at the lawyer's chambers in St Austell. Hal Tremayne, Morwen Killigrew and Randell E Wainwright had signed the papers that made them equal partners in all that parcel of land and rail tracks that made up the boundaries of Killigrew Clay workings. Notices had been posted at St Austell and Truro town offices and announced in *The Informer*, so that no one was in any doubt of the new ownership.

The clayworkers had taken to the new order of things suspiciously at first, and then welcomed the change, when Ran spoke to them with the same confidence as the Killigrews had always done, promising that the installation of new machinery to replace the old was to be his first priority. Together with attention to cottage repairs and proper maintenance of the rail tracks, which had been badly overlooked during the time of Ben's failing fortunes.

To Morwen, Ran was polite and businesslike. He never mentioned marriage, nor sought her company more than was necessary by way of being a family friend, relative and business acquaintance. Because of the ties that linked them, they were bound to meet, but to an observer, the tall likeable American was a perfect gentleman, and not one to take advantage of a pretty young widow.

It frustrated Morwen beyond words. She knew she had hurt him by her accusations. She too was hurt, still unsure whether to trust him completely. He had got what he wanted. He was taking over Killigrew Clay. Other women in similar positions to Morwen's might have carried on the business without a man by their sides. She had her father, of course… but Hal was no businessman, and Randell had all the qualifications needed to make Killigrew Clay the success old Charles Killigrew had always meant it to be. It was what everyone wanted, and she must be grateful…

Morwen seemed to cling to her family more and more lately. She was glad for Freddie and Venetia that their marriage looked set to being the happy-ever-after she had always hoped for him. Matt had begun writing to them all again, and now she could picture him and his family and feel that Matt was a part of them all once more.

Bess was more than relieved that Ran had bought into Killigrew Clay. It eased the burden on her man, and should take some of the problems away from Morwen. A young woman should be attending to home and children, not concerning herself with the workings of claypits. Bess smiled ruefully at the thought.

But for fate, both she and Morwen would still be working every day at the pits, scraping and stacking the clay blocks for drying in the sun and wind in the linhay, ready for despatching to the port.

She didn't often bother with thoughts of the past, but even now she sometimes found it hard to believe that their lives were no longer those of hardship, spent scratching for pennies. The old days, cheering off the clay blocks piled pyramid-high on the loaded waggons to go careering down St Austell's steep cobbled hills, were like something from another age. And best forgotten, Bess thought keenly.

Jack and Annie grew ever more anxious as the weeks passed; anxious, yet filled with hope and anticipation. Surely nothing could go wrong now… it was a daily silent prayer in Annie's mind, and a constant fear in Jack's.

The doctor said that Annie needed fresh air and gentle exercise, and it did her no harm to go visiting her St Austell relatives occasionally, as long as Jack took her in the trap, and providing she wasn't jolted over too many bumps in the road.

'We've a fat chance of missing bumps in these bloody roads,' Jack swore as the trap lurched over a deep rut on the way home from Killigrew House one fine Sunday afternoon in early August. He glanced at Annie, seeing the pallor in her cheeks as she clung to the side of the trap. 'I think 'tis time these jaunts stopped, dar, despite what Doctor Vestey says. The babby can get all the fresh air he needs when he's born—'

'I think 'tis time for stopping the trap while I try to decide if I'm suffering from indigestion or something more,' Annie said with a sudden small gasp.

Jack felt his heart jump in spasm. He reined in the horse at once and twisted to look at his wife.

'Christ, Annie, you're not telling me the babby's started, are you? There's two more weeks to go yet—'

'You try telling that to the babby,' she mumbled, trying to make a joke of it and ending up with a grimace as the sudden powerful wave of a contraction rippled through her.

Jack felt paralysed with fear for a few moments. They were roughly halfway between St Austell and Truro, and Annie's labour with the twins had been swift and furious. This pregnancy had been condemned by Doctor Vestey from the beginning, and the thought that his lovely Annie could die drummed through his head like a curse.

'If you'm sure, dar, we must get 'ee to Truro hospital.' In times of stress, Jack reverted to the old way of talking, telling Annie at once how alarmed he was. She shook her head quickly, and he saw that her eyes had darkened with the pains. He thanked God that they hadn't taken the children visiting that day, but had left them with their grandparents in Truro.

'No time,' she said with difficulty.

Jack looked around huntedly. 'But Annie, 'tis as far back to St Austell as 'tis to Truro, and we can't let the babby be born on the open moors!'

His brain panicked at such an eventuality. He was as strong as any man, but when it came to birthing, it was women's work, and the farther he was from the scene the happier he was.

'Take me to Ran's,' Annie gulped. 'He'll send word to Doctor Vestey to come to me there. I can't go further, Jack.' The words ended on a little scream that she tried hard to suppress. She knew that some women had long and dry labours... Morwen herself had told her that Justin had been born that way... but Annie thought fervently that anything would be preferable to this sharp and excruciating pain that seemed to cut through her with knife-edge keenness.

'Hold on, love,' Jack said through tight lips. He urged the horse forward, knowing that Annie chewed her lips with every rough bit of land they crossed. Ran's house seemed an endless distance away, its comforting square shape seeming to come no nearer as the sun began to sink low on the horizon and the shadows lengthened.

He wished desperately they hadn't stayed so long at Killigrew House. He hoped even more that Doctor Vestey would be at home when they sent the messenger, and not out on some evening's entertainment of his own.

At last they reached the approaches to New World. Jack told Annie to stay put while he hammered at the door. He hardly need have asked. She was convulsed with pain, trickles of sweat running down her back and between her breasts, praying that she would be able to bear each new contraction.

Was it ever this bad with the twins? Annie suddenly thought in fright. She couldn't remember. Time had dulled the agony, but now she had to make a desperate effort to remain conscious each time the waves of pain tossed her high and then threw her down again. It couldn't be happening so quickly, she thought in terror. There would be no time for the doctor to get here, and she couldn't deliver a child by herself…

'Jack—' she croaked.

In a second he was back with Ran. 'It's all right, Annie. We'll get you inside and into bed,' Ran said, in a voice as soothing as warm honey. 'My housekeeper will stay with you while Jack goes to Truro for the doctor, and if you want her, I'll send a maid for Morwen.'

'Oh, yes!' Annie moaned. 'But don't send a maid, Ran. You know how they dawdle. Go yourself, *please*! 'Twill be quicker.'

She could only speak in short, staccato sentences. Everything was such an effort. She wanted to reassure Jack, but his scared white face kept floating back and forth in front of her and wouldn't stay still.

She realized in a lucid moment that it was because he and Ran were carrying her up the stairs to a cool bedroom and laying her gently on a bed. Mrs Enders, Ran's elderly housekeeper, fussed round her, but Annie surmised correctly that the woman would be as useless as a chicken in helping to birth a child.

She tried to keep very still and let the waves of pain take her up and carry her along with them, feeling the welcome touch of a cooling cloth on her forehead each time the contractions came. She tried to smile her thanks at Mrs Enders, and tried even more to ignore the woman's mutterings that the doctor had best come soon or they'd be in a sorry state…

She felt the warm flood as her waters broke and felt herself being padded with a towel. She was becoming light-headed, trying to tell Mrs Enders that she must remove the towel to give her son room to emerge into the world, but somehow the words wouldn't come.

And anyway, the pains didn't seem so severe now. Nothing very much seemed to be happening any more. The pains dwindled to an irritating twinge every few minutes, as though they wanted to occur, but something was preventing them.

Annie didn't care. It was such a relief to be rid of the pains for a while that she didn't care about anything. She even drifted in and out of a restless sleep, while the daylight faded and the moon rose in the sky, and still the doctor didn't come.

It seemed a long while later that a cool hand gripped her plucking fingers, and she recognized it at once. Annie Tremayne wasn't the first to feel that strange sense of trust in those soft feminine hands.

'Morwen?' she croaked. 'Is that you? The babby don't seem to want to come after all. Do you think 'twas all a false alarm?'

'I don't think so, my love,' Morwen whispered. 'I think the doctor must see to 'ee, and I'm sure he'll be here soon.'

Annie gave a thin smile. 'Poor Ran. He never thought his house would be turned into a hospital, did he?'

She gave a sudden shriek, her nails biting into Morwen's hands as the pains returned more savagely than before, and she knew instinctively that something was badly wrong.

Her relief when Doctor Vestey and Jack appeared at the bedroom door was almost overwhelming. Jack gave a loud cry at seeing the way his wife's face was distorted, and after giving Annie a brief examination, the doctor sent him packing at once.

'The young woman will assist me,' he snapped. He looked directly at Morwen. 'You're up to it?'

'Of course,' she stuttered, wondering what he wanted of her. But Annie's sobs were so heart-rending, she knew she could never leave her until it was all over, one way or another.

'The baby's breeched,' Doctor Vestey said tersely. 'I'll have to help it out as best I can. If she was in hospital I could use instruments. As it is, we must manage the best we can, and your job is to hold her still, and pray she doesn't tear.'

Morwen's mouth went dry as the brutal instructions went on and on to the accompaniment of Annie's screaming. Morwen tried to close her ears to it, conceding that Doctor Vestey was nothing if not efficient. And it seemed nothing short of a miracle when at last the slithering child was held in his hands, and he was smacking its bottom and making it open its lungs and yell its own greeting to the world.

'Is the babby all right?' Annie mumbled weakly from the sodden pillow. 'Is it Jack's boy?'

Morwen turned to look at her. So much pain, and all she could think about now was the baby she and Jack wanted so much. So much pain, and yet, as she held out her arms to take the squalling, red-faced infant from the doctor's hands, Annie Tremayne was so beautiful that the tears stung Morwen's eyes at being privileged to watch such a moment.

'Aye, it's Jack's boy,' the doctor said. 'And a fine and lusty specimen he is. You're a lucky young woman, Annie, but this must be the last, do you hear? There are only so many times you can cheat the old reaper.'

Morwen shivered, but amazingly, Annie was laughing triumphantly as she cuddled the baby, still attached to her by the cord, and waited for the after-birth to come away before she was made presentable.

'We'll see, Doctor! We've cheated him this time, and I'll settle for that for the present.'

Half an hour later, Doctor Vestey was preparing to leave, and Morwen had washed her sister-in-law and tidied her, and Annie was sitting up in bed awaiting Jack's inspection, the baby wrapped in a clean towel for the night, until Jack took her home in the morning. Morwen promised she would stay, knowing Ran's hospitality would extend to her, and wanting to be at hand in case Annie should need anything.

As soon as he had seen that everything was well with his wife and son, Jack would go home to give his children the glad news, and those at St Austell must wait until morning.

Jack had a few private moments with Annie, and then invited Ran to take a look at the newest Tremayne.

'We're going to call him Sam after Jack's eldest brother,' Annie said, suddenly shy. 'But we want to give him a second name after you, if you've no objection, Ran.'

'I'd be highly honoured, Ma'am,' Ran said gravely, in that quaintly-worded mixture of the old world and the new that enchanted every Cornish lady who heard it.

'I think I'd like to go to sleep now,' Annie said suddenly, snuggling down carefully in the bed. Jack got up from the bedside at once, a hint of relief in his eyes. It hadn't been an easy time for him either, downstairs with the sound of Annie's suffering plain to hear. And he and Ran had taken more than their usual share of spirits to calm their nerves. He kissed his wife and said he'd be back in the morning to fetch her home.

'I'm to go to the hospital to see Mr Shiner first,' Annie reminded him. 'Just to see that everything's all right.'

But it was obvious from the love flowing between them that everything was more than all right. Everything was wonderful.

Morwen spent the rest of the night in Annie's room. There was a small couch where she could doze, to be ready in a moment if mother or baby stirred. Annie slept the blissful and exhausted sleep of a newly-delivered woman, but it was impossible for Morwen to sleep. She felt as though she teetered on a cliff-edge now, as though this new arrival to cement Jack and Annie's solid relationship emphasized her own insecurity.

She wandered to the window, where the ocean breezes wafted in. Out there, beyond the horizon, was America, where Matt had found his own haven. Everyone had someone, and she, who had once had everything, now had nothing. She no longer minimized the love she and Ben had once shared. It had been everything in the world to her, but it was a part of her life that was over, and in the months that passed, she could remember Ben now with love, instead of pain.

There was a small writing desk near the window, a block of paper, pen and ink in their separate grooves, for guests' use. For some reason, the words Ran had once said to Walter came floating back to her.

'It's a special privilege to get letters from the people you love. They can often say things in letters they find dificult to say out loud.'

It was as though some other hand was guiding her to reach out for the pen and dip it in the ink, and draw the writing block towards her. Telling her not to throw away the chance of love and happiness, for those who were offered it were the fortunate ones in this world, and shouldn't discard one of God's greatest gifts lightly. She wrote carefully, wishing she had the words at her command to say all that she felt, and knowing the sense of release at being able to say, if only on paper, all that her heart longed to say.

'My dearest Ran,

I call you that in all sincerity, because you are the very dearest man in all the world to me. My own foolishness has driven us apart, and I regret it more than I can say. I don't ever expect you to love me again, because you will probably always suspect that I still doubt your motives in wanting to marry me. I know I destroyed your love for me, and for that God is punishing me every day of my life.

Ran, I know that nothing matters but the feelings of a man and a woman, and to have your love again I would gladly give away Killigrew Clay and everything I own. It was never really mine, anyway. It was always Ben's and part of a man's world. I would only ever have played at being an owner, so what did it really matter?

You asked who put the idea into my head. It was my mother, and it was done in all innocence when I told her I loved you and thought I was going to marry you. She said I would be occupied with having babies and being a proper woman and would be glad to leave the running of Killigrew Clay to you, and that was when I began to mistrust you.

I should have seen the sense in her words, my dar. They're all that matters. Now that I know you're lost to me, I had to put things right, and to let you know I do trust you, Ran. I'd trust you with my life.

I'm tempted to tear up this letter, but that would be cowardly. So I'll leave it where you'll find it after I've gone home in the morning. I'm no good at being noble, though, so don't expect me to dance at your wedding to one of the Pendewy girls, because I shan't! I love you.'

Annie gave a small moan, and Morwen went to her at once, but the girl was only turning in her sleep. The baby was tucked up in a drawer on the floor by her side, and slept contentedly. Morwen's throat was full, just watching them. And even more so from saying all that she wanted to say to Ran.

She wouldn't be able to leave next morning until Jack had taken Annie and the baby home, but she suddenly felt desperately tired, and at last she slept fitfully, the letter safely tucked beneath her head. She would slip it beneath Ran's bedroom door before she left for Killigrew House.

–

The children were excited to hear the news. Walter had left for the works long ago, but Morwen sent one of the stable-lads with a message for Bess, and told him to go on to the Clay One to tell Walter and Hal. There would be a lot of rejoicing among the Tremaynes and the Killigrews from now on, she thought mistily, as the girls clamoured to know what the baby was like and what he would be called.

'He's to be called Samuel Randell Tremayne,' she said, feeling an absurd little twist of pride at the name.

'Samuel! That was our father's name, wasn't it?' Primmy echoed. Her face went suddenly scarlet. 'I'm sorry, Mother. I – I just don't know what to call him. I can't say Uncle Sam, can I?'

Morwen hugged her. 'He'll always be your father, my love, and he'd be so proud of his children.'

'Anyway, we've got a cousin Sam now,' Albert said. 'So in a way, our father's still here, isn't he, Mother?'

'In a way, love,' Morwen said.

Sometimes, to her, Sam had never gone away. Especially when she looked at the three older ones, who looked back at her with Sam's blue Tremayne eyes.

They spent the rest of the morning discussing when they could go and see the baby, and if it would be baptized in Truro or St Austell, and which one of them it was going to be most like. In the afternoon, Primmy and Albert and Justin begged permission to go and see Grandma Bess. Charlotte played outside, making daisy-chains on the lawn, while Morwen sat back in a wicker chair and let the sun warm her face.

She didn't see anyone approach until a shadow came between her and the sky, and then she opened her eyes and saw a tall stranger with sunlight like a halo around his face, and her heart leapt.

'Ran,' she breathed.

He dropped down on the grass beside her, while Charlotte whooped around them. She might have been on another planet for all the adults were aware of her. Morwen watched nervously as Ran slowly took a folded piece of paper from his pocket.

'Did you mean it?' he said quietly. 'Every bit of it?'

In the daylight, it was less easy to admit to the opening of her heart. But if it had been foolish to mistrust him, how much more foolish would it be to deny everything now? She gave a small nod.

'Of course I did. Everything,' she said.

Thinking that now he would surely take her in his arms. Thinking that everything would be restored between them as if by one magic stroke of an artist's brush.

'I should put you across my knee and thrash you,' he said, his voice edged with anger. Morwen blinked, and Charlotte came within her focus, her eyes saucer-round at this apparent quarrel between her two favourite people.

'Why?' she bristled at once.

'Because it wasn't until the end of the letter that it even sounded like my Morwen. All that humility made me cringe! It wasn't until you reverted to normal and said you were no good at being noble and that you had no intention of dancing at my wedding that I believed any of it.'

She was outraged until she realized he was teasing her. There were dancing lights in his eyes, and the laughter lines around them forced little ridges of pleasure at her annoyance. And there was something more in his face that made her heart begin to beat faster with a soaring feeling of hope…

'Are you going to marry Uncle Ran?' Charlotte shouted.

Before Morwen could say anything, the other children had come home and were running into the garden in time to catch the words. Primmy looked from one to the other of the adults, standing so stiffly together, her quick mind assessing the situation at once.

'*Are* you Mother?'

Justin spoke up. 'She can't, can she? She's married to our father—'

'No, she's not. You can't still be married to somebody when they're dead, you ninny,' Albert said. He looked at Morwen and Ran with all the wisdom of the adolescent.

'We wouldn't mind, Mother, really we wouldn't,' he said with some embarrassment. 'Uncle Ran could move in here—'

'No, he couldn't,' Ran told him. 'I have my own house, in case you've forgotten.'

But Morwen knew there was more to it than that, more than the children would understand. She could see it plainly in the sudden flash of pride in Ran's eyes. If he did intend to marry Ben Killigrew's widow after buying into Ben Killigrew's business, he certainly wasn't moving straight into Ben Killigrew's house as well. There was no way he wanted to walk so completely in Ben's shoes. Randell Wainwright's shadow was his own.

'It's simple then,' Primmy said matter-of-factly, and Morwen felt a stab of amusement as the four children crowded together, almost shutting her and Ran out as they thought out their own solution. They were extremely good at that, these Killigrew children, she realized... especially when Primmy the schemer initiated something...

'Justin wants to go to that Truro college, so he and Charlotte can move into New World with Mother and Ran. Albert and me like our school here, and Walter's already working at Killigrew Clay. So if Grandma Bess and Granddad Hal move in here, the three of us can all stay together!'

The four of them drifted indoors as Mrs Horn called them in for tea, still chattering like magpies over the proposed new order of things. Would it happen? *Could* it happen? Morwen's mind buzzed with the sweet simplicity of it all. It would still need her Mammie and Daddy to agree to it, of course...

She looked up into the eyes of the tall, powerful man at her side. The man who had called her 'honey' in a way that was special and exclusive. She loved him with a fierce and primitive passion that was almost pain, and her throat was suddenly dry. Because no matter how clever the plan, she wasn't certain yet if Ran still wanted to marry her.

Her spirit momentarily deserted her, and it was more than she could do to ask. But as always, her beautiful, expressive eyes spoke more than words ever could, and Ran's feelings matched hers as he answered the unspoken question in his own way.

'Your children have more sense than you, Mrs Killigrew,' he said, and then he opened out his arms to take her inside.

The Cornish Clay Sagas

Killigrew Clay
Clay Country
Family Ties
Family Shadows
Primmy's Daughter
White Rivers
September Morning
A Brighter Tomorrow